R U I N S

RUINS

DAN WELLS

BALZER + BRAY

An Imprint of HarperCollins*Publishers*

Balzer + Bray is an imprint of HarperCollins Publishers.

Ruins
Copyright © 2014 by HarperCollins Publishers
All rights reserved. Printed in the United States of America.
No part of this book may be used or reproduced in any manner
whatsoever without written permission except in the case of
brief quotations embodied in critical articles and reviews. For
information address HarperCollins Children's Books, a division
of HarperCollins Publishers, 195 Broadway, New York, NY
10007.
www.epicreads.com

Library of Congress Control Number: 2013953788
ISBN 978-0-06-207111-8

Typography by Alison Klapthor
16 17 18 19   CG/RRDC   10 9 8 7 6 5 4 3 2
❖
First paperback edition, 2015

This book is dedicated to everybody you hate.
Sorry. Life's like that sometimes.

PART 1

CHAPTER ONE

"This is a general message to the residents of Long Island."

The first time they heard the message, nobody recognized the voice. But it played every day, all day, for weeks, cycling through every available frequency to be sure that every human on the island could hear it. Terrified refugees, huddled in groups or alone in the wilderness, came to know it by heart; it blared from every radio relentlessly, burning itself into their minds and memories. After the first few weeks it haunted their dreams, until even sleep was no respite from the calm, methodical proclamation of death.

"We did not want to invade, but circumstances forced our hand."

The voice, they eventually learned, was that of a scientist named McKenna Morgan, and the "we" of her sentence referred to the Partials: unstoppable super-soldiers, created in labs and grown in vats to wage a war the humans couldn't win on their own. They fought, and they won, and when they came back to the United States to find themselves homeless and hopeless, they turned on their creators and waged a new war, the Partial War, the war that ended the world.

But the war that ended the world was not the last war that world would ever see, for twelve years later the humans and the Partials were both on the verge of extinction—and each species was willing to destroy the other to survive.

"We are looking for a girl named Kira Walker, sixteen years old, five feet ten inches tall, approximately one hundred eighteen pounds. Indian descent, light-skinned, with jet-black hair, though she may have cut or dyed it to help disguise her identity."

Only a few people on the island knew Kira Walker personally, but everyone knew her by reputation: She was a medic, trained in the hospital to study the plague known as RM. They knew Kira because she had found the cure; she had saved the life of Arwen Sato, the Miracle Baby—the first human infant in twelve long years to live more than three days. Kira was infamous because, in the process of finding the cure, she had led two unprovoked attacks on the Partial army, awakening, they thought, the monster that had lain dormant since the end of the Partial War. She had saved the world, and she had damned it. The first time the message played, most people didn't know whether to love her or hate her. Their opinions grew less complicated with every human death.

"Bring us this girl and the occupation ends; continue to hide her, and we will execute one of you every day. Please don't force us to do this any longer than is necessary. This message will cycle through all frequencies and repeat until our instructions have been complied with. Thank you."

The first day they killed an old man, a schoolteacher from back in the days when there were still children to attend. His name was John Dianatkah, and he kept a hive of bees to make honey candy for his students. Partial soldiers shot him in the back of the head in the middle of East Meadow, the largest human settlement on Long Island, leaving his body in the road as a sign that they were serious. Nobody turned Kira in because, at that time, they were proud and unbroken; the Partials could rattle their sabers all they wanted, but the humans would not bend. Yet still the message played, and the next day they killed a young woman, barely seventeen years old, and the day after that an old lady, and the day after that a middle-aged man.

"Please don't force us to do this any longer than is necessary."

A week went by, and seven people died. Two weeks; fourteen people. In the meantime, the Partials weren't attacking the humans, they weren't forcing them into labor camps; they simply corralled them in East Meadow and rounded up everyone who tried to escape. Attack a Partial and you were whipped or beaten; cause too much trouble and you might be the next night's victim. When a human disappeared completely, the rumors spread in hushed whispers: Maybe you'd escaped. Maybe Dr. Morgan had taken you to her bloodstained laboratory. Or maybe they'd simply find you in the street the next night, kneeling in front of a Partial while the endless message blared from speakers all across the city, until you sprawled forward with a bullet where your brain used to be. Every day another execution. Every hour another message, the same message, endless and unstoppable.

"We are looking for a girl named Kira Walker."

Still, nobody turned her in—not because they were proud,

but because they couldn't. She'd left the island, said some, and others said she was hiding in the woods. *Of course we'd give her to you if we had her, but we don't, can't you see that? Can't you understand? Can't you stop killing us? There are barely any humans left, can't you find another way? We want to help you, but we can't.*

"Sixteen years old . . . five feet ten inches tall . . . Indian descent . . . jet-black hair."

By the end of the first month the humans were as scared of one another as they were of the Partials, terrified of the witch hunt that swept through the refugees like a poison wind—*you look like Kira, maybe they'll take you, maybe that will be enough.* Teenage girls, women with black hair, anyone who looked like they might be Indian, anyone who looked like they might be hiding something. *How do I know you're not Kira? How do they? Maybe they'll stop killing us, even if it's only for a while. And how do we know you're not hiding her? I don't want to turn you in, but we're dying. I don't want to hurt you, but they're forcing us.*

"Continue to hide her, and we will execute one of you every day."

The Partials were bred to be stronger than humans, to be faster, to be more resilient and more capable in every way. They were trained as warriors since the day they were pulled from their vats, and they fought like lions until they turned twenty and their built-in expiration date killed them. They wanted Kira Walker because Dr. Morgan knew what the humans didn't: that Kira was a Partial. A model that they'd never seen before, that they never knew existed. Morgan thought Kira's DNA could help them cure the expiration. But even if the humans knew, they wouldn't care. They only wanted to live. A handful of resistance fighters survived in the wilderness, relying on their knowledge of the terrain to keep them alive while they fought a losing war against extinction. Partials outnumbered humans 500,000 to 35,000—more than ten to one—and outclassed them in combat by another order of magnitude. When they decided to kill humans, there was no way for the humans to stop them.

Until the leader of the resistance recovered a nuclear warhead from a sunken navy destroyer.

"We did not want to invade," said the message, "but circumstances forced our hand."

The resistance told themselves the same thing as they smuggled the bomb north toward the Partial homeland.

CHAPTER TWO

Senator Owen Tovar blew out a long, low breath. "How did Delarosa know there was a nuke in a sunken ship?" He glanced at Haru Sato, the soldier who'd delivered the news, and then looked at the island's intelligence officer, Mr. Mkele. "More to the point, how did you *not* know it?"

"I knew there was a sunken fleet," said Mkele. "I had no idea it had been carrying a nuclear warhead." Haru had always seen Mkele as a confident, capable man: terrifying when he and Haru were on different sides, fiercely reassuring when they were on the same one. Now, though, the intelligence officer seemed desperate and overwhelmed. Watching Mkele flounder for answers was even more disturbing, in its way, than the horrors that had brought them to this point.

"One of the people in Delarosa's resistance group knew about it," said Haru. "I don't know who. It was some old navy guy."

"And he's kept it to himself all these years?" asked Tovar. "What, did he want it to be a surprise?"

Senator Hobb tapped the table. "He probably had the very understandable fear that if he told someone, they'd find it and try to use it. Which, it turns out, is exactly what happened."

"Delarosa's claim is that the Partials are overwhelming us," said Haru. The four men were deep in the tunnels beneath the old JFK International Airport—a ragged ruin now, but one with a wide airfield around it that made encroaching Partials easy to spot. It had become the fugitive Senate's last, desperate hiding place. "Not just now, but forever—she says that the human race will never be able to rebuild properly while the Partials are still out there. And she's right, that's the terrible thing, but that doesn't mean detonating a nuke is going to make things any better. I would have stopped her, but she's got a whole army of guerrillas, and most of my unit joined them." He shook his head. Haru was the youngest of the four men, barely twenty-three years old, and he felt more like a child now than he had in years—than he had since the Break, really. The doom and the chaos were terrible enough, but it was the familiarity that really got to him—the sense that the doom and the chaos had all happened before, twelve years ago when the world ended, and now it was ending again. He had been a child then, and suddenly he was a child again, lost and confused and desperate for someone, for anyone, to step in and make it all better. He didn't like that feeling at all, and he hated himself for allowing it to enter his mind. He was a father now, the first father in twelve years to have a living, breathing, healthy child, and she and her mother were trapped somewhere in the middle of this mess. He had to pull himself together, for them.

"I liked Delarosa better when she was in jail," said Hobb.

"This is what we get for trusting a terrorist." He shot a glance at Tovar. "Present company excepted, of course."

"No, you're right," said Tovar. "We've made a habit of trusting fanatics, and it's rarely turned out well for us. I was a pretty savvy terrorist—savvy enough to get my label switched to 'freedom fighter' and wind up in charge—but I'm a terrible senator. We like people who stand up and fight, especially when we agree with them, but it's the next step that really matters. The part after the fighting." He smiled sadly. "I've let everybody down."

"The Partial invasion was not your fault," said Mkele.

"The final remnants of the human race will be glad to hear it," said Tovar. "Unless the Partial invasion's a big hit, in which case I'll totally claim the credit."

"Only if Hobb doesn't beat you to it," said Haru.

Senator Hobb spluttered an awkward defense, but Mkele merely glanced at Haru disapprovingly. "We have more important things to do than trade insults."

"Even true ones," said Tovar. Mkele and Hobb both glared at him, but he only shrugged. "What, am I the only one admitting my personal failings?"

"There's a convicted war criminal with a nuclear weapon loose on our island," said Hobb, "not to mention the army of super-soldiers murdering us like cattle. Can we maybe focus on that instead of personal attacks?"

"She's not going to use it on the island," said Haru. "Not even Delarosa's that bloodthirsty. She's not out to kill Partials, she's out to save humans—she's still going to kill the Partials, obviously, but not at the expense of the few of us who are left."

"That's a nice sentiment," said Mkele, "but a nuclear warhead is a very imprecise weapon. How do we know she'll use it wisely? Best-case scenario, she takes it to the mainland, blows it somewhere north of the Partials, and lets the fallout radiation finish them off; more likely, she takes it to their home base in White Plains and blows it there, killing all of us in the fallout instead."

"Which might be the only plan that works," said Hobb. "For all we know, they're not even susceptible to radiation poisoning."

"How close is White Plains?" asked Tovar. "Anybody have a map?"

"Always," said Mkele, and set his briefcase on the table, undoing the locks with a pair of soft clicks. "Traveling from here to White Plains would take days, because you'd have to go around the Long Island Sound." He unfolded a paper map and spread it flat on the table before them. "Even if she crosses the sound by boat, which is the route most likely to get her caught, it will take her a couple of days to get there, at minimum. Months, maybe, if she travels carefully enough to stay hidden. As the crow flies, though, it's not that far. White Plains to East Meadow is . . ." He studied the map, pointing out the two cities and measuring their distance with a well-worn plastic ruler. "Forty miles, give or take." He looked up. "Do we know what kind of nuke she has? What kind of payload?"

"She said she pulled it from a ship called *The Sullivans*," said Haru. "Plural like that, I don't know why."

"That's a destroyer," said Tovar, "Arleigh Burke class—an older ship, even twelve years ago, but very dependable; the navy used them for years. *The Sullivans* was named after five brothers who all died in the same battle in World War II."

"I thought you didn't know about the nuke," said Hobb.

"I didn't," said Tovar, "but you're talking to an ex-marine. Try to name a navy ship I *don't* know the specs of."

"Then tell us the specs of this one," said Mkele. "Would that class of destroyer be armed with nuclear missiles, or would they have just put one in the cargo hold for onboard detonation, like a suicide bomber?"

"Arleigh Burke destroyers would be outfitted with Tomahawks," said Tovar. "That's a nuclear cruise missile with a two-, maybe three-hundred-kiloton payload. Those are designed for long-range attacks, but the Partials had enough antimissile defense to shoot one down before it hit home. The reason it's sitting right off the coast of Long Island, I assume, is that they brought it close to detonate on site; it would have sacrificed the fleet, and most of New York and New Jersey and Connecticut, but it would have destroyed the Partials pretty decisively."

Haru grimaced, marveling again at how desperate the old government must have been to consider such a thing—though he supposed it was no more desperate than their situation now. Before the world ended, and knowing that it was about to, a nuke would have been a small price to pay: You'd kill everyone in range, and destroy the area for decades to come, but the Partials would have been gone. It might have actually been worth it. Now, though, with the last of the human race sitting just forty miles away . . .

"What's the radius of destruction?" asked Haru. "Is the entire island dead?"

"Not necessarily," said Tovar, "but we don't want to be here if we can help it. At that payload the initial fireball's going to be about a mile and a half wide—that's the part that's two hundred million degrees—and the physical shock wave will destroy everything within five or six miles. Everything in that zone is going to go up in flames, instantly, and that much fire starting that abruptly will suck in enough air to jump-start a raging hurricane with air temperatures hot enough to boil water. Every living thing within . . . ten miles of ground zero would be dead in minutes, and five or ten miles farther out you'd still kill enough of everything not to know the difference. Here on the island we won't have any of those primary effects—we might feel a thump, and anyone looking right at the detonation will be blinded, but that should be the worst of it. *Should be.* Until the radioactive ash cloud gives us all leukemia and we die in slow, crippling agony."

"And how big is the ash cloud?" asked Haru.

"A nuclear ash cloud doesn't radiate out like a shock wave," said Mkele. "It's a distribution of physical material, so the exact pattern will depend on the weather. The major winds in this region tend to blow northeast, so most of the ash cloud will drift that way, but we're still going to get some peripheral fallout— flurries around the edges, and castoffs from the winds in the firestorm."

"Anyone less than ninety miles downwind will be dead within two weeks," said Tovar. "We just have to hope the winds don't change."

"So the Partials would be effectively destroyed," said Hobb.

"Everyone on the mainland, yes," said Mkele, "but this close to the blast zone we're going to lose a lot of humans as well, even under ideal conditions."

"Yes, but the Partials will be gone," Hobb repeated. "Delarosa's plan will work."

"I don't think you're grasping the ramifications here—" said Haru, but Hobb cut him off.

"I don't think you are either," Hobb snapped. "What are our options, honestly? Do you think we can stop her? The entire Partial army has been trying to find Delarosa for weeks, and they can't; we can barely leave this basement without getting shot at, so I'm pretty sure we're not going to find her either. We could find her strike force, maybe, because we have protocols in place for that, but the team delivering the warhead is likely beyond recall. This bomb is going off, whether we like it or not, and we need to be ready."

"The Partials will catch her," said Mkele. "A warhead's not an easy thing to transport—it's going to compromise her ability to stay hidden."

"And if that happens, she might just blow it on sight," said Hobb. "As long as she's twenty miles from East Meadow, our major population center is safe, and then the winds will blow the fallout north to White Plains."

"If she makes it twenty miles," said Haru.

Tovar raised his eyebrow. "Are we prepared to risk the human race on a bunch of ifs?"

"What are we risking?" asked Hobb. "We send someone to stop her, and everyone else to evacuate the island—we're not risking anything unless we don't act."

"Hobb wasn't exaggerating about how hard it is to move around," said Mkele. "Haru can do it because he's been trained, and he knows the island, but how do you intend to carry out a mass evacuation without drawing attention?"

"We do it after the blast," said Hobb. "Spread the word, get everything ready, and when the bomb goes off and the occupation force is distracted, we rise up, kill as many Partials as we can, and run south."

"So your plan is to murder a superior enemy army," said Tovar, "and then outrun the wind. I'm glad it's so simple."

"We have to evacuate first," said Haru, "now, to avoid even the periphery of the nuclear fallout."

"We already talked about how that's not going to work," said Hobb. "There's no way to move that many people without the Partials seeing us and stopping us." He looked at the others. "Remind me why the kid is even here?"

"He's proven himself valuable," said Mkele. "We're not exactly in a position to turn away help."

"Which is also why you're still here," said Tovar.

"My wife and child are in East Meadow," said Haru, "and you know who they are—every human being alive knows who they are. And that means you know why we don't have time to waste. Arwen is the only human child in the world, and she's going to attract some attention—for all we know, they're already in Partial custody somewhere, ready to be cut open and studied."

"We can't lose that child," said Tovar, and Haru could see that the fear in his face was real. "Arwen represents the future. If she dies in that explosion, or in the fallout after . . ."

"That's why we have to evacuate now," said Haru, "before Delarosa detonates that nuke. There's got to be a way."

"Hobb's plan uses the explosion as a distraction," said Mkele. "But what if we distracted them another way?"

"If we could create a distraction big enough to overthrow the Partials, we'd have done it already," said Hobb. "The nuke is all we have."

Mkele shook his head. "We don't need to overthrow them, just pull their attention. Delarosa's guerrillas have been doing that already, more or less, but if we went all out—"

"We'd die," said Tovar. "It's like Hobb said, if we could do it safely, we'd have done it already."

"So we don't do it safely," said Mkele.

The other men went quiet.

"This is as final and as deadly as any situation can be," said Mkele. "We're talking about a nuclear explosion forty miles from the last group of human beings on the planet. Even our best-case scenario, where somebody finds Delarosa and stops her in time, leaves us trapped in the hands of an occupying species that treats us like lab rats. An all-out attack on the Partials is going to kill every human soldier who tries it—none of us hold any illusions about that—but if there's a chance that the rest of the humans could escape, then how can we possibly argue that it's not worth it?"

Haru thought about his family: his wife, Madison, and his baby girl. He couldn't bear to think of leaving Arwen without a father, but Mkele was right—when the only alternative is extinction, an awful lot of horrors become acceptable. "We're going to die anyway," he said. "At least this way our deaths will mean something."

"Don't go volunteering just yet," said Tovar. "This is a two-part plan: One group provides the distraction, and the other gets everyone as far south as humanly possible. No pun intended."

"Then we run," said Mkele. His voice was somber. "Away from our only source of the cure. Or did we all forget?"

The room fell quiet again. Haru felt a numbness creeping

up his legs and back—no matter how far they ran, they still had RM. Arwen was alive because Kira had found a cure in the Partials' pheromonal system, but so far the humans had been unable to replicate it in a lab. They'd have to start over in a new medical facility, and it could take years just to find one and get it working again—and there was no guarantee that they'd ever be successful. If the Partials died, the cure would almost certainly die with them.

Haru could tell from their faces that the others were thinking of the same insurmountable problem. His throat was dry, and his voice sounded weak when he broke the silence. "Our best-case scenario keeps sliding closer and closer to our worst."

"The Partials are our greatest enemy, but they're also our only hope for the future," said Mkele. He steepled his fingers and pressed them to his forehead a moment before continuing. "Maybe we should take some with us."

"You say that like it's easy," said Haru.

"What do you want to do?" asked Tovar. "Just keep a few in cages and pull out the pheromone when you need it? Doesn't that seem kind of evil to any of you?"

"My job is to protect the human race," said Mkele. "If it means the difference between life and extinction, then yes, I will keep Partials in cages."

Tovar's face was grim. "I keep forgetting you had this same job under Delarosa."

"Delarosa was trying to save the human race," said Mkele. "Her only crime was that she was willing to go too far in order to do it. We decided, briefly, that we didn't want to go along with her, but look at us: We're hiding in a basement, letting Delarosa fight our battles, seriously considering letting her deploy a nuclear bomb. We are long past the point where we can pick and choose our morality. We either save our species or we don't."

"Yes," said Tovar, "but I'd prefer it if we were still worth saving by the end of it."

"We either save our species or we don't," Mkele repeated, more forcefully this time. He looked at the other men one by one, starting with Hobb. The amoral senator nodded almost immediately. Mkele turned next to Haru, who stared back only a moment before nodding as well. *When the alternative is extinction, all kinds of horrors become acceptable.*

"I don't like it," said Haru, "but I like it more than everybody dying. We're out of time for anything better."

Mkele turned to Tovar, who threw up his hands in frustration. "Do you know how long I fought against these kinds of fascist policies?"

"I do," said Mkele calmly.

"I started a civil war," said Tovar. "I bombed my own people because I thought freedom was more important than survival. There's no point saving us if we lose our humanity in the process."

"We can change if we live," said Mkele. "A nation built on slavery can be redeemed, but not if we all die."

"This is wrong," said Tovar.

"I never said it wasn't," said Mkele. "Every choice we have is wrong. This is the lesser of ninety-nine evils."

"I'll lead your distraction," said Tovar. "I'll give my life to help the rest of you escape, and I'll sell that life as dearly as possible. Hell, I've always been a better terrorist than a senator anyway."

He stared at them pointedly. "Just don't give up on goodness yet. Somewhere out there there's a way to get through this." He opened his mouth to say something else, but instead just shook his head and turned to leave. "I hope we find it in time."

Tovar's hand was inches from the doorknob when suddenly the door shook, practically rattling on its hinges as someone pounded on the other side.

"Senator!" It was a young voice, Haru thought, probably another soldier. Tovar glanced back at the group curiously before opening the door.

"Senator Tovar," said the soldier, practically tripping over himself in his rush to speak. "The message has stopped."

Tovar frowned. "The message . . . stopped?"

"The radio message from the Partials," said the soldier. "They've stopped the broadcast. Every channel is clear."

Mkele stood up. "Are you sure?"

"We've scanned every frequency," said the soldier.

"They've found her," said Haru, stunned by the sudden blend of relief and terror. He'd known Kira for years, and the thought of her in Partial hands was sickening, but at the same time, Kira would be the first to say that one girl was more than a fair trade for the hundreds of people the Partials seemed willing to kill in their search for her. He'd come to hate her for not turning herself in, and eventually convinced himself that she couldn't possibly still be on the island; she must have either fled or died, or surely she would have come forward by now. No one could stand by silently while so many people were executed. *But now, if she's been captured, maybe that means she's been here all along. . . .* The thought made him furious.

"We don't know for sure that they've found the girl," said Mkele. "It's possible that their radio tower's just failed temporarily."

"Or maybe they just gave up," said Hobb.

"Keep monitoring the frequencies," said Tovar to the soldier. "Let me know the instant you hear anything. I'll join you when I can." The soldier nodded and ran off at a dash. Tovar closed and locked the door, keeping their conversation secret—nobody else knew about the nuke, and Haru knew it was wise to keep it that way. "How does this change our plans?" asked Tovar, looking back at the group. "Does it change them at all? There's still a nuke, and Delarosa's still probably going through with her plan. Even without the daily executions it's still just a matter of time, and this is still the strongest blow she can strike against them."

"If the Partials pull out, it makes the nuke an even more attractive option," said Mkele, "because it will catch more of them in the blast."

"And Kira too," said Haru. He didn't know how he felt about that.

Tovar smiled sadly. "Twenty minutes ago we were struggling to justify this attack, and now we can't bear to give it up."

"Delarosa will go through with her plan," said Hobb, "and we should go through with ours."

"Then I guess it's time to piss off the overwhelming enemy," said Tovar. He saluted them stiffly, the ex-marine appearing like magic from inside the form of the old, weathered traveler. "It's been a pleasure serving with you."

Mkele saluted him back, then turned toward Hobb and Haru. "You're in charge of the evacuation."

"He means me," said Hobb.

"He means us," said Haru. "Don't think you're in charge just because you're a senator."

"I'm twice your age."

"If that's the best reason you can come up with, you're definitely not in charge." Haru stood. "Can you shoot?"

"I've trained with a rifle since we founded East Meadow," said Hobb indignantly.

"Then get your gear ready," said Haru. "We're leaving in an hour." He left the room, deep in his own thoughts. Maybe the Partials really had found Kira—but where? And why now, after all this time?

And now that they had her, what would they do?

CHAPTER THREE

Kira stared up at the surgery robot, a massive metal spider looming down from the ceiling. Twelve sleek, multijointed arms swiveled into place, each tipped with a different medical instrument: scalpels and clamps in half a dozen different sizes, syringes with interchangeable barrels of brightly colored liquid, and spanners and spikes and other devices with functions Kira could only guess at. She'd been in medical training since she was ten—almost eight years ago now—but there were things in here she'd never even dreamed of.

They showed up all the time in her nightmares, though. This was the same facility in Greenwich, Connecticut, where Dr. Morgan had captured her and tortured her before Marcus and Samm had saved her. Now she'd abandoned them both and come back of her own free will.

The spider rotated silently, reaching toward her with sleek steel pincers. Kira suppressed a scream and tried to think calm thoughts.

"Local anesthetic to points four, six, and seven," said Morgan, tapping the locations on a massive wall screen, where a diagram of Kira's body hung motionless in the air. "Engage." The spider reached down without pause or ceremony and plunged its needles into Kira's hip and abdomen. Kira stifled another scream, gritting her teeth and compressing her fears into a low grunt.

"Such a glowing bedside manner," said Dr. Vale, standing by another wall. "It warms my heart, McKenna—you're like a mother hen."

"I started a war to find this girl," said Morgan. "You want me to ask permission every time I touch her?"

"A quick 'This will only hurt a little' might be nice," said Vale. "Maybe even an 'Are you ready, Kira?' before we start the surgery?"

"As if my answer would change anything?" asked Kira.

Morgan shot her a glance. "You made the choice to be here."

Vale snorted. "Another answer that didn't technically change anything."

"It changed a great deal," said Morgan, looking back at the wall screen. She plotted out lines for incisions. "It impressed me."

"Well, then," said Vale. "By all means, treat her like a lab rat."

"I was a lab rat last time," said Kira. "This time is better, believe me."

"That's the kind of answer that only makes this worse," said Vale, shaking his head. "You were always cold, McKenna, but this is the most coldhearted, dehumanizing—"

"I'm not a human," said Kira, and realized with a start that Morgan had said almost the same thing—"She's not a human"—simultaneously. They looked at each other for a moment, then Morgan turned back to her wall screen.

"In the interest of"—Morgan paused, as if searching for the right way to say it—"a peaceful working relationship, I will be more communicative." She tapped a few icons on the wall screen, which split into three sections—the line diagram of Kira's body on one side, and two half-size boxes on the other showing two sets of data: one labeled "Expiration" and one labeled "Kira Walker." "Dr. Vale and I were part of the Trust—the group of ParaGen scientists who created the Partials and the RM plague. We didn't intend for the plague to bring the human race to the brink of extinction, obviously, but the damage is done, and once I realized the humans were a lost cause, I turned my attention to the Partials instead. I've spent the last twelve years helping them build a new civilization, trying to find ways to overcome the sterility and other handicaps hardwired into their DNA. Imagine my surprise when they began dying, for no discernible reason, precisely twenty years after they were created."

Vale spoke up again. "The expiration date was—"

"The expiration date was the surest sign that 'the Trust' was a horrible misnomer," said Morgan. "Living, thinking beings that I helped create were preprogrammed to wither to dust in a matter of hours the moment they hit their biological deadline, and I knew nothing about it. I've been doing everything in my power to fix it, which brings us here."

"You think I can cure it," said Kira.

"I think something in your body holds the secret that will help me cure it," said Morgan. "The last time I had you in a lab, when we discovered you were a Partial—another secret the 'Trust' kept from me—my initial scans determined that despite being a Partial, you had none of the genetic handicaps the others have: no sterility, no fixed age, no inhibition of growth or any other human function. If it turns out that you have no expiration date either, there might be a way to reverse engineer certain fragments of your genetic code to help save the rest of the Partials."

"I've already told you that this is impossible," said Vale. "I'm the one who programmed the expiration date—I'm sorry I couldn't tell you at the time, but there it is. You were unstable, and no, we didn't trust you. It wasn't just you, though—Armin didn't trust me with some of the pieces, either."

Armin, thought Kira. *My father—or the man I used to think was my father. He took me home to raise as his own, he never even told me what I was. Maybe he would have, one day. Now nobody even knows where he is.* She wondered if he was dead. Everyone else in the Trust had survived the Break—Trimble and Morgan here with the Partials, Vale in the Preserve with a group of hidden humans, Ryssdal in Houston working on "environmental issues," whatever that meant, and Nandita on Long Island with the humans.

Nandita. The woman who raised me, who also *didn't tell me I was a Partial.*

Dr. Morgan tried to kill me, but at least she hasn't pretended to be something she isn't.

"Even if you can find something in there," Vale continued, "how are you going to incorporate it into the Partials' genetic sequence? Gene mods? You're talking about hundreds of thousands of people—even if we had the facilities and the personnel to mount that kind of a mass modification effort, we don't have the time to pull it off. How many Partials are left, half a million?"

"Two hundred thousand," said Morgan, and Kira couldn't help but gasp at the low number. Morgan's voice was grim and exhausted. "They were created in batches, so they die in them as well. The next wave is due in just a few weeks."

"And they're all soldiers," said Vale. "Infantry and pilots and maybe a few commandos, but the leaders are all dead—more to the point, the doctors are all dead. It'll be up to you and me, and we wouldn't be able to process even a tenth of what's left before their time runs out—even if we already knew how."

"That's why we have to do something," said Kira. She thought of Samm, and everything they'd shared, and their final, terrifying, passionate moment together. She loved him, and if her sacrifice here could keep him alive . . . "Everyone in the world is dying, humans and Partials, and I gave myself up because this is our best shot at saving anyone. So let's get on with it."

Vale's expression darkened. "I'm trying to help you, Kira, don't get snotty with me."

"You don't know her very well," said Morgan, and her voice softened.

Vale stared at her a moment, then snarled and turned away.

Morgan looked at Kira. "Last time, we scanned your reproductive system only peripherally—back when we thought you were human, it wasn't a priority. Today we're going to do several biopsies."

Kira's hips and abdomen already felt numb and lifeless from the anesthetic. She looked back at Morgan, steeling her resolve, and nodded silently.

"Engage," said Morgan, and the spider unfurled its knives.

CHAPTER FOUR

"**D**isengage that last hose," said Heron. Her voice sounded tinny and distant through the radio, and Samm bristled again at the oddness of trying to communicate without the link. Partials used pheromonal communication because it was efficient, folding words and emotions and tactical information into a single, silent package. Working side by side, yet communicating solely through the radios in their helmets, felt like being deaf and mute. He still didn't understand how humans did it.

As difficult as dealing with the repurposed diving gear was, though, it was necessary. If either of them breathed a whiff of the air in the laboratory, they'd be unconscious in seconds.

Samm slowly disengaged the final hose from the unconscious Partial's odd metal face mask. There were ten comatose Partials here in Dr. Vale's old laboratory, fast asleep in a secret subbasement of the Preserve. Vale had kept them here, unconscious, for thirteen years, tending them like plants and harvesting the Lurker pheromone from their bodies—an engineered chemical, naturally produced by all Partials, which served as the only known cure for RM. These Partials had kept the humans of the Preserve alive for over a decade, allowing them to raise healthy children—something the humans on Long Island had been completely unable to do. These ten Partials—*But no,* Samm corrected himself, *these nine Partials.* These nine Partials had given the Preserve a life and hope no other human had felt since the end of the world. Maybe even before that. They were saviors. But they were unwitting, unwilling, unconscious saviors, and Samm could not allow that to continue. The tenth Partial, this last one with the odd-looking face mask, had been modified by Dr. Vale to produce a different pheromone: one that would instantly render any Partial comatose. His mere proximity was a weapon.

Samm and Heron were disconnecting him, but they still had no idea what to do with him.

"That hose was pumping his sedative throughout the building," said Heron. "Now that we've cut off his access, the effect should be limited to his immediate presence."

"He's got a tag," said Samm, leaning in closer. "Williams." He flipped the dog tag over, reading the numbers on the back; he couldn't interpret them perfectly, but he knew the coding system well enough to know that Williams had been assigned to the third regiment. *The group we left behind, back in the rebellion, to guard Denver and NORAD after we'd taken them.* He guessed that the other Partials in the room had come from the same group. He flipped the tag over again, hoping to find something he'd missed, but there was nothing. It wasn't surprising, exactly—most Partials only had a first name—but it was odd to find one who only had a *last* name. He wondered what the man's story was, where his name had come from, what he'd done and what he'd thought and how he'd lived, but that information was lost forever now. His own genes would keep him sedated for the rest of his life.

It was the cruelest thing Samm had ever witnessed, and Samm had watched the world end.

"This mask is grafted on," said Heron, probing Williams's face mask with gloved fingers. Samm looked closer and saw that she was right—it wasn't really a mask at all, more of a cybernetic implant that covered, or perhaps replaced, the man's nose, mouth, jaw, and neck. Vents stood out on the side like gills, and the surface was covered with nozzles and valves. *His entire body was rebuilt for a single purpose,* thought Samm, *to spread this sedative,* but then he paused and considered his own body. *I was built for a single purpose too. All of us were. We're weapons, just like him.*

I'm even designed to destroy myself, when I reach my expiration date.

In eight months.

"We still haven't decided what to do with him," said Samm.

"We can leave him here for now," said Heron. "Vale kept him healthy for years, and he's still hooked up to life support. Now that the hoses are disconnected, we can access the rest of the building without these stupid helmets, and we can move the rest of the Partials up and out of range so they can wake up."

"And then what?" asked Samm. "We just keep him here forever?"

"Until his expiration, yeah," said Heron.

"He's like a living corpse," said Samm. "That's cruel."

"So is killing him."

"Is it?" Samm sighed and shook his head, looking around at the room full of atrophied, corpselike Partials. "Every single one of us is going to be dead in eight months—I was part of the last purchase order, and when we go, there's nobody left. The humans will live longer, but without the cure for RM their species won't propagate, and they'll be just as dead as we are. The entire world is on life support, and—"

"Samm," said Heron. Her voice sounded cold and clinical, and Samm wondered if she was really being terse or if all the consoling, sympathetic feelings were being cut off with the rest of the link. With Heron it was hard to tell, even under the best of circumstances. "Survival is all we have. If we end we end, but if we live a second day there's always a chance, no matter how slim, that we can find a way to live a third, and a fourth, and a hundredth and a thousandth. Maybe the world kills us and maybe it doesn't, but if we give up, it's the same as killing ourselves. We're not going to do that."

Samm looked at her, confused by the care she seemed to be taking for his welfare. It wasn't like her, and without the link to clue him in, he had no idea why she was behaving so strangely. He tried to read her face, the way Kira said that humans did—Heron was an espionage model, the most human of the Partial designs, and showed a lot of her emotions on her face. Even without the curved diving helmet distorting her visage, though, Samm was just too unpracticed to read anything.

The best thing he could do, then, was answer. "I'm not really considering it," said Samm. "I would never give up." He stared at Williams. "But he can't give up, even if he wants to. For all we know he's miserable—maybe he's in pain, or he's aware enough to feel trapped, or something even worse. We don't know. There's always a chance for us to find something new, like you said, but what about him? Vale said he lost the technology to make another Partial like him, and that includes the technology to turn him back. He will never be conscious or . . . alive, ever again. I just don't know if that existence, specifically, is worth preserving. Maybe euthanasia is the most merciful thing to do."

Heron paused a moment, looking at him, before answering softly. "Do you really want to kill him?"

"No."

"Then why are we even talking about it?"

"Because maybe what I *want* doesn't matter here. Maybe the best decision is the hardest one to make."

Heron turned away and started fiddling with one of the other Partials, the one next to Williams, checking his vital signs before carefully disconnecting him, tube by tube, from the life support system. She wasn't killing him, Samm knew, she was freeing him; this was the next step in their plan. He checked his own oxygen level in the diving helmet—a needless precaution, since there were several hours left—and read Williams's sensor readout one last time. He was alive, technically, and his body was as healthy as any long-term coma patient's would be. He turned to the other nine Partials and helped Heron unplug them from the machines.

They wheeled the first two gurneys to the elevator and took them upstairs. The humans who lived in the Preserve were waiting outside, led by the only two humans Samm was certain he could trust: Phan, the short, perpetually cheerful hunter, and Calix, the most skilled scout in the Preserve, now confined to a wheelchair from the gunshot in her leg. She watched Heron coldly as they brought the first two Partials out of the building, but when they actually reached her the coldness was gone, and she was all business.

"I didn't want to believe you," she said, staring at the comatose Partials.

"There are eight more down there," said Samm, taking off his diving helmet. The air was fresh, with no lingering trace of the sedative. "All as emaciated as these two."

"And this is where Dr. Vale got the cure," said Phan. He touched one of the unconscious Partials lightly on the arm. "We didn't know. We never would have . . ." He looked up at Samm. "I'm sorry. If we'd known he was enslaving Partials, we would have . . . I don't know. But we would have done something."

"We've had more than one thousand children born since the Break," said Laura, an older woman, and the acting leader of the Preserve now that Vale was gone. "Are you really saying you would have let them all die?"

Phan went pale, an impressive feat on his dark features. "I didn't mean that, I just mean—"

"Are you saying you want them back down there?" asked Heron, watching Laura like a snake about to strike. She still wore her helmet, and the radio gave her voice a menacing, mechanical sound. Samm interjected before the situation could get out of hand.

"I've already told you I'll fill in for them myself," said Samm. "You need the cure, and I understand that, so you can get it from me—willingly. The slaves go free, and everybody's happy."

"Until Samm dies," said Heron. He assumed she was being

flippant and sent her a scalding blast of WATCH IT before realizing that with her helmet on she was still cut off from the link data. He glanced at her instead, trying to convey the same sharpness he'd seen so often when Kira was mad at her. She smirked back, silently amused, and he assumed he'd done it wrong. *At least she knows what I meant, even if she doesn't care.*

Calix craned her neck over her shoulder, calling to the gathered humans behind her. "Take these two back to the hospital, and make sure they're ready for more." The crowd hesitated, and Calix barked another command that even Samm could tell was intended as a harsh verbal slap. "Now!"

An older man spoke. "These are Partials, Calix." His suspicious glance encompassed Samm and Heron as well.

"And they've saved one thousand of your children from RM," said Calix. "They've done more for this community than any of us, and they've done it all from the verge of death. Anyone who's got a problem with helping them will answer to me."

The man stared at Calix, a slim sixteen-year-old girl in a wheelchair. Her eyes hardened.

"You don't think I can back that up?" she whispered.

"Just take them to the hospital," said Laura, grabbing the first gurney. "I'll come with you. The rest of you go down with them, now that we know it's safe."

Samm let Laura pull the gurney away and slowly buckled his diving helmet back on for the next trip down. He knew this wasn't easy for the humans to do, but they were doing it, and that impressed him. In the back of his mind, though, he knew that Heron's quick, snarky comment was the truest statement any of them had made: Sooner or later, no matter what anyone did or sacrificed, the Partials were going to die. And then the humans would die, and it would all be over.

Kira had left to help try to find a cure. Would she and Dr. Morgan find it in time? And if they did find it, would they bring it back here?

Kira . . .

Would Samm ever see her again?

CHAPTER FIVE

Dr. Morgan took biopsies of Kira's uterus, ovaries, lungs, sinuses, heart, spinal fluid, and brain tissue. She built elaborate models of Kira's DNA, manipulating them on the molecular level through a massive holographic display, running so many simulations she actually slagged one of the hospital's central computer processors. Every Partial technician who might have known how to replace it had already expired, so they soldiered on with the two remaining processor banks and hoped for the best.

Hope, Kira realized, was quickly becoming their sole remaining asset.

Dr. Vale, for his part, spent his time poring over Morgan's copious records of Partial genetics, trying to reconstruct as much of his work on the expiration date as possible. When Kira wasn't on the operating table or in the recovery room, she sat with him, usually attached to a rolling IV, and tried to learn as much as she could.

"This is part of the aging sequence," said Vale, pointing to a segment of a DNA strand glowing faintly on the screen. He highlighted a series of amino acids with his fingers, and it glowed a different color. "A normal Partial grows to physical maturity in about ten months, all inside of a big glass tube; we called them vats, but they really looked more like those clear capsules you'd use at an express diner."

Kira shook her head. "I have no idea what that means."

"Sorry. How about a . . . skinny glass elevator?"

"I was five years old at the Break," said Kira. "I grew up after the world already ended. You're going to have to explain this without old-world metaphors."

"Okay," said Vale, pressing his fingers to his lips as he thought. "Okay. Imagine a clear cylinder, about seven feet long and two feet in diameter, with a metal cap on each end full of tubes and hoses and such. We had a few of them in the ParaGen building in the Preserve, I should have shown you; the rest were all at the growth and training facilities in Montana and Wyoming, but those were pretty heavily bombed during the Partial War. Anyway: The techs would create the zygotes in a lab and plant them in a nutritive gel Dr. Morgan invented, and by the time they were done growing, they more or less filled the tube; them and all the liquid we pumped in with them. I designed the entire life cycle," he said, pointing back at the glowing DNA strand on his screen. "They required a remarkable amount of energy to grow at such a rate, most of which they drew from Morgan's gel, though we had to keep them warm as well—the infant Partials were designed to be so energy-efficient that they lost virtually none of their energy as heat, which helped them grow quickly but kept them unnaturally cold. Once the accelerated aging was finished, the heightened metabolism slowed down, and they live relatively normal lives, but when the twenty years are up, the age accelerator kicks into overdrive—it looks like they're decomposing, but really they're aging a hundred years in a matter of weeks."

"And freezing to death at the same time," said Kira.

"Well, yes," said Vale. "The energy has to come from somewhere." He sighed. "I know you don't approve, and I assure you that I don't either. I didn't like it then and I don't like it now. But there was no other way."

"You could have refused."

"To create the Partials? ParaGen stood to make trillions of dollars—if we hadn't helped them, they would have found someone else. This way we could control the process."

"You could have refused to set an expiration date."

"It was supposed to be a temporary measure to buy us time: The government wanted a kill switch, the Failsafe I thought had been implanted in you, and if we'd gone with that plan, the Partials would all be dead by now, and the humans would have no hope at all. This way we had twenty years to find another solution, but the end of the world precluded that."

The Failsafe. Kira had crossed the continent looking for information on the Failsafe, only to discover that it was a twisted mess: The government had demanded a plague that could kill Partials if they ever got out of hand, and the Trust had built two versions. The first—the plague the government wanted, the one that would only affect Partials—was never implemented, intended solely as a decoy to make ParaGen think the Trust was following orders. The second, which would only target humans, was what eventually came to be known as RM, though for reasons even the Trust didn't understand, it had proven to be far more deadly than planned. They had tried to make the humans' well-being dependent on the Partials, giving them a disease only the Partials could cure. They'd thought it was the only way to keep the Partials safe from genocide. Instead, they'd committed genocide themselves.

Kira watched Vale in silence as he pored over the DNA images, reading them the way an archaeologist would read an ancient language—organic hieroglyphics that he studied with a low, intense mutter. After a moment Kira spoke again.

"What was your plan for those twenty years?"

"Excuse me?"

"You said you had twenty years to deal with the expiration date before it kicked in, and that you were going to try to deal with it before it became an issue. What was your plan?"

"It was Armin's plan," he said softly, still staring intently at the DNA. "We all had our jobs, and we worked in secret. That's why Morgan didn't know about the expiration date."

At the mention of his name, Kira was lost in another dark reverie. It was Armin who had formed the Trust, he who had suggested the rash plan to save their million Partial "children" from death. If he had a plan to overcome expiration, what was it? Was he just relying on the same genetic equipment Morgan was? Before the Break, with access to the full resources of ParaGen, gene-modding a million people might have been a feasible plan, diving into their DNA and carving out the expiration code like a patch of rot in an apple. What Armin would have done, she could only guess. She'd lived with the man for five years, give or take—she had no idea how long she'd gestated in a growth vat before popping out to be taken care of. Armin had raised her as his own, so fully she'd never even suspected she wasn't human, that she wasn't really his daughter. She didn't even know what her purpose was. Would she ever meet him? Would she ever get the chance to ask him?

Did knowing the truth about who he was, and what she was, make him less of a father? She remembered him with love—was that relationship any less meaningful now? She hadn't decided yet. She wasn't sure if she could. You didn't need a biological connection to be a family; all of the family relationships post-Break were ones of adoption, and the love they felt was real. But none of those adoptive parents had lied to their children about the fundamental aspects of those children's existence and species. None of those adoptive parents had synthetically engineered their children and grown them in a clear glass cylinder.

None of those adoptive parents had ended the world.

Well, except Nandita. I have all the luck with parents.

"Do you know where Armin is?" she asked softly.

"You asked about him before," said Vale, pausing to turn and look at her. "What's your interest in him?"

Kira wasn't sure she wanted to share that part of her life with Vale or Morgan—at least not yet. "He's the only one we can't account for."

"We don't know much about Jerry Ryssdal, either."

"But Jerry Ryssdal wasn't the one who created the Trust."

Vale shook his head helplessly. "Well, given the circumstances, I would assume Armin is dead."

Kira swallowed, trying not to let her feelings show, even as she was unsure of what those feelings were. "But the Trust are all immune to RM. You gene-modded yourselves for protection."

"There are plenty of ways to die that aren't related to RM," said Vale. "When things fell apart . . . he could have died in a looting scuffle, during a Partial bombing—"

"I thought the Partials didn't attack civilians."

"ParaGen was hardly a civilian target in that particular war," said Vale. "Many of our facilities were attacked, and he may have been in or near one at the wrong time."

"But you survived."

"Why are you interrogating me?"

Kira took a deep breath, shaking her head tiredly. "You're trying to work, and I'm . . . preoccupied. I'm sorry. You're in here practically twenty hours a day trying to cure this thing, and I should be helping you, not—"

Now it was Vale's turn to shake his head, refusing to meet Kira's eyes. "You're helping more than anyone." There was more anger in his voice than Kira had expected. "You're a sixteen-year-old girl and I'm letting Morgan treat you like a cell culture."

"I volunteered."

"That doesn't make it right."

"It's the only right choice there is."

"That doesn't mean I like it."

They sat in silence for a moment, and Kira smiled sadly. "I'm seventeen, actually. Almost eighteen."

Vale smiled back, though the smile seemed just as sad and forced as Kira's. "When's your birthday?"

"I have no idea. Sometime in January. I always just celebrate it on New Year's."

Vale nodded, as if that meant something profound. "A snow baby."

"Snow?"

Vale sighed again. "I forget you kids don't know about snow. When was the last time . . . ? I can't remember. . . . Even I must've been a kid the last time it snowed. Anyway: a New Year's baby, then." He turned back to his monitor. "That's good luck. We're going to need it."

Kira looked at the glowing DNA strand, trying to read it like he did, but it meant virtually nothing to her. She'd trained as a medic, so she knew the terminology, but genetics were not her specialty. She traced the tape holding the IV tube to her arm. "Are you sure there's nothing more I can do to help?"

"Find Armin," he muttered, staring at the screen, "and ask him what the hell we're supposed to do now."

Kira felt a surge of excitement at the suggestion, but she knew it was a hopeless plan—there was too little time left, and no idea even where to begin. And when it came right down to it, she wasn't even sure she wanted to find her father. What would she say to him? She didn't even know if she'd be angry or glad. "I've tried looking for the Trust already," she said at last. "I can do more good here, helping you and Morgan with your research."

"That's what you keep saying."

"I know you're just trying to help me," said Kira, "and I appreciate that, but I'm serious about this." She felt a flutter of fear, as she always did thinking about her situation, but forced it down. She thought about Samm, and steeled her resolve. "I don't go back on my promises."

"Even if they have no purpose?"

Kira frowned. "You don't think Morgan will find anything?"

"I think she's looking in the wrong place. All she's going to find in you is a basic Partial template, an example of a Partial genome with no expiration triggers."

"Which is exactly what she's looking for," said Kira.

He dismissed that notion with a wave. "It's a solution she can't implement. Even if she finds the right genes, what then? We don't have the time or the means to disseminate the cure to more than a handful of Partials, let alone every Partial in the world. I've talked to her about it, but she's determined."

Kira started to speak but trailed off, uncertain and terrified. "But if I'm not . . ." It was a fear she hadn't even realized she had, but which sprang up in her mind like a nightmare, shaking her to the core.

I'm not a cure for RM, and I don't have any special powers or abilities that anyone can find. I'm not even the Partial Failsafe, according to every test they've been able to run. I thought I was created for a purpose, but I've tried everything else, and curing expiration is the only purpose left.

But if I'm not the cure for expiration, what good am I to anyone?

She tried to control her tears, but they burst out in a flood. Vale looked up in surprise, his face a mask of confusion; he looked like he wanted to help but had no idea what to do or say, and Kira stood up quickly, grabbing her rolling IV stand and walking away before he could try to comfort her. She was still sobbing, so much she could hardly see, but she knew that a single word from anyone, even a kind one, would wreck her completely. She staggered out of the room, closing the door behind her, and sagged against the wall in a torrent of tears.

I thought the Trust had a plan to save everyone, and the more I looked the more it kept coming back to my father, to me, to the questions that no one could answer. Why did he make me? Why would anyone hide a Partial among the humans? What was I intended to do or be or accomplish? What was I . . . She sobbed, completely unable to even articulate the thought anymore, even to herself. She'd dared to believe that she was the plan—that her father had created her for this time, for this purpose, to cure both species and save the world. To lose that dream was hard enough, but the sheer arrogance of having that dream in the first place broke her in half.

Dr. Morgan found her twenty minutes later, curled on the floor and shivering in her hospital gown.

"The spinal fluid was another dead end. I want brain tissue."

Kira didn't bother to ask why, or what her methods were, or how much brain tissue Morgan needed. She dragged herself to her feet, clutching the IV stand like a cane, and shuffled toward the operating room. The biopsies were invasive and painful, more like torture than a medical procedure, but Kira set her face grimly and lay down under the spider. The hospital was so empty, they hadn't passed a single other person in the halls. Too many of the Partials were dead.

The needles gleamed, piercing her like daggers, but Kira embraced the pain. It was all she had left.

CHAPTER SIX

Ariel tapped her fingers on the stock of her rifle, watching Nandita as the women in the house readied themselves to leave. It would be so easy to kill her—half a second to aim, another to pull the trigger. Boom. Dead. So easy to rid the world of its most heartless, deceitful, irredeemable denizen. Nandita Merchant had created the Partials, she had created RM, she had kidnapped Ariel and three other girls and experimented on them for years, right under everyone's noses, lying to them about their true nature. Ariel was a Partial. Her adoptive sisters—Kira and Isolde—were Partials. The enemy.

In Ariel's mind it felt as if Nandita had changed her with a sentence, like a magic spell, stealing her humanity to leave her gasping in the darkness. She had made her a monster, with the blood of the world still dripping from her talons. She didn't know what to think, or even how. It was too much to take in. The world had shifted, and it would never be the same.

Only one thing remained after the announcement: She had

hated Nandita before, and she hated her now. She touched the trigger, just lightly, not even pointing the rifle in Nandita's direction. The curve of it gave her a dark, illicit thrill. *It would be so easy.*

Isolde walked into the room, a stuffed backpack in each hand and Mohammad Khan, her red-faced, screaming baby, in a tight sling across her chest. Ariel moved her hand back to the stock.

"I have blankets, clothes, and everything in the house that can be used as a cloth diaper," said Isolde. Her eyes were bloodshot, and her voice was raw from emotion and fatigue. "I think that's everything, but I don't know. I'm convinced I'm forgetting something."

"You're fine," said Nandita, stroking Khan's cheek ineffectually. He was five days old—an outright miracle in the world after the Break, when most children died in three—but his apparent immunity to RM wasn't saving him from the other disease he'd had since birth, a mysterious illness that spiked his fever and ruptured his skin with boils and rough, leathery patches. Nandita thought she could save him, that Khan's human/Partial hybrid DNA would make him more resilient. But Ariel knew the truth. Being a hybrid hadn't saved her baby two years ago, and it wouldn't save Isolde's now.

Isolde set her backpacks on the couch, next to Xochi's and that of Xochi's adoptive mother, Senator Erin Kessler. Madison's bag was on the floor, packed mostly with supplies for Arwen, her baby, and the only healthy human child since the Break.

Isolde froze in terror when a sudden knock sounded sharply on the front door. Every woman in the house looked up with wide, wild eyes, for a knock on the door meant only one thing.

Partial soldiers.

Ariel took stock of the room in a single, practiced glance—almost everything in the house was liable to get them arrested, starting with Arwen. The Partials had heard rumors of a thriving human child, nearly one year old, and they wanted her for their experiments. Khan would probably mean nothing to the average observer—his condition made him appear as just another doomed baby—but the guns were contraband and the loaded backpacks were a clear sign that they were about to make a run for it. Nobody was allowed to leave East Meadow, and if the Partials thought they were trying, they'd arrest them all just to be sure.

Ariel stashed her gun behind a bookcase, still in easy reach if she needed it, and caught the bags Xochi threw to her. Nandita, who the Partials had been searching for almost as eagerly as Kira, hid herself in a back room, while Senator Kessler did the same—she wasn't necessarily a criminal, but if the Partials recognized her as a senator, they might take her anyway. Isolde struggled to calm her screaming baby, and far in the back, beneath a false panel in the floor, Madison quietly shushed Arwen. Ariel hid the last of the bags in a kitchen cupboard; barely ten seconds had elapsed since the knock on the door. The soldier outside pounded loudly again, and Ariel opened it.

"What do you want?" Her voice was more surly than she'd intended; she was trying to act innocent and unnoticeable. When the Partials didn't react to her anger, she realized that maybe anger was the most innocent reaction of all in an occupied city. She allowed herself a fierce scowl, surprised at how good it felt.

The pair of Partial soldiers on the porch were both

young—about eighteen years old in appearance, as they all were, though she knew they were closer to twenty. She wondered if she'd seen these two around the city anywhere, maybe guarding a street corner when she'd been out scavenging for food, but they all looked so similar she couldn't tell. The Partials weren't clones of one another, but they may as well have been. Ariel found them completely indistinguishable. It made her wonder if the Partials thought the same thing about humans.

Which only made her grimace, nauseated anew by the realization that "us" and "them" meant completely different things than they had three days ago.

"Miss," said the first Partial, "we heard a baby crying on the premises. We've come to see if there's anything wrong."

You mean you've come to see if it's Arwen, thought Ariel. She glanced at Isolde, who flashed a look of impotent fury before gritting her teeth and giving a small, almost imperceptible nod. They had prearranged a plan to use Khan to hide Arwen, and while Isolde had agreed with it, she hated it intensely.

"Yes," said Ariel, pointing toward the swaddled infant. "Can you help? We've done everything we can, but he's dying." The Partials glanced at Isolde and her baby, and Ariel stepped closer. "It's RM, and it's killing him." She felt more anger boiling to the surface and unleashed it like a flamethrower. "Don't you have any medicine? They told us the Partials had the cure—can you help him? Or are you just here to watch him die?"

The first Partial stepped inside and walked to Isolde, examining Khan up close. Isolde took up the act as well, though she was less angry and more pleading. Ariel studied the second Partial, still in the doorway, covering his partner like a good wingman;

his rifle wasn't aimed, but it was ready to bring up at a moment's notice, and they all knew from experience just how fast a Partial could be.

It occurred to Ariel, not for the first time, that she could give them Nandita. The old woman was concealed in a closet, trapped like a rat if Ariel decided to lead them to her. What would they do if they found her—torture her? Kill her outright? Nothing good, she knew, or Nandita wouldn't be so intent on staying hidden. Ariel wanted to speak up so desperately she had to clench her fist to keep from blurting it out, but there were two reasons she forced herself to keep quiet: first, because the inevitable questions that followed might possibly expose Arwen, or even Khan's unique parentage. Second, and more frustrating, was Nandita's mysterious power over the Partials—she seemed to be able to control them, and exposing her to these two soldiers would do nothing but give her a new pair of pawns.

The control, she knew, came through something called the link—Kira had discovered that the Partials used a system of chemical communication, like pheromones in an ant colony, breathing one another's thoughts and feeling one another's emotions. Ariel, however, could never sense any of it. She breathed deeply, trying not to be obvious about it. Nothing. It made her wonder if Nandita was simply lying to them—if they weren't some alternate Partial model, but human after all. She'd lied about everything else, why not that?

"Hi," said the Partial in the doorway. "I'm Eric. That's Chas."

Ariel stared back, furious at the soldier's attempt at conversation. How dare he treat them like friends—like equals—in the middle of an enemy occupation? In the middle of an armed home invasion? She wished she could use the link just so she could blast him with the full force of her rage.

Caught by a sudden impulse, before she knew it she was blowing out a long, slow breath, right toward his face. Any harder and he'd feel the wind of it. Her heart seemed to stop as she waited, watching his eyes for any reaction, but she saw nothing—no sudden alarm, no glimmer of recognition. If she had the link at all, he was as deaf to hers as she was to his. She didn't know if she should feel triumphant or disappointed, and the confusion only made her feel sicker. She scowled, and gripped the door frame for support. The Partial in the doorway shot her a quick glance, saw nothing important, and continued with his scan of the living room.

The Partial named Chas inspected Khan, presumably trying to determine for himself whether this fevered newborn was the fabled Miracle Baby. The women's plan, posed by Xochi, was to present Khan to any Partial scouts in the hope that they wouldn't bother looking for a second baby. The only problem would come if one of their neighbors—perhaps someone starving, or hoping to free a loved one from the Partials' prison—had sold them out. All the humans knew about Arwen, and where she was hiding, but none of them would dare to betray the Miracle Baby. *She hoped*. Ariel held her breath, trying not to look as scared as she felt, waiting for the Partials to leave.

"What are these blisters?"

Ariel felt her chest grow tighter; she was still facing the doorway, but she could hear the sharp intake of breath as Xochi or Isolde, maybe both of them, reacted in sudden fear to the question. Had the Partials noticed their fear? Did they suspect the girls were hiding something? She wanted to spin around, to see what was happening in the room, but forced herself to stay calm. She studied Eric in the doorway, looking for a sign of alarm in his face, but saw nothing. *That might not mean anything,* she told herself. *The link makes them express emotions differently from us. He could be on the verge of killing us, and we'd never know.*

The silence dragged on, the soldier's question hanging in the air unanswered, and Ariel realized that Isolde was too shocked to speak. Maybe the Partials would miss a sudden intake of breath, but a failure to answer a direct question was bound to arouse suspicion.

Ariel turned around slowly. "He's sick. I told you already."

Chas adjusted his rifle and leaned in closely over Khan; the baby whimpered slightly, too exhausted from its constant pain to keep screaming. Chas reached toward one of the dark-yellow blisters. "This doesn't look like RM."

"RM's not the only disease a baby can get out here away from a hospital," said Ariel, her anger laced with fear. *Why won't they just go away?* She swallowed nervously.

Isolde turned and stepped back, shielding the baby from the soldier's hand. "Don't touch him," she snapped. "The blisters are painful."

Eric raised his rifle—not all the way, but just enough to signal that it was still there, and that the Partials still had all the power. Ariel felt things spiraling out of control, the situation turning dark and desperate and ready to snap. She raised her hand to reach out, but she didn't know where or to whom. Chas reached for Khan again, more aggressively this time, and saw Isolde raise her hand.

"Isolde!" Ariel tried to force her voice to be bright and chipper.

The blond girl looked up, her hand frozen halfway through what might have been intended as a slap or worse. "Can I get you a drink of water?"

Isolde glared at her, her pale face practically red with rage, but she allowed the soldier to touch Khan's face, probing carefully at the rough patches of hardened skin. Isolde seemed to swallow a scream and nodded to Ariel as mechanically as she could. "Thank you."

Ariel walked toward the kitchen, but Chas barked a sudden order.

"Stop."

Ariel froze. She could just see Xochi from the corner of her eye, edging toward the curio cabinet where she'd hidden her handgun.

"No one's allowed to leave the room," Chas continued, his voice grim and serious. "You all stay exactly where you are, where we can see you."

Ariel looked the other way, still frozen in place, and counted the steps to her own rifle's hiding place. *Three steps, and cover when I get there.*

It still won't be enough.

If they started a fight, Senator Kessler would be here in seconds, surprising the Partials and, if they were lucky, taking one out of the fight. If the fight went long enough, Nandita would expose herself as well, using her power over the Partials to stop it—she didn't like to use her control out of fear that it would attract too much attention from the rest of the Partial army, bringing out forces they couldn't hope to deal with, but for a situation like this she might step in. But Xochi or Isolde or both might already be dead by the time Nandita came out, and maybe even Ariel herself.

At last Chas turned away.

"Let's go."

He walked to the door, and that was it—no warnings, no parting words, no acknowledgment of Khan's illness or Isolde's desperate cries for help. They were looking for Arwen, and this wasn't Arwen, so they left. Isolde clutched her baby close to her chest, and Xochi closed the door the soldiers had left hanging open.

Ariel grabbed her rifle, checked the barrel, and tried to slow her breathing.

"We've got to get out of town tonight," said Kessler, stepping into the room with her own rifle gripped tightly in her hands. "That was too close."

"I think we handled it pretty damn well," Xochi snapped.

Kessler growled, rolling her eyes. "I never said you didn't."

"Be quiet or you'll make him start crying again," said Isolde, and hurried out of the room. Ariel slowly peeled her fingers off the rifle, though she still couldn't take her eyes off the locked door, or the windows they'd so carefully blocked to keep from being spied on. Xochi and Kessler pulled the bags out of the cupboards in the kitchen, running last-minute checks to make sure everything was ready. Ariel set her rifle on the table beside her but couldn't bring herself to take her hand off it.

"You may have saved their lives, Ariel," said Nandita, so close behind her that she almost jumped when she heard the old woman's voice. She shot her a dark glance over her shoulder, then walked into the kitchen to help with the bags.

"The other girls froze," Nandita continued. "You didn't. I thank you for that."

Kessler glared at Xochi, but neither of them spoke.

"You still haven't told us where we're going," said Ariel.

"Does it matter?" asked Madison, walking in with Arwen on her hip. "We need to get out, I don't care where."

"Where this group goes matters more than almost anything else in the world," said Kessler. She had a soft Irish lilt in her voice; Xochi, her adopted daughter, was Mexican by birth, but had lived with Kessler so long that the same lilt crept into her voice when she was angry.

It was fully evident now. "You know that's not what she meant, Erin."

"Yes, we have to get the children away from the Partials—" said Madison, but fell abruptly silent almost before she could even finish speaking. Ariel felt everyone's eyes on her but said nothing. "The Partial soldiers," said Madison, correcting herself. "We had the perfect cover today, and it still almost fell apart."

"I'm not suggesting we stay," said Kessler. "I'm just agreeing with Ariel. We need to know where we're going."

"To the same lab where I spent most of the last year," said Nandita.

"That doesn't tell us anything," said Ariel.

Nandita sighed. "And what if one of you is captured? They could torture you, and get the location, and cut the rest of us off before we even arrive."

"What are you expecting this trip to be like?" asked Ariel. "Two infants, an old woman, and barely enough survival training to go around. We're sticking together just to stay alive, and if they find one of us, they find us all."

Nandita glared back at her, but after a moment of silence she spoke. "Before the Break there was a government laboratory on a tiny island off the eastern tip of this one, the Plum Island Disease

Research Center. Being separated from the rest of the continent made it the only safe place to study the most contagious organisms, but it turns out that same isolation saved it when the rest of the world fell apart. It has its own power source, its own air and water recycling system, and a hermetically sealed interior— it hasn't fallen apart the way everything else has. That's where I made this." She held up the hand-sized leather bag that hung around her neck, containing the small glass vial with a chemical trigger; the trigger that would release . . . something inside Ariel's and Isolde's bodies. Nandita had thought it was the cure for RM, but given everything unexpected that had happened with Khan, they could only wonder. "If there's any facility in the world where I can study and cure Khan's illness, it's there."

Ariel found herself instinctually assuming that Nandita must have other motives as well, but she didn't have time to dwell on it. Isolde entered the room, and Khan, in a rare moment of surrender, was passed out from fatigue, asleep on her chest. Isolde looked just as exhausted.

Ariel looked back at Nandita, fixing her with her stare. "Can you actually save him?"

"I will stop at nothing."

They stared at each other, sizing each other up. Ariel wondered what the old woman was thinking, what she was reading in Ariel's face and attitude.

"If you can really help him," said Ariel, "then I'll stop at nothing to help you do it."

And as soon as he's safe, I'll kill you.

CHAPTER SEVEN

General Shon, leader of the Partial invasion force, climbed down from his horse in the yard outside the Dogwood outpost. He handed the reins to his assistant, Mattson. The human Defense Grid had used Dogwood to patrol East Meadow, keeping threats at bay, and Shon now used it for the opposite purpose of keeping the humans contained inside the city. As the most remote outpost, it was also a handy place to keep certain things he didn't want anyone, human or Partial, to find. The link data in the yard crackled with anxiety—Shon could feel edginess and uncertainty in the soldiers, just like the rest of the army, but here they were outright terrified, and with good reason.

The humans, it seemed, had released a biological weapon, and Dogwood was where Shon had been keeping the corpses of his Partial brethren who'd died from the disease.

"Are you sure it's safe here, sir?" asked Mattson.

"I wouldn't have anyone here if it wasn't," said Shon. "Let's go inside." He tried to project as much strength and certainty as he could, hoping his example would bolster the soldiers. Ideally it would be a real general here, not Shon—he was just another infantryman, like them, created to be a sergeant at the most—but he was the one Dr. Morgan had promoted when the other officers expired. Authority was more than just rank for the Partials, it was a biological fact: A general could command those under him through link data that enforced their obedience, and they passed those commands down with link authority of their own. Everyone knew where they fit, and why, and it worked. Now the entire army was flailing, leaderless, and Shon felt it more than anyone. He forced the thoughts out of his mind, determined again to present the most confidence he could muster.

"General," said the guards, saluting as he approached. They were men he'd handpicked for Dogwood, and they knew not to be confused by an infantryman in a general's uniform. He saluted back, and they opened the door to the main building. The strong scent of antiseptic wafted out, and the guard offered Shon a paper mask to cover his mouth and nose.

Shon hesitated, not wanting to muffle the link by restricting his air, but the guard shook his head. "Trust me, sir, you'll want it. The link still functions, it's just weaker."

Shon took the mask, and motioned for Mattson to do the same. They walked inside, where an old friend of Shon's met them with a crisp salute.

"Sir, welcome to Dogwood." Michelle, a sergeant herself, had driven Shon's armored personnel carrier in the Isolation War, and they'd fought together in ten or twelve military campaigns since, most of them against other Partials after the Break. Since Long Island had no easy access to fuel for the APCs, Michelle had been scheduled to return to the mainland after the initial invasion was successful, but Shon had asked to keep her as a tactician. Now she ran Dogwood. The weary tinge to her link data told Shon she was as exhausted by the demands of emergency promotion as he was.

Shon saluted back. "Sergeant."

"Thank you for coming, General," said Michelle. "I wish I had better news."

"More victims?"

"Two more, though all the victims were stationed inside East Meadow. I have the bodies isolated, and I've sent everyone in their units to Duckett Farm."

Shon sighed. "Do they know they're in quarantine?"

"They know they're not allowed to leave; maybe they suspect the truth, I don't know. Even if they do, they might not suspect it's a bioweapon."

"We're genetically engineered to fight off all disease," said Shon. "Now that there's a disease we can't fight, I don't know what else they'd think it is."

"I'm just hoping for the best, sir," said Michelle. "So far none of them have gotten sick, just like the previous units we put under quarantine, so unless they're carrying the disease and haven't manifested yet, I think we've saved them all."

"Not all, though," said Shon heavily.

Michelle shook her head. "Not all. Come with me." She led them to a small room full of white plastic bodysuits, talking as they pulled the protective coverings on over their uniforms. "The doctor arrived only two days ago, but he's already made some excellent headway toward figuring out what the bioweapon is."

"That's good."

"I suppose it's progress," said Michelle, "but as news goes, it hardly classifies as 'good.' The blisters seem to be caused by an autoimmune response—the bioweapon affects Partial biology in such a way that the body becomes allergic to its own skin; the skin cells can't connect to each other properly, and the entire epidermis starts to disintegrate. There's a word for it that I can't remember; something big, at least five syllables."

Shon glanced at her sidelong, confused by the self-deprecation. "You know plenty of five-syllable words." Almost immediately he felt her embarrassment through the link data. She was trying to stay on top of everything, and she'd learned the word, but this was so far outside the realm of her expertise and she hadn't slept in days and there should be a doctor or a general handling this outpost, not a driver, and—

He held up his hand. "It's okay, Michelle, I know you're doing your best."

"Acantholysis," she said quickly, and her link data returned almost immediately to a professional calm. "I'm sorry, sir, it won't happen again."

"It's not your job to know the names of the diseases," said Shon. "That's what the doctor's for. So if this . . ." He shook his head, struggling to remember the word, and eventually gave up. "If these blisters are caused by an autoimmune response, I assume that makes it harder to cure?"

"Much harder," said Michelle, opening a door to a basement stairwell. The antiseptic smell was stronger here, and the plastic-lined steps were puddled with disinfectant. Shon pressed his face mask tighter against his mouth and nose to keep from coughing.

"But I haven't told you the worst part yet. The other primary symptom is rough, scaly skin, something the doctor can only diagnose as icthyosis."

Shon parsed the Latin roots of the word and frowned in confusion. "Fish. Because of the scales, I assume?"

"Exactly. But icthyosis isn't communicable, it's genetic."

Shon stopped short, one hand on the stairway railing. "This is a genetic disease?"

"Somehow the humans have found a way to make a genetic disorder contagious."

Mattson swore, and Shon couldn't help but agree with the sentiment; the link data from both Mattson and Michelle was sharp with fear, detectible even through the face mask. Shon looked at the door at the bottom of the stairs, which Michelle's team had converted to a makeshift air lock, shrouded with plastic and ringed with rubber seals. Shon felt a surge of trepidation, stopping just for a moment; the urge to turn and flee almost overpowered him. It occurred to him that if he could still sense link data through the mask, it probably wasn't protecting him from an airborne disease, either. He kept it on anyway.

"Let's do this."

Michelle opened the door and they followed her through.

The basement was as carefully sealed as the door, not only the windows but the walls themselves covered with layers of protective plastic. The room was crammed with bulky medical computers and the two hospital beds, each one bearing a Partial covered with boils and rough, scaly skin. Shon had considered housing the victims and their researchers in the East Meadow hospital, but he was concerned the disease would get out, and wanted it as far from the Partial population on the island as possible. Instead he'd brought several of the hospital's solar panels and set them up here, to power the medical equipment and air recyclers.

He'd also sent Dogwood the hospital's best human doctors, since all the Partial doctors had already expired.

"This is Dr. Skousen," said Michelle, leading him to an old man in a medical gown and a face mask of his own. The human looked up from a twitching, sweating patient and scowled at Shon.

Shon nodded but didn't bother to extend his hand to shake. "We've met," said Shon. "Tell me, Dr. Skousen, have you had any luck isolating the cause of the disease?"

Shon was only beginning to understand the full range of human facial expressions, but the hatred on Skousen's face was easy to read. "The only reason I'm even looking for this germ is to shake its hand for killing you so spectacularly."

Shon radiated irritation on the link, even though he knew the human couldn't sense it. "But you are looking for it?"

Skousen simply scowled at him, and after a moment Michelle answered for him. "As far as we can tell, yes," she said. "He may as well be doing magic down here for all we understand it."

"He's not hurting anyone," said Shon, meeting Skousen's stare. "That's not who he is." He looked back at Michelle. "You're giving him time to study our RM resistance in return, like I said?"

"Two hours a day," Skousen snarled, "with no access to my notes or my team from the hospital."

"I can give you some of that," said Shon. "If Michelle vouches for your work, I can bring some of your notes from East Meadow."

"And my team."

"I can't take the risk that you'll collude against us."

"I thought you said that's not who I am."

Shon shook his head. "I trust you, Doctor, not your colleagues."

"More time, then," said Skousen. "Two hours a day is nothing—my people are dying, and I might be the only man alive who can help them."

"He only sleeps four hours as it is," said Michelle. "We expect him to collapse in exhaustion any day now."

"I can do the work if you'll give me the time!" Skousen growled.

"Your priority is to cure these Partials," Shon ordered.

Dr. Skousen laughed coldly. "That's not even close to my priority."

"You can't cure anyone if you're dead."

"You already tried to kill me," said Skousen. "Thirteen years ago when I cared for an entire hospital full of RM victims. You think this is bad?" He gestured wildly at the dying Partials, his hands shaking with age and anger. "When the bodies pile so high in this room that you have to step on the dead just to reach the dying, then you can tell me how serious this is. Then you can tell me I'm working too hard and I need some *rest*. Then you can see what it's like to watch an invisible monster kill everyone you've ever loved, assuming you love anything at all."

Skousen's chest was heaving, his old frame out of breath and shaking from the tirade. Shon watched passively, moving only to grab Michelle's arm when she advanced on the doctor angrily.

"Tell me again why we trust you at all," Michelle said, her voice neutral but her emotions raging like wildfire on the link. "This is a weapon your people created—"

"We still don't know that for sure," said Shon.

"—and you're the only one on this island with the medical expertise to create it," Michelle continued, tugging against Shon's grip on her arm. "You should be hanging from a traffic light being eaten by crows, not hiding down here laughing while we parade your victims past you like a highlight reel."

"He didn't create it," said Shon.

Dr. Skousen sneered. "Why do you think you know me so well?"

"Because when my platoon arrived in East Meadow, you were treating our wounded outriders in your hospital. Because you continued to treat them even after we started Morgan's daily executions." Shon spoke simply and softly. "Because you're a healer, and you hate us, and you heal us anyway. You remember RM too well. You couldn't create a new disease even if you wanted to."

Skousen looked back fiercely, but soon he began to sag. "I've dreamed of your deaths every night for thirteen years, but not like this. No one should die like this."

Michelle stopped trying to reach the old human, and Shon relaxed his grip on her arm. The air recyclers hummed loudly in the background, filling the dark plastic room with an unfeeling hiss. Shon gestured at the dying Partial soldiers. "Do you know how to cure it?"

"I barely even know what's causing it," Skousen whispered.

"Michelle said something about it being a genetic disorder."

"Two different ones, if I'm reading the data correctly," said Skousen. "It might be a bioweapon, but at this point you have to consider the possibility that this is a . . . malfunction. A factory error in your DNA, possibly related to your expiration date."

"Expiration doesn't look like this," said Shon.

"Nothing in your history looks like this," said Skousen. "We have to base our theories on analysis, not precedent."

"So what's causing it?" asked Shon. "Why is it only appearing in East Meadow, and why only in specific quadrants? Every victim we've seen has come from one of two patrol assignments, overlapping in a very specific region of the city—that has to be environmental."

"Every victim we've seen has appeared in the last four days," said Skousen. "This disease is too new to make any assumptions about—something that looks like a trend might just be a quirk blown out of proportion by a small sample size."

A muffled alarm sounded down through the insulated ceiling, just loud enough to hear. Michelle looked up sharply.

"New victims."

"Damn." Shon moved to the door, but Michelle blocked his path.

"The disinfection procedure to get out of this room takes ten minutes. We might as well just wait." She sighed. "They'll bring them right to us anyway."

They waited, agonizingly helpless, listening to the shouts and footsteps above them. Finally the door opened, and two gas-masked soldiers dragged a stumbling, blistered Partial into the basement laboratory. Skousen helped them get the man onto a table, and Shon used the link to demand a report.

"Same patrol as the others," said the first soldier, saluting as he spoke. "Symptoms are about two hours old; we grabbed him as soon as his unit reported them."

"The others have been quarantined?"

"They're in the yard," said the soldier. "We knew you'd want to talk to them first."

Shon nodded and walked to the sick man. "What's your name, soldier?"

"Chas," said the man, grunting the word through gritted teeth. "The pain, it's—"

"We'll do everything we can for you," said Shon, and turned to Michelle. "Stay here; learn everything you can from him. I need to get upstairs and debrief the others." He looked at Skousen. "Figure out why this is happening."

The human's voice was firm. "Bring me my notes."

"We don't have time for this."

"Then give me what I want," said Skousen.

Once again Shon felt the impossible weight of his assignment bearing down on his shoulders, threatening to grind his bones to dust against the ground. Invade the island, subdue the humans, find the girl Kira, kill the humans, control the humans . . . and now silence. Morgan's orders had piled up like corpses, and then she had found the girl and closed herself off, with no new orders at all. Shon was undertrained, understaffed, and completely on his own, and now the situation on the island was breaking down faster, and more catastrophically, than he could possibly keep up with. He nodded curtly to Skousen, promising the old man his notes, and raced to the decontamination chamber, where he and Mattson and the two arriving soldiers scrubbed themselves and their boots and their plastic bodysuits with sharp, harsh chemicals. Shon threw away his face mask with disgust and grabbed a new one before racing outside to talk to the rest of Chas's patrol.

What he found in the yard was not remotely what he had expected.

The soldiers in the yard were braced in a wide semicircle, the Dogwood guards and the visiting patrol mixed together almost haphazardly, their rifles up and their sights trained solidly on some . . . *thing* . . . in the middle of the open yard.

Shon drew his handgun as he approached, staring in shock at the thing before him. It was man-shaped, at least vaguely—two arms, two legs, a torso and a head—but it was at least eight feet tall, with a broad, solid chest and thick, powerful arms. Its skin was dark, a kind of purplish black, and plated like the hide of a rhinoceros. Its fingers and toes were clawed, and its thickset head was the most inhuman part of all—hairless, noseless, with a jagged mouth and two dark pits for eyes, which watched them all silently. Shon drew even with the soldiers in the semicircle, his gun level, his mind barely comprehending what he was seeing.

"What the hell is that?"

"No idea, sir," the soldier next to him breathed. "It's . . . waiting for you."

"It talks?"

"If you want to call it that."

Shon looked over his shoulder, seeing Mattson there with his own gun drawn. Shon looked back at the creature and swallowed, stepping forward. The thing watched him, never moving.

Shon took another step and spoke. "Who are you?"

"I am here to speak to your general." The thing's voice was deep, rumbling through Shon's chest like an earthquake and reverberating in his mind with shocking clarity. It didn't seem to have used its mouth at all.

Shon reeled in shock. "How are you using the link?"

"I am here to speak to your general."

"I am the general." Shon stepped forward again, lowering his gun slightly to display his uniform. "You can speak to me."

Wide holes opened on the thing's neck, sniffing like nostrils, or a blowhole. "You are not a general."

"Battlefield promotion," said Shon. "All our generals are dead."

Shon felt a wave of confusion so crippling he nearly dropped his gun, and saw in his peripheral vision that the other soldiers were staggering under the same effect. He righted himself, trying again to project as much strength and confidence as he could.

"What do you want to say to us?"

"I am here to tell you that the Earth is changing," the thing rumbled. It shifted its weight from one massive leg to the other, and still its mouth never opened as it spoke. "You must prepare yourselves."

"For what?"

"For the snow."

The giant turned and walked away.

"For snow?" Shon took a step to follow it, confused at the strange pronouncement, and even more so by the sudden departure. "Wait, what do you mean? Winter? What are you talking about? What are you?"

"Prepare yourselves," said the thing, and Shon saw the slits over its collarbones flare open again, and suddenly he was staggering from fatigue, his body going numb, his eyes struggling just to stay open. He tried to speak, but the world grew dark, and all around him the soldiers were sinking to their knees, collapsing in the dirt.

Shon managed one more "Wait" before the crippling need for sleep overpowered him, and his eyes forced themselves shut. His last view was the monster's back as it plodded slowly away.

CHAPTER EIGHT

"**Y**ou're useless," said Dr. Morgan. She was staring at the wall screens, filled to overflowing with data on Kira's biology, Kira's immune system, Kira's DNA, Kira's everything. They had spent weeks studying her from every possible angle, Morgan and Vale and Kira together, and they had found nothing. There was nothing in her genes that could stop or reverse or even slow expiration, no way to save the Partials from dying. For Kira it was a devastating loss, and she lay on the operating table with no energy left—not physically, not mentally, and certainly not emotionally. She felt like a raw nerve, exposed and despairing, every bit as useless as Morgan said she was. She looked across at her face on the wall screen, sideways to her perspective, gaunt and gray and checkered with scars and bandages from a dozen different invasive surgeries. Her face was a doppelgänger that had betrayed her—her own body an unsolvable riddle, and an implacable enemy.

For Morgan, the realization hit like a tidal wave. She

screamed in frustration, finally giving up, and in a sudden fit of rage pulled out her sidearm and shot the screen, fracturing it into a jagged web of bright, vicious fangs. The image remained, split in serrated shards, and Kira saw her face abruptly cracked and refracted—an eye on this piece, a strand of hair on that one, the corner of a mouth made large and separate and meaningless.

"Useless!" Morgan screamed again. She stood up, spinning around with the gun extended, and Vale jumped in front of Kira, desperately trying to calm the raging scientist. Kira, for her part, was too despondent to move.

"Be reasonable, McKenna."

"How much time did I waste on her?" Morgan demanded. "How many Partials have expired while I was in here wasting my time on a dead end!"

"That's not her fault," said Vale. "Put down the gun."

"Then whose fault is it?" Morgan seethed, thrusting the gun in Vale's face, then turning back to the damaged screen and firing three more rounds into it: *bam bam bam*, a therapy of destruction shattering the remnants of Kira's projected face. "It's our fault, if it's anyone's," she said, more softly this time, though every bit as furious. "Even mine, though I only knew half the plan at the time. Armin's fault, maybe, because he seems like the only one who knew the whole thing, but he's gone." She snarled and threw the gun on the floor. "I can't shoot him." She gripped the edge of a small rolling table, and Kira braced herself, waiting for the woman to throw it aside, scattering scalpels and syringes across the white tile floor, but Morgan's rage seemed to be subsiding. Instead of throwing it, she was gripping it for support. "It doesn't matter whose fault it is," said Morgan. "All we can do now is look for another lead." She stared at her computers, or through them to something else beyond, but there was no hope in her eyes.

Kira clutched the thin operating blanket tighter around her shoulders, rolling sideways on the table and curling into a ball. She watched Vale, his mouth open, preparing to speak but holding back, looking at Morgan as if trying to build up the nerve. His hesitance made Kira angry—far more than the action merited, she knew, but her nerves were worn raw. She sneered and croaked at him.

"Just say it."

He looked at her. "What?"

"Whatever you keep trying to say. You've been on the verge of it all morning, just get it out."

He took a deep breath. "It's just that . . ." He grimaced, still staring at the back of Morgan's head. "Look, I don't want this to sound wrong; I'm not trying to say 'I told you so'—"

"Don't even start," said Morgan.

"But I do think we need to consider the possibility that we've backed the wrong horse, so to speak," said Vale, pushing forward despite her warning. "Both species are dying, and we know the cure for one of them—let's just focus on that one, and save as many humans as we can—"

"And let the Partials die?" Morgan demanded. "Two hundred thousand people that we helped create—practically our children—and we should do nothing? Or worse yet, enslave them? Like your master plan? Lock them up in some basement dungeon as . . . what, feed stock? A temporary cure for the lucky species we deigned to save?"

"We're past the point of options we can all agree on," said Vale. "*Everyone is dying.* We're running out of time, and this is a dead end, and I don't think I'm being a monster to suggest that we need to use what little time we have left pursuing the only solution that any of us have managed to uncover."

"The cure for RM is just as much of a dead end," said Kira. "In another ten months every Partial will be gone, and the cure will be gone with them, and none of this will matter." She thought again of Samm, and longed to see him again before he expired. But he was on the other side of the continent, with a toxic wasteland and a pair of solemn promises keeping them apart.

"That's why we have to act now," said Vale. "Extract as much of the cure as we can and store it for the future, to give us a buffer while we try to find another solution."

"We have ten months left—" said Morgan.

Vale sighed, as if his argument was self-evident. "Ten months is nothing."

"But we could still do it," hissed Morgan, "and the humans will still be there when we're done."

"Both of you shut up," said Kira, forcing herself to sit. She wanted nothing more than to lie down, to heal from her weeks of surgeries, to close her eyes and let this whole problem go away, but she couldn't. She'd never been able to let go of anything, and no matter how much she cursed herself now, she pushed herself up, gritted her teeth, and stepped down to the floor. "Shut up," she repeated. "You fight like my sisters, and I'm not in the mood." She gathered the blanket around her, shivering in the cold room, and walked to one of the undamaged wall screens.

"We're doctors, dammit, let's act like it."

"We've been acting like it for weeks," said Vale. "I think we've earned a little break for self-pity."

"And only two of us are doctors," said Morgan snidely. "Neither of them are you."

"Only two of us figured out the cure for RM," Kira countered, studying the monitors. "Go ahead and remind yourself which two."

Morgan sneered, but after a moment she stalked to the door. "Have your little pity party," she said to Vale. "I have work to do." She stormed into the hall and slammed the door behind her.

"I delight in anyone who stands up to that harridan," said Vale, "but she's arguably the most powerful person in the world right now. You need to keep a civil tongue."

"People have been telling me that my whole life," said Kira, only barely paying attention to him. She stared at the vast screen, cataloguing the data in her mind, searching for some kind of order in the chaos—some final, perfect key that would pull it all together and make sense of it. "What do you see here?"

"Your entire life, reduced to numbers," said Vale. "Cellular decay rates, gene sequences, pH levels, white cell counts and bone marrow samples—"

"The answer's not here," said Kira.

"Of course it's not here."

She felt a tiny spark of excitement, the familiar thrill of solving a riddle slowly coming back to her. "But this is the most exhaustive biological study I've ever seen. It's not just my data, it's years' worth of studies about expiring Partials and healthy Partials and human test subjects and everything else. Whatever else you want to accuse her of, Dr. Morgan is spectacularly thorough."

"You're acting like that's good news," said Vale, "but everything you're saying only makes our situation worse. Morgan's a brilliant scientist, and she's been collecting this data for over a decade, and the answer's still not here. If you've already looked everywhere and you can't find your answer, your answer doesn't exist. There is no cure for expiration."

Kira spun around, her eyes alive with eagerness. "Do you know how I found the cure for RM?"

"By capturing a Partial and experimenting on him," said Vale. "Kind of puts your current situation into an interesting karmic light."

Kira ignored the jibe. "We did everything for RM that Morgan's done for expiration, and we ran into this same wall—we'd tried everything, we'd failed at everything, and we thought we had nothing left. We found the cure because we looked in a Partial, and we looked in a Partial because he was literally the only thing we hadn't looked in yet. It didn't make sense, it didn't follow from any data we'd previously collected, it was just a hunch—an absolute Hail Mary—but it worked, by pure process of elimination. If you've already looked everywhere and you can't find your answer, you haven't looked everywhere yet."

Vale walked toward the screen, studying the glowing words and numbers as he did. "I know the Trust kept a lot of secrets from one another," he said, engaging more actively in her brainstorm. "But I can assure you there are no more mysterious species out there we can gather up and poke around in."

"Not strictly true," said Kira. "On our trip to the Preserve we were attacked by talking dogs."

"The Watchdogs aren't a cure for expiration," said Vale, tapping the screen to call up a file on the semi-intelligent animals. "Believe it or not, Morgan's already studied them, trying to see if they had the same expiration date the Partials did. They don't carry any more potential cures than you do."

"Which is exactly why this giant, useless data dump is such a godsend," said Kira. "It's like a road map that only shows ninety-nine percent of a country—all we have to do is figure out what *isn't* on the map, and that's where the answer is. The one percent of the territory that we haven't studied yet."

"Okay," said Vale halfheartedly, flicking through a list of digital folders, "what's not in here?" He stopped, watching as his simple touch created a cascade of innumerable folders flying past him on the screen. "How are we even supposed to know where to start?"

"We start by thinking about the people, not the numbers," said Kira. "This isn't just data, it's Morgan's data, collected by her based on her own suppositions. And she wasn't looking for a natural, random phenomenon, she was looking for something created by another person—by Armin Dhurvasula. He had a plan for everything, you said he did, so all we have to do is figure out what it was."

"If your plan relies on us reading the mind of a dead mad scientist who *might* have come up with a plan to save the world, *maybe*, I'm going to suggest that we'd be better off looking for another plan."

"It's not mind reading," said Kira, "just . . . think about it. What were the resources Armin had to work with?"

"The entire industry of genetic engineering."

"Divided into a specific subset of tools," said Kira. "Each of you in the Trust had a specific job, right? What was his?"

Vale narrowed his eyes, as if suddenly caught by the viability of Kira's line of thought. "He did the pheromones—the link system."

Kira grimaced, pulling up the folders about Morgan's pheromonal research. It was one of the biggest subsections in the databank. "Morgan has researched every aspect of the pheromones she could think of," she said, shaking her head as she flicked through the list of subjects: Communication; Tactics; Vulnerabilities. Dozens of folders, each with dozens of subfolders, sitting on top of a mountain of notes and experiments and images and videos. "There's no way she missed something in all of this."

"She missed the cure for RM," said Vale.

Kira almost laughed. "Yeah, okay, I'll give you that one. That still doesn't make this any easier to figure out."

"So now we need to think like McKenna Morgan," said Vale. "Why did she miss the cure under all this data?"

"Because she wasn't looking for it," said Kira. "She was trying to solve Partial expiration, not the human RM susceptibility, so she never thought to look in the other species."

"So maybe we should be looking in the other species, too." Vale put his hands over his mouth, breathing through his fingers—a nervous tic Kira had noticed several times over the last few weeks of research. He stared at the data. "Let's approach it from this angle: Morgan missed the connection because she didn't expect Armin to make one species the cure for the other.

But this can't be as simple as reversing that same situation, because that's impossible—he could hide the cure for humans inside the Partials because he built the Partials. He built the pheromone system that carries the human cure. But he obviously didn't build the human genome, and unless he ran some kind of massive gene mod program we don't know about—"

"Holy shit," said Kira.

"I told you to keep a civil tongue," said Vale.

"He did run one," said Kira. Her body was practically shaking with excitement as the revelation rushed over her. "A massive program, worldwide, that reached out to every human and altered them, right under our noses—he seeded them with active biological agents, each carrying his own, custom-built DNA. If he wanted to hide the Partial cure inside humans, he had a perfect opportunity to do so."

Vale stared at her, his face twisted in confusion, until suddenly his jaw dropped open and his eyes went wide. He struggled to speak, but he was completely dumbfounded. "Holy shit."

"No kidding."

"RM," said Vale, turning back to the wall screen and clutching his head, as if expecting his brain to burst right out of his skull. "Every human being in the world is a carrier for RM. He used the world's most contagious virus to plant the cure in the last place anyone would ever look."

Kira nodded. "Maybe. We don't know for sure. But it's a start."

"Then let's get to work."

CHAPTER NINE

Kira read through Dr. Morgan's archive without sleeping, without leaving the room, not even pausing to eat. The grim scientist had studied RM, but only peripherally, and never in the context of Partial expiration. Most of her research on the subject was related to Pheromone 47, the mysterious particle that Kira had dubbed the Lurker, because it didn't seem to have any purpose. Morgan's hypothesis had been that the Lurker could cause RM, or somehow trigger it in a human who was carrying RM but had not yet manifested symptoms. Kira had deduced—over a year ago now, she realized—that the Lurker was in fact the cure for RM, but she had only made that connection because she'd spent months studying RM itself. Morgan had never done that.

The records also contained a fair bit about the other Partial factions, the ones who still held out against Morgan's consolidation, and Kira read these now and then as breaks between the endless string of biology studies. Each rival faction was too small for the larger armies to bother with, and now that Trimble's forces had been brought into her fold, Morgan seemed to be ignoring them completely. Each one was marked with an approximate location, and one or two lines explaining their reasons for not supporting Morgan: "disagrees with our methods"; "opposed to medical experimentation"; "formed a new, pacifist cult"; and so on. The nearest was a group called the Ivies, somewhere in northern Connecticut. She read each new entry with fascination, astonished not just at the variety, but at the one thing that made each group the same: Faced with the issue of supporting Dr. Morgan or dying of expiration, they chose the latter. None of them had firm plans to solve it on their own—or at least if they did, it wasn't recorded in Morgan's files. Kira wondered if Morgan's records had a prideful blind spot, or if the other factions were really just ready to die. Trimble, it seemed, had been holding out for something to step in and cure it all for her. Were the others the same?

Did anyone, in the end, have any hope of being saved?

Scrolling through the medical records, Kira's mind turned just as often to Arwen, the baby she'd saved from RM. But no, she wasn't a baby anymore—that had been over a year ago. She'd be a toddler now. Setting aside her cursory glances of the children at the Preserve, Kira hadn't seen a toddler since the Break, more than thirteen years ago, and though she had studied pregnancy and childbirth in excruciating detail, she realized she knew next to nothing about childhood itself. How fast did children grow? Would Arwen be walking by now? Talking? The entire concept of early childhood development had never come up before, for her or for anybody. Madison would be learning everything for the first time.

Kira felt a wave of despair, thinking that Arwen's tiny, precious life wouldn't even matter if she couldn't find a way to cure everyone completely.

She dove back into her studies, determined to do just that.

RM was a shockingly complex virus that passed through multiple stages over the course of its life cycle. When she'd been studying Samm—*well over a year ago,* she thought grimly— she'd named these stages the Spore, the Blob, and the Predator. The Spore was the most basic version of the virus, created inside of the Partial respiratory system, where it passed into the air and, eventually, into a human body. As soon as it entered the bloodstream, usually by being absorbed through the lungs, it transformed itself into the Predator—a vicious killer that sought only to reproduce itself and build more of the Spore, attacking the host and practically eating it alive, breaking down every cell and tissue it could find in a mad rush to spread the disease to as many new hosts as possible. Carried to its extreme conclusion, this process could reduce a human body to goo, but obviously the infected person would die long before, as her organs and internal systems broke down. Most hosts actually died from fever, as their bodies fought back so violently they ended up frying themselves from within.

As deadly as the Predator was, human doctors knew very little about it, simply because it killed too efficiently. Anyone who lived long enough to be properly studied was either inherently immune—a staggeringly small percentage of the population— or infected with the third stage of the virus, which Kira had named the Blob. She had thought the Blob was the killer, but the Blob was in fact a combination of two different particles: just as the Spore reacted with human blood to become the Predator, so the Predator reacted with the Lurker, the mysterious Pheromone 47, to become the Blob—a fat, harmless, almost completely inert version of the virus. The Partials breathed out the disease, but they also breathed out the cure, which they could pass along in proximity to a human. Vale and Morgan insisted that the Trust had never intended for RM to destroy the human race, and it was the Predator they were probably referring to—RM was simply too good at its job, far better than anyone had ever expected, and the disease spread too quickly among people far from any Partials. Graeme Chamberlain had designed it, and killed himself soon after, so whether he'd done it on purpose was anyone's guess. But the key interaction, the most important part of the process, was that third stage. The Blob. It said so much about the Trust, and about their plan, and about the man who'd come up with it.

Armin Dhurvasula. Kira's father.

Kira had yet to find any solid connection between RM and expiration, but she had leads. First of all, she knew from Dr. Vale that the purpose of RM had been to tie humanity intrinsically to its engineered children. The Partials were thinking, feeling people, and the human race couldn't be allowed to cast them aside like used tools when it was done with them. By putting the cure for RM inside the Partials, it seemed as if they were making a clear statement about the solution to this problem—the humans who cast the Partials aside would get sick, but the humans who embraced them would be fine. The Partials would breathe out their cure, the humans would breathe it in, and everyone would be healthy. And if the Predator had been less deadly, that plan probably would have worked.

Would the same plan have saved the Partials as well?

If Kira was right, somewhere in the life cycle of the RM virus there was a cure for expiration. Obviously it wouldn't be in the Spore, because then the Partials could heal themselves; it wouldn't be in the Predator, either, because the mere presence of the Partials removed the Predator from the bloodstream. No, the cures seemed to be designed to activate only when the species intermingled, so what she was looking for would be buried in the Blob. The Partials would give humans the Lurker, thus saving them, and then the humans would turn around and give something back to the Partials and save them . . . but what? Was there a fourth stage of the virus she hadn't encountered yet? Was there another interaction she hadn't seen? It was possible that some of the Partials who'd spent a lot of time around humans would have already been exposed to the cure, but the only way to test that was to wait until their expiration date and see if they died. She opened a new file on her medicomp and made a note to check the records for something like this, but she didn't hold out much hope for it—if any of the Partials had survived their expected expiration, it would be bigger news. Very few of the Partials had come into contact with the humans anyway, not for nearly eleven years. The Partials involved in the East Meadow occupation had received plenty of human contact, but was it enough? How much did it take? How quickly could it take effect? There were too many variables, and they were running out of time—observational data wasn't good enough. She would have to test her theory directly, and that meant hands-on experimentation: She had to obtain a sample of the Blob and expose it to Partial physiology.

It was a good plan. It was the only plan she could make. But the steps she would have to take to carry it out made a part of her die inside.

"We need to kidnap a human."

Dr. Vale looked up from his medicomp screen; another iteration of the same data Kira had been poring over for days. He stared at her a moment, blinking as his eyes refocused from the screen to her face. "Excuse me?"

"We need a human test subject," said Kira. "We have to study the interactions between the stage-three RM virus and a living Partial, and the only way to get stage-three RM is from a human. I'm not human, and you've already used gene mods to make yourself immune. The only way to get what we need is from a human—I don't like it, but it's a medical necessity. What we learn in this experiment could save the world."

Vale stared a moment longer, his face blank, before finally furrowing his brow and turning fully toward her. "Forgive my incredulity, but is this the same young woman who called me a monster for keeping Partials imprisoned under the pretense of medical necessity?"

"I told you I didn't like it. And I'm only talking about taking blood samples, not inducing a comatose state in our subject for years on end—"

"Is this also the same young woman," Vale continued, "who was herself kidnapped and studied? In this same facility?"

Kira gritted her teeth, frustrated both with him for resisting, and with herself for suggesting it in the first place. It tore her apart even to consider it, but what other options were there? "What do you want me to say?"

"I don't know," said Vale. His voice sounded lost and weary. "I'm not fishing for a specific response, I'm just . . . surprised. And saddened, I suppose."

"Sad because this is our only option left?"

"Sad because I may have just witnessed the death of the world's last living idealist."

Kira clenched her fists, trying to calm herself as tears threatened. "If we can find the interaction between the species, with RM as a catalyst for both cures, we can save the world. We can save everybody. Isn't that worth every sacrifice we can make?"

"When you gave yourself to this research, it was a sacrifice," said Vale. "I didn't like it, but I admired you for it, but now—"

"Now we have even less time to debate the ethics of it—"

"Now you're talking about someone else," said Vale, raising his voice to talk over her. "Now I see I was wrong about you, because you weren't giving yourself for a cause, you were just obsessed, as obsessed as Morgan is, and you only gave yourself because you didn't have anyone else to give."

Kira's tears were real now, streaming hotly down her face as she screamed back at him. "Why are you fighting me so much?"

"Because I know what it feels like!" he roared. He stared at her, his chest heaving with the force of his emotion, and she looked back in stunned silence. He took a few more ragged breaths, then spoke more softly. "I know what it's like to betray your ethics, your humanity, everything that makes you who you are, and I don't want you to go through that. I destroyed ten lives in the Preserve—ten Partials that I didn't just enslave, I tortured. I loved them so much I betrayed the entire world to give them the life they deserved, and when that plan went as wrong as it could possibly go, I betrayed them in return, all to save what, a thousand humans? Two thousand? Two thousand humans who are just going to die alone once the only source of the cure expires anyway."

"Not if this experiment works."

"And if it does?" asked Vale. "What then? Say the humans can't live without the Partials, and the Partials can't live without the humans—how will that possibly end well? Are you expecting some kind of glorious cultural marriage between the two? Because that's not what happened before, and it's never going to. The group with the power has always oppressed the group without—first the humans, by making Partials in the first place, and forcing them to fight and die and come home to a life of second-class subservience. Then the Partial War. Then my work in the Preserve. Dr. Morgan's experimentation with live subjects. Even you captured a Partial for study and were captured in return. Now Morgan's invaded East Meadow and the humans are fighting tooth and nail, and Kira the Partial wants to capture a human. Don't you see the futility of it all? You know both sides better than anyone. If *you* can't live in peace, how can anyone else hope to do it?"

Kira tried to protest, knowing that he was wrong—that he had to be wrong—but completely failing to find any reasons why. She wanted him to be wrong, but that wasn't enough to make it so.

"There will be no cultural marriage," said Vale. "No meeting of equals. The future, if we have one at all, will be a mass cultural rape. Tell me with a straight face that that's good enough, that that's acceptable on any conceivable level."

"I . . ." Kira's voice trailed off.

There was nothing to say.

CHAPTER TEN

Samm shouted into the hallway, "I think this one's waking up!" He heard a flurry of activity and raced back to the side of the bed where Partial Number Five was slowly stirring. The Partials from Vale's lab had been free of the sedative for weeks now, but the effects had lingered, and their bodies, unconscious for nearly thirteen years, seemed reluctant to wake up. Many in the Preserve had given up hope that they would wake up at all, but Samm had refused to abandon them. Now Number Five— they did not know their names—was moving, not just shifting in his bed, but fidgeting, coughing, and even groaning around his breathing tube. Samm had watched with growing excitement all morning, but when Five finally started to flutter his eyelids, as if struggling to open them, Samm called for the others. They came flooding into the room: Phan and Laura and Calix, who was now on crutches as Heron's bullet wound slowly healed in her leg. The girl pointedly avoided even looking in Heron's direction.

Avoiding Heron was all too easy these days, as she seemed to have withdrawn herself from the community—not completely, but almost. Instead of disappearing from sight, she simply hovered along the edges, lurking in shadows and hallways, detached from the others. She stood now against the back wall of the hospital room, practically in reach of the humans but somehow miles apart from them. Samm knew without looking that she was as curious about the humans' behavior—and Samm's—as she was about the slowly waking Partial. Her link data was typically analytical, but with a tint of the growing confusion that Samm had started to sense from her more and more frequently.

WHY?

Samm did his best not to respond, focusing his thoughts—and through them, his link data—on the stirring Partial. He had approached Heron about her apparent confusion before, but every time he did, she left immediately. He didn't know what she was trying to figure out, but she wasn't interested in talking about it—but neither did she seem interested in leaving the Preserve entirely. The one thing he knew for sure about Heron was that if you saw her lurking in the shadows, it was only because she wanted you to. What did she want now? He would have to think about it later, when the link wouldn't give him away.

Partial Number Five had been sending out link data of his own, and Samm returned his focus to that. It was both fascinating and tragic. The link was designed to carry tactical information in the field of battle, informing your squad mates of both danger and safety and syncing everyone to the same informed, efficient emotional state. One of the side effects of this system was that it was triggered from an imaginary stimulus as easily as it was from real life, making Partial soldiers vaguely aware of their sleeping companions' dreams. The effects were more muted—a simple dream about pizza or a flashback to basic training wouldn't usually register for anyone else—but an intense emotional experience would often spread through the squad like subtle magic, until they were all sharing the same, or a similar, dream. Like a contagious vision. If one soldier had a nightmare, soon everyone had one; if one soldier dreamed of a girl, the entire squad might wake up with an awkward mix of high fives and embarrassed chuckles. Samm's sergeant had once dreamed of falling, and the entire group had woken up in the same terrifying moment, gasping with one loud, unified breath as the half-remembered terror subsided. A Partial soldier with a history of good dreams—or simply a very strong memory of a woman—was welcome in any squad, while a soldier haunted by darkness and nightmares was sometimes looked upon as a curse.

The comatose Partials from Dr. Vale's lab were a pit of darkness Samm could barely stand to be next to. It wasn't that Number Five's dreams were dark, for there were many bursts of active, tense, and even happy data that Samm had come to identify as the sleeping Partial's dreams. What broke his heart was the rest of the time—all the long, troubled, hopeless hours where Five wasn't dreaming at all. The soldier seemed to exist in a state of constant pain and despair, sensing on some unconscious level that something was deeply and horribly wrong, but lacking the observation and the rational thought to decipher what it was. The other sleeping Partials were the same, with only small variations in the length and magnitude of their brief dreaming respites. Samm could feel their dark pall hanging over the entire floor of the hospital, and he worried about the turmoil they might bring with them when they finally woke up. You couldn't spend thirteen years in that kind of a pit without being horribly, perhaps irrevocably, scarred by the experience. What would they do when they awoke? Would they be cheered by their recovery, or marked for life by their trauma? Samm had no way of knowing.

As he watched the waking Partial, thinking these thoughts, Samm couldn't help but feel again inadequate to the unsought task that seemed ready to crush him: the leadership of the Preserve. He was not a leader, not by design and not by nature; he was an underling at best, the perfect soldier, ready to follow his commander through the gates of hell but choked by doubts when it came time to lead the charge himself. And yet here he was, stronger and better informed than almost anybody else in the Preserve, and they had started to look to him for leadership. Laura was technically in charge, but Samm was the one who knew about the sleeping Partials; Samm was the one who knew where Kira and Vale had been taken, and why; Samm was the one who gave his own breath and body to produce the RM cure and save their newborn infants. He had all the power, and they knew it—he could probably beat any ten of them in a fight, too, and he supposed they knew that as well. Even Heron followed him, often wordlessly, though he supposed that was less out of subservience than a simple distaste for taking any leadership herself.

Samm watched the Partial twitching back to life, sensing the horror in its soul, and wondered again if it was a good idea to bring them back at all. Nine Partials could destroy a community like this; nine angry, possibly unhinged Partials would cut through it like a rain of blades. *It should be Kira deciding this,* he thought, *not me—she was the leader, the thinker, the visionary. I'm just some guy.*

Like it or not, though, it was his decision, and he wasn't going to make one against his own people. Thus the Partials were nursed back to health, risks and all, and when they woke up, they'd find some guy named Samm waiting to say hello. He would do his best. He brought children into their rooms sometimes, and tried to send happy thoughts over the link and hoped those actions could counteract their thirteen years of darkness. It was a simple plan, but he was a simple man, and sometimes simple was good. He hoped this was one of those times.

"Here he comes," said Heron. Samm glanced at her, surprised that she would be the first to announce the final step of Number Five's awakening, but a sudden cry from Calix made him look back. Heron was right. The gaunt soldier was struggling actively now, not just waking up naturally but striving, practically clawing at the universe to force himself awake by choice. He coughed and sputtered, and Samm jumped up, reaching for the breathing tube and pulling it from Five's throat. The soldier's eyes flew open, and his hand shot up to grab Samm's arm, clamping down with surprising strength for someone so atrophied.

"Help." His voice was ragged from disuse, thin and raw, but the link data slammed into Samm like a moving truck. The newly opened eyes were wild with terror, and Samm felt the same terror welling up in his own gut—a numbing, crippling, overwhelming sense of wrongness, of helplessness, of boundless fear. Samm raced to sort through his thoughts, trying desperately to separate his own mind from this irrational fright before the link overwhelmed him; he closed his eyes and repeated every comforting detail he could think of, one after the other like a mantra.

You're safe. We're your friends. We're protecting you. We're healing you. You're safe. He realized the soldier probably thought he'd been captured, waking up abruptly with none of his companions nearby and no officer to reassure him; any of his squad mates he could sense on the link would be broadcasting the same catastrophic confusion that he was. *We're your friends. We're protecting you. We're healing you. You're safe.*

"Help." The soldier's voice was painful to hear, as if the words themselves were bleeding. "Arm."

"What does that mean?" asked Calix. "Does his arm hurt? Why did he say 'arm'?"

"He knows he's unarmed," said Phan. "He's afraid."

"He's still waking up," said Laura, shaking her head. "He's not rational. Give him time."

"He might never be rational," said Heron. "We don't know what kind of brain damage he's sustained from being asleep for thirteen years."

"You're not helping," said Calix.

"I could shoot you again," said Heron. "Would that help?"

"You're safe," said Samm. "We're your friends. We're protecting you. We're healing you."

"Hole," said the soldier. "Blood."

One of the hospital's few nurses burst into the room. "One of the others is waking up." She looked over her shoulder, listening to a distant shout, then turned back with a frantic mania. "Two of them."

▽ ▽ ▽

Five of the nine were awake before morning, though all but one of them had to be restrained. They seemed insane, mad and squalling like superpowered children; Laura thought their minds had been destroyed by Vale's enforced coma, while Calix, more charitably, suggested that their minds were simply still asleep, and only their bodies had awoken. Samm thought about it just long enough to decide that he didn't have enough information to decide, and that his course of action would be the same no matter what was wrong. He helped to hold their thrashing limbs while the nurses tied each Partial down with sturdy leather cords.

He worried, briefly, that the damage to their minds was his own fault, having somehow harmed them when they disconnected the Partials from their life support systems, but he pushed that thought away. There was no turning back now, and nothing he could do. He could only solve so many problems at once, so he would spare no time worrying about things he couldn't change.

When the sun rose and the next shift of nurses arrived at the hospital, Samm briefed them in full before sending the night shift back to their apartments. He murmured his thanks as they left, but stayed himself; there were still four Partials set to wake up, and while they had been preemptively bound, he still wanted to be there when they woke up.

I don't want them to wake up and think they're in prison, he thought. Phan urged him to get some sleep, but Samm was fine—fatigued, yes, but not overly so. He had been designed for far worse physical punishment than a single sleepless night. Emotional punishment, on the other hand . . .

That was another problem he couldn't solve, and so he pushed it away. Others could help the Partials as they awoke, whispering and soothing and calming their unfocused agitation, but only with words. He was the only one who could speak to them through the link, and so he stayed. The air itself, thick with the link data of nine traumatic disasters, hung around him like a poison. He sat in the room of Partial Number Three, the next one they expected to rise, and tried to think happy thoughts.

WHY?

The thought rang in his head for nearly a minute before he realized it was not his own. He looked up and saw Heron standing in the corner behind the door, though he was certain she hadn't been there before. Either he was going crazy, or she was specifically trying to be mysterious. He guessed it was the latter, and wondered what petulance would spark such an odd behavior. Or maybe she simply didn't want anyone else to see her.

"You're not a ghost," said Samm. "I know you didn't walk through that wall."

"And you're not as observant as you think," said Heron. She stepped out of the darkness and walked toward him, padding across the floor like a cat. Samm imagined her pouncing on him with her teeth bared, tearing the flesh from his face, and realized that he was probably much more exhausted than he realized. Partials were rarely struck by such colorful daydreams. Heron turned the room's other chair and plopped into it with a distinct lack of grace. She was exhausted as well. "I suppose it's a wonder you saw me at all, with so much hell in the air."

"I linked you," said Samm, then paused, too exhausted to explain himself clearly. "Though I guess there are even more link distractions than visual ones."

"You don't have to do this."

Samm looked around. "I'm just sitting in a room. That's all I'd be doing if I went home."

"Home is a few thousand miles away."

"You know what I mean."

"No, I don't," said Heron. "You think of this place as home? We shouldn't even be here."

"You didn't have to stay."

"Neither did you."

"I promised I would," said Samm. "That means I have to, as surely as if I was chained here."

"If promises are chains," said Heron, "you should learn not to make any."

"You don't understand," said Samm. He watched Partial Number Three as he lay in the hospital bed, his eyes blinking rapidly—he was dreaming, and from the intensity of his link data Samm knew it was something terrible. The Partial was running, as fast as he could, blasting the room with his fear.

GET OUT

And underneath it, softer but ever-present, Heron's unspoken question: WHY?

Samm looked at her, tired of games, and asked her directly, "Why what?"

She narrowed her eyes.

Samm leaned forward. "You really don't understand why I'm here, do you? That's what you keep asking about." He peered into her face, lost in the link and trying to read her eyes, her mouth, her expressions. The way humans did. But it was just a face.

Maybe Heron didn't have any emotions, on her face or the

link. Just questions in an empty shell.

"You stayed too," he said. "You sold us out to Morgan, but you stayed. Why are you still here?"

"You only have a few months left to live," said Heron. "Dr. Morgan is looking for a cure, but you can't get it out here."

"So you stayed to help me get back?"

"Do you want to go back?"

Yes, thought Samm, but he didn't say it out loud. It wasn't that easy anymore. He hesitated, knowing his confusion would be clear to her on the link, but there was no helping that.

GET OUT, linked the soldier, writhing in his restraints, trapped in his own nightmare.

Samm took a slow breath. "I promised to stay."

"But you don't want to."

"It's my own choice."

"But why?" Her voice was louder now, and the question hammered into him on the link. "Why are you here? You want to know what I'm asking? I'm asking why you're here. You want to know why I stayed? Because I want to know why *you* did. We've known each other for almost twenty years now, we fought together in two wars, I followed you through a toxic hell because I trust you, because you're the closest thing I've ever had to a friend, and now you're going to kill yourself with inaction. That's not a decision a rational person makes. Your expiration date will come, and you'll die, and . . . why? You think you're saving these people, but you're only buying them, what, eight extra months? A few more infants saved, a slightly larger generation lives, and then you die and they stop having children and their slightly larger generation grows up and they can't have any children and the whole world dies. Eight months later than it would have." Her voice was hot and angry, spitting the words through clenched teeth. "Why?"

Samm pointed at Number Three. "I'm helping them, too."

"By putting them through this?" Heron yanked on the leather cords.

GETOUTGETOUTGETOUT

"Their expiration dates are even sooner than yours," said Heron. "You're waking them up, detoxing them from whatever mind warp Vale put them under, forcing them through this torture, just so they can wake up and die?"

"I'm helping them."

"Are you?"

"I'm giving them a chance," said Samm. "That's more than they had before."

"Then give yourself the same chance," said Heron. "Live now, and figure out how to keep living tomorrow. These people are gone, so give them up—come with me back to Morgan and get the cure and live through your expiration. Let's go home."

"We don't even know if she's found a cure."

"But if you go home, there's a chance!" Heron roared. "Go home and you might die anyway, stay here and you die no matter what."

"It's not just about living—"

"What the hell else is it about?"

"It's about living right."

Heron said nothing, staring at him with fire in her eyes.

"These soldiers kept the Preserve alive for thirteen years," said Samm. "There are thousands of children who are alive today because these nine men helped them—maybe not willingly, maybe not even knowing what they were doing, but they did it, and they went through hell to do it, and I can't just leave them to die for that. Let's say only half of them wake up sane, and only half of those are in shape to make the journey back to Morgan; that's still two of them she can give the cure to, and two is twice as many as me. Staying here doubles the number of Partials I can save from expiration, at the very least, and even your emotionless calculator brain has to see that that's worth the trade."

His fervor grew as he spoke, and he spit the final words like an indictment, feeling good to let his emotions out. He sat watching Heron, waiting for a response, but the link was empty. The soldier had fallen asleep, and Heron was a blank page. An empty shell.

"You can save more Partials. . . ." Her voice trailed off. "But none of them are you."

She stood up and left, as silent as a shadow, and as Samm watched her go, he couldn't help but wonder if he'd completely misinterpreted the conversation.

CHAPTER ELEVEN

Marcus watched the forest through the broken glass of an old window frame, holding his breath. Commander Woolf had chosen the hiding spot just outside of Roslyn Heights, and it was a good one—a house so covered in vines that no one outside would even know there was a window in this part of the wall, let alone that four people were hiding inside. Galen, one of Woolf's soldiers, was watching the front door with their biggest gun—an assault rifle they'd salvaged from a dead Grid patrol—while the fourth man in their group, a Partial named Vinci, kept watch from a different window. Their ragtag group were the only survivors from Woolf's ill-fated diplomatic mission to the Partials. They had been hoping to form an alliance with the largest of the Partial factions, in a desperate bid to fight back against Dr. Morgan's invasion, but a schism in the Partial ranks had destroyed that plan almost before it could start. The friendly faction fell, and now Morgan ruled them all—all but Vinci, and a handful of tiny, independent factions scattered through the mainland.

Woolf's new plan was to unite those factions to oppose Morgan's army, but they couldn't do it alone. They needed to find the only successful group of human resistance fighters.

They needed to find Marisol Delarosa.

Marcus saw a movement from the corner of his eye—just the shake of a leaf, but he'd learned from experience not to take anything for granted. He watched the leaf, and the foliage around it, with a keen intensity, his mind racing with any number of horrifying possibilities: It might be one of Delarosa's guerrillas, or it might be a Partial soldier; maybe a whole squad of Partial soldiers, slowly surrounding them, getting ready to attack. Maybe it was a Partial sniper, buried in leaves and sticks and camouflage, lining up the perfect shot to drill Marcus right through the eye.

This is when the little bird hops into view and I chuckle derisively at my own paranoia, thought Marcus. Nothing moved. *Come on, little birdie. You can do it.* He stared at the foliage for two minutes, for five minutes, for ten, but no bird appeared, and no soldiers. *Probably just as well,* he thought. *If I chuckled at my paranoia, I'd probably give myself away and get sniped. Thanks for throwing me off my guard, hypothetical bird.*

Commander Woolf crept up beside him, settling into position where they could whisper the latest report.

"Anything?" asked Woolf.

"Just cursing imaginary animals."

"Crazy or bored?"

"Well," whispered Marcus, "it's so hard to pick just one."

"Vinci hasn't linked any other Partials," said Woolf, "so we're pretty sure there are no patrols in the area. I don't know if that makes us more or less likely to find Delarosa, but there it is."

"It makes us a lot less likely to be killed by Partials," said Marcus, "so I'll take what I can get."

Delarosa's White Rhinos, as she called them, had been evading the Partials for months, thanks to a combination of keeping her groups small, sticking to familiar terrain, and executing a clever system of decoys and distractions—all classic tactics of a defensive guerrilla force, and all devilishly effective. Marcus and his companions had had no more luck than the Partials in finding the elusive army, but they had a few tricks the Partials didn't. Now and then they'd come across other human refugees, just lone fugitives, lying low from the occupation, who assured them that the White Rhinos were heading north, in a slow, secret march toward the shore. Some of the refugees had been rescued by the Rhinos, others had been fed or given other supplies, but all told the same tale. The human resistance had a plan, and they were coming this way. All Marcus's group had to do was wait for them.

But they'd been waiting for days, and they were running out of supplies.

"You're due for sleep soon," said Woolf. "Go early and try to get some rest; I'll take over your watch."

"How much food do we have left?" asked Marcus.

"A day's worth," said Woolf. "Maybe more. I don't think Vinci is eating a full share."

"Maybe he doesn't have to," whispered Marcus. "For all we know he's . . . photosynthetic or something. Or he's been eating these." Marcus picked at the vines growing across the interior wall. He pulled too hard, the leaf failed to break away like he expected, and the whole section of tendrils shook—inside and out. Marcus looked up in shock at the unexpectedly massive display. "Crap."

A flurry of bullets slammed into the brick wall, punching through and sending a shower of broken clay shards spraying wildly through the room. Marcus threw himself to the floor, Woolf diving down beside him, and they covered their heads as they crawled for the hallway. The gunfire was quieter than usual—not silent, but more like a nail gun than the harsh gunshot explosions Marcus was used to. They reached the hallway, taking cover behind the extra layer of wall, just as the hail of bullets ceased.

"Can they see us?" asked Marcus.

"Let's find out," said Woolf, and stuck his hand back into the open doorway. Nothing shot it. "Probably not."

"Or they don't want to bother with just your hand," said Marcus.

"If they could see us that clearly, they'd have hit us," said Woolf. "More likely they were passing close by, saw the sudden movement, and thought it was an ambush."

"All the shots I heard were silenced," said Marcus. "That means Galen didn't shoot back."

Woolf shook his head. "They wouldn't have hit him, they were shooting at your movement."

"Good yet embarrassing news," said Marcus, nodding. "But then why didn't he shoot? From where he's stationed he should have had a good angle on the source of that attack."

Woolf rose to a crouch, checking his own weapon as he prepared to run. "In that case, this is the best news we've had all month. Who would Galen see but not shoot at?"

Marcus grinned. "You think?"

"Let's go find out."

They scurried down the hall to the stairs, and from there to the main floor, where Galen was crouched in another concealed gun nest. "Humans," Galen whispered.

"How can you tell?"

"Too many body types," said Galen. "Partials are all young men, like Vinci; this group has women, one of them pretty old."

"Smart," said Woolf. "You haven't hailed them?"

"Waiting for you."

Woolf nodded and moved away from Marcus's window to a separate window—partly for the different angle, but Marcus realized nervously that it was also a safety precaution. If the enemy fired again when Woolf hailed them, he was the only one they'd hit. Marcus admired the wisdom of the move, but the need for it twisted a dull knot in his stomach.

"Rhinos!" Woolf shouted. He wasn't looking out the window, but lying below it, using a small credenza as an extra layer of makeshift armor. All three of them held their breath, waiting for the reply—would it be words, or bullets?

"Stay quiet!" It was a woman's voice, and Marcus almost thought he recognized it, but it wasn't Delarosa. *Too young*, he thought.

It was the only response. Marcus peered through the gaps in the kudzu, but saw nothing. Galen shook his head. "They've disappeared. Now that they know we're here, it's too easy to hide from us."

"You heard from Vinci?" Marcus whispered. Even if this was Morgan's group, they would want to keep Vinci's true nature a secret at first. A Partial ally was a valuable asset, but they needed to explain it properly first.

Galen shook his head. "Still upstairs, I think. Staying quiet."

"Hey," said Marcus, "it's not my fault I gave us away."

Galen looked at him, raising his eyebrow. "You gave us away?"

Marcus rolled his eyes. "It's also not my fault that I told you that."

"I can't believe you gave us away."

"Not on purpose," said Marcus. "Next time you don't know about something stupid I did, let me know you don't know before I say it out loud."

"How can I—"

There was a sudden thump from the back room of the house, and a strangled shout that got cut off just before it became loud enough for the sound to carry outside. Marcus spun to face the sagging kitchen door, his rifle up and ready, but stopped in surprise when he heard Vinci's soft voice.

"It's just me."

Marcus furrowed his brow, confused. "What on earth?"

"They sent flankers through the back of the house," said Vinci. "I don't know if they're Delarosa's people, but they're definitely human."

"So you attacked them?" asked Woolf.

"Just disarmed them," said Vinci. "Don't shoot, I'm opening the door now." He pushed open the kitchen door and led two cloaked figures into the front room. Marcus stared at them in surprise, then jumped up eagerly as he recognized the girl in front.

"Yoon?"

The cloaked girl looked at him, a slow smile spreading across her face as she realized who he was. "Marcus?" The smile disappeared almost immediately, and she frowned at him sternly. "Are you trying to get yourself killed?"

"We're trying to find Delarosa."

"By scaring the hell out of us," asked Yoon, "and then shouting loud enough to attract every Partial in the forest?"

"Sorry," said Marcus. "None of that was really how we intended this to go."

"I recognize you," said Woolf, standing up. "You're one of the Grid soldiers who went with Kira and captured the Partial named Samm. I remember you from the disciplinary hearing."

"I was reassigned to an outpost on the North Shore," said Yoon. "When the Partials invaded we fled south, and the unit broke apart, and eventually I ran across the Rhinos." She pointed to her companion, a young man who looked sixteen years old at the most; Marcus realized with a start that this made him one of the youngest humans left in the world. "This is McArthur."

Marcus shook the boy's hand. "You have a first name?"

"No, sir," he said, and Marcus nodded. It had become common for some of the youngest humans to drop their first name altogether, preferring their surname because it linked them to the past. A three-year-old kid who lost everything he ever loved usually remembered that he *had* parents, but wasn't likely to remember much of anything about them. Identifying himself by his surname told people like McArthur that he came from somewhere, and helped him feel connected. Sometimes that was more important than an individual identity.

"Well then," said Marcus. "Yoon, McArthur, say hello to

Galen, Vinci, and Commander Asher Woolf. We've been look-ing for you everywhere."

"We're not easy to find," said Yoon. "Though there's prob-ably a better way to say hello than just shaking the hell out of the kudzu on the side of the house. We thought it was an ambush."

"That was an accident," said Marcus, giving a small, embar-rassed nod. "It did work, though, so there's that."

McArthur frowned. "How are you still alive? We thought you all died months ago."

Woolf clapped the young man on the shoulder. "I like this kid. But we've made enough noise here to attract every Partial scout in the forest, so what do you say we get back to your group and continue this conversation where it's safe?"

Yoon looked at Vinci. "Can we have our weapons back?"

Vinci handed them over freely—two sturdy rifles and a wide, curved blade. "Just making sure we didn't have any more acci-dental ambushes."

Yoon took a rifle and the knife, sliding the latter into a slim leather scabbard on her back. She stepped to the window, whis-tled a short birdcall, and waited silently for an answer. Marcus was expecting another whistle but was surprised to hear a low, rumbling growl. Yoon opened the door and a massive black cat peered in, yawned, and stalked away into the trees.

"That's a pet?" asked Marcus. Small cats, the kind the old world kept as pets, had adapted perfectly to the post-Break world and were practically ubiquitous across the island, but Marcus had never seen one so large. "It looks like a panther."

Yoon grinned wickedly. "That's because it's a panther."

"You keep panthers?" Vinci's voice was calm and even,

though Marcus had come to know his moods well enough to view this as surprise.

"Not typically, no," said Marcus. "Yoon is . . . special."

"We found wild ones in Brooklyn," said Yoon. "I think they escaped from a zoo. On patrol last year I found this one as a baby, and I've been raising him. He's pretty tame."

"Until Yoon tells him to rip somebody's head off," said McArthur. "Then everybody has nightmares for a few days."

A man in a dark-green cloak stepped up to the doorway, a rifle in his hands and a pair of night-vision goggles pushed up across his forehead. "You sounded the all clear. What's going on in here?"

"Commander Asher Woolf," said Woolf, holding out his hand to shake. "We're looking for Delarosa."

The soldier looked over the group quickly, sizing them up. "You and you I recognize from the Grid," he said, pointing at Woolf and Galen; then he looked at Marcus. "You look like Marcus Valencio."

"I am," said Marcus. He'd become a minor celebrity after helping Kira bring back the cure.

The soldier frowned at Vinci, though, and Marcus felt a pang of nervousness. Did they know what Vinci was? Did they suspect?

"You I don't know," said the soldier.

"I vouch for him," said Woolf. "Now we need to get out of here."

The man thought a moment longer, and finally nodded. "Let's go." Marcus and his companions grabbed their packs— little more than bedrolls at this point, with their food and ammo almost completely gone—and followed the White Rhinos into the trees. Though they called it a forest, it was really just an overgrown subdivision; derelict houses and weathered fences crumbling from thirteen years of disuse, with the neighborhood's old trees and an explosion of new young ones growing up in the abandoned yards. Woolf had chosen their house because it sat on a small rise, giving a slightly better view of the path they'd expected Delarosa to take; that the White Rhinos had come right past them instead of sticking to the more obvious route was, Marcus thought in hindsight, a big part of why the group had been so hard to find. They knew the Partial army was looking for them, and they knew how not to be seen.

The rest of the group was farther out in the trees, arranged in attack formation around Marcus's hiding place, safely concealed in cover. Delarosa herself was near the center of the group, near a low wagon. Marcus frowned at this, wondering what could possibly be so important—and so heavy—that they would risk the ruts and tire tracks of a wagon in order to haul it around. He didn't get a chance to ask, for Delarosa recognized Woolf and nodded brusquely, cutting off all conversation with a single question.

"The Senate sent you?"

"We haven't heard from them," said Woolf. "We assume they've been taken."

"We'll talk later," said Delarosa, tossing each of them a dark cloak mottled with green and brown. "Wear these, and stay as quiet as you can. If you attract any Partials, we'll leave you to them."

"Understood," said Woolf.

Marcus threw the cloak over his shoulders, covering his pack and weapon and everything, and pulled the hood up over his head. The White Rhinos moved almost silently through the trees, Yoon's black panther ranging ahead like a malevolent shadow. Marcus did his best to stay as quiet as they did, but found himself constantly stepping on twigs or clattering chunks of broken concrete into one another. Delarosa glanced at him angrily on more than one occasion, but she seemed to glare at Woolf and Galen just as often. Vinci was far more stealthy, though still outclassed by Yoon and some of the more experienced guerrillas. It made Marcus wonder again about the different abilities of the various Partial models—Vinci was infantry, likely not built for infiltration. Heron, who had once terrified Marcus by appearing ghostlike from the shadows, definitely was.

While they walked, Marcus studied the White Rhinos. Most of them were in Partial uniforms—old, weathered uniforms, but still recognizably Partial. *Claimed from fallen enemies?* he wondered. He also noticed that all of them carried a gas mask, hung from a belt or dangling from their backpacks. That seemed odd, as the Partials didn't seem to be using any chemical weapons, but when he looked again at the Partial uniforms he smiled, realizing with a burst of excitement exactly what was going on. At the first rest stop he approached Yoon about it.

"You're disguising yourselves as Partials," he said, keeping his voice at a barely audible whisper. "The gas masks block the link, so you put them on and wear those uniforms and the Partials can't tell from a distance that you're human."

Yoon smirked. "Pretty clever, don't you think?"

Marcus whistled softly. "It's amazing. Everyone's wondering

how you've managed to hide for so long, but with a disguise like that you could walk right up to them."

"Only the ones who look like Partials," said Yoon. "McArthur's too young, Delarosa's too old, but I can pass pretty easily—they think I'm a tank driver, for some reason."

"Samm said the drivers and pilots are all petite girls," said Marcus, marveling at the deception. "Apparently they saved the government a lot of money, building smaller tanks and jets. So you've actually talked to them? And they didn't suspect anything?"

"It was hard at first," said Yoon, "because they usually only wore the gas masks to fight each other—against humans there's no need for them. We planted the story that the humans were using some kind of biological weapon, and it seems to have caught on." She laughed. "We've even heard rumors of Partials dying from it in East Meadow, so it seems the legend has taken on a life of its own."

"That's hilarious," said Marcus. "Do you use the disguises just for emergencies, like if a group of Partials finds you in the woods, or do you actually seek them out for information and stuff?" Yoon tried to answer, but Delarosa whistled a birdcall, and the group was back on the move.

They walked for hours, almost until dark, and stopped for the night in a thick outdoor grove. This surprised Marcus, because he'd always learned to camp in the abandoned buildings that covered the island—they gave you shelter, they kept you hidden, and they were more defensible if you ever got attacked. Even the Partials used them. Once again, though, the White Rhinos seemed determined to defy expectations, and Marcus decided that they were probably avoiding the houses precisely because that was where everybody expected them to be. Delarosa chose a spot near a babbling stream, to mask any errant sounds with the white noise of the water, and kept everyone low to the ground to reduce the camp's profile. Guards stayed along the outer perimeter, while the mysterious wagon was brought in near the center of camp.

"Help me dig a fire hole," said Yoon.

Marcus's eyes went wide. "You're lighting a fire?"

"One of the benefits of staying outside," said Yoon. She held up a pair of rabbits. "How else are we going to cook these?"

"But that's the whole problem," said Marcus. "We're *outside*. Anyone in the area can see it."

Yoon rolled her eyes. "Watch and learn, city boy. Hold these." She thrust the rabbits into his hands, pulled a small shovel from her pack, and surveyed the ground around the camp. "That's the best spot for it," she said, pointing at the slight depression where Delarosa had left the wagon, "but we can find another."

"We could move the wagon," Marcus suggested.

"The Wagon Has Priority," said Yoon, in a tone of voice that gave each word the weight of law, if not an outright religious commandment. "And trust me—you don't want to build a fire even remotely close to it. Let's try over here." She walked ten paces east of the wagon, maybe twenty-five feet, and knelt down to start digging.

Marcus knelt next to her, keeping his voice even lower than usual. "So what's in the wagon?"

"Secrets."

"Well, yeah," said Marcus, "but are you going to tell me what they are?"

Yoon kept digging. "Nope."

"You do realize that we're on the same side," said Marcus, readjusting his grip on the rabbits. They were soft and furry, and cuddly enough to creep him out when he remembered they were dead.

"The Wagon Has Priority," Yoon repeated. "When Delarosa tells you, she'll tell you, and she'll probably tell you tonight, so stop worrying. Until that happens, however, I am a soldier and I will keep my commanding officer's secrets."

"Your commanding officer is a convicted criminal," said Marcus.

"So am I, remember? We all have our baggage." Yoon paused in her digging and looked up at him. "Delarosa does what nobody else is willing to do," she said. "It's kind of her thing. Last year that made her a criminal; now she might be the only hope for the human race."

Marcus thought about this, leaning closer. "Have you really been that effective? Everything we've heard suggests you're a thorn in their side, causing just enough trouble to keep the army off balance but not strong enough to gain any serious ground. Do you really think you can fight them off?"

"Not yet," said Yoon. "But eventually, yes. After."

"After what?"

Yoon smirked. "The Wagon Has Priority."

"Good," said Marcus, nodding. "I was hoping you'd say that again. Cryptic answers are the *best*."

Yoon finished the hole—a narrow pit, like a posthole, about eight inches across and at least twice that deep. She moved over a few inches and dug a similar hole, keeping the piles of displaced dirt close at hand, and when the second hole was finished she knocked a tunnel between them, connecting them at the base. McArthur brought her a collection of twigs and sticks and bark, and the panther, alarmingly, brought a dead cat held lightly in its jaws. It left the thing at Marcus's feet, eyed him mysteriously, and padded back into the twilight.

Yoon could barely suppress her laughter. Marcus stared at the mauled cat in shock. "You taught it to bring food back for you?"

"That's a dog behavior," she said, struggling to keep her laugh quiet. "When cats bring dead animals it's because they think you're helpless, and they're trying to teach *you*. I had a cat in East Meadow that left dead mice on my porch all the time." She grinned and patted his head. "Poor widdle Marcus, too helpless to hunt his own kitties."

"I don't know if I can eat my own kitties, either."

"I know exactly how you feel," Yoon confided. "But meat is meat, and as little as cats have, two rabbits weren't enough anyway. I'll keep an eye on Mackey while she cooks, and let you know which bits are which."

"I've never felt a more conflicted sense of gratitude," said Marcus.

Yoon packed the first hole with sticks—the biggest at the bottom, the smallest, toothpick-size fragments at the top—and pulled out a match. "The moment of truth." She shielded it with her hand, struck it, and dropped it on the wood. It caught almost immediately, the fire spreading slowly from the twigs to the bark to the thicker sticks below, and the second hole acting as a chimney to suck in air to the bottom of the blaze. In moments the fire was burning hot and steady, completely smokeless, and well below the rim of earth that kept the flames hidden. "One match," said Yoon proudly. "Bow before my greatness."

"Just help me skin these," said another woman, and took the rabbits from Marcus's hands. She started on one and Yoon on the other, keeping the blood and fur and organs buried deep in a third hole nearby. The broken cat lay on the ground beside them, waiting for its turn. Marcus was a surgeon, or at least he'd been in training to become one before the whole world had gone crazy, and blood had never bothered him before, but somehow two bunnies and a kitty was too much. He wandered back toward Woolf and the others, already deep in whispered conversation with Delarosa.

"That's why we need your help," Woolf was saying. "We can recruit the smaller Partial factions and put up a meaningful resistance, but we can't do it alone. You and your guerrillas have the expertise we need to get through Morgan's lines and find the pockets of resistance on the other side."

"You've done fairly well yourselves," said Delarosa, but shot a quick glance at Marcus. "Most of the time."

"One little vine," said Marcus.

"The more people we have, the faster we can work," said Woolf. "We don't know for sure how many Partial factions there are, but either way we need your extra manpower. Time is running out."

"You've heard the rumors?" asked Delarosa.

Woolf shook his head, and Marcus leaned in closer. "We've been pretty out of touch," said Marcus. "Is Dr. Morgan escalating the invasion?"

"Not the Partials," said Delarosa. "Something new. Some of the outlying farms have mentioned it, and we've heard it from the Partials as well when we gather intel." She looked at Woolf. "There's some kind of . . . thing."

"That sentence wasn't as helpful as you probably intended it to be," said Marcus.

"What kind of thing?" asked Woolf.

"I don't even know what to call it," said Delarosa, shooting a glare at Marcus. He could tell he was stepping over the line, but mouthing off was an instinct when he got nervous. He resolved to rein it back in. Delarosa grimaced, like she was struggling to find the right words. "A monster? A . . . creature? None of it makes sense, but the stories are remarkably similar: a man-shaped . . . thing, eight or nine feet tall, and the color of a new bruise. It walks into villages, settlements, anywhere there's people, and warns them."

"Warns them of what?" asked Woolf.

"Snow," said Delarosa.

Marcus nodded slowly, trying to form a response that wouldn't get him smacked. Woolf was apparently thinking the same thing, though his tone was diplomatic: "And you believe these stories?"

"I don't know what to believe," said Delarosa. "I won't deny that it sounds completely insane—more like a folktale than real news." She shook her head. "But the reports, like I said, are too similar to discount. Either an island full of war-torn refugees got together to play a giant practical joke on us, or something's really going on."

"An island full of Partials," said Marcus. "Maybe they're spreading these rumors for some reason of their own."

"The Partials are just as confused as we are," said Delarosa.

"The thing's appeared to them as well, and I believe their stories more than anyone's. If they knew our agents were humans, they would have just captured them instead of spreading the same insane story."

"Trimble didn't have any creatures like that," said Vinci. "I don't think Morgan did either."

Delarosa shot him a sharp look. "How do you know that?"

"We'll get to that in a minute," said Woolf. "When you say he's warning about snow, what do you mean?"

"Winter hardly seems like the kind of thing to warn someone about," said Marcus. "Maybe the giant monster wants us to put on a sweater?"

It was Woolf's turn to look at Marcus, but instead of derision, his eyes were full of sadness. Marcus frowned at this, wondering what he should feel guilty for, and realized that Delarosa had the same odd expression. "What am I missing?"

"We haven't had a real winter in thirty years," said Woolf. "Maybe that's what it means."

"A real winter?" asked Marcus.

Delarosa nodded. "With snow."

Marcus had heard of snow, but he'd never actually seen it in person. "It never snows this far south."

"We're on Long Island," said Delarosa. "It used to snow here all the time—'this far south' used to mean places like Florida or Mexico. But the climate shifted, and by the time of the Break even Canada was too warm for a real snowstorm."

"It happened after the war," said Woolf. "Not the Isolation War, but the one before it, when we lost the Middle East. It was a side effect of the weapons they used to destroy it." His face was solemn. "The planet's cold zones grew warm, the warm zones grew hot, and the hot zones grew intolerable. They told us it was permanent."

"Nothing's permanent in geologic terms," said Marcus.

"Permanent from the human perspective," said Delarosa. "Nothing that's measured in geologic time could reverse itself in thirty years."

"Then it's got to mean something else," said Marcus. "Why would a giant red monster show up to warn us about a weather pattern we haven't seen in decades?"

"Why would a giant red monster show up at all?" asked Delarosa. "I told you, it makes no sense, and I'm not saying it means one thing or another or anything at all. It's crazy." She shrugged. "But it's there."

"Where has the thing been seen?" asked Vinci.

"South, but slowly moving north," said Delarosa.

"Is that why you're moving north as well?" asked Woolf.

"That's for other reasons," said Delarosa, gesturing toward the mysterious wagon. "We're going north because we're going to end the war."

Marcus cocked his head in surprise. "You're going to help us recruit the other Partials?"

"Better," said Delarosa. "We're going to destroy them."

Marcus eyed the wagon again. "It's full of guns?"

"Guns wouldn't do it," said Galen. "It's got to be bombs."

"Only one," said Delarosa.

Woolf's face went white. "No."

Delarosa looked at him sternly. "It's the only way to win. They outnumber us ten to one at least, and their combat capabilities outclass us by much more than that. If we're going to survive this war, we need to even the odds, and this is the only way to make that happen."

"You want to let the rest of us in on this?" asked Marcus.

"It's a nuclear warhead," said Woolf. "She's going to blow them up."

"That is a very bad idea," said Vinci.

Marcus was suddenly intensely aware of Delarosa's guerrillas, surrounding them with weapons close at hand. If this became a fight, they didn't stand a chance, not even with Vinci.

"I don't see how you're going to stop me," said Delarosa.

"Those are—" Vinci stopped before giving himself away. "No matter which side of the war they're on, I can't let you—"

"You can't let me?" asked Delarosa sharply. The tension in the camp grew even heavier than before, and Marcus felt the pressure like a stone weight on his lungs. Delarosa looked at Woolf with fire in her eyes. "I asked before who he was," she hissed. "Tell me now."

"I'm a Partial," said Vinci calmly. "I'm an enemy to Dr. Morgan and an ally to these men. I came here to be your ally as well, but I cannot allow you to do this."

The guerrillas' guns seemed to fly into their hands, and Marcus and his companions found themselves at the center of a circle of aimed and ready rifles. Even Yoon had drawn a bead on them, her face grim, her rabbit-skinning knife still dripping with blood. Delarosa's voice was a controlled tornado of fury.

"You brought a Partial into my camp?"

"He's on our side," snarled Woolf. "Not every Partial is an enemy."

"Of course they are," said Delarosa. "They're not even capable of making their own decisions—that chemical link they have enforces obedience."

"I've sworn on my honor to help," said Vinci.

"Until a Partial officer shows up and commands you to spill all our secrets," said Delarosa. She looked at Woolf, and Marcus was shocked to see tears forming in the corners of her eyes. "They're biologically incapable of disobedience, damn it, and we can't risk this plan by consorting with the enemy!"

"You can't risk this plan at all," said Woolf. "There's nowhere you could nuke the Partials that wouldn't decimate the human population with them—we're too close."

"Not to mention all the Partials who'd die," said Marcus. "But I'm guessing that part of your evil plan is nonnegotiable."

"Tie him up," said Delarosa.

"Don't touch him," said Woolf.

"We're taking him prisoner no matter what you do," said Delarosa. "The only choice you can make is whether we take you prisoner, too."

The camp fell silent, each group staring tensely at the other. Finally Marcus stepped forward. "If you insist on going through me to get him, it's your call. But I warn you, I will probably cry when you hurt me, and you'll feel bad about it later."

Vinci looked at him. "That's your defiant speech?"

"Get used to it," said Marcus. "There's a lot more useless heroics where that came from."

CHAPTER TWELVE

Kira stood in the hallway outside Dr. Morgan's office, her hand poised above the doorknob. If she explained her plan, the scientist would go for it; they would capture a human, extract the virus, and test it for anti-expiration properties. Kira was certain they would find some; in a world where nothing seemed to make sense, this did. The secrets she'd spent years uncovering, the plan she'd traveled halfway across the world to reveal, the unsolvable secrets buried inside every human and Partial and viral RM spore—they all pointed to this answer, this complex, hidden, brilliant interaction of biology and politics and human nature. Working together was the answer: Partials could cure humans, and now humans could cure Partials. She was sure of it. All she had to do was prove it, and Morgan could help her do that.

But was that as far as it would go?

Dr. Vale had enslaved Partials to help keep his tiny band of humans alive, and Morgan was more than capable of doing the same thing in reverse. Kira thought about the Partials in the

Preserve, eternally sedated, tended like a human garden and harvested like gaunt, skeletal herbs. Unwilling victims, forever on the precipice of death. Morgan would do the same to humans—her records of early experiments already told horror stories of humans kept in cages, starving and naked, subjected to horrible tortures, all in the name of saving the Partials. She had the power to make it happen again, and Kira was about to give her the reason. It didn't have to be that way—it didn't have to be one side ravaging the other—but it would be. It always had been, and this new revelation was only going to make it worse. The situation wouldn't change.

Unless Kira changed it herself.

But how?

The hospital corridor was empty; there were a handful of Partial soldiers Morgan had pressed into service as lab assistants, but they were in other parts of the complex today. The building was powered, but the rooms and halls were hollow and abandoned, devoid of life and sound and movement. No one would see Kira standing here, locked in indecision . . . she could turn around and leave if she wanted to. She could probably leave the whole complex without even being seen or raising an alarm, as Morgan had lost all interest in keeping her here. She was a failed experiment; a shattered dream.

I could go, she thought, *but where?* What was left to do in a world this ruined? What answers could she even try to look for, what hope could she possibly find? She had an answer here, practically in the palm of her hand, and she had the means to take it and mold it and make it a reality. The implications were terrible, and the fallout would be catastrophic, but if she was right, civilization would survive—humans and Partials, enslaved and immoral and unconscionably compromised, but alive. Things would be bad, but they would get better; maybe not for generations, but someday.

Is that enough? thought Kira. *Is survival really all that matters? If I tell Morgan, and Morgan enslaves the human race to save the Partials, they'll live—but they'll live in hell. How can I make that decision? If I have the chance to save even one life, and I don't do it, am I a killer? If I have the chance to save the entire world and I let it die, how much worse am I? Yet I would be responsible for the greatest oppression ever forced upon the human species. Every person I saved would curse my name, from now until the end of time.*

I can't think of any other way, but I can't bring myself to go through with it.

Her hand hovered over the doorknob, an inch and a half from making her decision. The heat from her palm was warming it, hot blood pumping through her veins, radiating out in an aura of vitality. If she left now, that heat would remain, a ghostly afterimage of her presence, here and gone in an instant. Another few months for the Partials, another few years for the humans. The rain would fall, the plants would grow, the animals would eat and kill and die and grow again, and the ghost of sentient life would fade away, an insignificant blip in the memory of the Earth. Someday, a million years away, maybe a billion, when another species evolved or awoke or descended from the stars, would they even know that anybody had been here?

There might be buildings, or plastic residue, or something to say that we existed, but nothing to say why. Nothing to say what made us worth remembering.

I could go, she thought again. *I could find Samm, or Xochi or Isolde or Madison. I could see Arwen one last time. I could find Marcus.*

Marcus.

He wanted to marry me, and I wanted him. What changed? I guess I did. I had to find out what I was, and what I meant, and now I know that I'm nothing. Just another girl who can't save the world.

Well, not unless I damn it.

Marcus wanted to accept the end of the world, to enjoy our time together because it was all the time we had. Was he right? I said no, and I left, and what do I have to show for it? I'm just as lost and hopeless as I ever was—more so now, because I've tried and failed.

But at least I tried.

And Samm. He taught me to accept as well—not the end of the world, but the end of myself. To sacrifice myself because it was the only moral choice when every other option was too terrible to consider. I made that choice, and I gave myself up, and yet here I am, no better off than before. The world is still ending. The heat of our presence is still fading from the Earth.

But even that's not true: The world ended thirteen years ago, and now the human race, and the Partials with us, are nothing but an afterimage. We're dead already, like a severed head still blinking on the ground.

I've never given up on anything, Kira thought. *But I've always had options I could follow. Other choices I could take, and roads I could try, and . . . something. Do I have any of that now? Is selling out my people, my family, the entire human species, really the only answer? Can I live with myself if I do this?*

Can anyone live at all if I don't?

She put her hand on the doorknob, gripping it firmly, feeling the smooth metal curving in the palm of her hand. It was time. It was now or never.

She let go of the knob and backed away a step.

She backed away another.

If extinction is the only option left, she thought, *the choice you would never consider becomes the only moral choice you can make. Slavery is hell, but it's not annihilation. We could still come back. Sometimes the wrong choice is still right.*

But sometimes it's just wrong.

She took another step back.

The human race is more than blood and bones, thought Kira. *The Partials are more than a double helix and an engineered phero-mone. These are people; these are people I know. This is Samm and Xochi and Madison and Haru and Arwen and Isolde and Marcus and everybody I've ever met, everybody I've ever loved or hated or anything. It's Vale and Morgan. It's me.*

It's not enough to save us. We have to be worth saving.

She took another step back, standing now in the exact center of the wide hospital hallway, staring at the closed door.

There are other Partials, she told herself. *Other factions living out in the towns and the woods and the wasteland. They haven't sided with Morgan, and I don't have to either. If I can get even some of those groups, even one of those groups, to join me; if I can get them to help the humans like Samm did, to join them and live with them and work together, then we can do it. We can save the world. Not just our lives, but the reasons our lives are worth saving. Our thoughts and our dreams.*

Our hopes.

Kira turned and walked back down the hall, striding purposefully now, her hesitance gone and her decision made.

She could only hope that her decision was the right one.

CHAPTER THIRTEEN

Ariel ran, clutching her rifle, her heavy pack thumping frantically against her back. The others ran ahead of her, gasping desperately for breath, never daring to look back: Isolde with her baby, Madison with hers, Nandita surprisingly spry, and Xochi and her mother leading the way. They didn't know what had given them away, but it didn't really matter: A routine patrol had found them in the wilderness, and now the Partials were close behind them, roaring through the broken streets in Jeeps and motorcycles, and behind them a flatbed truck, barred with iron and bound with chicken wire.

A cage.

Kessler turned left into an overgrown yard, leaping ahead as she sought for a path to escape, and Xochi stayed behind, waving the others through the gap in the fence. Khan and Arwen were screaming, reflecting their mothers' fear. Ariel caught up as Nandita struggled stiffly through the fence, and she spun around, risking a look behind. The Partials were practically on top of them. Xochi fired a burst from her rifle, shattering the lead Jeep's windshield and forcing the driver to duck; it slowed them just enough to get through the fence, and then the women were running again, weaving through the bushes and saplings and overgrown debris. This yard was full of old appliances, a repair shop maybe, dishwashers and fridges rising up like monoliths. Ariel heard a bullet ping against one as she passed it.

"They're too close," Xochi panted, barely able to speak as she barreled headlong through the weeds. "We're not going to get away this time."

Ariel grabbed Nandita's arm as she ran, pulling her through the maze of obstacles. "Think how easy this would be if our crazy witch lady would use her magical Partial mind control powers."

"You know I can't do that," said Nandita, wheezing from exertion. "They'll know they've been controlled, which means we either keep them with us forever or send them home with the knowledge that one of the Trust is on the island."

"Can't have that," snapped Ariel, diving for cover as another burst of bullets flew by. "If they start hunting us, this might start to get serious."

"This is a patrol team rounding up strays," said Nandita. "A dedicated hunt would be orders of magnitude worse."

Xochi fired over the rim of a rusted dishwasher, slowing the pursuit by forcing the Partials into similar cover. "In another minute or two we won't have any choice," she said. "They're better at this, and there are more of them."

"Wait," said Ariel, cocking her head as she listened. Something had changed. Xochi fired again, and Ariel shushed her with a wave. "Quiet, can't you hear that?"

Xochi dropped back into cover, and the three of them listened carefully as the others ran ahead. Ariel closed her eyes, trying to concentrate on the sound. *What was it?*

"The engines," said Nandita. "They're idling."

Yes, thought Ariel, *the sound of the engines has changed, but there was something else first. Something bigger, like a . . .* She couldn't put it in words.

"Remind me what idling means," said Xochi. "I've heard, like, four engines in my entire life."

"It means they're waiting for something," said Nandita. "They're not pursuing us anymore."

"They can't get the vehicles through this junkyard anyway."

"They revved them again," said Ariel, still concentrating on the sounds. "But it sounds like they're . . . leaving."

"How can you tell?" asked Xochi. "I can hear engines, but none of this deep emotional nuance you two are pulling out of them."

"You're human," said Nandita. "And you don't have a fraction of the gene mods I do."

"They can't be giving up," said Ariel. "They were too close. You think they're trying to surround us?" She looked ahead, trying to see the rest of their group, but they'd gone around a corner and out of sight. "We have to catch up. Kessler can't defend the mothers by herself."

"There still might be Partials behind us," said Xochi. "Moving out of cover might get us killed."

Nandita shook her head. "They're here to capture us, not kill us."

"That was before we shot at them," said Ariel. "Now we're enemy combatants."

"Give me a moment," said Nandita, and closed her eyes, drawing in a long, deep breath. She held very still, as if concentrating, and Ariel knew she was trying to sense nearby Partials on the link. She took a breath of her own but didn't notice anything; she never could. *Maybe with practice?*

Nandita's eyes snapped open. "Ahead of us," she gasped. "Run to the children!"

All three women jumped up and ran, pelting forward to the rescue. Ariel spared a quick glance behind, but saw nothing. *Why would they abandon us? Even if they sent men forward to cut us off, why pull away from their position behind?*

Ariel outpaced the others, slowing at the corner of the next big building to bring up her rifle before stepping out carefully, the barrel already lined up at head level for any enemies that came into view. All she saw was a boot and ankle, disappearing through a doorway as a Partial walked inside. A moment later she heard the cry of an infant and bolted back into a run just as Xochi caught up with her.

"Where?" asked Xochi.

Ariel pointed to the open doorway, and Xochi nodded. They were each armed with an M16 assault rifle, taken from their personal collection as members of the old East Meadow militia; every teen on the island had been trained in firearms as part of their schooling, and the rifles had enough punch to take down an armored Partial if they hit it in the right places. *We can do this,* thought Ariel.

Except we don't know how many there are, or where.

They were almost to the doorway. Ariel whispered as softly as she could while still running, "Do we sneak in quietly, or charge in guns blazing?"

"Too late for either one," said a stern male voice, and Xochi and Ariel both froze in their tracks. "Drop the rifles and step against the wall," said the man, and they did, all the while Ariel cursing herself for her recklessness. She glanced back the way they had come but couldn't see Nandita anywhere. She heard the children crying inside, and then footsteps behind her and the clank of metal, as the Partial soldier kicked their rifles farther out of reach. "Tell us what you know about the resis—"

He stopped abruptly, as if alerted by something Ariel hadn't heard, followed a split second later by another Partial shouting from inside the building.

"Ced, you need to see this."

"Two combatants in custody," their captor responded, "position unsecured."

"Bring them in here," said the other Partial, "and ask them what they know about a year-old human child."

Ariel swore under her breath and heard Xochi doing the same. She looked to the side again, but Nandita was still in hiding.

"Who are you waiting for?" asked their captor.

Ariel swore again, though she kept it in her head this time, and hoped she hadn't completely given Nandita away. "There was another group of you chasing us," said Ariel. "I'm just surprised they haven't caught up yet."

"They're holding position while we flanked you," said the Partial, though Ariel knew he was lying. *The others left,* she thought, *and at full speed in their transports. That can't be standard*

procedure—even the cage truck drove away. How were they plan-
ning to bring us in? What's going on?

"Through the door," said the Partial, "and don't try anything stupid."

Xochi and Ariel filed through the door into the ruin beyond, their hands held high above their heads. It was some kind of warehouse, holding more of the heavy appliances they had seen rusting outside. The interior was shady, but not dark, as much of the roof was collapsed and open to the sky. There was only one other Partial inside, holding his own rifle and Senator Kessler's, while Kessler, Madison, and Isolde crouched in a corner with the two children. The Partial watched them warily as they came in, but he couldn't keep himself from glancing back at Arwen, again and again and again. A one-year-old was too rare, too shocking to ignore. He motioned them into the same corner, and as they passed, Ariel scanned the floor as subtly as she could, looking for any other guns. There were none. She, Xochi, and Kessler had all been disarmed, but Madison and Isolde might have their semiautomatic pistols.

And Nandita was still outside, where their captor had left their rifles lying in the grass.

"That's a year-old child, Cedric," said the second Partial.

"That's . . ." The Partial who'd captured them followed them in, but the sight of Arwen stopped him cold. He peered at the girl in awe, his back to the door, letting his guard down for just a moment, and Ariel half expected Nandita to step in behind and shoot him. Nothing happened. He recovered his wits and moved to a defensive position where he could watch both the women and the door. Ariel was fairly certain it was just the two

Partials, left alone to capture six women. Those numbers would make bringing them in very difficult, even for Partials, and the idea that capture might not be their goal suddenly chilled Ariel's blood.

"Tell us everything you know," said Cedric.

"I know Partials are heartless killers too stupid to pick their own noses without an officer around to show them how," said Kessler. "Is that the kind of stuff you're talking about? Or do you want to narrow that idiotic question down a little?"

"Start with her," said the other Partial, pointing at Arwen. "We thought all human children died instantly."

"You certainly did your best to make it that way," said Isolde. Kira had told them that the Partials hadn't released the plague, but few people believed her. Ariel wasn't sure what she believed about it. The two Partials didn't offer anything to confirm or deny it.

"Is this the one you saved?" asked Cedric. "The one Kira Walker cured?"

"We don't know anything about Kira Walker," said Ariel, deflecting the question. She forced herself not to glance at the door, not to give her thoughts away so easily again. Even if Nandita didn't want to use the link to control them, she could pick up the dropped rifles and attack—a surprise shot that dropped one was all they needed, and in the confusion Ariel could take Isolde's pistol and finish the other one. *Or if we're going to shoot them anyway,* she thought, *just use the damn mind control and make it easy on us.* Was Nandita really that careful—that paranoid and secretive—that she'd risk losing them all in a firefight just to keep her best weapon hidden?

Of course she is, thought Ariel with a snarl. *This is Nandita—she's always been like this, and she always will be. She'll sell out every one of us to protect herself.*

"We don't know why my daughter didn't die," said Madison, telling the lie they'd agreed on in case they ever got caught. "She's immune, just like we are. Please leave us alone."

"We had a program called the Hope Act," said Kessler. "We created as many pregnancies as we could—statistically, some of them were bound to share their parents' immunity. This one did."

"Are there more?" asked Cedric. The other Partial watched the door, and Ariel watched him.

Kessler shrugged. "We don't know. I'd heard that maybe there were, way out in the east, but we don't know where."

"That's where we were headed," said Madison. "We thought maybe if there were more children there, we could meet up and try to stick together. That's all."

"There's no one left in the eastern part of the island," said Cedric. "We've gathered everyone into East Meadow."

"Why?" asked Ariel. She held no hope that the soldiers would answer, but she couldn't help herself. Why gather the humans to a single location? What were they planning to do once they had them all? As expected, the soldier ignored her question completely.

"Tell us what you know about the resistance," said the other Partial. Ariel recognized this as the first question Cedric had asked, while they were still outside. She hadn't been aware that there was a resistance movement, but it seemed to be a pretty big deal.

"There is no resistance," said Xochi. "Maybe a few groups

like us, trying to get out of East Meadow, but that's it."

"The humans have been running a guerrilla campaign for the full length of the occupation," said Cedric. "Tell us about the biological weapon."

"What biological weapon?" asked Ariel.

"Tell us about the rocket strikes in Plainview," said Cedric. "Where did they get the rockets? Where are the ringleaders hiding?"

"We don't know any of this," Ariel insisted. "We're not part of any resistance—we're just trying to protect these children."

"You're fleeing the site of the largest human counterattack in the history of this occupation," the Partial said firmly. "You are involved, and you will tell us what you know."

Ariel tried to visualize the map in her head, the old roads of Long Island laid out in her memory. They had left East Meadow through Levittown, and then Bethpage, and then . . . Plainview. *We were in Plainview this morning,* she thought. *There was no rocket strike, no attack of any kind. Maybe it happened since we left? But that's only been a few hours—*

The noise I heard, she thought suddenly. *I heard a noise, something big and distant, and then the engines stopped, and then a minute later they left. Was that the attack? A human resistance movement attacked Plainview, barely minutes ago, and the patrol chasing us was called back to help. These two aren't here to capture us, they're here to interrogate us.*

She opened her mouth to respond, but Cedric and the other Partial stood up, in almost perfect unison, glancing at each other and then all around the room. Ariel couldn't tell if they looked scared or just confused.

"What the hell is that?" asked Cedric.

"It's getting closer," said the other.

Ariel glanced at the other women, crouching lower and huddling closer for protection. Ariel pressed herself to Isolde's side, feeling the gun tucked under the girl's shirt. "I'm taking this," she whispered.

"They're feeling something on the link," whispered Isolde, nodding as Ariel took the handgun.

"Think it's Nandita?" asked Xochi.

Ariel shook her head. "I've seen Nandita do her thing once before, and it was nothing like this." She looked at the Partials again and saw them consolidating into better cover.

"Do you have any more weapons?" asked Cedric. It took Ariel a moment to realize he was addressing them.

"What's going on?" asked Ariel.

"Something's coming," said Cedric. "If you have weapons, get them ready."

"It's got to be Nandita," whispered Isolde.

As if in answer, Nandita stumbled through the door, practically walking backward. To Ariel's shock the Partials noted her only mildly, keeping their weapons trained on the door. "Get down!" they shouted. She scrambled for cover, her eyes wide. Cedric's voice was hard as steel. "Did you see it?"

"No," said Nandita, "what is it?"

"We don't know," said the other Partial, "but we've heard stories."

Ariel stared at them in shock, wondering what could be so terrifying as to make the Partials abandon their interrogation, and Nandita abandon her hiding spot. A heartbeat later she decided it didn't matter what it was—if they were scared of it, she was too. She brought up Isolde's handgun, a thick semiautomatic, and saw Xochi do the same with Madison's. They waited, crouching in the ruins, their eyes trained on the door.

And then it came.

Ariel felt it first—not with her body, but somewhere in her mind. It was a presence, simultaneously massive and invisible. She staggered, and saw Isolde do the same. *It's the link,* she thought. *We're feeling it on the link.* Khan, quiet a moment ago, began screaming, almost as if he could feel it too.

A shadow crossed the doorway, and moments later a massive shape appeared—humanoid, but wildly inhuman. It was dark red or purple, covered with what looked like rough plates of hide armor; Ariel couldn't tell if they were part of its body or something removable. It was so large it had to stoop to look through the door, and considered them a moment with tiny black eyes. Its voice was deep, though Ariel saw no mouth.

"It's time to get ready," said the thing. "Prepare yourselves for snow."

"Who are you?" Cedric demanded, but the creature ignored the question.

"Tell the others," it said, and straightened to leave. Cedric fired a single shot from his rifle, hitting the thing's leg. Ariel couldn't tell if it did any damage. The creature stooped back down in the doorway, its pace measured and deliberate, and Ariel saw some kind of flaps flare open on its shoulders, like giant nostrils. The two Partials dropped unconscious, and Ariel felt a moment of wooziness, like she was about to pass out. She grabbed Xochi for stability, struggling to keep her eyes open, and noted with numb interest that Isolde and Nandita seemed just as unstable. The creature watched them for a moment, as if waiting to see whether they'd fall, then spoke again. "Don't follow me," it said. "I already know. You have to tell the others." It paused a moment, and Ariel got the sudden and unmistakable impression that the thing was surprised. Its surprise washed over her like a thick, viscous wave, and it was all she could do not to yelp in reflected terror.

"Nandita," said the creature. Ariel didn't know where its surprise ended and her own began.

"Who are you?" Nandita demanded.

"It's almost here," said the creature. "I'm fixing it, and it's almost done."

"What are you fixing?" demanded Nandita. "Who are you?"

"I'm me," said the creature. "The world will be fixed. There will be snow again."

It turned and walked away.

CHAPTER FOURTEEN

Samm stood in the center of the hospital cafeteria, watching the Partials react to their latest bit of news. All nine were awake now, gathered here in wheelchairs and hospital beds, most of them still too weak to walk and some of them far worse. Number Eight, a soldier named Gorman, was still on oxygen, his lungs too atrophied to function completely on their own. None of them were officers, but they'd served together before the Break, and they all looked to Gorman as their leader.

"Twelve years," said Gorman. His face was gaunt, his eyes watery and sagging. He was physically eighteen, like every Partial infantryman, but he was so sickly he looked decades older. "That's . . ." He paused, lost for words. "Twelve years."

"Almost thirteen," said Samm. "I don't know exactly when you were sedated, but it's 2078 now." He glanced at Heron, silent in her corner, and then at the door—it didn't lock, but Calix had promised to keep everyone out so they could have some privacy. So far she'd done her job well, and the meeting had remained Partials-only.

"The rebellion started in 2065," said a soldier in a wheelchair. "We might be a month or two off, but that's close enough to thirteen to make no difference either way." Samm had learned his name was Dwain.

"The last thing I remember was coming here," said Gorman. He gestured feebly at the complex in general. "It was when RM was in full swing, when the brass finally decided the humans weren't coming back from it. We'd been assigned to search the ParaGen compound, to see if there was something we could do about the plague, and then . . . well. Here I am."

"You don't remember who sedated you?" asked Samm.

"There was no 'who,'" said a soldier named Ritter. "I was in full gear when it happened—I don't remember exactly, but it must have been on a patrol. I think it was . . ." He flashed a burst of frustration across the link. "I don't remember. In one of the lab buildings, maybe this one, for all I know. It was like a chemical attack."

The other Partials linked their agreement, and Samm nodded. "The same man who imprisoned you had one other, a soldier named Williams, who he modified to produce a targeted Partial sedative in his breath. We . . . have no way to change him back."

Everyone shifted uncomfortably.

"The world you woke up in is not the world you left," Samm continued. "I've already told you about the Break, and RM, and the Preserve. What happened to you was done out of a fear of extinction, and while that doesn't make it excusable, it at least makes it understandable. Outside of the Preserve, the world is empty. The only other settlements on the continent—and as far as we can tell, the entire world—are back east: the humans have gathered on Long Island, in a town called East Meadow, where there's approximately thirty-five thousand of them."

The room filled with surprised link data, followed almost immediately by a crashing wave of confusion as the full implications of the Break finally hit home. Dwain was the first to speak.

"Only thirty-five thousand humans? As in, anywhere?"

"That's the entire world population of the species," said Samm. "There may be small pockets here and there, but within the next hundred years, at the most, they'll be extinct."

"So where are the Partials?" asked Gorman. "We were immune to RM, and there's no way a group of thirty-five thousand could subdue all million of us in the army."

Samm felt his chest constrict, and he hesitated before speaking, as if there was some way he could save them from the news he was about to give. "The Partials are just north of them," he said, "in our old headquarters in White Plains. All"—he paused—"two hundred thousand of them."

"Two hundred thousand?" asked Ritter. "You're joking."

"I am not."

"What happened to the rest of us?" demanded Gorman. "Did the humans attack? We heard rumors of a naval assault, but then we came here and . . ." His voice broke, and the swirl of link data through the room turned bitter with sadness. "They did it, didn't they? The Last Fleet broke through and slaughtered our army."

"The Last Fleet was stopped," said Samm. "The humans didn't kill anyone."

"At least not directly," said Heron.

Gorman shot her a look, then turned back to Samm. His voice was weak, still wheezing on the respirator, but his link data practically sparked with indignation. "Then what happened?"

"About three years ago the first generation started dying," said Samm. "The first wave of Partials they built for the war, all the veterans who were first on the shores in the Isolation War, just . . . died. Healthy one day and then rotting the next, like a piece of fruit left out in the sun. We discovered that every single one of us was built with an expiration date. On or around our twentieth birthday, every Partial dies." Samm paused a moment, giving them a moment to absorb it. "The next batch goes in one month; the final batch—my batch—has about eight. Depending on when you came out of the vats, you have between four and thirty-two weeks to live."

The room was silent, each Partial sitting quietly, thinking. Adding. Even Heron was silent, watching Samm with deep, dark eyes. Link data crackled through the air in a disjointed blend of confusion and despair.

"You say it kills everyone?" asked Gorman.

Samm nodded. "It's not a disease, it's built into our DNA. It's unstoppable, incurable, and irreversible."

"Twenty years?"

"Yes."

"And you say this is 2078?" asked Gorman.

Samm frowned, confused by the string of questions. He had expected some disbelief, but Gorman's linked confusion was growing less heartbroken every second. "October. Why?"

"Soldier," said Gorman, "we're Third Division. Out of the vats in 2057." He opened his eyes wide, as if even he could barely believe what he was about to say. "Five months ago we all turned twenty-one."

Samm stared at him. "That's impossible."

"Obviously not."

"No one has ever lived through expiration," said Samm, "we've tried everything—"

"How do we know this expiration date is even real?" asked Ritter.

"I'm not making this up, if that's what you're implying," said Samm.

"If he's lying about this, he could be lying about everything else," said Dwain.

"I'm not lying," said Samm. "It is 2078, and the world is dying, and somehow you've been saved from that and we need to figure out how—"

In a blur of motion Heron stepped out from the wall, pulled a combat knife from a sheath on her belt, and grabbed Ritter by the shoulder. Before Samm could even blink, Ritter was down on the floor, his chair clattering away across the tile, Heron's knee on his chest and her knife pressed down against the skin of his throat. "Tell me the truth," she said.

Samm jumped to his feet. "Heron, what are you doing?" He was joined by a chorus of cries from the others, most of them too weak even to stand up. Gorman struggled against the breathing tubes around his neck, trying to rise, but the effort was too much and he sagged back into bed. Outrage coursed across the link in waves.

"How old are you?" asked Heron. She pressed the knife closer against his throat. "Don't make me show you how serious I am."

"He can barely breathe," shouted Dwain. "How's he supposed to say anything with you crushing his rib cage?"

"Then somebody answer for him," said Heron, "before I put him out of his misery and start looking for a new hostage."

"We're twenty-one," said Gorman, coughing out the words between deep, thirsty breaths from the respirator. "Everything we've said is true. We're twenty-one years old."

Heron stood up, dropping her knife back into her sheath almost as quickly as she'd drawn it. She offered Ritter a hand up, but he batted it away with a scowl and lay gasping on the floor.

She looked at Samm. "Something here is keeping them alive."

Samm raised an eyebrow. "Something in the life support?"

"Is it really going to be that simple?" asked Heron.

"How do you know it isn't the coma?" asked a Partial named Aaron near the wall.

Samm glanced over at the soldier. He considered the idea. "It could have been, but I think it's unlikely. If slowing a person's metabolism postponed expiration, we'd have seen more variation in the dates."

"Not the coma itself," said Aaron, "I mean the coma's cause. The sedative. What if the humans who did this to us built in a way to keep us going?"

Heron still hadn't taken her eyes off Samm. "Is Williams the cure?"

"That would be ironic," said Samm.

"That would be useless," said Gorman. "You've seen what that thing did to us. Even if it gives us thirteen new years, is that really a solution? We'll still die after twenty, plus a massive stretch of physical and mental torture in the middle of it."

"Different usage could have different effects," said Heron.

"Use it in small doses and it's just a really good sleep aid that helps keep you alive longer."

"He's not a sleep aid," said Dwain, "he's a member of our squad, and you can't use him like this."

"That can't be it anyway," said Samm. "Dr. Morgan took Vale specifically to look for a cure for expiration. If he already had one, he would have said something."

"Saying something would have forced him to reveal what he'd done to these ten," said Heron. "Morgan would have flayed him alive, and half the humans in the Preserve."

"I have half a mind to do the same," said Gorman.

"They've done nothing to you," Samm snapped.

Gorman waved his hands in a feeble gesture that included the respirator, the gurney, and the entire room full of sickly, crippled Partials. "You call this nothing?"

"I call it Dr. Vale's work," said Samm, "not theirs."

"We're not just talking about the coma," said Gorman. "What about everything else? We started a war to get away from human oppression—a war that you're telling us literally ended the world—and now, thirteen years, later we wake up to what: more oppression. Worse oppression. Our entire species is dying, and you come in here like somebody's pet Partial trying to tell us how bad the humans have it. Do you have any spine, soldier? Do you have any self-respect at all?"

Samm said nothing. He didn't even have to look at them to feel their disgust, their anger, their pity filling the air like a poison cloud. He'd tried to be their friend, their guide to the new world they'd woken into, but all they saw him as was a traitor. He opened his mouth to protest, to tell them that he wasn't just a human tool, to explain everything that had happened and all his reasons, but it was . . . It was too much. He looked at Gorman, but shouted to the hall.

"Calix!"

He waited, wondering if she'd wandered away, praying that she hadn't locked the door. It felt like a lifetime, but it was barely a second before the door opened. Calix stood in the doorway, balancing on her good leg.

"You need anything?"

He kept her in his peripheral vision, his eyes on Gorman. *Listen closely,* he thought, hoping that the soldiers were paying close attention. "Have the hunters reported back yet?"

She blinked, a tic Samm had come to recognize in her as confusion. It wasn't the question she'd expected, but she answered it. "Phan bagged a deer; he and Frank are bringing it back. Should be here soon."

"And the harvest?"

She blinked again. Her voice was more hesitant this time, probing him for answers. "Everything's picked, they're still . . . canning the fruits and beans and stuff, is . . . everything okay?"

"Everything's great," said Samm, watching Gorman closely. "How about the beehives? We getting enough honey?"

If she was still confused by his questioning, she kept it to herself this time. "Yields aren't as high as last year, but we're doing okay," she said. She paused a moment, then added, "Certainly enough to feed ten extra mouths."

"Great." Samm phrased his next sentence carefully—not a request, but not a command. "I know I told you to keep these guys' diets light and bland for the first little bit, but they've been through a lot, and I think they deserve a little something extra. That honey candy Laura makes is amazing. Let's get them some."

Calix grinned; she'd helped Laura make the most recent batches and loved showing them off. "Lemon or mint?"

Samm looked at the Partials. "Lemon or mint?"

Dwain shook his head in disbelief. "You're bribing us with candy?"

"We'll take mint," said Gorman. Calix nodded and closed the door, and Gorman scowled at Dwain. "That wasn't a bribe, it was a demonstration." He shot a hard glance at Samm. "He's showing us they're equals."

"We're working together," said Samm. "Partners, friends, whatever you want to call it."

"What do *you* want to call it?" asked Heron. Samm gave her a quick glance but didn't answer.

"But why?" asked Gorman. "After everything that's happened, after everything you've told us about the humans and the world and all the million things wrong with it . . . Why?"

Samm was still looking at Heron when he answered. "If you want to survive in this world, you need to stop asking why people work together, and just start working together."

CHAPTER FIFTEEN

Kira crouched in the shade, surveying the destruction before her. She guessed the ashes were at least a month old, maybe more. Animals—maybe foxes, probably cats, and by the looks of it at least one wild pig—had already ravaged the site, dragging clothes and backpacks through the dirt, scattering the remnants of old, weathered equipment. Picking clean the bones.

Kira picked up a scrap of an old armored vest and turned it over in her hands before dropping it with a thump back into the dust. Dr. Morgan's records of the smaller factions were accurate, but apparently out of date; she had sent a patrol out in this direction, but there was no report of this battle. The corpses might be Morgan's soldiers, rival soldiers, or a mix of both. Kira wondered if there were newer, more complete records hidden in a drive somewhere, encrypted and secret, or if Morgan had simply stopped bothering to complete them. They were both equally possible, but Kira's gut told her the latter was more likely. Morgan was obsessed, pursuing the cure for expiration with fanatical zeal. Everything else was being left by the wayside, including the people Morgan was trying to save. This forgotten battleground might very well be the last attack she'd ordered. Kira prayed that it was.

A small breeze lifted the ashes from an old grenade blast. Kira sat on a fallen log, staying under the trees and keeping her back to the water, where attack was less likely, and pulled out her map. She was in a thick beech forest on the shores of the North Stamford reservoir—about ten or twelve miles from Morgan's headquarters in Greenwich—where Morgan's scouts had marked the location of a possible recon camp for a faction of Partials called the Ivies. Obviously the recon camp was gone, but what about the rest of the Ivies? Kira hadn't been able to find clear data on each faction's beliefs or alignments, but the file on speculation listed the Ivies as "strongly opposed to medical experimentation." That marked them as potential allies for Kira, and their suspected territory was relatively close.

She examined her map, scavenged from a high school library on her way out of Greenwich. She had transferred Morgan's records to a data screen, purely in the interest of speed, but the battery wouldn't last more than a few days, and as soon as she was out of Morgan's reach, she'd sat down and painstakingly copied as much of the info as she could into a musty paper notebook. The map, too, she had heavily marked with pencil, denoting all the possible faction camps and her most likely routes to travel between them. Some were weeks away, either north along the Hudson or east through Connecticut and Rhode Island. One group had allegedly traveled all the way to Boston, fleeing the faction war almost completely. The Ivies, if Morgan's scouts were correct, had retreated to the wilderness in between, making their home by a place called Candlewood Lake. Maybe twenty miles away, as the crow flies. Kira checked her supplies—a bedroll, a poncho, a handgun, a compass, and a knife. A bag of apples. Only what she could glean from the hospital without arousing suspicion. She'd look for more on the road.

She filled her canteen in the reservoir. *Time to go.*

The first leg of her journey ignored the highway and cut across the countryside, through a wooded stretch of land that the map said was more empty forest, but that turned out to be broken asphalt roads that wound through a loose collection of massive homes, each with its own fetid swimming pool, and most with their own tennis court. Kira kept to the trees when possible, just in case someone was following her, but when she reached the town of New Canaan, she turned north on Route 123 and made much better time. It was late enough in the year that most of the leaves had changed color, and foliage seemed to burn with bright yellows and oranges. Most of the leaves would fall soon, a callback to the old days when the winters were fierce and heavy, but the beeches kept theirs well into the spring. Kira wondered if they'd always been that way or if it was a new development, nature's way of adapting to the new, winterless world the humans had created.

She passed a golf course, the long, open greens overgrown by saplings. It always felt like such a waste when she saw that—old golf courses were some of the easiest fields to clear for farming. A good sign, she decided, that the Ivies were nowhere near.

Kira camped for the night in a fire station; the giant bay doors were open and the trucks gone, making Kira wonder if the firefighters had succumbed to RM while out on a call. The disease didn't normally kill that fast, but if they were already infected and working while sick . . . She hadn't seen an infected adult in thirteen years, but she knew the disease was painful, and she couldn't imagine the strength it would take to keep going in those final stages. She had to admire anyone who'd try to fight fires while dying of the plague. She rolled out her blanket in the barn-like cavern of the open station, protected from rain but smelling the cool night air, and fell asleep to dreams of fire and death. In the morning she felt like she hadn't slept at all. She repacked her bedroll and started walking again.

She followed Route 123 north until it ended, then traveled east on something called the Old Post Road. Her route seemed to weave back and forth between New York and Connecticut, and she couldn't help but wonder how those ancient divisions had been decided, and what they meant for the people who'd lived there. There were no gates or walls, no clear delineations of where one state ended and another began. She didn't even know what that division meant. It had been so obvious to the adults, and so meaningless to the post-Break children, that they'd never bothered to teach it in school.

However the state relationship had worked, it was over now, the houses empty, the cars rusted and falling apart, the roads buckling and breaking as new plants and trees encroached relentlessly back into their ancient territory. Birds roosted in the upper windows of sagging houses, while deer and other animals stepped lightly through the overgrown lawns, nibbling the new young leaves that grew up between the ruins. In another hundred years, Kira thought, these houses would crumble and fall completely, and the forest would swallow them up, and the deer and the boars and the wolves would forget that there had ever been anyone here at all.

The thought of wolves made her worry about Watchdogs—the bizarre talking hounds that ParaGen had made as scouts and companions for the Partial soldiers. There were none on Long Island, but she had been attacked by a feral pack of them on her trip to Chicago with Samm. He had assured her that they weren't fully intelligent, at least not to a human level, but Kira couldn't decide if that knowledge made her more or less nervous; more or less disturbed. She had no idea how widespread they were, but prayed she wouldn't encounter any on her trip to Candlewood Lake.

Eventually the Old Post Road ended as well, and she turned north on Route 35 toward the town of Ridgefield. The town wasn't large by any means, but it was far more developed than the forest and scattered houses she'd been walking through since Greenwich, and the heightened visibility gave her pause. In all likelihood there was nobody here, nobody for miles—and if there were, it would probably be a scout or spotter for the Ivies, not a far-ranging agent of Dr. Morgan. Even so, the urban center scared her. Instead of trees and dirt on the edges of the road, there was simply more concrete, which meant the forest hadn't regrown as heavily. The sight lines were longer and more open. An enemy would be able to see her from blocks away, instead of the few dozen feet allowed by the woods; she would be easier to ambush, or simply snipe from long range. She hesitated on the outskirts of the thinning forest, trying to convince herself she was being paranoid, but in the end she backtracked and cut through the trees and yards, pushing her way through dilapi-dated fences and dashing across each open street. The detour was barely an extra mile, maybe two, but she breathed easier when she finally passed the last shopping center and rejoined the narrow forest highway.

Eventually 35 merged into Route 7, and Kira made her camp in a small house just outside the crossroads. The windows were all broken—most were, outside the maintained areas—but the roof was holding, and despite a few cat prints in the hallways, it didn't seem to have become a den for any animals. Two human skeletons lay in the bedroom, their bony arms resting loosely around each other, the decayed remnants of a blanket clinging in tatters to their ribs. Two victims of RM. She cleared a space in the living room and fell asleep looking at the old, faded photos of the family on the wall.

CHAPTER SIXTEEN

The next day would take her to Candlewood, but the route passed through a city called Danbury—several times larger than the town that had scared her so much the day before, and right on the shores of Candlewood's southern tip. If the Ivies were really there, they'd see her coming for sure.

"That might not be a bad thing," she mused to herself, falling into her old habit of thinking out loud. She'd spent a few months alone in Manhattan, the only living soul for miles in any direction, trying to track down an old ParaGen office; by the end she'd been carrying on entire conversations with herself, as if desperate for any kind of companionship. She felt silly doing it, but just as silly forcing herself to be quiet. When she got to the city she'd be quiet, but here in the wilderness, why not talk?

The question was, how much of the city should she actually pass through? She munched on an apple in the early morning light, sitting not in the living room but out on the porch, away from the skeletons and their ghostly faces staring down from the photos. She had the map out, spread across her knee, but it wasn't nearly as detailed as she wanted.

"If the Ivies are there, and see me, that's good," she said, "because I want them to see me. That's the whole reason I'm here." She swallowed her bit of apple. "Unless, of course, they shoot me on sight. Which they probably won't do, but what do I know? Do I want to take that chance? If they get close enough to link me, which they can't do because I'm not on the link, they'll think I'm human." She took another bite of her apple. "But for all I know, thinking I'm human might make them more likely to shoot me, not less. I don't know anything about them." She swallowed her apple. "And what if Morgan really does have spies up here? What happens if they see me first? I think I need to stay hidden as long as possible. I need a more detailed map to plan this route."

She repacked her scant possessions and headed back to the crossroads, where one corner held a weathered gas station. The wide metal awning had collapsed over the pumps, and this and the scattered hulks of rusting cars gave her cover as she dashed across the parking lot. The entire front wall had been glass, now shattered and crunching under her feet; years of rain had blown in, wrinkling the magazines in the rack by the front and washing out their colors. Kira picked her way through the shelves looking for road maps, finding them at last in a rotating wire rack that had long since toppled to the floor. Many of the maps were damp, and some had been nibbled by rats, but she found a Connecticut road map that seemed to be in pretty good condition. She found a spot of metal shelving, clear of broken glass, and sat down to inspect her route.

The highway she was on continued straight up to Danbury, where it widened and merged with Interstate 84, a massive multi-lane road that seemed to skirt the edge of Danbury and then curve up toward Candlewood Lake. "That will be the easiest route," she said quietly, "but also the most obvious. If they're watching anything, they'll be watching that." She searched through the city itself, following the major roads and looking for other options, and marked the two major hospitals with her pencil. All the post-Break settlements, human and Partial, tended to cluster around hospitals, and the Ivies might be the same. "*Might* be," she reminded herself. Morgan's records had reported them farther north, on or around the lake itself, and with lake and city so close together it was telling, she thought, that the scouts had placed them specifically at the lake. "Maybe they don't like cities," she mused. "I'm not a big fan, either, but I'm an outsider—if this is their home territory, they could secure the city and get a lot of defensive advantages the lake can't offer. Unless they're searching for advantages I'm not considering." She looked closer at the lake, wondering what those advantages might be. Fresh water, certainly, and maybe the longer sight lines across the water. Any hunting or farming they wanted to do in the wilderness would be just as easy in the city; she had grown up doing the same in the dense urban areas of Long Island. It didn't seem to make sense. She looked at her notes again: the Ivies were "strongly opposed to medical experimentation." That was all the information she had. She stared at the map, still completely unsure how best to approach it.

"Better to be safe," she decided at last, and plotted a course that curved west, around the edge of the city, and approached the lake through the smaller, suburban area called New Fairfield. She would be staying off the roads almost the whole way, and she worked out enough of the details to guide herself by compass instead, landmark to landmark, starting with the western edge of a place called Bennett's Pond. The forest was thicker there, with steeper hills than she'd passed through before, and she found herself tiring more quickly in the rougher terrain. She crossed I-84 around ten in the morning, a wooded stretch of road well west of the city, and then tramped across a narrow stream and through another thick, old-growth forest. By noon she had reached another wide pond, ringed by a series of golf courses long ago gone to seed. The western edge of the water was a low marsh filled with empty nests. Cold or not, the need to migrate south was too ingrained in the birds' tiny minds, and the wetland was still and quiet. She saw a cluster of small, gleaming curves, surprised to find a clutch of eggs, but when she drew closer they were simply golf balls, yellowed and cracking in the sun.

She kept heading north through the forest, skirting the invisible line between the states, until a cluster of homes signaled it was time to curve eastward again. More and more houses appeared as she drew closer to New Fairfield, the buildings fading and forlorn in the midst of the trees. Kira imagined them not as houses but as spirits of the houses that used to be here, persisting stubbornly, ethereally, long after the structures themselves had disappeared. She skirted the edge of Corner Pond, crossed a narrow road, and turned almost straight east. Her undeveloped forest was running out quickly.

And then she saw a bright white mark in the trunk of a tree;

a recent carving, maybe three days old at the most. The roman numeral four. IV.

The Ivies.

It made so much sense, and so abruptly, that she marveled she hadn't thought of it before: the Ivies hadn't named themselves for the plant, but for their old military designation. IV. The fourth division or regiment or some such segment of the Partial army. They were real, and they were here; this was either a border sign or a trail marker, and she couldn't help but wonder if they used this same forested corridor to avoid the developed areas on either side. It was possible, maybe even likely, but why? What did a defensive army have to fear from the homes and open streets of a long-abandoned suburb?

A sudden thought consumed her, and she crept closer to the mark to examine it. Dogs and other animals used smells to mark their territory, and the Partials' link system was similar in a lot of ways. Could their data pheromones persist in the same way? It was possible that this sign was more than visual, that the mark merely pointed out where the real data could be found. She'd practiced with Samm to develop her own small connection to the link; if there was something there, she might be able to sense it. She walked up cautiously to the mark on the tree, breathing deeply as she went. She sensed nothing. When she reached it she touched the bark gently, feeling the edges of the three white lines: IV. They looked like they'd been hacked in with a hatchet, two quick chops per line to break through the bark and expose the white wood underneath. White except for an odd discoloration at the bottom of each letter, like something had dripped there, or been smeared on purpose.

It was blood.

Kira hesitated, glancing nervously at the forest around her. Nothing moved, not even wind in the leaves. She looked back at the bloody letters, wondering why the blood was there at all. Was it an accident? A warning? Was that the best way to make the link data persist long-term? She leaned in, steeling herself, taking a deep breath.

DEATH PAIN BLOOD BETRAYAL—

She staggered back, gasping for breath, rubbing her nose to get the smell out.

DEATH BETRAYAL PAIN THEY'RE KILLING US—

She tripped over a tree root, yelping as she fell, rolling to her feet and grabbing handfuls of dirt and leaves and grass as she came up. She ran through the forest, irrationally, helplessly terrified, clutching the ground cover to her face and sucking in the smell, trying desperately to drown the signal out.

DEATH PAIN—

DEATH

And then it was gone. Kira collapsed to the ground, her heart still racing, her blood pounding in her ears. The link was designed as a combat tool, a fast, wordless way for the Partials to warn one another of danger and coordinate their movements on the battlefield. When one soldier died, he released a burst of death pheromones, warning his companions that something was wrong; Kira had sensed it before, but it was nothing like this. That had been data, in its truest form: an announcement of what had happened, and where. This was a frantic, overwhelming warning, a pheromonal scream. A normal death would produce nothing like it, and she didn't even want to think about what could. Partials had been murdered here, probably tortured, perhaps solely for the purpose of creating that data. She'd had to walk right up to smell it, but her link connection was weak.

Did the whole forest smell like that? Was this warning spread around the entire lake?

In her mad race to escape, Kira had gotten disoriented, and she pulled out her compass with trembling hands. North was behind her, which meant she'd been running south; obviously not too far, as she hadn't run into any houses. She looked up, trying to get her bearings. *Do I keep running, or stay on track?* She was too scared to speak out loud. *The Ivies are "opposed to medical experimentation," and if this is how they tell people to stay away, it looks like they're a lot more opposed than I realized. And maybe that's not all they oppose. Morgan's record focused on experimentation because that's all she cares about—they don't want to help with her work, and they're too far away to interfere with it, so she forgets them and moves on. Never mind the details.*

She slowed her breathing, calming herself, forcing herself to think clearly. It was harder than it should have been, and she wondered how much of the warning pheromones were still in her nose, still filling her bloodstream with adrenaline. She closed her eyes, trying to focus. *They still might be my allies,* she told herself. *They post these as warnings to Partials, to Morgan's forces. Their community might be sympathetic to the humans, and almost certainly amenable to a plan that opposes Dr. Morgan. And if nothing else, they're expiring. I can offer a possible solution to that.* She thought again about the pain and fear it must have taken to produce that warning on the link, and shuddered. *Is that really who I want to align myself with? All the things I was worried about*

Morgan doing—would they do the same?

She shook her head. *I might be misinterpreting everything, not just how they created the border marker but the fact that it's a border marker at all. For all I know, one of the Ivies was ambushed by Morgan's soldiers and carved that mark as a warning to his friends. I can't judge them without more information.*

She checked her compass, set her jaw, and hiked east toward the lake.

CHAPTER SEVENTEEN

Marcus sat as still as he could, trying not to pull against the handcuffs tied around his wrists to a metal bar behind him—he'd struggled a lot the first night, hoping to get out of them, and rubbed his skin raw in the process. Now any movement at all brought lances of pain so sharp they made him bite the inside of his cheek. Woolf, Galen, and Vinci were tied up next to him, sitting silently against a wall in the back room of an old supermarket, but none of them seemed to be in quite as much pain. Marcus wondered if they were better at masking it, or if they'd just been smarter about their wrists in the first place. Either way he felt stupid.

Which was to be expected, he decided, when you found yourself tied up by a terrorist you went looking for in the first place.

"This is what we get for trusting her," said Marcus.

"She was our only option," said Galen.

"She is also a convicted criminal," said Marcus. He looked at the others with as bemused a grin as he could muster. "I kind of feel like we should have given that point more weight when we made our plan to find her."

"She was working with the Senate and Defense Grid," said Woolf. "Since the start of the invasion she hadn't done anything suspicious or illegal—that we knew about," he added.

Marcus closed his mouth, swallowing his snarky comment.

Woolf shook his head. "Obviously if we'd known she'd managed to round up a nuclear warhead, we would have thought twice about it."

"If we'd known she had a nuclear bomb, we would have done exactly the same thing," said Vinci. "We just would have handled the meeting a little differently. Infiltrating her army would have been the best bet."

"I suppose it's too late for that now?" asked Marcus, looking at the guard on the other side of the room.

The guard nodded. "Yes, it is."

"Bummer," said Marcus. "Thought we had something there."

"Why is she doing this?" asked Vinci. "A bomb big enough to destroy the invading Partial army would kill almost every human on the island in the same instant. Ninety percent of both groups are in East Meadow—she can't possibly consider that an acceptable loss."

"She won't set it off on Long Island," said Woolf. "She'll take it north to White Plains, or as close as she can get it, and detonate it there. Even out the numbers, like she said."

"It's genocide," said Vinci.

"You mean like RM?" asked the guard. "You mean like exactly what you did to us thirteen years ago?"

"The Partials had nothing to do with RM," said Vinci, his

voice calm and matter-of-fact. He wasn't arguing, Marcus realized, simply explaining. A quick glance at the seething guard showed just how unlikely he was to listen to reason.

"You're talking to a man ready to set off a nuclear device fifty miles from the last human survivors," said Marcus. "Let's just assume he doesn't believe you and move on."

"The Partials need to be destroyed," said the guard, lifting his rifle. "Every one of them. I can't believe she hasn't let us execute *you* yet." He stood up, his face hard as stone, and Marcus pressed as far back against the wall as he could.

"See?" said Marcus, trying to keep his voice from cracking with fear. "I told you this would be more fun." The guard's eyes were red with fury, and Marcus half expected him to shoot all four of them in one long burst of bullets.

The door to their back room opened, revealing Delarosa flanked by Yoon and another guerrilla. Marcus breathed an audible sigh of relief. "You have awesome timing."

"Unless she wants us dead as well," said Vinci.

"Still good timing," said Marcus. "It'd be a bummer if this guy shot us and she didn't get to see it."

"No one's going to shoot you," said Delarosa. She stepped forward into the room and looked down at them, not arrogant or angry, but businesslike. "We're not monsters."

"And we're more valuable to you alive," said Marcus.

Delarosa cocked her head to the side. "How?"

"Because, um . . ." Marcus grimaced. "I don't actually know, I just assumed because that's what people typically say at this point."

"You've seen too many movies," said Delarosa.

"I've never seen any," said Marcus, shrugging. "Plague baby. But I've read a lot of spy novels: They don't need batteries."

"Either way," said Delarosa. "We have no reason to keep you alive but our own human decency, and nothing to gain from killing you but convenience."

"Is that a phrase?" asked Vinci. "'Human decency'?"

"You find it insulting?" asked Delarosa.

"I find it confusing," said Vinci. "Especially considering your plan."

"I'm not happy about it," said Delarosa. "I've lost a lot of sleep trying to think of an alternative. The Partials are all dying—can I just wait a year and let them die, and free ourselves without lifting a finger?"

"I vote we try it," said Marcus. "Are we voting? Hands up, everybody, don't leave me hanging here." He moved his hands to raise them, and winced at the sudden stab of pain in his wrists.

"That plan won't work," said Delarosa. "The occupying army in East Meadow is killing too many humans, and now they might not die at all because they've found Kira—"

"Holy crap," said Marcus, "they found Kira?"

"They stopped the broadcasts," said Delarosa. "The hostage scenario is over. The most likely explanation is that they got what they wanted."

"We need to go get her," said Marcus.

"The Partials think they can use Kira to cure their expiration date," said Delarosa. "I don't know how she'll help them do that, but there it is. The longer we wait, the less likely it becomes that this situation will ever end—if we want to get rid of the Partials, we have to strike now, and with overwhelming force. We don't have the army for it, so a nuclear weapon is our only choice; it can be delivered by a single person, under their radar, and finish them off in a single blow."

"The invading army will still be here," said Galen. "A bomb on the mainland won't end the occupation here."

"Vinci," said Delarosa, "what will the Partial army do when White Plains goes up in a fireball?"

"They'll go back there," said Vinci calmly. "They'll try to find as many survivors on the mainland as possible."

"Even if they don't leave, they'll die a few months later," said Marcus. "Any research they've done on a cure for expiration will be destroyed in the explosion, along with anyone skilled enough to continue it."

"It has to happen," said Delarosa, "and it has to happen now. We upset the balance of nature when we created the Partials, and now we have to put it right."

"You can't trigger that warhead remotely," said Woolf. "Which of these brainwashed saps have you tricked into setting it off for you?"

"I'm not a monster," Delarosa said again. "This is my plan, and my responsibility."

"You're going to do it yourself?" asked Marcus.

"I came to say good-bye," said Delarosa. "I don't want to kill you, but we can't transport you effectively without attracting too much attention. I'm leaving tonight, and I'm leaving Yoon Bak in charge of this outpost, with explicit orders that you not be harmed."

"Tell this guy, too," said Marcus, nodding at the guard. "You heard her, right? No harm."

Vinci studied her. "Why are you leaving me alive if you're just going to murder my entire species?"

"Because it's not about murder," said Delarosa, "it's about necessity."

"That doesn't make it not murder," said Marcus.

"Why, Marcus," said Delarosa coldly. "I thought all you did was tell jokes."

She turned and left, and Yoon stared fiercely at the guard with the rifle until he grudgingly sat down.

"You're alive," said Yoon, "but you're still considered enemy combatants. We'll keep you in here, under guard."

"Until we die of old age?" asked Woolf.

"Until you're not a threat," said Yoon. "Or until it doesn't matter anymore."

"You can't agree with this insane plan," said Marcus. "You don't want this nuke to go off any more than we do."

"There's a lot of things I don't want," said Yoon. "Sometimes we have to accept them to get the things we do."

Marcus pleaded with her. "If getting what you want means killing a ton of people, is that really worth it?"

"I don't know," said Yoon. She glanced at Vinci. "Is it?"

"I'm not ashamed of what we did," said Vinci. "But eradicating your species was never part of our plan."

"You Partials keep saying that," said Yoon, turning to look right at him. "Considering where we are now, do you think maybe it should have been?"

Vinci was silent. Yoon stood and left the room.

CHAPTER EIGHTEEN

Ariel planted herself in front of Nandita, refusing to budge an inch. "Tell us what that was."

"I told you," said Nandita, "I don't know."

"It knew you."

"I've never seen anything like that before in my life," said Nandita. "Not here, not before, not anywhere."

"Something like that would have to have come from Para-Gen," said Kessler. "You made all kinds of genetic freaks before the Break—Watchdogs and dragons and who knows what else. And you've told us that all you people in the Trust gene-modded yourself to hell. Longer life, sharper brainpower, increased physical abilities. That twisted abomination sure looks like your handiwork to me."

Ariel considered Xochi and Kessler, who were usually fighting tooth and nail but at the moment were completely unified. They even stood alike, expressing their anger with the same fierce gestures and posture. They did everything they could to be different, yet here they were. *Do Nandita and I look like this?* Ariel wondered. *For all my hatred, how much of me is just a reflection of her? She raised me for eleven years—more than twice as long as my real parents.*

Except they were never my real parents. I have nothing left that's truly my own.

Not even my anger.

"I assure you," said Nandita, "if I'd worked on a project like that, or even seen one, I'd remember it."

"You told us before that some of the Trust didn't trust the others," said Isolde. "You worked on projects without telling each other. What if it's something like that?"

"Some kind of proto-Partial?" asked Nandita. "A model one of the others miraculously kept secret for thirty-odd years? Impossible."

"Then somebody else," said Madison. "Another genetics company, making their own version of the same technology?"

"Then it wouldn't know Nandita," said Ariel. "This did, which means it came from ParaGen, which means she knows something she's not telling us."

Nandita sighed, looking behind them. "If I talk while we walk, can we at least keep moving? We're too exposed here."

"We have to cut south now," said Kessler. "We're coming into Commack, and we had two old farms in this region. We have to assume the Partials have a presence here, even if it's just a few scouts."

"That means crossing the Long Island Expressway," said Xochi, looking at her map. "If you don't like how exposed we are now, that's really going to get you."

"If we have to, we have to," said Ariel, jogging to catch up with Nandita. "Now talk."

"That creature was almost definitely ParaGen," said Nandita. "But I don't recognize it, and I truly don't know who had the skill to make anything like it. Furthermore, the fact that I don't recognize it almost guarantees that it was created after the Break."

"Who has that kind of technology?" asked Ariel.

"I didn't think anyone did," said Nandita, "but finding the facility at Plum Island has forced me to reevaluate. If that lab could continue, there may be other labs as well, remnants of the old green movement, designed to run entirely on self-sustaining power. The obvious first guess is the ParaGen facility itself."

"ParaGen was bombed pretty heavily in the Partial War," said Kessler.

"I know," said Nandita icily. "I was there. But it was a rugged facility, and something may have survived. ParaGen had the equipment to make a creature like that—though in the old days we would have made the changes more subtly, more human-like—and also to do whatever else the creature was talking about. Fixing the world, the climate."

Ariel sneered. "How could ParaGen 'fix' the climate? You were a genetics company—you can't just gene-mod the wind."

"You can use genetics to fix anything, given enough time and energy," said Nandita. "Genetic engineering is the most powerful force on the planet. The ParaGen facility was built on an old radioactive materials site, and we built bugs designed to absorb the radiation and neutralize it; we made other bugs to nourish the soil and plants. By the time of the Break, it had become a paradise. I'm not saying this is what happened, because I don't know, but someone with the time and the means could alter the climate by engineering bacteria designed to radiate or absorb heat, or to unlock water tied up in certain areas or aquifers. On a large enough scale you could change the weather patterns, and eventually the seasons themselves, but it would require an unbelievable amount of energy to create and distribute that kind of bacteria on anything less than a geologic time frame. Para-Gen's old facility might still have power, but they don't have that much."

"So somebody made a bunch of germs to alter the weather," said Isolde, "and a creepy monster thing to tell us about it. The fact that that sentence explains anything says a lot about how little sense the world makes right now."

"That doesn't explain how it recognized Nandita," said Ariel. "This wasn't some random vat-born monster; it knew you. It had seen you before, and the way it talked, it was expecting you to recognize it."

"What if it was gene mods?" asked Xochi. "Not a new creature, but someone you used to know . . . modded up and . . . weirdified. You know what I mean."

"That many gene mods would drive a person mad," said Nandita. "We've seen it happen before, and on a much smaller scale. Something that drastic would break the subject's mind in half."

"That might actually explain it," said Ariel. "Do you know who it might be?"

"There's the expressway," said Kessler. They'd been following a trail at the base of some telephone poles, cutting a thin forest path between the homes and businesses on either side, but the trail had run out. The few telephone wires still attached stretched out over a wide gully, filled with asphalt and cars—Ariel shoved her way through the undergrowth to get a good look and counted ten lanes, plus four open shoulders separating them from the edges of the road. "Two hundred feet across, minimum," said Kessler, "and not enough vehicles to provide any meaningful cover. If we go for this, we have to go fast and lucky."

"Last time we crossed this expressway, we went under it," said Isolde. "I liked that better."

"There's nowhere like that anywhere around here," said Kessler. "Just bridges over it, like that one, which has no sides and leaves us probably more exposed than just running across here."

"I've done this before," said Xochi. "We made it just fine."

"What do we get into if we stay on this side?" asked Madison. "Is crossing it really worth the risk?"

"Partial patrols are more likely on this side," said Kessler. She took Xochi's map and held it open for the group to see. "On top of that, in another mile or two we'll hit this interchange, and beyond that this entire area is a commercial district: wide roads next to wide parking lots. We'll be more exposed there. If we cross now, though, we can lose ourselves in a string of residential areas, and camp for the night in this community college campus—it has some open areas, but they're lawns instead of parking lots, so they'll likely have plenty of foliage to hide us, and we never used them for farming, so there shouldn't be any settlements or Partials in the area."

"The odds anyone will be watching this exact stretch of road at this exact time are low," said Xochi. "Not as low as we'd like, but low. If we just go for it, all out, we can do this."

"Then let's do it," said Isolde. "Khan's going to wake up soon;

when he does, we'll want to be as far away from Partial patrols as we can."

Ariel nodded, glancing at the sleeping baby—the sedated baby, really, as his constant screaming had led Nandita to start administering low levels of drugs for safety. But the sedatives wouldn't last forever, and they needed to be well hidden by the time he got noisy again. The group shoved their way through the trees—heavier here, it seemed, than in the wooded track they'd just passed through—and worked their way down to the edge of the wide-open expressway.

"Everybody ready?" Ariel whispered. She listened carefully as each other woman in the group said yes. She took a deep breath. "Go."

The group dashed out, backpacks slamming up and down against their spines, their feet slapping furiously across the asphalt. The edge of the road was cracked and broken, as the plants struggled to reclaim their ancient territory, but the road was so wide that the center remained smooth—covered with dead leaves and windblown dirt, but still one piece. They ran behind a delivery van, and then in front of a pickup. Three lanes across. Four lanes. Ariel was almost to the center barrier when she heard a shout, and looked up to see figures on the nearby bridge.

"Partials!" she screamed. "Keep running!" She crouched down by the rusted hulk of an old SUV and started firing, trying to force the soldiers into cover. The figures disappeared, but Ariel kept her eyes on the bridge, ready to fire at the first head that popped up. "Just keep going!" she called. "We have to move south!"

Xochi reached the barrier first and launched herself over it, then reached back to hold Arwen as Madison passed her over.

Both girls ran for the southern trees, while Kessler, close on their heels, found more cover in the lee of a moving van and laid down another burst of fire.

"Ariel," she shouted, "I'll cover you! Catch up!"

Nandita jumped nimbly over the barrier, then paused to help Isolde clamber over with Khan still strapped to her chest. Ariel heard the baby scream, probably woken by the shooting. She reached the barrier just as Isolde cleared it, and leaped over without pausing.

A voice called out from the bridge during the brief moment of quiet. "Don't shoot!"

"The hell we won't," snarled Ariel, running past Kessler to take cover behind a faded white sedan skewed sideways in the road. A skeleton slumped over the wheel. Ariel drew a bead on the bridge and shouted for Kessler to move up. "Get into the trees!" She fired another burst. "We can lose them in the houses on the other side!"

"There's a chain-link fence!" Xochi called back. "You've got to buy us more time to knock it down!"

Ariel gritted her teeth and fired again. "Come on, you little bastards, stick your heads out." She fired again. "Come on, I dare you."

"Don't shoot!" shouted the figures on the bridge. "Madison!"

Ariel frowned in confusion. Madison whipped around. "Did it just say my name?"

"How do all these things keep knowing our names?" Kessler demanded, reaching the far side and throwing her weight against the fence.

"Madison," the voice shouted, "it's me! Madison, we've found you!"

Madison ran back into the street. "That's Haru!"

"It's not Haru," Ariel snarled, "it's just a trick. Get your head down before you get shot!"

"We're through the fence!" shouted Xochi.

"Madison, tell them not to shoot." The voice echoed through the tree-lined gully. "It's me, I'm standing up!"

"Don't shoot him," hissed Madison, "that's my husband."

"It can't be," said Isolde.

A figure stood up on the bridge, and beside him another, then another. They were more than a hundred yards away, and hard to distinguish, but Ariel could tell they weren't wearing Partial uniforms.

"That's him!" Madison fell to her knees, racked with sobs. "That's him, he's alive."

"Meet us on the far side," said Haru, and ran south across the bridge. A few other figures joined him, while some hung back, dropping down to take up firing positions and cover the women's final push across the street. Ariel didn't know what to think and stayed crouched in cover, aiming right back at them.

"Come on," said Isolde. "If they were bad guys, they would have shot us."

"Unless they want us alive," said Ariel.

"That's Haru," Isolde insisted. "You don't know him like we do—I recognize his voice."

"Get off the road," Kessler yelled. "No matter who it is, we have to get out of the open."

Ariel growled in frustration but realized Kessler was right. She took one last look at the shooters on the bridge before jumping up and running to the trees. Xochi and the others had knocked down enough of the fence that they could scramble over it, and Kessler and Nandita were helping Isolde. Khan was screaming piteously, awakened again to his life of endless pain. Isolde cleared the fence, with Kessler and Nandita close behind. They hadn't even pushed through to the service road at the top of the hill when Haru came crashing through the underbrush, screaming Madison's name. She called back and ran to him, rushing into his arms with Arwen pressed between them: the first reunion of a real family in thirteen years. Ariel saw Isolde and Xochi crying; even Kessler's eyes were wet. Ariel wanted to cry too, but the tears didn't come. Nandita was as emotionless as ever.

"I found you," said Haru, "I found you. I found you."

"I thought you were dead," said Madison.

"We have to go to ground," said Haru. "We've made too much noise already. Every Partial on the island can hear us, and—" He stopped abruptly, looking back and forth between Arwen and Khan. "The screaming baby's not Arwen? There are two babies?"

"This one's mine," said Isolde. Her eyes were sunken, and her voice dripped with fatigue. "Nearly a month old."

"Then this is about to get real interesting," said Haru.

Madison frowned. "What's wrong?"

Haru's companions burst through the foliage, with Senator Hobb in the lead.

"We need to hide," said Hobb. "Can you get that kid to shut up?"

"Congratulations," said Haru dryly. "You're a father."

CHAPTER NINETEEN

Isolde stared at Senator Hobb in shock. "What are you doing here?"

"Isolde?" Hobb looked half-surprised and half-terrified.

"We can't stay here," said Ariel, pushing past them through the trees. "A Partial patrol could be here any minute; we have to keep moving."

"Is that . . ." Hobb stared at the screaming infant, too stunned to move. "My . . . child?"

"We can talk about it while we run," said Nandita. She looked at Haru. "Did you come from the north or south?"

"South," said Haru. "We haven't seen any Partials in two days."

"Then we keep heading south," said Nandita. "Xochi, find us a place to hide for the night."

"We saw a good place not far from here," said Hobb. "It was a middle school, straight down this road, maybe four blocks—"

"Thank you," said Nandita crisply, "but we can find our own

hiding places. The infants require us to use a very specific kind of camp, and a school won't do."

The men fell in line with the women, Xochi and Kessler leading the way. Haru's shooters from the bridge joined them a minute later, taking up rearguard positions at the back of the column, so Ariel jogged forward to catch up with Isolde. There were six men in total, an even match for the six women.

"Is it a boy or girl?" asked Hobb.

"Boy," said Isolde, not even deigning to glance at him.

Hobb's voice was reverent. "I have a son."

"You made it very clear you had no interest in me or the baby after you knocked me up," said Isolde. "That means I have a son, and all you have is a memory of something you'll never have again."

"You act like I turned you away," said Hobb. "I'm a busy man. You can't think I hate you just because I didn't have time for a heartfelt conversation every day."

"I worked in your office," said Isolde. "You didn't even have time for 'Good morning, Isolde,' which seems to me like a pretty strong hint."

"We were working under the Hope Act," said Hobb indignantly. "Getting you pregnant was our civic duty—yours and mine—but I never expected the child to live. They never live. If I'd known—"

Isolde cut him off. "Do you honestly think that anything you're saying is working in your favor?"

"But I—"

"I think it's time for you to shut up now," said Ariel, stepping between them. "We can talk about this later."

"Or never," said Isolde.

"Never's good too," said Ariel. Hobb scowled but stayed quiet.

Xochi led them off the main road at the first good cross street, winding through a series of narrow, tree-lined roads before finally finding a house tucked back behind the others, surrounded on three sides by thick woods. The group trekked around to the back, entering through a wide broken window so the door looked undisturbed, and slipped into the basement. It was dank and musty, but they closed the basement doors and pulled up mattresses to stand against them, blocking as much sound as they could. Arwen got down to play, excited to see her daddy and babbling wordlessly as she sat on the mildewed carpet. Isolde pulled Khan from his sling and tried to nurse, but the screaming baby was too bothered to suck, and Isolde worked instead to calm him down. Ariel thought his blisters looked worse than usual, but it was hard to tell.

Hobb stared at the boy in alarm. "What's wrong with him? He's sick!"

"He was born with it," said Nandita. "We have some pain-killers and fever reducers to help keep him comfortable, but it's the best we can do for now."

"You know what that looks like," said Hobb, peering in closely.

"It's the bioweapon," said Haru, leaning forward as he noticed the same thing. "The symptoms look identical."

"What bioweapon?" asked Isolde.

"We don't know exactly," said Haru. "The Partials are getting sick—we used to think it was part of their expiration, but everything we've managed to overhear says otherwise. They're calling it a bioweapon, and they think it's us fighting back."

"The two we ran into outside Plainview said the same thing," said Ariel. "Why do they think it's a bioweapon and not just a plague?"

"Because it targets very specific areas," said Haru. "We got the full story from two victims of it, also near Plainview; they were scouts, I think, who contracted it on a mission and never made it back to base. When we found them they were too sick to fight back, so we got as much info as we could in exchange for a merciful death."

Madison paled. "They asked you to kill them?"

"It's apparently very painful," said Haru. "They think the bioweapon was deployed in East Meadow, in the district by Nandita's old house, and then whoever had it moved east along a path the Partials haven't been able to decipher yet. The symptoms look like more or less the same thing your child has—scaly skin, yellow blisters, high fever, plus the two we talked to were obviously hallucinating. They kept talking about a giant monster, and snow—"

"No way," said Ariel. She was staring at Isolde, who was staring right back with the same stunned expression. Ariel looked at the other women, her heart sinking as she saw that each of them had apparently come to the same conclusion.

"This is a very scary sudden silence," said Haru. "What's going on?"

"It can't be him," said Isolde.

"It absolutely can be," said Kessler. "Everywhere we've gone—"

"I know," growled Isolde. "I know that it's probably Khan. I just don't want it to be."

"That's what you named him?" asked Hobb. "Khan?"

"It doesn't make sense that Khan would catch it, too," said Haru. "It's designed to target Partials—"

"He is a Partial," Isolde snapped. "So am I." She gestured to Ariel. "We both are—ask Nandita."

Then men looked at Ariel, then at Nandita. "What?" asked Hobb.

"It's a long story," said Ariel, "and Nandita's really bad at telling it. Here are the bullet points: Nandita was a geneticist at ParaGen. They made the Partials and loaded them up with a bunch of weird diseases, including RM and an alternate disease that kills Partials. When the Partials rebelled, the wrong one got released, because the Partial-killer was only inside a handful of certain late-model Partials designed to mimic a regular human life cycle. Me, Isolde, and Kira."

Hobb stared at her blankly. "What?" he said again.

Haru shook his head. "I think you mean 'What the bloody hell?'"

"Ariel left out the reasons behind our actions," said Nandita, "but the basics are all there. Isolde's DNA is coded with the blueprints for a Partial-killing plague, and when that DNA mixed with Hobb's to conceive Khan, it looks like it may have . . . gotten loose."

"Gotten loose?" asked Hobb. "My son is dying of a plague you built, and all you say is that it 'got loose'?"

"I might be able to cure him," said Nandita. "His human half seems to be keeping him alive, and if I can get to the lab on Plum Island, they have genetics equipment that could remove the disease altogether."

Isolde was holding Khan tightly now, rocking him gently, her eyes filled with tears.

Hobb's face was still aghast. "You're a Partial?"

"You need to get past that part," said Ariel. "None of us knew until a few weeks ago."

"Let's take a step back to think about this," said Kessler. "We were headed to Plum Island—and we should still go there eventually—but if he's a bioweapon . . ."

"No," said Isolde.

"If he killed those two soldiers outside Plainview that fast," Kessler continued, "think what he could do if we got him into the middle of the Partial army."

"Not a chance," Isolde hissed. "He's a baby, not a bomb!"

"The Partials have ruined everything we ever loved," said Kessler. "We could end it all right now—the war, the occupation, even the hunt to find us—"

Ariel scoffed. "You want to end their hunt by just turning ourselves over?"

"We'd be in custody for a couple of days at the most," said Kessler, "then everyone hunting us would be dead, and everyone they worked with, and we could race to Plum Island without having to stop and hide every few hours. We might be able to cure him sooner."

"You are not using my son as a weapon!" said Isolde.

"It doesn't matter anyway," said Haru. "That's why we've been following your trail all over the island—we have to get off now. There's no time to attack the Partials and definitely no time to visit some lab."

"If we don't get there, he'll die," said Nandita.

"If we don't head south as fast as we possibly can, he'll die anyway," said Haru. "You heard about the rocket attack in Plainview?"

Ariel nodded. "The soldiers thought we did it."

"Wrong place at the wrong time," said Haru. "That was the first strike of a military campaign designed to distract the Partial army and lead them north, away from East Meadow and everything south of it. We're evacuating every human we can: out of East Meadow, off the island, and then down the coast as far as we can get."

"We can't run away from the Partials," said Xochi. "We need their pheromones to cure RM."

"I'm sure some of them will follow us," said Haru. "There's not going to be anywhere else to go."

"What are you talking about?" demanded Ariel. "What's going to happen?"

"Former senator Marisol Delarosa is carrying a nuclear device to White Plains," said Haru. "The radius of the fallout will include a lot of Long Island—we don't know how much, or where, so it's safer to just be gone. Traveling north and east toward your lab is just following the wind, and taking you farther into trouble."

"How on earth did she get a nuke?" asked Kessler.

"Does it really matter how?" asked Xochi. She looked at Haru. "How long do we have?"

"We don't know that, either," said Haru. "She's probably traveling slowly to stay hidden. I don't know how big a nuclear warhead is, but I can't imagine it's easy to haul around. That said, your group is traveling even slower because of the children. If you want to get to a safe area, you have to start now."

"We can't just leave," said Isolde. "If we're caught in the fallout, Khan might die, but if we don't get to that lab, he *will* die.

I'll take my chances in the fallout."

"I . . ." Madison's voice trailed off, soft and guilty. "I can't take Arwen into danger."

The room was silent. Ariel looked from one mother to the other, feeling trapped in a vise.

"You know I'd follow you to the ends of the earth if I could," said Madison. She looked up at Isolde, her eyes wet with tears. "I'd do anything to help your baby, but I can't just think about myself anymore. I have to save Arwen, and if that means . . ." She closed her eyes. "I think we need to split up."

"We can't do that," said Haru.

Madison fumed. "I won't drag Arwen into danger—"

"I'm not saying that we should," said Haru. "I'm saying we need to get out of danger, all of us, together." Isolde started to protest, but Haru shouted her down. "I know you want to help your son, but your plan to do that is a long shot anyway. *If* you can make it through the Partial army, and *if* you can find this lab, and *if* Nandita can find a way to fix him—that's too many ifs. It's completely unfeasible. Come south with us, get clear of the blast, and we'll find another way to help him—"

"If we wait that long, he'll die!" shouted Ariel.

"Not too loud," said Xochi. "We're trying to stay hidden."

"We'll never find another lab like the one on Plum Island," said Isolde. "It's self-sustaining, it's self-powered, and it was designed to work with diseases. If we're going to save his life, we do it there."

"We should split up," said Senator Hobb. His face was solemn, and Ariel saw in him a spark of the old Hobb, the charismatic leader who led the island through the worst days of its civil war.

He looked at Haru. "You take your wife and child, and anyone who wants to go south with you. Meet up with the other refugees and get off the island. I'll take Isolde and Nandita to their lab, and we'll catch up with you as soon as we can."

"You'll die," said Haru.

"Then I'll die protecting my son," said Hobb. "It will be more than worth it."

"I'm staying with Isolde," said Ariel.

Xochi nodded. "Me too."

"That means I'm staying as well," said Kessler, and looked at Xochi. "I'm a mother too, you know."

"That's not the same," said Xochi, but Kessler shook her head.

"Just because I don't like you very much doesn't mean I don't love you," said Kessler. "I raised you for ten years; you're my daughter whether you like it or not."

"I'm so sorry, Isolde," said Madison, wiping tears from her eyes. "I wish I could go with you."

"Protect Arwen," said Isolde. "You're doing exactly what I'd do in the same situation. It's okay."

"I love you, Isolde," said Madison, and wrapped her adopted sister in a mournful hug.

Isolde hugged her back. "I love you too, Mads."

"I won't make anyone else come with us," said Hobb, addressing the four Defense Grid soldiers in their group. "These girls have handled themselves just fine this far; you can do more good following Haru back south, rounding up as many humans as you can."

"Then we leave first thing in the morning," said Haru. "Rest while you can, because we have a lot of ground to cover."

CHAPTER TWENTY

Kira's map showed a prison. It was near the shores of Candlewood Lake, on a long southern finger of water called Danbury Bay. That, she determined, would be the most likely place for a group of rebel Partials to set up their headquarters: The same defenses that kept the prisoners in could be used to keep the enemy out, and the Ivies would be well set up to fight off Morgan's forces. She left the trail she'd thought of as safe, winding through the residential streets instead of the forested strip between them, hoping to avoid any more of the terrifying warning markers—and the people who'd set them. She still didn't know what to think of the Ivies, and when she finally met them she wanted it to be on her terms.

Even though she tried to avoid the forests, they were still so prevalent that she ended up tramping through a number of thickly wooded hills and gullies. Crossing a stream near Padanaram Road, she found another bright IV carved into a tree and gave it a wide berth. The land rose steadily from here, a gentle but continual slope, and a quarter mile later she passed a fallow farm, the fields completely overrun with ten-year-old trees. Across the field lay the prison, and she crept through the underbrush slowly, cautiously, practically crawling, and stopping every few seconds to listen for any sounds, either ahead of or behind her. She heard nothing, and when she dared to use the link, she felt nothing there either. The crossing seemed to take hours, and the sun was well past its peak when she drew near to the prison. *The light's behind me now,* she thought, lying low in the weeds as she planned her approach. *If I stand up I'll be silhouetted for everyone to see, but if I stay low they'll have the sun in their eyes, and I'll be hidden in shadows.* She crept forward silently, holding her breath.

The prison was as empty and decrepit as every other building she'd passed.

She watched it for another hour, just to be sure, forcing herself to be patient and avoid giving herself away. Only when the sun sank low behind the horizon did she dare move out from her hiding place at the edge of the trees, slipping across the buckling parking lot to the ragged prison fence. It was torn and warped, and the inside was lined with skeletons wrapped in faded orange jumpsuits—a thirteen-year-old prison break stopped in its tracks as the last dying prisoners tried to claw their way out before the plague claimed their lives. She wondered how many had escaped, only to collapse and die in the field behind her. The bodies behind the fence had been picked by crows, their clothing ripped and torn; where the fence had gaps, wild dogs had gotten in, and the bodies had been worried and dragged across the field. No living person, human or Partial, had set foot in the compound since the Break. Kira walked the full perimeter, just to be sure, but the story was the same on all sides. There was nowhere to look but the lake itself, and whatever homes around it the Ivies had chosen for their community.

She slept that night in the prison, not daring to light a fire, and ate her last apple. Her stomach growled, but she didn't dare go looking for more food. The linked message from the bloody tree still haunted her.

DEATH.

BLOOD.

A narrow forest road wound out from the prison toward a dock on the bay, but when Kira crept out in the morning she cut through the trees, still trying to stay off the obvious paths. The bay was wide, perhaps five hundred feet at its narrowest point, and while the near side was nothing but trackless forest, the far shore was rimmed with houses, each with a private dock. The homes she could see were shrouded in foliage but appeared empty. She walked north along the western shore, keeping a few dozen yards back from the water to stay hidden, watching alertly for any sign of life or movement.

After a mile she hit a wide promontory, where the bay ended and the lake began, and at the end of it stood a small pier. She walked toward it cautiously, trying to get a better look across the water, and stopped in shock at the sight of the pier itself. Standing tall on the edge of the cracking wood was a thin log, perhaps an old signpost, but the sign was gone, and in its place was a hand—human or Partial—pinned to the post with a thick, feathered arrow.

Kira felt her eyes go wide, and covered her mouth with her fingers to stifle a cry. She crept forward a few steps, trying to get a better look at the hand without giving herself away. The hand was severed at the wrist, the palm pressed tightly to the log, the arrow plunging straight through the back of the hand. The wood below the wrist was dark and discolored, and Kira thought she could see a blade mark in the wood itself—someone had pinned the hand to the wood while it was still attached to a body, then chopped it off and let it bleed out. The skin was gray, but not decomposed. This had happened within the last few days.

She took another step forward, looking for the body, but stopped herself and retreated farther into the forest, crouching down in the lee of a giant boulder and shaking her head compulsively. "This isn't right," she whispered. "It isn't right." She drew her handgun, just for the comfort of holding it, and peered out through the trees. A soft breeze stirred the fletching on the end of the arrow. "It's just a warning," she told herself. "A warning against Morgan's forces, which are the only enemy they have in this part of the country. They might still be friendly to me— they might be friendly to the humans—"

She rolled her eyes. "Who am I kidding? I'm not this stupid." She stood up. "There are other Partial factions I can talk to; I'm going to go find one that doesn't dismember their enemies and use their body parts as decorations."

Kira turned to leave, but from her new position she could see a foot down on the dock; a foot that seemed to still be attached to a body. She stopped. If she could get a glimpse of what the corpse was wearing, that might give her a clue as to who had killed him, and which side he was on. She looked again at the arrow and the graying hand. *Morgan's people don't use arrows. But it might not be the Ivies either.* She groaned. *It doesn't matter who the dead body is—I need to get out of here, now—*

And then the foot moved.

Kira swore under her breath, gritting her teeth and staring at the grisly dock. If someone was alive, she had to try to help him . . . but the dock was beyond the tree line. Everyone on the lake would be able to see her. She still didn't know which part of the lake the Ivies lived on, and which other groups might be here fighting them. She tried to turn and go, but she couldn't do it. If this victim was alive, he needed her help. She checked her handgun, making sure she had a full magazine and a bullet in the chamber, and crept forward.

The lake glistened in the morning light, the sun to the east—putting her in the opposite position than she'd been in last night, fully exposed and blinded by the bright flashes on the water. She took another step forward, her eyes darting wildly. Had something moved in the trees? On the water? She held her gun with trembling hands, trying to reassure herself: *This isn't an ambush. They cut off the man's hand and then left. It's the only explanation that makes sense.*

Right?

She reached the trail that passed in front of the dock; probably an old hiking trail kept clear by deer or foxes. She looked left and right, crouched on the edge of the narrow clearing, but the forest was thick, and the trail curved away in both directions, limiting her view. She looked back at the body on the dock, half-hidden by a stand of trees but coming slowly into view as she moved forward. The leg moved again, feebly, but she could swear it looked deliberate—not the random twitching of a dying nervous system, but a purposeful movement. The man was alive, and maybe even partly awake.

She stopped at the edge of the trees, standing silently behind a trunk. One more step and she'd be in the open, visible across the full width of the lake. "If I ever see Dr. Morgan again, I'm going to punch her in the mouth," she said softly. "'Opposed to medical experimentation'? That's really all you could say about these people? Not maybe 'psychopathic savages murdering people on a haunted lake'? That's not worth writing down?"

The leg moved again. She saw another movement in the corner of her eye and spun around, her training and adrenaline taking over, her pistol sight locking in on the motion. It was just a branch, swaying in the wind.

She stepped out onto the dock. She could see the whole man now, sprawled out, clutching his arm stump with his one good hand. He wore the standard gray uniform of the Partial army, just like all of Morgan's soldiers. Crusted blood mixed with bright red smears of flesh. She stepped around the arrow, linking to the struggling man as she came closer: PAIN BLOOD HELP ME HELP. The wide lake stretched out before her, disturbingly idyllic next to the gruesome scene. She slid her handgun back into her pack and knelt down by the man, probing his neck for a pulse. He jerked when she touched him, but he was too weak to move away.

"Don't . . . ," he croaked.

"I'm here to help you," she said, ripping a strip from his tattered clothes. She wrapped it tightly around his wrist as she spoke. "Do you know who did this to you?"

BETRAYAL, said the link. The man tried to speak, but his voice was cracked and raw. BLOOD.

"You have to tell me," she said. "Was it the Ivies? Where are they? What are they doing?"

"It was the . . . Blood Man."

"The Blood Man?" Kira tied off the bandage and started

probing the rest of his body for wounds. There was too much blood to have come just from the wrist . . . and then she found it, a gaping hole in his gut where blood mixed with viscera. She reeled back at the stench. "This stab wound perforated your intestine," she said, swallowing her disgust. "You need antibiotics."

"The Blood Man," he croaked. "They serve the Blood Man."

"The Ivies?" asked Kira. She looked around wildly for something to stanch the bleeding in his abdomen, but she knew he wouldn't make it. They were too far from anyone who could help, even if she could find a way to move him. She grunted in frustration and simply ripped her own shirt, several inches off the bottom hem, and shoved the wad into his wound.

"You have to run," he said, his raw voice painful just to listen to. "They'll want yours too."

"My hand?"

"Your blood."

She saw a flash of movement from the lake—not on the water, but under it, the dark black shadow of a massive fish.

"What's going on here?"

DEATH

The water erupted in a geyser, a pale white figure bursting up by the edge of the dock and grabbing Kira's arm. She screamed, backing away, fumbling for her gun, but the pale figure yanked her forward and she lost her balance, tumbling toward the water. The last thing she saw was his neck flaring open, wide fishlike gills flapping delicately in the open air, and then her face hit the water and the world went black.

CHAPTER TWENTY-ONE

Samm dreamed about Kira.

They were walking together through the ruins of old Illinois—not the flooded necropolis of Chicago, and not the toxic badlands west of the Mississippi River, but the rolling fields and wide, flat nothingness between them. They walked, hand in hand. Birds circled lazily in the sky above them, and herds of wild mustangs roamed from field to field, trampling the fences that separated the vast checkerboard of empty farms, running free in a world that didn't remember the war, the Break, or anything but sun and wind and rain and stars. They drank from cool streams and lay on their backs staring up at the moon, finding shapes and faces in the craters. The world was still and ancient and new, and they were together.

The dreams never lasted. Samm woke up, bleary-eyed, and stared numbly at the faded walls of the old business office he used as an apartment.

"Today I'm going to leave it all and go find Kira," he

whispered. He said it every morning. He pulled on his shirt and shoes and trudged down the stairs and across the compound to the hospital. His body built up a measurable amount of Particle 223 every six days, and he was due for another extraction. Calix had started volunteering in the hospital, still too unsteady on her feet to go back out as a hunter, and she greeted him in the lab with a smile. Samm smiled back wearily, easing himself down onto the homespun blanket covering the cracked plastic surface of the examination bed.

"Good morning," said Calix. She prepped a syringe of local anesthetic; the procedure involved a very long needle spending a very long time very deep in Samm's nasal cavity, and while he didn't like the drugs, he liked the needle even less. Samm lay on his back while Calix applied the first shot—a tiny sting, and a slow, spreading numbness. They waited for the shot to take effect, and Calix chatted idly. "Gorman was walking pretty well last night."

That was good news; the soldier's health seemed to have plateaued over the last few days. "How far?"

"Just to the bathroom and back," said Calix. "He didn't even call us for the first leg, just the return trip."

"He doesn't like being dependent," said Samm.

"Nobody does." Calix picked up the syringe again. "Time for number two." Samm held still, and she slid the needle deep into his nostril. Another sting, much farther back, and Calix sat down with a mischievous smile. "Want to see the needle?"

"No," said Samm, "but show it to me anyway."

Calix laughed and held it up—the needle on the end of the syringe was about four inches long. "You always ask to see it."

"That's because I swear you're shoving it halfway into my brain," said Samm.

"I barely put it in that far," said Calix, placing her gloved finger about halfway along the slim metal line. "Wait for the third shot when we hit the back wall, that's the doozy."

Samm closed his eyes. "Always my favorite."

"Any good dreams last night?"

"Dreamed about Illinois."

"Odd choice," said Calix. "What's in Illinois?"

Samm thought about Kira, and the horses and the moon. "Nothing."

Calix chattered a bit about the hospital, and the other Partials, and her soccer team's standing in the current tournament—she couldn't play since she had gotten shot, but she cheered harder on the sidelines than any other fan. Samm smiled and nodded, genuinely happy for her, but he was too . . . *busy? Too busy to care? That's not the right word,* he thought. *Weary? Lonely?*

Lost, he decided. *I feel lost.*

Calix gave him the third shot of anesthetic, and after a few minutes called in a more experienced nurse to help with the long process of finding the right gland and extracting the pheromonal cure for RM. Samm couldn't talk during the extraction and spent the next forty minutes cataloguing his day, planning out the jobs he had to do and the order in which he could do them most efficiently. Phan called him a walking day planner, but it never struck Samm as an odd behavior: He had a lot to do, and a limited amount of time to do it. What was wrong with a little planning? His first order of business would be the maternity ward, saying hello to the new mothers and hearing a report on the children. He had no specific responsibility there, but he liked to do it anyway. He liked to see what these sessions in the lab had wrought.

When the nurses finished the extraction, the older one took the vial to be processed, and Calix helped Samm sit up. The anesthetic always made him a little woozy, and he munched on a piece of flatbread while he waited for his head to realign. Calix watched him, more pensive than usual, and after a moment asked a question.

"Do you like it here, Samm?"

"It's wonderful," said Samm automatically. "You have food and water, you have electricity, and people aren't killing each other. It's great."

"And yet you're not happy."

Samm chewed slowly, thinking. "I'm helping people," he said at last. "The pheromone we just extracted saves lives, and we're helping the other Partials get back on their feet. I'm happy to be a part of that."

"You're proud of it," said Calix, "but you're not *happy*."

"The total amount of happiness in the Preserve is greater with me in it than out," said Samm.

"That's the saddest definition of happiness I've ever heard."

"What other choice do I have?" asked Samm. "It's not like I can leave."

"It's exactly like you can leave," said Calix, "and nobody could stop you. We might try, but let's be realistic. Especially if Heron's helping you—that chick makes the monster under my bed have nightmares."

Samm smiled. "She feels bad about shooting you."

"She'd do it again in a heartbeat."

"She would," said Samm, nodding. "I was just trying to make you feel better."

Calix laughed and swatted his arm. "Now let me be clear about this: We are incredibly grateful that you've stayed. You're giving us a future. But you don't have to . . ." She trailed off, and Samm looked up, finishing her sentence for her.

"I don't have to stay here?" he asked. "Of course I do. I gave my word, and that's a stronger bond than any chains you could use to lock me down, or any walls you could put up to keep me in."

Calix bit her lip, thinking, and finally nodded. "I realize that, and I thank you. We all do. But . . . I asked if you were happy here, and you talked about leaving. You told me how wonderful it is here, and then talked about leaving. How do you think it makes us feel that your only conception of happiness involves leaving? You could be happy here, Samm, I know you could. We would do anything we can to make you happy here."

She stopped talking abruptly, wiping her cheek with her hand so quickly that Samm couldn't tell if there'd really been a tear on it or not. He instantly felt bad, thinking about how insulting his attitude must be to the humans of the Preserve. They needed him for the pheromones, but they treated him like a person. They'd accepted him as one of their own, just like Samm had shown Gorman. And yet for all their efforts to include him, Samm wasn't working to include himself. He didn't know if he could.

Calix looked at the floor, avoiding his eyes, and he realized something else. Calix had wanted him once, back when he'd first arrived. He'd told her he was in love with Kira, but now Kira was gone. What was to stop Samm and Calix from being together now? Had she been waiting this entire time, too polite to exploit Kira's absence, but counting the days until Samm came to the same realization? He'd promised to stay here forever. What was he waiting for? What was he holding out for? If this was really his home—not just the place where he lived, but a real home, with a new family—why was he still acting like a visitor?

Calix was kind, she was smart, she was funny, and even with a bullet wound in her leg she'd been more than capable of contributing to the Preserve. They'd been spending more and more time together over the last few weeks, until Samm had come to think of her as one of his best friends. And he had to admit she was beautiful. Calix wasn't Kira, but Kira wasn't Calix, either.

And Kira wasn't here.

Calix looked up, as if sensing his gaze. He looked at her, studying her face, her eyes, remembering their kiss. Was it really so wrong? He was staying here anyway—was it really so bad if he stayed here with her?

"Samm." Her voice was hesitant, probing.

"Calix," he said.

"I'm sorry—"

"Don't be," he said quickly. "You've made me realize something."

She bit her lip again. "What?"

He took another long look at her, then shook his head. "I've promised to stay," said Samm. "The other Partials haven't." He sighed and stood up. "I can't expect them to make the same choice, or to stay here forever. I need to ask them what they want."

Calix nodded. "And then?"

"Then we give it to them."

"And then?" asked Calix. She stood carefully, favoring her bad leg. "What's the next big crisis you can put your life on hold for?"

Samm put his hand on her shoulder. "You're the best friend I have."

"I bet you say that to all the girls."

"I've never said it to anyone."

Samm walked through the halls to the recovery wing, which the nine healing Partials called home. The air linked a mixture of hope and restlessness; it was a typical morning. Gorman was sitting up in his bed, holding the respirator cannula in his hand.

"That works better if you actually put the air tubes in your nose," said Samm.

"And beds work best when you lie down in them," said Gorman. "It's not the equipment I want to work right, it's my body."

"Keep practicing, then," said Samm. "I heard you went walking last night."

"They tell you about the dump, too? If they're going to tell the whole Preserve what I do at night, they'd better not leave out the real excitement."

"You can give me the details later," said Samm, looking around the room. Only three Partials were there, Gorman in his bed and two others sitting in chairs by the open windows, soaking up the sunlight. "Where's everybody else?"

"Dwain's still in bed," said Gorman. "I think he's got the hots for the nurse, so he's milking his convalescence for a lot more than it's worth."

"Calix or Tiffany?"

"Tiffany."

"Wrong tree," said Samm. He paused. "Not that I want him chasing after Calix, either."

Gorman eyed him. "Are you and she . . . ?"

"No," said Samm. "How about the others?"

Gorman ignored the deflection. "What about Heron?"

"How many girls do you think I'm hooking up with?"

"Not as many as you could, if I'm interpreting the signs right." He took a breath of air from the cannula. "Calix follows you around like a puppy, and Heron . . . Well, I guess it sounds wrong to say she follows you around like a snake, but you get my meaning."

"Heron is an old friend," said Samm. "We fought together in the Isolation War."

"And now?"

"Now we . . ." Samm didn't know how to describe their relationship. Over the last week or so he'd barely seen Heron at all, but he knew she was nearby. Just like before, she'd been making it obvious that she was watching him. Apparently Gorman had noticed it too. "Heron's a good friend," he said again. "That doesn't mean I have any idea what she wants. She's an espionage model; she's hardwired for secrecy and misdirection."

"Trained in seduction, though," said Gorman, pointing at him with the cannula. "That's got to count for something."

"If a woman trained in seduction were into me, I think I'd know it by now," said Samm. He turned the conversation back to Gorman and his squad mates, gesturing at the mostly empty room. "Where are the others?"

"Outside walking," said Gorman. "Ritter's as healthy as you are; he has no business being in a hospital anymore. Aaron and Bradley, too."

"That's what I wanted to talk about," said Samm, pulling a chair next to the soldier's bed. "You're getting better now, minor setbacks notwithstanding." He gestured at the cannula, and Gorman rolled his eyes. "It's time to move past recovery and into real life. You can't stay in the hospital forever."

"Knock on wood," said Gorman. He pursed his lips, thinking for a moment. "What about the Preserve?"

"You're certainly welcome to stay," said Samm, "but no one's keeping you here."

"They could get a lot more of that pheromone with all nine of us pitching in to help you. They could stock up before we expire, assuming we ever do, and last for another few years."

Samm nodded. "They're good people," he said. "I don't exactly want to leave them without a source of the cure, but they feel the same way I do: If they have to enslave you again to get it, it's not worth getting."

"That sounds an awful lot like a guilt trip."

"That's not my intention," said Samm. "Sooner or later they're going to run out anyway, whether it's my death next year or your death . . . whenever. Don't feel obligated."

"So it's too much of a lost cause for me to bother with," said Gorman, "but you're still giving your life for it."

"I gave my word," said Samm. "You're welcome to stay as long as you want, and you're welcome to contribute the cure pheromone if you want, but those choices are yours to make." Samm rubbed his nose, still numb from the extraction. "As jobs go, though, an hour a week in a lab chair is a pretty lightweight one." He smiled. "And frankly, all you might be able to handle right now."

Gorman held the cannula to his nose, taking a deep breath, then dropped his hands heavily back to his lap. "I do want to give something back," he said. "I was suspicious in the beginning, but they've been good to us. They deserve whatever we can do to help them."

"They'd be grateful," said Samm. He glanced to the two soldiers by the window, and the sunny courtyard beyond. "Have you talked to the others?"

"I think I'm stuck here no matter what," said Gorman. "The healthier ones are itching to get back."

"To White Plains?"

"To wherever," said Gorman. "The world's changed, and they want to see it. And if things are really as bad as you say, they want to help. Partials killing Partials, humans still dying of RM, the war still raging between the species . . . it's hard to sit here in a paradise on the wrong side of the world knowing that the rest of our species is going to hell."

Samm raised an eyebrow. "Tell me about it."

"We could stop it, you realize that?"

"What?" asked Samm. "The war?"

"The plague," said Gorman. "These are good people, like you say, but they're just a fraction of the humans left alive, and the community in East Meadow doesn't have you around to keep them healthy. We have a new baby in this hospital every week or so, sometimes more; the people in East Meadow probably have at least that many, and because they don't have the cure, they all die. All of them. We could stop that."

"I've thought the same thing," said Samm. "What we have . . . if we could get there, and if they'd listen to us, and if they'd ever accept our help . . . we could do a lot of good."

Gorman nodded. "And if they haven't all killed each other."

"You couldn't make the journey," said Samm. "The Badlands are hell on earth, and they're only half the distance."

"So you go in my place," said Gorman. "Take Ritter and Aaron and Bradley and whoever."

Samm knew the air was filled with his conflicting emotional data—a sudden rush of fear and worry and desperate, overwhelming hope. Could he really leave? He'd given his word to stay.

"Take that little hunter," said Gorman. "Phan, or whatever his name is. He could handle your Badlands just fine, even for a human—if there's a storm on the face of this earth that could kill him, I'd like to see it."

Samm rubbed at the acid scars on his arm. "No, you wouldn't."

"I'm serious about this," said Gorman, leaning forward. "I can't leave. The doctor said my lungs might never fully heal, and it's not like I can take one of these oxygen tanks on a trip through unforgiving terrain. Even when I can walk again, even when I can run, I'll be sleeping in this building with this cheap plastic noose around my neck for the rest of my life." He shook the cannula for emphasis. "There's nothing I'd like more in the world than to find that bastard Vale and kick him in the nads, over and over and over, but these people aren't him, and they've given everything to help me. I want to help them." He paused. "Let me stay here, in your place, donating Particle two-twenty-whatever-the-hell-it-is, and you go back home. Go to East Meadow and save the humans. Go to White Plains and slap some people around. And sure, if you see Dr. Vale, feel free to castrate him with a steel-toed boot, but first things first."

"You'd really do this?" asked Samm.

"What else am I going to do?"

Someone banged loudly on the door, and Samm barely had time to look up before Calix threw it open, barging in breathlessly. "You gotta see this."

Samm leaped to his feet. "What's wrong?"

"There's nothing wrong," said Calix, grabbing his hand and heaving him toward the door. "It's Monica's baby, the one that was born last night."

"You gave her the shot?" asked Samm.

"She doesn't need it," said Calix. "She's not sick."

Samm stopped in his tracks, staring at her, glancing back at Gorman. "She's not sick?"

"She never got feverish," said Calix. "They've been watching her all night, waiting for your extraction this morning, but she never got sick."

Samm broke into a run, hurtling down the hall so fast he left Calix hobbling anxiously in his wake. He reached the maternity ward in less than a minute and pushed his way through the babbling crowd of nurses and onlookers surrounding the nurse's station. Heron was already there, standing apart in a corner.

"Where is she?" asked Samm.

"Right in there," said Laura, pointing to a mother staring in awe at her sleeping baby in a private room off the hallway. "Strong as an ox."

Samm stared as well, not comprehending what was happening. Why hadn't the baby gotten sick? Was she born immune?

Surely RM was still in the air—all these people were carriers. So why wasn't she sick?

A doctor rushed up to them, holding a small glass data screen in Laura's face. "The blood test just finished: She already has the pheromone in her system."

"Who gave it to her?" asked Laura.

"Nobody," said the doctor.

Samm looked at the data screen, reading the results as best he could. "One of the other Partials, maybe?"

"She's been under constant observation," said the doctor. "We don't leave their side for a second in the days after birth, and we record everything that happens. Nobody's given her anything—just general antibiotics and some milk from her mother."

"It's airborne," said Heron.

Calix finally arrived, gritting her teeth as she hopped toward them. "What's airborne?"

Samm looked at Heron, slowly realizing what she meant. "Nine Partials have been living in the hospital for a month," he said. "Ten, since I'm here more often than not. We've been injecting the pheromone directly to the bloodstream because that's the way Vale did it, but it's a pheromone—it's designed to be transmitted through the air. Now that you're living with us twenty-four hours a day, you're breathing it in, and it's just . . . everywhere."

Calix looked at the data screen, then the baby, then back at Samm. "How many of us are going?"

"Going where?"

"To East Meadow," said Calix. "This is the answer; we have to tell them."

"We need Samm if we're going to keep this whole pheromone incubator working," said Laura.

"Gorman will stay," said Calix, "and others. Most of them still can't make the journey."

"None of you can," said Heron. "The Badlands will kill you."

"It's worth the risk," said Calix.

Samm shook his head. "It's too dangerous—"

"You'll get to see Kira again," said Calix.

Samm fell silent.

Calix's eyes were hard. "If this system can work, if Partials and humans can live together, side by side, we can save the other humans, and who knows—maybe the Partials too. Gorman and his team are still alive, even if we don't know why." She looked down, just for a moment. "And we can save Kira, too. This is what she came here for."

Samm breathed deep, trying to think of something to say. He looked at Laura. "She's right."

"I know she is," said Laura. "If there really are more humans out there, we have to do what we can for them."

"I don't know if I'll be able to come back," said Samm.

"*We*," said Calix fiercely. "I'm going with you."

"Not with that leg," said Samm.

"You'll have to shoot me again to stop me."

Heron fingered the butt of her semiautomatic. "Same leg, or the other one this time?"

"I'm the best wilderness explorer in the Preserve," said Calix hotly, "even with a bad leg. Frankly, I don't think you can make it without me."

Samm thought about the Badlands: the swirling pools of

poison water, the endless miles of bone-white trees. He and Heron were more resilient than any human, but neither of them were scouts; someone with targeted survival training would be useful. He rubbed his acid scars and frowned. "Shooting you might be kinder." Calix started to protest, but Samm stopped her with a gesture. "We leave tomorrow morning. If you're prepared to die for this, be ready to go at dawn."

PART 2

CHAPTER TWENTY-TWO

"**G**eneral."

Shon looked up from his maps, trying to plan the next wave of their hunt for the human terrorists. The resistance had ramped up their attacks over the last few weeks, striking harder and in more places than ever before, only to fade away like ghosts into the forests and ruins. They were getting bolder, too: His camp had spent the night and morning pinned down by sniper fire. He looked at the messenger with weary eyes. "What news?"

"We found the sniper's nest, but no one was there—just a rifle rigged up to an alarm clock."

Shon raised his eyebrow. "You're kidding."

The messenger's link was completely sincere, blended with disbelief. "I saw it myself, sir. The trigger had been removed and connected to the gears of an alarm clock—one of the old wind-up ones, sir, completely handmade. We think it was set to fire into the camp at regular intervals, and the tripod was loosened just enough that the recoil adjusted the aim with each shot, so it wasn't hitting the same spot over and over. The scouts think no one's been up there since the first shot last night."

Shon clenched his fist, linking his rage so fiercely that the messenger staggered back.

"That explains why no one was actually hit, sir," said the messenger. "We thought it was just because humans are bad shots, but . . . now we know, I guess. It wasn't even aiming, just firing every half hour or so. Maybe they just set it up and hoped they got lucky."

"All they were hoping to do was slow us down," said Shon, "which they've done brilliantly. Just when I thought we'd figured out these White Rhinos' tactics, they switch them up completely."

"That's the other thing, sir," said the messenger. "We don't think this was the Rhinos—or if it was, it was some kind of splinter group. There was a note." He stepped forward and handed it to the general.

Shon frowned, taking the wrinkled piece of paper. "They've never left a note before."

"Exactly, sir. Everything about this strike is different from what we've seen before."

Shon read the note: "'Sorry we couldn't wait around. We have some more surprises to set up. Love and kisses, Owen Tovar.' What on earth?"

"We don't know who Owen Tovar is yet," said the messenger, "but we're working on it."

"He was one of the senators," said Shon. "We thought they'd all gone into hiding. But why . . ." He stared at the note, turning it over in the halfhearted hope of finding another clue on the back. There was nothing. "Why identify himself? Is it just a taunt, or is there a deeper message to it?"

"Maybe he's trying to rile us up?" asked the messenger. "After all those sniper shots into the camp, the soldiers are ready to burn the forest down to find them."

Shon sighed and rubbed his eyes, feeling the strain of the long day more keenly than ever. "What's your name, soldier?"

The messenger straightened to attention. "Thom, sir."

"Thom, I want you to follow the scouts trying to track whoever set up that rifle. Report to me immediately when you find who's responsible. You have a radio?"

"I can get one from supply, sir. Our battery packs are dwindling, though."

Shon nodded. "We have prisoners hand-cranking the generators twenty-four hours a day, charging new ones." *And with any luck, we'll get new orders from Morgan any day now, calling us home. Until then . . .*

"May I ask a question, sir?"

Shone considered him a moment, then nodded. "Yes."

"Why not flush them out with more hostages, sir? There are more guerrillas in these woods almost every day, but we still have East Meadow locked down. If we threaten to kill a few of them, it might get these rebels to stop—"

"We're not murderers, soldier." Shon's words were accompanied by a harsh sting across the link, and he noted with satisfaction that Thom flinched when he sensed it. "The rebels are enemy combatants, and fighting enemy combatants is literally in your DNA. We were built to win wars while protecting innocent lives, and if you can't do the one thing you were designed to do, maybe you're not fit for this army." It was a ferocious counterattack, the cruelest insult a Partial could give to another, but Shon had seen this same attitude growing in the ranks and he was determined to stamp it out. Thom recoiled, his link data a mixture of shock and shame, but barely a moment later his data was overpowered with rage, and he shot back a comment of his own.

"Dr. Morgan had us killing civilians, sir, and she had more right to her authority than some jumped-up infantryman—"

"Soldier!" He sent his anger thundering across the link, so powerful that his guards came in from the room beyond, hands on their guns and ready for trouble. "Have this man court-martialed," said Shon, "and held in custody for the duration of the occupation."

The guards linked their shock at the order but obeyed without question, taking Thom's weapons and leading him away. *Off to one of the cages,* Shon thought. Out here in the wilderness, the modified trucks were the only form of prison they had. *We've never used them to lock up one of our own before. The way things are going, that might become a lot more common.*

Shon looked at the note again. Why the name? Why the flippant attitude? And what, in the end, was their plan? The day full of sniper shots had kept the entire camp on eggshells: hiding from the shots, searching for the shooter, returning fire when they could—fruitlessly, he realized now. But what purpose did that serve? The recent string of guerrilla attacks had been almost deliberately random, apparently not even decoys designed to lead them in a certain direction. *But of course not,* Shon realized. *If we could tell that they were trying to lead us in one direction, we'd go directly in the other, and they know that. They're not trying to lead us anywhere, just keep us busy. So it is a decoy tactic, but for what?*

Keep us busy long enough, he thought with a sigh, *and sooner or later the whole army's going to fall apart. We have insurgency in the ranks, the bioweapon's still destroying our patrols, and we haven't heard from Morgan in weeks. I don't even know if my messages to her are getting through. All we have are the same old orders, the last orders she ever gave us: contain the population, and hold the island. No explanation of what we're holding it for, just . . . hold it. It doesn't make sense.*

According to his scouts, the mysterious giant creature had finally left the island—he'd moved north, talking to everyone he could, and when he'd reached the North Shore he'd just . . . walked into the sound, still heading north. *That's one less thing to worry about,* he thought. *And maybe if Morgan sees it for herself, she'll realize how disordered things have become over here. Maybe she'll finally take command again, tell me* something *about what I'm supposed to be doing here. Anything.*

But I'm not Thom, he thought. *I don't question my orders. She told us to hold this island, so we're going to hold it.*

Or die trying.

CHAPTER TWENTY-THREE

Kira woke to the sound of dripping water. She tried to move, only to feel handcuffs on her hands and feet. The small chains rattled as she scraped her limbs across the floor, struggling to sit upright. Her face and body were wet, pressed onto something soft and damp, like a layer of slimy growth. The scent of mold filled her nose. She opened her eyes, but it was too dark to see.

She coughed, hacking up water, and tried to right herself. Her hands were trapped behind her back, and when she rolled faceup to get a real breath, her fingers squished deep into the soft something covering the floor. She coughed again, staring around wide-eyed yet blind. Dark shapes emerged as her eyes began to adjust: a wall, a window, a dim blue star. She looked away from it, trying to penetrate the inky black corners of her prison.

Something moved, slow and heavy.

"Who's there?" Kira's voice was barely a whisper, the words rasping from her throat with another cough and a spurt of filthy water. She retched and backed away, only to realize that she didn't know where the sound was coming from; she might be backing blindly toward it. "Who's there?"

Another movement, closer now. A dark black shadow moving in the darkness.

Kira tucked her legs up close to her chest and scooted her bound hands down past her hips and around to the front of her body. Her feet were cuffed too tightly to properly stand, so she crawled on her hands and knees to the wall with the window. Something was coming after her, moving much more quickly than she could. She stood up and found the window glassless and open. She braced herself against the sill, ready to vault out, but a pair of thick hands grabbed her from behind, one on her stomach and one on her mouth, clamping down over her scream, dragging her back to the floor. She kicked and thrashed, and felt hot breath on her ear.

"Stay down and be quiet. They'll hear you."

Kira kept kicking, fighting as hard as she could to get away. The man holding her was strong, and his arms were like iron bands.

"I'm on your side," the man hissed. "Just promise me you're not going to scream."

Kira couldn't escape, so she tried to hold still despite her pounding heart and the adrenaline surging through her like fire. She clenched her hands into tight fists, forcing herself to concentrate. Her mouth was covered, but she took a deep breath through her nose.

FEAR

The room was saturated with it. The man was a Partial, and

he was just as scared as she was. She tried to slow her breathing, and finally nodded her assent.

The man let her go. She rolled away instantly, but only a few feet, and stayed out of view from the window. With her eyes better adjusted to the dark she could see him now, a standard Partial infantry model. His uniform hung in tatters, and his face, while difficult to see clearly, was covered in grime.

"You're human," he said.

She didn't bother to correct him. "You're not in handcuffs."

"They don't care about the cuffs," he said dismissively, holding up a small metal key. "They just use them to transport us."

"They don't care if we escape?"

"Where you gonna go?" he asked. He scooted toward her, and after a moment she held out her wrists for him to unlock. "You'll understand when you look outside. But be careful—if they see you awake, they'll come back."

He unlocked her, and she rubbed her wrists while he opened the cuffs on her ankles. "They want us unconscious?" she asked.

"They don't care either way," he said again. "But you're new—if you're awake, they'll come for you. We may as well put that off as long as we can, right?"

He unlocked her ankles, and she drew her legs in close, suddenly chilly in the damp air, her clothes wet and her body soaked to the bone. She took a moment to feel for her equipment—all gone—and looked around to see that she was in a house, just like any other wealthy pre-Break home; the damp, squishy surface that had disgusted her so much was just a carpet, completely saturated with water, and indeed the entire building seemed suffused with extra moisture—the corners were shaggy with moss, the walls were ringed with mold stains, and even the ceiling seemed to sag and drip.

"Where are we?" she asked.

"Come take a look." He crawled across the floor to a set of squishy stairs and led her up to a second and then a third floor. It was drier up here, though it still showed signs of water damage. The room at the top of the stairs had windows on three sides, all covered with blankets, and a hallway on the fourth led to more rooms. There was a low wall around the open stairwell, and Kira glanced over to see a long drop down to the second floor. The wooden furniture had all been broken down, stacked like firewood in the corner, and it seemed like every mattress in the house had been shoved against the walls. Kira guessed it was for insulation; it was colder here than she'd expected.

"I live up here," said the Partial. "So did the others, before they were taken. You can peek out the windows, but be careful— move the cloth too much and they'll see it. With a newbie in here, they're bound to have someone watching."

Kira walked slowly to the nearest window, putting a hand on the stiff blanket and pulling it just slightly to the side, barely wide enough to peer through the gap. There were trees outside, just below the level of the windows, and beyond that the dark black water of the lake. Tiny wavelets reflected the starlight. She couldn't see the ground, and guessed that the lake came almost to the base of the house. The view from the other windows was the same, and when he led her to another room to look out the last side, she realized they were on an island—no roads, no bridge, just water. The front side of the house looked across to another island, maybe two hundred feet away, and the back window showed another at least three times the distance. The water between was dark and ominous, and Kira remembered the pale, gilled man bursting up from the deep. She shivered and sank to the floor.

"That's why they don't tie us up," said the Partial. "No one is dumb enough to cross that water."

"Have people tried?"

"And died." His voice was barely a whisper in the darkness. "We figure this was some rich human's vacation house, a mansion on a tiny little island. There's a dock outside and everything, but of course the boat's gone."

"I suppose we're lucky," said Kira. "This island is the best prison around, whether or not there's a house on it." She shrugged. "At least this way we get a roof."

"I guess so."

She crawled to the side window and peered out again, seeing the faint white glimmer of a dock on the far shore. She couldn't tell if it was the same one she'd been pulled from. She sat back down and looked at the Partial, a man-shaped outline in the darkness. "What's your name?"

"Green."

Kira nodded toward the wall and the dark black lake beyond it. "Let's start with the obvious question: what the fat holy hell?"

Green laughed dryly. "The things that captured you are Partials, but some model we've never seen before."

Kira frowned. She'd run into gilled Partials before, and Heron hadn't known what they were either, assuming they were Morgan's "special operatives." "They're not on Morgan's side?"

Green shook his head. "I've been with Morgan practically

since the Break, and I've never seen anything like them. She's done some interesting gene mods on select Partials, heightened senses and things like that, but never gills."

Kira remembered the short entry about the Ivies in Morgan's files, now more sure than ever that she had no clue what they really were. "They actually live in the lake?"

"They have some kind of modified temperature regulation system in their bodies, so they can stand the cold. I think they prefer it."

Kira frowned, trying to parse the information. "Some kind of amphibious soldier, then? The Isolation War kicked off with two different ship-to-shore assaults; maybe this was a special model, designed specifically for those battles."

Green cocked his head to the side. "You're not nearly as over-whelmed by this as I expected."

"I've been around."

"Apparently," said Green. "I didn't think humans ever left Long Island; you're pretty far from home."

Kira smiled. "This is nothing. What would you say if I told you this isn't even the first time I've seen gilled Partials?"

"I'd ask where you saw them."

"Chicago."

Green whistled softly. "Now I know you're either lying or—" He stopped abruptly. "What did you say your name was?"

"I didn't," said Kira. "And I don't know if I should. Are you still with Morgan?"

"Not since I went AWOL."

"In that case, hi." She extended her hand. "I'm Kira Walker."

"That explains a lot. Last I heard, Morgan had found you."

"Her experiments didn't pan out," said Kira. "I left her labs a week ago."

Green's voice was quiet. "Damn. AWOL or not, I was still hoping she'd find a way to cure expiration."

"Why'd you leave?"

"My whole squad left," said Green. "We figured we'd join one of the other factions still holding out from her authority, and the Ivies seemed like a good choice. You can see how well that turned out."

"But why?" asked Kira. "You'd been with her for so long."

Green didn't answer.

Kira drummed her fingers on the damp carpet. "I found another Partial out there," she said, "on a dock on the lake's edge. I assume he was one of yours."

"Still alive?"

"Only barely. Probably not anymore." She put her hand on his. "I'm sorry."

"That might be Alan," said Green. "He tried to swim for it about five days ago. I saw them pull him under, and then . . . well, he was the last one. I've been alone since."

Kira couldn't bear to tell him the grisly details. "I tried to help him, but it was too late." She sat up suddenly, remembering his final words. "He tried to warn me—he said something about 'the Blood Man.'"

"That's what we call him," said Green, nodding. "The gilled soldiers seem to obey him, though he's not one of them, as far as we can tell."

"That's a pretty dramatic name," said Kira. "I didn't realize Partials were superstitious."

"We're not," said Green. "We call him the Blood Man because he literally takes blood from us. We think he collects it."

"What does he look like?"

"We've never seen him," said Green. "The Ivies, or whatever they are, came and took some of our group, one every few days. Our sergeant, our driver, and one of the infantry."

"One each of the surviving Partial models," said Kira.

"Exactly."

"That sounds like he's collecting DNA," said Kira. "And no one's ever talked to him? The Ivies didn't say anything about him?"

"Just that he needed their blood," said Green. "And then they told us he'd left to find more."

Kira's heart sank. "Don't say he went south."

"Where else?" asked Green. "They told us he had all the Partial blood he needed, and it was time to visit the humans."

"He's going to hunt humans now? Why does he need their DNA?"

"Why does he need anybody's?" asked Green, his calm exterior cracking with fear and frustration. "He's a psychopath with a blood fetish, and an army of super Partials to back him up."

"We have to stop him," said Kira, but her words froze in her throat when she heard a loud, sharp click from somewhere below.

"That's the door," Green whispered. "They're here."

CHAPTER TWENTY-FOUR

Kira looked to Green with wide eyes.

FEAR.

"Come out," a voice called from downstairs. "We only want to talk."

"What do we do?" Kira whispered.

"They'll be armed," said Green. "And probably wearing body armor."

Kira nodded, remembering the fight in Chicago. "They'll link you and know we're up here. Is it worth trying to fight?"

"If they wanted you dead, they would have killed you already."

"Or they'll kill me after they interrogate me," said Kira. "With the Blood Man gone, they have no reason to keep us alive."

"That we know of," said Green. "They haven't killed me yet."

"So you're just waiting until they do?"

"Don't make us look for you," said another voice. "You know that only makes us angry."

"What am I supposed to do?" Green hissed. "Even if we can overpower multiple armed soldiers, what then? For all we know, this whole lake is crawling with them—there could be hundreds more just under the water."

A stair creaked, loud and haunting. *They're coming up to find us*, Kira thought. *We're running out of time and they'll have guns and—*

"Wait," said Kira. "You said they're armed, right?" She thought back to the soldiers in Chicago, who'd been carrying both tranquilizer darts and standard assault rifles. "The Ivies might be fine underwater, but their guns aren't. Normal firearms can't fire when wet."

"We had waterproof rifles in our armory in the Isolation War," said Green.

"Have you seen any since then?"

"Maybe these guys have them all."

"Or maybe those weapons are too rare, and the Ivies are carrying the same thing as everybody else." Kira grabbed his shoulder, whispering urgently in his ear. "They have to store them on land, and they've got to transport them somehow."

Another creaking stair. Green stared at her. "You think they came in a boat? Sometimes they have one when they move prisoners, but—"

"Not only do they have a boat," said Kira, "but any more of them watching from underneath the water won't think twice when they see that boat leave the island. We only have to make it what, two hundred feet, to the other island? There's a causeway from there to the mainland, if I remember the map right. Then we're on solid ground again and we can make a run for it."

"Until they realize what's going on, and the whole lake rises up to get us."

"Do you want to escape or not?"

A gun clicked, a slide racking back. They sound close enough to be on the second floor now, and almost to the final set of stairs. Green's link was boiling over with terror. "What do we do?"

Kira didn't have time to plan; she had to wing this as best she could. She put her face against his ear, whispering softly so the Ivies couldn't hear. "They can't link me. Lead them out the window." She pushed away from him and slipped away on all fours, her toes and fingertips barely touching the floor as she stole around the corner to the hallway. Green hesitated, but seemed to understand her plan; he jumped up suddenly and ran to the window, tearing down the blanket and climbing out onto the slanted roof beyond. He disappeared past the edge of the window frame just as the first Partial came into view up the stairs.

"They've gone out the window," said one.

"Check it."

Kira pressed herself back against the wall, out of sight around the corner, trying to tell how many Ivies there were. She'd heard only two speak, but without looking there was no way to tell for sure. She had to act fast. This part of the hallway contained more broken furniture, neatly stacked like firewood, and the room beyond held the disassembled metal shell of a dryer, which the prisoners had folded out into a flat platform to contain their fires. A table leg in the pile of wood looked like it might make a good weapon, but Kira knew she had no chance in a club-versus-assault-rifle fight. She needed something better, something that used the only advantage she had right now: surprise. There was a large, ornate mirror leaning against the wall, which would be deadly but far too unwieldy to fight with, and an old 3D projector, which would be too lightweight to do any damage. She swore silently and reached for the table leg, knowing she was running out of time.

"They've jumped down to the balcony," said a voice from near the window. They were talking softly, rather than coordinating over the link, but that made sense: They were chasing Partials, so the link would give them away. They didn't know Kira was listening in. "I'll follow—you go back down and cut them off."

Kira saw the scene clearly in her head—one Partial gone out the window, the other walking back down that deep well of a staircase. She made her decision in a flash, grabbing the giant mirror with both hands and heaving it up, holding her breath to keep from puffing with the effort, padding across the floor as fast as she could without making any noise. The frame weighed at least forty pounds. She reached the wall around the staircase and hefted the mirror up and over, pausing only half a second to aim before letting go. The Partial heard her, or saw the motion, but it was too late; he looked up and the mirror crashed into his face, the full forty pounds focused in on a single edge right on the bridge of his nose. His faced caved in, his body crumpling to the stairs below, and Kira raced down after him.

DEATH

Already the link was broadcasting his death; even outside the building, his partner would know. Kira grabbed his gun and turned to look back up the stairs, bringing the rifle in tight to her shoulder. The starlight through the open window made a small trapezoid of light, and she watched it intently, her finger hovering over the trigger, waiting for the other Partial to come into view.

She didn't know if that was Green or the gilled Partial; the cold blast of FEAR that followed could have been either as well. She thought about Green, trapped outside with a scared, angry warrior, and moved slowly backward. After a few steps away from the stairs the window disappeared from view, and she spun around to confront any other horrors lurking in the darkness. No one had approached her from behind, so she assumed there were only two Partials—or that any others were waiting in the boat. The hallway was dark, with few openings to the light outside, and after the starlight upstairs, her eyes had to readjust. She held still, listening for footsteps or breathing, trying to sense on the link who might be lying in wait beyond the next shadow. All she could feel was the lingering DEATH, bitter as old metal on her tongue.

She looked into the first room she passed; a bedroom, she guessed, the furniture gone and the clothes piled up in the corner. A little girl's clothes, pink and frilly and eaten through by worms. The next room was an office; the next another bedroom. The house was empty and silent and choked out the light.

A tendril of link data tickled her nose: SOMETHING'S HERE. She moved swiftly to the next room in the hallway, a master bedroom leading out to the balcony. The wide glass doors were all broken, but the curtains still hung across them, thin and frail as ghosts. They billowed gently in the night air, and Kira almost fired her rifle when the shadow of a figure passed across one. The silhouette of a man outside on the balcony, too ill-defined to distinguish.

"Don't move."

Another shadow, facing the first. Neither seemed to be holding a gun; either could be wearing a helmet. She moved her rifle back and forth, locked in indecision. *Which one is Green?*

"Don't shoot me."

"Where is the other?"

"I don't know, she ran ahead."

"She is in the house."

"I said I don't know."

Kira brought the rifle to her cheek, holding it tightly, focusing her aim. She only had one shot—she had to pick the right target, and she had to hit it. The curtains billowed again, and she realized with shock that she didn't even know where the men were standing; depending on where the moon was, those shadows could be cast from anywhere. She stepped backward quietly, retreating to the hall. She had to find another vantage point. She stood a moment at the top of the stairs leading down to the first floor, but backed away from those as well; she didn't want to give up the high ground. But she didn't want to give the last soldier an open path to the boat, either, so she crept back up the hall toward the third-floor stairs. Stepping around the dead Partial, linking once again to the powerful DEATH particles, she remembered the link data she'd felt on the border marker two days before. It had completely overpowered her, the liquid pheromone so concentrated she'd barely been able to function until the smell of it cleared from her nose. A real Partial, with a more sensitive link mechanism, would be even more affected. She glanced behind her, set aside the rifle, and pulled the dead soldier into the little girl's bedroom.

"I'm very sorry about this," she whispered. She pulled off

her shirt and wrapped it tightly around her face, already gagging from the body odor and mildew, but hoping desperately that they'd be enough to protect her. *The face is too mangled,* she thought. *I'll have to go in another way if I want to find the right spot.* She pulled the soldier's combat knife from the sheath on his belt and thought back to her medical training, picturing the diagram of the nasal cavity and calculating the approximate location of the pheromonal glands. She placed the knife gently in the corpse's mouth, lined up the tip against the center of the soft palate, and shoved.

FEARBETRAYALDEATHBLOODRUNHIDEDEATHSCREAMFEAR-
BLOOD

The link data overwhelmed her, a rush of thoughts and feelings and even memories that threatened to drown her in a dead man's mind. She held her breath, trying to control her own brain, focusing on her own thoughts, her own movements. She pulled the knife out of the soldier and found it covered with liquid—blood and lymph and dark brown data, the liquid form of a dozen different pheromones jumbled chaotically together. The air seemed to vibrate, shapes and colors and smells and voices flickering madly across through the darkened room. She staggered to her feet and back down the hall.

"What's that?"

The voices were closer now, but they weren't the only one in the house, not anymore—

The bombs were falling now, she was back on the beaches of the Isolation War—she was sleeping in the water, looking up at the moon melting shapelessly on the surface of the lake.

DEATH

She heard a gun clatter to the floor. The hallway laughed at her, shadows twisting into faces telling her to RUN HELP STOP GO KILL. Voices screamed, but she couldn't tell if they were from the present or the past; real or hallucinations. She stumbled into the master bedroom and saw them, the gilled Partial and Green, clutching their heads and sobbing and shouting and there was her father between them, his hands dripping blood, and she blinked and he was gone.

"Garrett," sobbed the Partial. Link data slid from her dagger in dark drops of liquid thought, so thick in the air she could hardly see. She walked forward, pushing aside the haze of nerve gas from a Shanghai bunker, the artillery smoke from an assault on Atlanta, the bloody mist from the White Plains coup. She wanted to cower behind the trees, to hide behind the wall, to dive back into the cold, dark lake where she could be safe.

I am Kira Walker, she told herself. Identities ran through her mind like streams, rushing and blending and thundering together. She looked at the two men, now writhing on the floor, and couldn't tell which was the enemy. *I am Kira Walker,* she thought again. *I will not lose myself. Green is my friend.* She found the other Partial, gills flapping wildly on his pale, wet neck, and drove the knife home through the gap in his body armor right beneath his arm. The linked declaration of DEATH barely registered in the haze of super-concentrated madness. Kira fell to the floor, crawling toward Green, and dragged him out the door to the balcony. Fresh air rushed in like a healing angel, and she felt her mind begin to clear. Wooden stairs led down from the balcony; they wouldn't have to go back inside.

"I don't want to," Green mumbled. "I don't want to."

"It's okay," said Kira, her voice still muffled by her makeshift mask. She looked across the yard to the low stone dock on the island's edge, where a boat, half-obscured by shadows and trees, rocked gently in the water. Her theory had been right. There really was a boat. And it was empty.

"It's going to be okay," she said. "We're leaving."

CHAPTER TWENTY-FIVE

Dark shapes moved in the water. Kira helped Green into the boat, pulling it as close to the little stone dock as possible before easing him down into the center. The night air was slowly clearing her head of the concentrated pheromones, but Green was still lost in chemical memories, curling into a fetal position down in the aluminum belly of the boat. Kira stepped over the slim black line of the water, but stopped with her foot in midair before turning, gritting her teeth, and walking back to the house. She needed a weapon.

She clambered back up the wooden stairs to the balcony, took a deep breath, and ran into the bedroom, feeling her way through the sudden darkness. The dead Partial lay on the floor, his rifle beside him, and she grabbed it and ran back out. She didn't dare to breathe until she was back down the stairs, and sucked air greedily in the cool darkness of the wooded yard. When she reached the boat Green was still lying on the floor and panting, but his eyes were open. She stepped in carefully, trying not to think about what might be lurking in the water beneath.

"Where am I?" asked Green.

"Outside, on the boat," said Kira. "Stay quiet." She picked up an oar and dipped it gently in the water, all the time expecting a gilled Partial to grab it and yank, pulling her over the side. She untied the boat and it drifted away from the dock—ten inches, twenty inches, five feet, ten. The shore fell away sharply, the inky lake deep and impenetrable. Who was down there, watching? How many of them? What did they see or think? All it would take was one Partial, one pale and clammy hand, to reach up and tip the boat, and then both she and Green would be in the water, sinking and helpless, dragged down by dead-eyed monsters. She rowed carefully, evenly, not daring to rush. If the enemy Partials got suspicious enough to come up and check, they'd link their dead companions immediately, and Kira and Green would be exposed. The interrogators had rowed out to the island, and she had to make the others think that now they were rowing back, returning their weapons to dry storage before diving back down to their home.

Why would they live under the water at all? she wondered. *They can obviously survive on dry land, at least for a while.* Morgan and Vale had both told her that heavy gene mods can degrade a person's sanity. Was that what had happened here—Partials living underwater, killing other Partials and nailing their hands to pikes like savages? *How much of their minds is man, and how much is . . . something else?*

Two hundred feet to the closest island. One hundred. Fifty. Twenty. A small wooden dock sat low in the water ahead of them, and beyond it another house lost among the trees. Her map was gone, and all her equipment, but she remembered the bay's basic geography; if this was the large central island she thought it was, there would be a causeway about two miles down connecting it back to the western shore of the lake. They could cross there . . . if the causeway was still up.

Ten feet left. Five.

The boat bumped up against the dock and Kira leaped out, looping the rope around a short pole and reaching out a hand for Green. The wooden planks under her feet and the dark black water all around her brought back sharp, terrifying memories of the dock where she'd been captured, and she imagined another pale Partial bursting up from the lake to seize her outstretched arm, but nothing did. Green grabbed her hand and stood up, steadier now than before. She checked the rifle slung over her back, nervously reassuring herself that it was still there, and led Green up toward the house. The path here was well-worn, further proof that the Partials stored their water-sensitive gear on dry land nearby.

Which means there might be more of them waiting here, she thought. Kira tried to feel them on the link, but without the heightened awareness that came with combat or terror, the data—if any existed—was too weak for her limited abilities to detect. She whispered to Green. "Can you link anyone up here?"

"Not right now," he said softly, "but they come here often."

"Tell me if it gets stronger," said Kira, and pressed forward. The path led up from the dock through a wooded backyard, a former lawn now thickly overgrown with weeds and vines and saplings. The home there was large, old and once luxurious, now sagging and decrepit but obviously used by the Ivies;

the windows were boarded over, and the footpath through the underbrush led straight to the door. Green didn't alert her to any Partials hiding inside, and she could sense none herself but chose not to enter, just in case. They were clear now; their best plan was to put as much distance between them and the lake as they could before the Ivies realized they were gone.

They left the trail to give the house a wide berth and broke through the trees onto a cracked asphalt road that wound north through a parade of faded lakeside homes. By silent agreement they broke into a run, the only sound their shoes slapping wetly against the road. They ran half a mile before Green risked speaking.

"Do you know where we're going?"

"Sort of."

"That's good enough?"

"I had a map before I was captured," said Kira. "There's a causeway up here—if we're on the right island."

"And if we're not?"

"Then we have to cross the water again," said Kira. "So let's hope we're on the right island."

They ran in silence for a moment, and then Green asked another question. His voice was dark and worried. "What happened back there?"

"In the house?"

"I thought I was back in China again. Like, I literally thought I was there, in the middle of the Isolation War, in one of the subway tunnels we used to take their larger cities, except . . . I never had to fight in those tunnels. Other units did, but not mine."

"I got the drop on the first guard because they didn't know I was there," said Kira. "The only way to get the second was to use the link against him."

"I thought you weren't on the link."

"It wasn't my data," said Kira. She hesitated. "I borrowed it from the other dead Partial."

He shot her a probing look. "Borrowed?"

"Extracted via combat knife," said Kira. He looked horrified, and she felt queasy at the memory. "Look, I wish I didn't have to do it, but it was the only way. Normally you don't link the data until it's out in the air, diffused, but inside the pheromonal glands it's still liquid, and intensely concentrated." She shrugged helplessly. "Apparently his unit *did* fight in the subway tunnels, and we remembered it through his link data."

"Who—" said Green, stopping abruptly. Kira checked her steps, almost tripping, and looked back at him. He peered at her in confusion. "Did you just say 'we' remembered it?"

Crap, thought Kira. It wasn't that she desperately needed to keep her nature secret, it was just that she hadn't told him before, and she didn't want it to look like she'd been withholding something from him. She cleared her throat.

"You're not on the link," Green insisted. He walked toward her, furrowing his brow. "Maybe it's the concentrated data, like you said—when it's that strong, maybe humans can sense it too?"

This could be a way into recruiting Green to my cause, she thought. *If he thinks humans can sense link data, even only in a case like this, he could see a stronger connection between the species. He might be more open to helping me, helping the humans.*

Except it's not true. If we're going to work together—the two of us, or the two species—we have to trust each other. We can't start that relationship with a lie.

She shook her head. "I'm not a human."

"You said you were."

"I thought I was," said Kira, "for my whole life. I grew up with them. I still feel human. But I'm a Partial."

"Partials link," he said simply. "Partials don't age. You don't look like any Partial model I've ever seen."

"I was a new model," said Kira. "A prototype for a new line, after the war. That's why Dr. Morgan wanted to study me, because she thought my DNA would help her cure expiration. But it didn't work. I don't have any of your heightened abilities—none of the strength, none of the reflexes, maybe some slightly accelerated healing. And I can link, sort of, but only one way."

Green looked shocked. "You mean you can . . ." His mouth hung open, and he covered his mouth and nose with his hands, almost like he was protecting his breath. "You mean you can link me but I can't link you? You can feel everything I do, without giving anything back?"

"Not all of it," said Kira, though she was definitely linking him now: a confused mixture of shock and disgust. She realized that as naked as she felt knowing Green knew her secret, he must have felt even worse knowing that she could shamelessly, imperceptibly, unstoppably eavesdrop on his every emotion. The Partials were accustomed to sharing everything with one another, living in a permanently communal emotional state, but to have that state invaded by an outsider—one who didn't share her own emotions in return—must feel like a violation.

"I'm sorry," said Kira. "I'm sorry I didn't tell you. I should have."

"Just . . . run," said Green, breaking back into a jog as he ran past her up the road. "We need to get out of here before anyone notices we're gone."

Kira followed him but kept a respectful distance where she couldn't link him. Even so, running in his wake, she caught the occasional whiff of confusion or sadness or fear.

Samm never reacted like this, she thought, *but he had time to get used to it. We practically lived together for weeks before we found out I was a Partial. And Heron . . . who knows what Heron thinks about anything? She used to deal with humans all the time, so maybe it's not a big deal for her.*

But it is a big deal. To Green, and likely to others.

They reached the causeway a few minutes later, and Kira practically shook with relief to see it still intact. They kept to the center as they crossed, staying as far from the water as they could. As a gesture of goodwill, Kira deferred the next decision to Green.

"Where to now?"

Green grunted softly as they jogged past a boathouse with an open parking lot. "If we cut south, we'll have miles to run before we're clear of the lake," he said. "Obviously they can come up on land just fine, but I figure the more we can avoid water, the better." Sure enough, the road curved more and more to the left, before finally just turning sharply and leading them straight south. The road appeared to be the edge of the little lake community, with nothing but forest on the far side, and the two of them plunged into the trees to cut across and leave the lake behind.

"Watch out for border markers," said Kira. "I found them on my way in—they used link data, concentrated like in the house, to set up a perimeter and warn people away. If you start to get freaked out for no reason, that's the reason."

Green said nothing but nodded in acknowledgment.

They picked their way silently through the thick forest, and it wasn't long before they reached another road, but soon this, too, turned south, and they set back off into the woods. They crossed two more hills and a narrow stream before the sun began to come up, and when the next road turned out to be a wider, two-lane highway, they decided to risk a little southward travel. Almost immediately, though, the road cut back east toward the lake, as if the land itself was determined to twist them around and lead them back to danger. They struck out into the trees once more, but Kira was exhausted and starving and cold. Finally she stopped them in the backyard of an abandoned house.

"We need to figure out where we are."

Green nodded toward the house. "Think they have a map?"

"You check the bookshelves, I'll check for a den or an office."

Green shook his head. "You never look in a house for a map, you look in the cars." He led her around to the front, where two cars sat in the driveway. Kira started toward them, but he shook his head. "Too nice—all the rich humans had maps on computers, especially in their cars, and a lot of the middle-class ones, too. You want to find a paper map, find the oldest, nastiest car you can see."

Kira thought the plan was ridiculous, but Green was talking to her again, and she didn't want to ruin it. She followed dutifully down the wooded residential road, him on one side and her on the other. The houses in this neighborhood were all large, and set back from the road, which made the cars harder to see;

it also made Kira despair of finding an older-looking car, but she persevered. The road turned south, as all of them seemed to, but they were miles from the lake, and they were making better time here than in the trees. Finally she spotted one—no more rusty than the other cars, but with a notably different shape; longer lines and squarer corners. She caught Green's attention and the two trotted over.

"I've been scavenging old-world ruins for as long as I can remember," said Kira, "but I've never bothered with cars."

"Humans practically lived in their cars," said Green.

Kira nodded. "Sure, but we were always looking for food and medicine. Sometimes you get lucky and find a survivalist who died halfway home with a trunk-load of canned food, but it was rarely ever worth our time."

"Watch and learn." Green walked to the passenger side and leaned in the window, pressing a button on the dashboard to pop open a small box. "This is called a glove compartment," he said, rifling through it. "Aha." He pulled himself back out and held up a folded Connecticut road map, in better condition than Kira had ever seen. "The compartment has a watertight seal, so the items were protected from the weather. Let's figure out where we are."

"Rita Drive," said Kira, reading a weathered road sign. "A little horseshoe street off a larger road."

Green spread the map on the hood of the car, and after some searching finally found it. Kira's heart sank when she tapped the spot.

"We're surrounded by lakes."

"They're all over this area," said Green. He traced a winding path. "I think our best bet is to cut across this field, then follow this road, this road, and . . . this road. We might have to jump some fences, but we'll be clear of the lakes without getting close to any of them."

"One problem," said Kira, and tapped her finger on a portion of his proposed route. "I came in through this gap here, trying to avoid the major roads, and that's where I ran into the very first border marker."

"That puts the border a lot farther from the lake than I expected," said Green.

Now that they were out of combat, Kira's link sense was dulling again, and she couldn't tell how he felt about their situation—frustrated? Scared? His voice was impassive. "I wondered why we hadn't run across any yet."

"Be grateful that we haven't."

"Maybe this way," said Green, "off the edge of the map. We can find a New York map when we cross the border."

"That's no good," said Kira, thinking back to the map she'd had before. "West of here is just more lakes—there are hundreds of them. I don't know if the Ivies patrol them, but I want to avoid them just in case. Our best bet is south."

"South to where?" asked Green. "We may as well have this conversation now, if we're planning our travel. I'm a deserter, so I can't go near Morgan's territory, and after the Ivies I'm a little leery of trying to meet up with any of the other factions."

"I know how you feel," said Kira. "My plan was to visit as many of the smaller factions as I could, but now . . ." She hoped the others weren't as violent as the Ivies, and hoped even more that none of them had anything as creepy as a "Blood Man," but how could she be sure? Should she risk it? *If even one more faction captures me for some kind of . . . ritual sacrifice . . . is it worth it?*

I'm trying to save the world, she thought. *That's worth anything.*

She looked at Green. "I've never told you why I came here."

"I was wondering about that."

"Dr. Morgan is dangerous," said Kira. "I assume I don't have to tell you that, seeing as how you ran away from her."

Green said nothing, and Kira continued. It was the first time she would propose her plan to anyone, and she was grateful it was just one person instead of a big group. She didn't know how to present it. She already felt weird about starting with Morgan, and backtracked a bit.

"The humans are dying of RM," she said, "and the Partials are dying of expiration. What I discovered while studying Morgan's files is that the cure for one is the same as the cure for the other: Partials produce the cure for RM, and humans in turn are able to produce a particle that inhibits expiration in Partials. Both of the cures were engineered this way. So the only way to save both species is to live together. In peace, preferably."

Green's silence betrayed his skepticism. Kira went on.

"I mean we have to coexist, closely. Live in the same area, work together . . . basically just act like we're one species instead of two."

"That doesn't make sense."

"I'm trying to explain it," said Kira. "The transmission of the particles would be almost impossible to replicate in a lab, not on the scale we're talking about—tens of thousands of humans and hundreds of thousands of Partials. The two species can cure each other, but they'd have to be constantly breathing the same air. They'd have to live together without fighting."

Green said nothing, thinking. After a moment he looked at her again. "And Dr. Morgan?"

"What about her?"

"You started this by saying she's dangerous."

"Right," said Kira. "When I figured this out I left, because I didn't trust her. She's more likely to enslave humans than work with them."

"So you didn't trust Morgan, and you came out to try to find other groups of Partials who'd be more amenable to the idea of coexistence."

"Exactly."

Green paused for a long moment. "You're sure that this process you're describing works? That it's really all this simple?"

"I crossed the entire continent looking for the people who built RM—the same ones who built the Partials—and the only thing I learned for sure is that everything they did was part of a plan. That plan has gone horribly, terribly wrong, and the people who made it have all gone crazy or just . . . given up. But the plan is still there, written on our DNA. And it's all we've got."

"So Partials cure humans and humans cure Partials." He looked at her. "Where does that leave you?"

Kira took a breath, feeling a shadow of the same despair she'd felt in Morgan's operating room, convinced that she was useless. "I can't cure anything," she said softly. "And I don't think I expire. I don't know where that leaves me."

Green looked up at the sky, the blue growing lighter as the

sun rose. "We need to rest, but I don't want to stop before we get out of Ivie territory."

"That's probably wise."

"We'll go west, like I said before—maybe there are lakes over there, but if the Ivies have marked a border around this lake, I'm hopeful that means the others are safe."

Kira felt leery of the idea, but she had to admit that cutting straight west was the fastest route away from their captors. "Maybe west for now," she said, "but as soon as we're out of danger, I have to get back to this mission. With or without you."

He folded up the map, not saying anything. "Do you know where you're going next?"

"As much as I want to talk to the other factions, I lost everything in that lake," said Kira, "all my maps, all my notes, everything. I don't know where any of the other factions are, and even if I did, I don't know if I can spare the time to walk to where they are. Some of them are weeks away."

"That's not an answer to my question," said Green.

"What I'm saying is that I have to go back to Long Island," said Kira. "I don't trust Morgan, but her soldiers might listen to reason. The ones in the occupation have already been living with humans for months now—perhaps they're even seeing the effects of the process I just told you about. If I can convince anyone, it's them."

"And the humans?"

"They'll be just as hard to convince," said Kira, nodding. "But either way, they're on Long Island. I have to go there."

"You realize this isn't taking us out of danger," said Green. "We'll have to go through Morgan's territory, and into a war zone. We won't even be getting away from the Ivies, because they're headed in the same direction. The Blood Man said he was going after humans next."

"Then I'll stop him too," said Kira, but paused. "Wait. Did you say 'we'?"

"You're talking about saving the world," he said simply. "Of course I'm coming."

CHAPTER TWENTY-SIX

Owen Tovar ran through the streets of Huntington, heedless of making noise, trying only to get as far from the coffee shop as he could. His bad foot made him lope along unevenly, and he pushed himself to go faster. The Partials had hunted most of his group to nothing; he'd sent Mkele east with what soldiers they had left, and stayed behind to draw the Partials away. It was a strategy that had worked well so far, but it wouldn't work much longer. They had no men, no time, and no explosives.

Technically I have a ton of explosives, he thought, pelting between the cars. Partial soldiers had seen him now, and a few bullets whipped past him. *But that's all going to change in three, two, one—*

The coffee shop behind him exploded, the force of the shock wave so great that it threw him to the ground, even a block and a half away. The Partials behind him were shredded by the blast, and Tovar rolled onto his stomach, covering his head with his hands as shrapnel rained down around him. His ears rang, leaving him temporarily deaf; he gambled that the Partials couldn't hear either, and scrambled to the nearest side street before standing up and bolting off again. The soldiers would be too preoccupied to chase him for another few minutes at least; he needed to use that time to get as far away as he could.

Even as he ran, though, he knew he didn't have any options. Delarosa's forces had survived against the Partials through guerrilla tactics—harassing their flanks, hitting their supply lines, and then fading away into the wilderness. Tovar had needed to do more to get their attention, to draw them away from the human refugees fleeing south, and thus he had been more aggressive. And now they'd chased him all the way to the North Shore for it. He was surrounded on three sides by water, and on the fourth by Partials. He had nowhere left to run.

If I can make it to the water, I might have a chance, he told himself. *Maybe I can find a boat, or a piece of driftwood big enough to keep my head above water. Maybe I can just hide somewhere, and stay there for a week or whatever it takes.* He chanced a look back over his shoulder and was encouraged to find that he was still alone. They would find him eventually, but finding him would hold their attention. That was the goal. *Anything that keeps them here, on me, so the others can get out of East Meadow and off the island.*

I knew I was going to die when I signed up for this, he thought. *Dad always told me never to volunteer for anything—you'd think I'd learn to listen—*

A light flared in front of him, bright and white and blinding. He stumbled on his bad foot, turning to flee, but something slapped into his back, sharp and painful like a sting from a giant bee. He dropped instantly, his body convulsing as a jolt of electric current ran through it. When his mind cleared he was lying on the ground, his face in a grassy gutter, his limbs twisted like a rag doll and completely immobile. He tried to talk, but his mouth felt like lead.

The Partials don't use stun guns, he thought. *Who has the electricity to spare for a stun gun?*

A pair of hands, surprisingly gentle, turned him over. The man standing over him was a dark silhouette, framed by the bright lights behind, and Tovar couldn't discern any features. "I want you to know that this is not an attack," said the man. His voice was soft, with a nuance of expression that marked the speaker as human. Tovar tried to answer, but his jaw moved feebly, and no sound came out. "This will hurt you," said the man, "but it will save you, in the larger sense. 'You' as a people. The human race."

The man set a plastic case on the ground next to him, opening it with a click. Tovar couldn't see what was inside, but the shadowy man pulled out a glass jar and unsealed the lid. "Everyone is going to die. I assume that's not a surprise." He set the open jar on the ground and reached back into the case to pull out a long, sharp knife. Tovar tried to move, but he was still paralyzed. "I say that to let you know that you dying right here, right now, is an honor. You were going to die anyway, but it would have been meaningless in any other circumstance. This way you can be a part of the new beginning. The new life that will replace the old. Little sting here." The man placed the knife on Tovar's hand and pressed down, chopping off his longest finger. Tovar screamed in his mind, the pain burning through him like a fire, but no sound came out. The man dropped the finger into the jar, and went to work on another one. "There was a plan, you realize, for everyone to survive." *Chop.* "Not just survive but prosper—human and Partial, everyone together. It wouldn't have been hard. But that plan's gone now, and I've had to adapt." *Chop.* His voice remained calm the entire time, as if he were simply talking to a toaster while methodically taking it apart. "Now, this is the part that's going to hurt the most. Speaking biologically, I mean—I don't know if it will cause more pain than the fingers, but it will certainly cause more damage. This is the part you won't live through, is what I mean to say." He held up the jar and shook it gently, rattling the three fingers at the bottom. "I need to fill the rest of this with blood."

Tovar's voice returned just in time for him to scream.

CHAPTER TWENTY-SEVEN

Kira was colder than she'd ever been. They'd stopped in a town called Brewster Hill for rest and new clothes, and then again in North Salem for warmer clothes and jackets, but even that wasn't proving to be enough. Green was more resistant to the effects of the weather, and faster on the road, but even he was feeling it now. They'd gone nearly thirty miles in three days, all the way to Norwalk, and in that time the temperature had dropped twenty degrees at least. Kira was accustomed to a bit of a chill in the winter months, but nothing like this. Her breath came out in visible puffs, and her nose felt numb as she rubbed it with red, tingling fingers.

The streets of Norwalk were a deep metal canyon, just like Manhattan had been, but now there was frost on the deep-green kudzu that covered the buildings and crept in through the long-broken windows. She held out as long as she could, enduring the cold in silence, but finally decided that it wasn't worth it—getting to Long Island one day or even one hour earlier wouldn't do her any good if she died of hypothermia. At the next clothing store they passed, Kira led them in and they searched for heavy coats, but there were none to be found anywhere in the building.

"I guess the Break came in the summer," said Kira. "Nobody's stocked for this kind of weather." She paused. "That never occurred to me before, but I guess I've never needed a coat before."

Green shook his head, looking out the broken windows at the dark-gray clouds. "When was the last time you remember it being this cold?"

"Never," Kira admitted. She recalled Vale's wistful thoughts about the old winters, the real winters, and shivered. "Do you think it'll last?"

"If it does, we might even see snow." Green turned back from the window. "We need to find a hardware store—they'll have work gloves at least, which is better than nothing, and then maybe a furniture store so we can burn some tables for warmth. I don't want to cross the sound until this clears up."

"What makes you think it's going to clear up?"

"We haven't had a storm like this in my entire life," said Green. "Weather patterns that long-standing don't reverse overnight. We might get a freak storm, but that'll be it."

"I hope you're right." Kira hopped down from the counter where she'd been sitting and walked back out into the frigid street. The wind had picked up, and blew her hair wildly around her head. "You know where to find a hardware store?"

"No idea. Seems more likely outside of town than in it, though."

"That means backtracking," said Kira. "There's nothing

ahead of us but the city and the sound."

Green shook his head. "I don't want to backtrack—we're better off finding a boat and sitting out the storm in the building nearest to it. Then as soon as things are back to normal, we can jump in and race across the water."

Kira nodded. "Keep your eyes open for parks, playgrounds, and schools. Anywhere with grounds had groundskeepers, which means they'll have a shed or a garage somewhere with tools and work gloves."

"Clever."

"You know how to find maps, I know how to find gardening tools. My adopted mother was an herbalist." The thought of Nandita quelled her cheerful mood. Nandita had helped create Kira, she knew everything about her, and yet she'd never said a word. Why? Why deceive her? Had she just hoped that the problems would all go away on their own, and that Kira would grow up and grow old and die, and never have to face the truth about who she was and where she came from? *If she'd really cared,* thought Kira, *she'd have given me something to go on. Some help or guidance or advice that would help me to deal with all of this. She would have told me what I was built for, and why, and what I was supposed to do.*

With a flash she remembered an old conversation—nearly two years ago now, one of the last times she'd ever seen Nandita before the old woman disappeared. Kira had just come home from the salvage run in Asharoken, the one where they'd triggered a bomb, and Nandita was putting away her herbs. *I was troubled about something,* thought Kira, *probably the bombing, and Nandita said . . .* Kira shook her head in disbelief, the words

247

flooding back to her. *She said exactly what I needed to hear—not then, but now. Every life has a purpose, Kira. But the most important thing you can ever know is that no matter what your purpose is, that's not your only choice.*

"Groundskeeper," said Green. Kira looked up and saw a large brick building, the white gabled roof now cracked and yellowing with age; all around it was a wide green lawn, now overgrown with bushes and weeds and a loose forest of ten-year-old trees. There was a sign buried in the middle of the foliage, but it was too vine-choked to read.

"Looks like a government building," said Kira. "City hall or something. They don't always have groundskeeping equipment on site, because they handled all their properties from a central location."

"Maybe this is the central location," said Green. "Doesn't hurt to check." They walked around the side and back, finding a parking lot but no toolshed. Behind the building there was a baseball field, but this, too, had no tools or gloves or anywhere to store them. They made their way back to the main road, ready to press on and look for another park or a school, but Kira stopped in front of a house. Green shook his head. "Too fancy; they didn't do any of their yard work themselves."

"Not yard work," said Kira, "but look at the sign. 'Home Theater Design and Installation.' I don't know what a home theater is, but I bet they used gloves to install them."

They started their search in the front room, moving quickly through the building; it had been converted from a home to a business and was mostly empty. The back room held a lost fortune in holovid projectors, but those were useless now. She'd have traded the entire thing for a single pair of gloves. Finally in the back parking lot they found a rusted white van, weeds growing up around the flat, deformed tires, with the company's logo faded and peeling off the side. Kira wrenched the door open and found the back full of power cords and old projector parts, and four pairs of canvas work gloves in the top drawer of a tool chest. They pulled on two pairs each and jogged back to the main road to make up for lost time. The sky was darker now, far darker than it should have been for the time of day, and the wind was practically howling.

"We need to find shelter," said Kira.

"We need to find a boat," said Green. "I told you before, the instant this clears up we need to get on the water."

"Are you afraid it's going to start up again?"

"I'm afraid that we're running out of time."

"Look," said Kira, "I'm every bit as anxious about this as you are, but we're not going to do any good if we're dead of exposure. It feels like it's dropped another five degrees in the last few hours—this weather is well below freezing, and Partials or not, we're in a very real danger of hypothermia."

"We don't have time to sit around waiting," Green snapped, and picked up his pace.

"We'll live a lot longer if we get inside—"

"Really?" said Green.

Kira stopped, trying to figure out what he meant, and the answer hit her like a fist to the gut. She wrapped her arms tightly over her freezing chest and ran to catch up with him.

"How long do you have?"

His voice was emotionless—all the more eerie considering his words. "It just now occurred to you to ask?"

"I'm sorry," said Kira. "I've been focused on expiration as a concept, as an enemy to overcome. . . . You left Morgan's army. Does that mean you didn't think she was going to cure it fast enough to matter?"

Green walked silently, head down.

"The youngest batch has seven months left," said Kira. *Samm's batch,* she thought. She swallowed nervously, feeling tears creep up behind her eyes. "Do you have half that?" Green didn't answer, and she felt her heart sink. "Two months?"

"One," said Green. "I'll be dead by the end of the year."

"That might be enough time to help you," said Kira quickly, practically racing through the words. "The sooner we get across and find humans, the sooner we can—"

"Then stop arguing with me and look for a boat."

Kira fell silent, trying to imagine what it would feel like to know you were going to die in one month—and worse, that you knew there was nothing you could do about it. *But we can,* she thought. *This plan will work.*

I think.

Green stopped suddenly, putting up his hand to stop her too. "Do you feel that?"

Kira concentrated on the link but felt nothing. "What is it?"

"I have no idea," said Green. "Something big—like a whole squad's worth of link data, that kind of signal strength. It's just that . . . it feels like a single person." He turned his head slowly, as if trying to pinpoint the exact source of the data. "This way, come on."

Kira ran a few steps to catch up with him. "Wait, you're going to look for it?"

"Of course."

"But we're in a hurry," said Kira. "We don't have time to stop and maybe get captured by a patrol squad."

"I'm telling you, it's one Partial," said Green, still walking.

"But you're dying," said Kira. "What changed?"

"Don't you see? We have to find it because . . ." His voice trailed off, and he shook his head. "Because we have to. Because he has something to tell us."

"That doesn't make sense."

"How can it not make sense?" Green sounded almost frustrated, as if he were explaining that that water was wet to someone too thick to understand.

Kira shook her head. "Green, listen to me. This is the link—whatever you're sensing right now is luring you in, on purpose."

"Maybe. We can handle it."

"No, we can't," said Kira. She thought about Morgan's arrival in the Preserve, when she and Vale had used their own fierce control over the link to force the nearby Partials to obey them. "I've seen this kind of intensity in the link before, and it only comes from a member of the Trust. The people who made the Partials. There are two of them in this area—Dr. Morgan and Dr. Vale—and we don't want to meet either one of them." She planted herself in front of him. "If you keep going, we'll be caught and imprisoned, maybe executed. You do not want to do this."

He pushed past her and started running.

"Green, wait!"

She took off after him, but he was running at full speed now, arms pumping at his sides, and she struggled to keep up. Kira had something of a Partial's physical prowess, but she wasn't trained like he was. She sucked in breaths of freezing air, feeling her arms and chest grow sweaty with effort, and shivering almost immediately after as the sweat cooled and evaporated.

They approached an underpass and Green swerved right, scaling a stepped stone wall and then pelting onto the railroad tracks above. Kira followed, desperate to reach him and stop him, until a gust of wind brought the link data rushing into her lungs, coursing through her brain, stronger than she'd ever imagined, and then she was racing not after him but with him, convinced above all else that she needed to go now, to find this person, to hear his message. They ran along the tracks and then swerved off, down a hill and through a parking lot, crossing streets and jumping fences, until at last a vast field opened up before them. An ancient park, trees shaking in the freezing wind, and beyond it the roiling gray sea. They ran past benches and bushes and old baseball diamonds, barely visible in the new growth that had reclaimed the park. Beyond the field was another road, and beyond that a strip of sand rimmed with rocks and crashing waves. They'd run nearly a mile from where Green first felt the command. Others had apparently felt the same, for a ten-man squad of Partials sat scattered on the rocks, their expressions blank, their link data as stunned as Green's.

At the front of the group, staring out at the ocean, sat a giant creature, dark red, with skin like rhinoceros hide. Kira slowed to a stop, the sight a shock to her senses, momentarily giving her clarity as her brain fought to determine which feelings were her own and which were coming from the link. It was a clarity that she alone experienced; the rest of the Partials stood in rapt attention.

"You're just in time." The thing's voice rumbled. "It's starting now."

Green staggered forward, rubbing his chest to keep warm, taking up a position in the same loose semicircle as the other ten Partials. Kira walked forward as well, not stopping in the circle but pressing through it, approaching the creature directly.

"Who are you?"

"I've called you here to warn you," said the creature. She couldn't see its mouth move, but felt its voice rumbling powerfully in her chest. "I warned the people on the island, and the Partials in White Plains, but they did not heed me."

"You've been to White Plains?" asked Kira. "You've seen Dr. Morgan?"

"It was not a happy reunion," said the thing, and looked down at its chest. Kira followed its gaze and found that the creature's chest was riddled with bullet holes. One arm hung uselessly at its side, and the other clutched a gaping wound in its gut. "This body can regenerate most of the damage it takes, but not this much all at once. I am dying." It turned to look at her, and Kira saw a pair of nearly human eyes buried deep in the thing's monstrous face. "But I have delivered my warning."

Kira stepped forward, trying to see the wounds better. "What warning?"

"I have repaired the climate," said the creature. "I've fixed the planet we broke so long ago. Now the world can heal again."

Kira shook her head, barely understanding what he was trying to say. "You're saying you're the one who made it cold?"

"I cleansed the air, the water, the atmosphere. Earth's protective layers. Undid all the damage from our weapons in the old war. I've restored balance. We'll have seasons again. The first winter will be hard, and none of the people are ready. I warned them to help them survive."

"You're one of the Trust," said Kira. She ran through her mental list, cataloguing every member she knew and which ones she didn't, to puzzle out who this might be. There were only two unaccounted for, and one was her father, Armin Dhurvasula. Her mind reeled at the thought that this impossible creature—so altered by gene mods that he'd lost his humanity completely—might be her father.

She tried to speak, but her voice was lost. She coughed, shivering in the cold spray of the ocean sound, and tried again. "Who are you? What's your name?"

"No one has used my name in . . . thirteen years."

She stared at the wounds, at the dark blood seeping out onto the cold gray rocks below. She barely dared to speak it. "Armin?"

"No," said the creature. It watched the coming storm with sad, wistful eyes. "My name was Jerry Ryssdal."

Kira felt a rush of emotion—loss and sadness, that the man she'd found was not her father, and joy, that her father was not this thing dying slowly on the beach. Guilt, that she took joy in any aspect of another man's death. She wondered if some of those emotions were his—his sadness at dying, his joy at fixing the weather. His guilt for destroying the world.

Jerry Ryssdal was the one she knew the least about; Vale had said he lived in the south, near the eternal fires of old Houston. He'd changed himself, Vale said. Kira had never known what to make of that, but it was obvious now. A brutal barrage of gene mods to help him survive in the toxic wasteland. He'd dedicated his life to restoring the world—not the people in it, but the world itself. Somehow, impossibly, he'd done it.

The first winter will be hard, she thought, repeating his words. She'd never known a real winter; very few people had. There hadn't been one since the old war, before the Isolation War, when buttons were pushed and hell was unleashed and the world had been changed forever. *Not forever,* she thought. *It's changing back now. But any change this drastic will be painful to endure.*

She looked up and saw the first snowflake fall.

CHAPTER TWENTY-EIGHT

"It's not enough to go after Delarosa," said Marcus. "We have to warn the rest of the island as well."

"Agreed," said Vinci. "We need to do both."

"You can't do either one," said the guard. "You're still handcuffed and locked in the back of an old supermarket."

"Um, you're not really a part of this conversation," said Marcus.

"I'm sitting ten feet away from you."

"Then plug your ears," said Marcus. "And sing to yourself for a few minutes, too. We're about to discuss our plans for escape."

"Shut up, Valencio." Woolf sighed and turned to the guard. "Soldier, if you're in a talkative mood, I'd love to hear your justification for going along with all this. I don't care where Delarosa sets off that nuke, it's going to kill what few of us are left."

The guard glowered at them and returned to his former silence, leaning back in his chair and folding his arms with a frown.

"How about this," said Marcus, still addressing the guard. "You're stuck here guarding us, which isn't helping our plans or yours. How about we find some common ground: Let's all start traveling south, to warn everyone about the nuke, and we promise we won't slow you down or cause any trouble. Even as a loyal fan of the nuclear solution, surely you agree that people need to be warned."

"We're not going to just warn the humans and ignore what Delarosa is going to do to the Partials," said Vinci.

"Well—" Marcus stopped, trying to find the right words. "I was—that was kind of going to be the part of the scheme I didn't tell him out loud. Like, he would come over to free us because he was swayed by my brilliant and well-considered plan, and then when he got close you could jump up and . . . knock him out or something."

Woolf groaned.

"You're a Partial," said Marcus. "You could beat up a guy while still in handcuffs, right?"

"That was a terrible plan," said Vinci. "I can say without exaggeration that that's actually the worst plan I've ever heard."

"That's not entirely fair, though," said Marcus. "All the other plans you've ever heard have been designed by Partial strategists, and I'm just like a regular . . . guy."

"The worst part," said Vinci, "was when you revealed the entire plan right in front of the guard. You were intending to trick him, and then I asked you *one question* and you said everything out loud, right in front of him."

Marcus stuttered, trying to protest.

"Maybe that was actually the best part of the plan," said

Vinci, "since it meant that we never attempted to carry out the actual plan, which as I mentioned was terrible. This way you just look stupid instead of all of us getting killed."

"None of us would get killed," said Marcus. "It was a great plan." He made vague karate-style movements with his hands, though no one could see them with his hands still cuffed behind his back, and the raw skin on his wrists burned from the effort. "Super Partial combat prowess, you could totally have—"

"Will you please shut up!" said the guard. "Holy hell, it's like listening to my little sisters."

"You have little sisters?" asked Marcus.

"Not anymore," said the guard, "thanks to that mongrel sitting next to you." He pointed at Vinci, his face growing tenser and angrier. The room fell silent for a moment, but then Marcus spoke softly.

"Technically, he's less mongrel than anyone else in this room. He was grown in a lab from custom-engineered DNA; he's like a perfect . . . specimen, and all the rest of us are the mo—"

The guard leapt to his feet and crossed the narrow room in a single step, lashing out with the butt of his rifle to crack Marcus hard across the side of his face. Marcus reeled back from the blow, bright lights flashing behind his eyelids, his skull ringing, his entire consciousness focused on the intense, mind-ripping pain.

Somebody slapped him, and he struggled to open his eyes. Woolf knelt in front him, his hands free; behind him the guard lay unconscious on the floor, and Vinci and Galen were stripping him of his weapons and gear.

"Holy crap," said Marcus. "How long was I out?"

"Just a minute at the most," said Woolf, examining his head. "You're going to have a massive bruise here. If you remember back when we made this plan, *Vinci* was the one who was supposed to get hit in the face. He heals faster." He reached behind Marcus and unlocked his handcuffs.

"Vinci didn't take it far enough," said Marcus, examining his chafed wrists before touching the side of his head gently. It was already swollen, a rigid band of raised blood and tissue as hard as bone. "We got him all riled up and ready to pounce, and then Vinci didn't step up with the final insult. The moment was passing; I had to do *something*."

"You didn't have to push him quite that far," said Woolf. "That little speech about a Partial being a 'perfect specimen' would have gotten you punched in a nunnery."

"I didn't realize he needed further incentive," said Vinci, checking his rifle. "I'm sorry. I suppose I'm not very good at insulting humans."

"Marcus is a damned expert at it," said Woolf. He claimed the guard's sidearm, a semiautomatic pistol, and gave the combat knife to Galen. "Now let's get out of here before he wakes up."

"One thing first," said Marcus, crouching back down by the guard's feet. His head swam slightly as he did, and he paused a moment while the room stopped spinning.

"What are you doing?" asked Vinci.

Marcus began untying the guard's shoelaces. "Buying us an extra thirty seconds." He began tightly knotting the shoelaces back together, tying one shoe to the other; Galen groaned as soon as he realized what Marcus was doing.

"Oh, come on," said Galen, "it's taking you at least thirty

seconds just to do that. You're not buying us anything."

"I'm buying a happy memory," said Marcus. "I didn't like this guy even before he tried to crack my skull open." He looked at the fallen guard and grinned. "Have fun falling down idiotically twice in one day." He stood, reaching out a hand as the world swam again. Woolf grabbed him and held him firm. "Tell me about the first time he fell," said Marcus. "I missed it."

"Vinci swept his legs and then head-butted him on the way down," said Galen.

"Was it awesome?" asked Marcus. "Tell me it was awesome."

"Both of you shut up," said Woolf. "We're leaving now." He put a hand on the back door—it was locked, but the guard had held the key in his shirt pocket. The guard took the prisoners out through it at regular intervals to pee, which had given the three others their brief time alone to plan this escape. Woolf listened cautiously at the door, slid in the key, and turned it with a scrape and a rusty click. They froze, listening again for any sign that the noise had been noticed, but there was nothing.

Marcus shivered, ignoring the pain of the air brushing the skin around his wrists. "Are you sure I was only out a few minutes? I'm freezing—it feels like it's already night."

"One minute only," said Vinci. "It's late afternoon."

"But it is cold," said Woolf. He turned the creaky handle, as slowly as he could, and pulled the door open. "Holy . . ."

The parking lot outside was half-filled with cars, old and rusted, the pavement run through with seams and cracks as plants pushed up from underneath—and over it all, white and ethereal, was a gauzy curtain of falling snow.

"What on earth?" said Galen.

"Well, now we know one thing," said Marcus. "That crazy story about the big red giant was apparently true." He made a face, staring at the snow. "Actually the big red giant was easier to believe than this part. Is this really snow? I've never even seen it except on old holovid shows."

"This is the real thing," said Woolf. "Now come on." He stepped out into it, leaving a boot print in the thin layer of white that covered the ground.

"That's going to make us easy to follow," said Vinci.

"Only if they're right behind us," said Woolf. "Another few minutes and our tracks'll be completely covered. We couldn't have asked for better conditions."

"Then let's get going," said Marcus. "I want to be at least a hundred yards away when Yoon's giant panther hunts me down like an alley cat."

CHAPTER TWENTY-NINE

The Preserve sat against the base of the Rocky Mountains, on the outskirts of the Denver ruins. Before the Break, the sprawling city had become a megalopolis stretching all the way from Castle Rock to Fort Collins, from Boulder to Bennett. In the years since, it had become an acid-drenched hell, the western edge of the vast poisonous Badlands that consumed the Midwest. Every gutter and depression was filled with cracking salt pans, smoldering phosphorus, or the scattered dust of crystallized bleach. Not a single living plant or animal remained.

Samm and his group set out early in the morning on their journey back to East Meadow—back to bring the humans the cure, and the incredible news that the cure was self-sustaining. He worried about how, if at all, they would convince the humans and Partials to work together, but he supposed their group was a good demonstration: himself, Heron, Ritter, Dwain, and two more recovered Partials named Fergus and Bron; Phan had come with them as well, and Calix on one of their two horses.

The Preserve had no horses of its own, just the two that Samm and Heron and Kira had brought with them from New York. Kira had named them, and Samm allowed himself a brief, wistful moment to think of her. The other Partials looked at him, immediately aware of his thoughts through the link. He thought of the horses again, worried about their ability to find food in the Badlands. Calix was riding Bobo, Kira's horse, and following behind her on a lead was Oddjob, Afa's curious, disobedient mount, now relegated to a pack animal. He'd always hated being ridden, stubbornly going his own way and ignoring their commands, but he seemed content to follow Bobo. Samm hoped it would last.

Thinking of Oddjob made him think again of Afa, the childlike genius they'd brought with them through the wilderness, the only human on their journey out—and, not coincidentally, the only one who hadn't made it. He'd been injured in Chicago and finally died in the toxic fields of Colorado. Samm still didn't know if any human could survive the journey, and Calix was particularly at risk. Her injury made her slower and tied up her body's resources in healing; if anything happened to her it would slow down the entire group, making them all more vulnerable. Worse still . . . *I would miss her,* he thought. *Afa was my responsibility, but Calix is my friend. If it becomes a question of abandoning her or dying myself . . . I don't know if I'll be able to make that choice.*

He glanced at Heron as they walked through the corroded city. Several times during the Isolation War he'd envied her detachment, her ability to let all her pain, both physical and emotional, slide off her like she was changing clothes. She had lived through the worst that war had thrown at them, and the worst times since; she could face any problem they came up against, and could make any decision she needed to survive. Even if all of them died crossing the Badlands, she would live. She would make it home, because that was the mission. She was frightening, even to Samm sometimes, and she was hard to understand and even harder to befriend, but she was the group's best hope. He would have to talk to her in private and put together a contingency plan.

It took them three days to cross the city, and when they reached the eastern fringe, the Badlands spread out before them as far as the eye could see: flat, featureless, and dead. Here and there a bone-white tree twisted up from the poisoned soil, murdered by the rain and baked brittle by the sun. No longer forced to weave between buildings, they were able to pick up speed, and their first day east of Denver they traveled nearly as far as they had in the first three days combined. Heron took the lead, ranging far ahead to scout out the territory. Phan kept up admirably, not quite as resilient as Samm but still managing to show more endurance than the four Partials still healing from their comas. The horses were the slowest, built not for speed but for distance; they fell behind in the morning, Calix and Dwain staying with them, but then gradually caught up again as night began to fall. The group had been traveling northeast all day, following I-76 as it curved to follow the path of the South Platte River, and Samm couldn't help but notice that the night air was abnormally cold. Calix caught up to the others along the side of a foul-smelling river. She was shivering.

"We need to camp soon," said Dwain, accompanying the

statement with a silent link message: THIS HUMAN'S NOT DOING WELL.

"It's cold," said Phan. "Much colder than usual. We'll need shelter."

"We'll need shelter from more than just cold," said Heron. "If we're caught outside when it rains, we'll be dead in minutes."

"It's not going to rain," said Calix. "I've been reading these skies since I was four."

"Color me unconvinced," said Heron. "We go forward or we go back; we're not staying outside."

Now that he'd stopped walking, Samm felt the chill air creeping through his arms and chest. "Is it supposed to be this cold?"

"No," said Phan. "The last few weeks have been cooler than usual, but this is like nothing I've ever felt. Is this always like this out in the Badlands?"

"It wasn't when we came through here before," said Samm.

"The horses need to stop," said Calix. "They can't keep this pace much longer."

"We should have stopped in the last town," said Ritter. He looked at Heron sharply, his displeasure strongly evident on the link. "Too bad our scout led us into the middle of nowhere."

"This is the Midwest," said Heron. "Everywhere is the middle of nowhere. The next town is only another two miles, maybe less if we can find an outlying farmhouse."

"Keep moving," said Samm, and the group fell back into step. They kept an even pace with the horses now, tired and thirsty and rubbing their arms in the cold. The temperature seemed to plummet even further as they walked, and when they finally saw a row of low houses, they left the road eagerly, numb and exhausted. The highway was on a slight elevation, and the hill running down to the buildings was covered with dry, brittle grass that crunched like eggshells under their feet. It was an old farming community, like Heron had predicted, the fields now barren and desolate. The first house in the row was too ruined to serve as a proper shelter—a sliding glass door in the back had broken years ago, and a decade of windstorms had filled the interior with toxic dirt and dust. The next house was better, but too small to house them all. Samm left the Partials there, telling them to seal the doors and windows as well as they could, and took the horses and humans to the third house down. Heron followed him, and he sighed. She was never good with orders.

"You need to show them how to cover the gaps," said Samm. "I can show Calix and Phan."

"They're big boys," said Heron. "They can deal with it."

"So you want to deal with the horses?"

"I want to see if this godforsaken hole has anything resembling a downtown," said Heron. "We'll use almost all the water we packed just on the horses, and we need to find more."

"Take Ritter," said Samm. "We shouldn't go anywhere alone."

"I'm taking you."

Samm glanced at Calix, but she was apparently too tired to have been paying attention. Even Phan seemed ready to collapse. "I need to take care of the horses."

"So take care of them," said Heron. "Just don't take all night."

Samm linked his frustration, but said nothing and got to work. If Heron wanted to get him alone, it was almost certainly because she wanted to talk, and given how rare that was, he decided it was a good idea to know what she was thinking. He took Phan and Calix inside and set them up in the basement storage room—there was no food or water, but more important there were no exterior windows, and the surfaces were clear of toxic buildup. The horses he set up in the living room, doing his best to cover the floor with plastic tarps—not to keep them from fouling the carpet, but to keep them from eating it. He found some metal pans in the kitchen and filled them with the water they'd brought with them, then wearily unloaded their packs and saddles while they drank. It was more than half an hour later when he trudged back outside; the sky was dark and starless, and the freezing air bit at his nose and cheeks.

"This way," said Heron, hopping down from the hood of the rusted van she'd been sitting on. "There's a school about a mile down the road, with three big plastic jugs of water in the teachers' lounge."

"I told you not to go anywhere alone," said Samm, walking beside her down the road. "What if you'd gotten injured and nobody knew where you were?"

"If I get injured in an empty town a thousand miles from any possible enemy, I deserve to die."

"Well . . . we wouldn't leave without you."

"Then what's the problem?"

Samm linked his exasperation. "I assume I'm here because you wanted to talk about something."

"Interesting," said Heron. "What do I want to talk about?"

"I have no idea," said Samm. "Since you're playing coy, I'll start with the items on my own agenda. I need to know how dedicated you are to this mission."

"I'm here," said Heron simply.

"Here for how long?" asked Samm. "Here until something flips your loyalties backward again?"

"The Third Division survived for thirteen years because something in that Preserve kept them alive," said Heron. "Whatever it is—maybe Williams, maybe their life support system, maybe the microbes in the dirt that keep the plants healthy—could keep me alive as well. The secret to my survival is back there, in the Preserve, along with all the food and water and shelter I could ever need. And yet I'm here."

Samm understood. Survival was all she cared for, and for her to leave that behind was more meaningful than he'd given her credit for. "You're here," he agreed. "You wouldn't have left the Preserve if you weren't truly dedicated to something even more important." His emotions wrestled inside him, guilt and etiquette warring with the importance of his mission, until finally the latter won out. "Heron, I doubt it comes as much of a surprise to you when I say that I rarely have any idea what you're thinking and what you are trying to accomplish. But I still trust you, and most of the time that's good enough. Right now, though, I need to know what you're trying to do by accompanying us. Maybe you want to help us on our mission to save the species, or maybe you just want to get back to Dr. Morgan. Maybe you'll use us to get through the Badlands and then abandon us as soon as we're back on safe ground. Maybe you'll do something else I haven't thought of yet. But . . . this is important. The information we have might save the human species, and you might be the only one strong enough to deliver it. What I need to know is if you will."

Heron was silent a moment, and Samm sensed nothing

through the link. He marveled once again at her ability to hide her emotions so completely. Why would the espionage models even need to do that? Why give them the power to deceive their own companions, when they were designed to deceive humans? Only after she turned a corner, and they started eastward down a long, bare stretch of road, did she speak.

"Badlands is a Preserve term," said Heron.

"Excuse me?"

"We called it the toxic wasteland before," said Heron. "That's what Afa called it, and it's the most descriptive term. Badlands is the term the humans in the Preserve use, and now you use it."

"Are you saying I'm becoming one of them?" asked Samm. "Is that what's bothering you?"

"I never said anything was bothering me."

"Then why are you acting so strange?" asked Samm. "You wanted me to hurry, but you wouldn't help me with the work; you brought me out here alone, but you don't want to talk."

"We're talking."

"Does this count?"

"I don't know."

Samm's link crackled with frustration. "What is that supposed to mean?"

They walked a moment in silence, the dark clouds blotting out the moon. "You're cold," said Heron. "Let me help you stay warm." She put her arm around him.

Samm was too surprised to speak, and faltered a step as he walked. He was acutely aware of Heron's body against his, her arm around his shoulders, the side of her breast pressed softly by his arm. The cold breeze lifted her hair, black strands wafting across his face and ear. He slowed to a stop.

"What are you doing?"

She curled around in front of him, keeping one arm behind his back and encircling him with the other. She pulled him close and kissed him, her lips soft and moist, her fingers twining gently in his hair. He froze, too stunned to move, then grabbed her arms and pushed her away.

"What are you doing?" he asked again.

"It's called a kiss," said Heron. "You did it to Kira once, so I know you know what it is."

"Of course I know what it is," said Samm, his link data a jumbled mess of confusion and shock and arousal. "Why are you doing it to me?"

"I wanted to know what it felt like," she said. Her link data was as blank as ever. "Calix said you kissed her, too."

"Calix told you that?" Calix hated Heron; that was almost as unbelievable as the kiss.

"I can be very persuasive." She turned east again and started walking. "I was trained to use whatever means I could to extract information from humans—male or female. None of those techniques even work on Partials, because you never developed the ability to read the same cues."

Samm ran to catch up. "Heron, tell me what's going on." He grabbed her arm. "We've known each other for almost twenty years, and that . . ." He looked at the clouds. "I don't even know what to say."

"Your decisions are stupid," said Heron. "Our only operational goal is survival, by any means necessary, and you've had that in your hands a dozen times now just to throw it away. Your plans don't lead toward that end; your tactics don't support it. You're dying in seven months if you don't do something, and yet you're leaving behind your best chance to stay alive. Now Calix says you're in love with Kira, and that's the only thing that explains anything you're doing. They taught us in our training that love makes you stupid, that we could use that against our enemies, but you . . ." She turned to face him. "You're not even happy. You're throwing away your own life because you love someone who's not here anymore, and you hate it, and it's killing you. Love is the worst thing that ever happened to you, but you still love her."

She paused just long enough that Samm thought she was finished, and then spoke again.

"I . . . ," she began. "I wanted to see what that felt like."

Heron fell silent, but her eyes never left Samm's, and his mind swam. He didn't know how to respond or where to start, or even what he felt about Kira or Heron or anyone else.

"Kissing isn't love," he finally mumbled.

"Crossing the wasteland is?"

"Maybe," said Samm. "Heron, love isn't a weapon."

"Everything's a weapon."

"Everything can be *used* as a weapon," said Samm, "but that's not the same thing. Love is when you have the opportunity of turning someone's feelings or trust or vulnerability against them, but you don't. You make promises you don't want to keep, but you keep them because they're right; you help people who can't help you back." He turned up his palms, trying to describe something he could only barely define for himself. "You . . . call it the Badlands instead of the wasteland."

"You kill yourself," said Heron.

"You lose yourself," said Samm. "Love is when you find something so great, so . . . necessary, that it becomes more important to you than your own goals, than your own life—not because your life has no meaning without it, but because it gives your life a meaning it never had before."

"Life is its own meaning," said Heron. "We live because otherwise we die. There is no meaning in death, no hollow gestures, no glorious sacrifices. Love ruins your ability to make those decisions properly."

Samm shook his head. "Do you realize I used to envy you? I used to think how great it would be if nothing ever got to me, and I never got sad and I never lost anything I loved, and my heart never broke over any of the stupid, meaningless tragedies that have defined our entire existence. Did you know ParaGen built us to love? To empathize? They gave us emotions specifically to make us value human life, to love them. All it did was make it hurt that much more when we finally realized they didn't love us back. And you . . . you never let that or anything else ever bother you. I used to think that was something to strive for. But you've pushed your emotions so deep inside that I can't even feel them on the link. Tactical data, health data, location and combat, that's all there, but your emotions are gone. You're like a black hole, Heron, and that's not good. That's not healthy."

"The espionage models were built differently," said Heron. "You don't feel my emotions because I don't feel them either. And you're right about me—I'm a black hole. I'm a hollow shell. You think I'm being mysterious but I'm just . . . confused. I thought that maybe if I kissed you, if I felt what Kira felt, or

Calix, then maybe . . ." She turned away. "It didn't work."

Samm stood in shock, trying to process what she'd said. "Why would anyone do that?" he asked. "Why make a person, and then take away everything that makes them a person?"

Heron's link data was as empty as always. "Because it helps us survive."

CHAPTER THIRTY

Some of the Partials Kira met by the seaside were from Morgan's faction, out on patrol; by the time Jerry Ryssdal died and the first great snowflakes fell, they were all deserters like Green, too shocked by what they'd seen and felt to ever go back again. The world had changed, pivoting too far, and at too violent a velocity, to ever be the same again. Some of them fled east, trying to find old friends from other divisions who'd already joined the outlying factions. Three others joined Kira, swayed by her promise of a cure for expiration. She was open with them, and with Green, telling them that no matter how certain she was, there was still a chance that her plan wouldn't work. The leader of the squad, a soldier named Falin, simply scratched his head and looked out across the sound.

"If it doesn't work, and we die, at least we tried." He looked at Kira. "I don't know that we can expect any better than that. Not now, not ever."

"Not everyone's going to be so open-minded," said Kira.

"The humans are just as likely to resist this as the other Partials."

"The sooner the better, then," said Falin. "I'm only one batch away."

One batch away, thought Kira. *Green will die in a month, and Falin the month after.*

How much longer does Samm have? Will I ever even see him again?

They buried Ryssdal by the side of the ocean, laying him in a shallow grave and covering him with rocks. It took long enough that he was already blanketed with snow by the time they finished. Kira wondered how long the storm would last, but she didn't dare to wait any longer. The park Ryssdal had called them to sat at the head of a long, narrow bay leading out to the sound, and a quick run across a bridge brought them to a large pier crowded with boats. Many of them had long ago come loose from their moorings, and the years of waves had washed them into a massive pile on the edge of the wharf, or out into deeper water where they dotted the bay like tiny white shipwrecks. Several were still tethered tightly to the docks, but none of them looked seaworthy enough to risk sailing. They walked through the vast lot of beached boats, safely stored for an off-season that had lasted thirteen years, and cut off the tight plastic wrapping that covered them, searching for one that would suit their needs. No one in their group knew how to sail, but one of the larger yachts, sixty feet at least, was equipped with wide, black solar panels, and a console that leapt dimly to life almost as soon as the panels were uncovered.

"We're not going to have much sun to rely on," said Green, looking up at the clouds. "It's late afternoon already, and those clouds aren't going anywhere."

Falin looked in the gas tank and waved his hand in front of his nose as the foul stench rose up. "The gas is almost completely settled out—mostly resin now, probably won't even turn the motor. The solar panels will still work until nightfall, but that's probably not enough to get us across the sound."

"Let me show you a little trick I learned," said Kira with a smile, and pointed across the lot to a tall AUTO BODY sign a few blocks away. "If that place has any turpentine, we're good to go."

"Paint thinner?" asked Falin.

"What do you think gasoline resin is?" asked Kira. "Come on."

Falin glanced at Green, who only laughed. "Trust me, she knows her stuff."

The auto body shop did indeed have turpentine, and they brought it back in heavy metal cans and pushed the boat down the ramp into the water. It took them an hour to get through the press of broken and overturned boats, clambering over them and cutting them loose while the snow grew heavier and wetter. When they reached open water Kira cranked the engine up to full power, pulling from both the panels and the gas tank, and roared out into the bay.

"Stay away from the exhaust vents," she called back, "and be careful if the wind changes and starts to blow it toward us. That turpentine smoke is poisonous like you wouldn't believe."

The mouth of the bay was choked with small sandbars and islands, and they maneuvered through them carefully. By the time they reached the sound it was already night, and they were forced to rely solely on the gasoline as they thumped through the choppy water. The boat had a convertible canvas awning that raised up over the pilot's station, but the years had not been kind to it, and it cracked nearly in half when they tried to unfold it. Green found a baseball cap belowdecks and gave it to Kira to keep the snow out of her eyes while she steered, and when she needed a break she passed both controls and hat to him. They steered slightly westward as they drove, and made land in Huntington Bay sometime around midnight. The beach was wide and pebbly, and they beached the yacht carefully in case they needed to use it again, tying it to a sturdy upright log that had once been part of a dock.

The snow was getting thicker, and with the storm clouds blocking out the moon, they could barely see enough to walk. They took shelter in a massive mansion just off the water, sleeping soundly in a small bedroom with all five of them huddled together for warmth. In the morning they scoured the house for canned food, finding some garbanzo beans that hadn't gone bad yet, and shared the meager fare before trudging back outside into the snow. The world was covered with a thick, white carpet, with more still falling in a slow, steady curtain. They didn't walk far before Falin stepped on a small bump and jumped back with a curse.

"That's a body."

Kira looked up quickly, glancing around to see if there was danger she hadn't registered yet, perhaps some ambush from the storefronts, but she saw nothing. She walked to the group, clustered around the prone body, and knelt down next to it. Now that she was looking closely, she could tell it was a vaguely man-shaped outline, lying on his side in a fetal position.

"Not a Partial," said Green. "No death stamp on the link."

Kira brushed away the snow and frowned as she uncovered

more and more dark, frozen blood. Whoever it was had died violently. She wiped the snow from the dead man's face and gasped in horror.

"You know him?" asked Green.

"His name is Owen Tovar," said Kira. "He was a member of the group that rebelled against our government a couple of years ago, and then a senator after his rebellion was successful. I didn't know him well, but . . ." She shook her head. "I liked him. He was a good man."

"He's missing three fingers," said Falin, clearing away the snow from his hands. "And it looks like the kill shot was in the gut. No reason for a Partial to have done any of that."

"No reason for a human, either," said Kira.

"What I'm saying is that a Partial's more accurate," said Falin. "We would have hit him up here, in the chest or the head—"

"There's no exit wound," said Green. He was crouching on the other side, by the body's back, and Kira stepped over to look. "That looks like a gunshot in his stomach, but whatever it was didn't come out the back. I don't even know what would make a wound like this. The entry hole's too big for a knife."

"Oh no," said Kira, and tried to roll him over to see the wound; he was frozen to the ground, so she scrambled back around to examine it more fully. She felt her heart sink. "Oh no."

Kira could sense their alarm on the link; they were already fanning into defensive positions, cued by her words that something was wrong. Green crouched next to her. "What is it?"

"I've seen this kind of wound before," she said. "Once. On your squad mate I found on the dock back at Candlewood."

Green held her gaze for a second, his mind adding up the

ramifications, and he came to the same conclusion she had. "The Blood Man."

"I'm not saying it is," said Kira, standing up. "It could be a coincidence."

"Who's the Blood Man?" asked Falin.

"We don't know," said Kira. "Some kind of . . . murderer? Collector? We escaped from a group of modified Partials that seemed to take orders from him, but we never saw him. He killed a bunch of Partials and drained their blood, and the last Green heard he was headed south to do the same to humans. We don't know why."

"Modified Partials?" asked one of Falin's soldiers.

Green placed his hands on either side of his neck, and flapped them up and down. "Gills."

"There are only two good reasons to collect blood," said Falin. "One is you're crazy, and two, you need it for a transfusion or something. Maybe he's dying."

Kira shook her head. "If all he needs is a transfusion, he wouldn't hop around taking a pint or two each from a dozen different people. He's definitely collecting it, almost like he's curating it, trying to get a variety of different samples. In Candlewood he took at least one each of the three Partial models he had access to." She looked up. "I've done a lot of blood tests in my work as a medic, and experiments and all kinds of things. Maybe he needs it for that?"

"Whatever's he's doing, and for whatever reason he's doing it, we need to get out of the open," said Green. He waved them toward the sidewalk, out of the snow-covered road. "Stick to the storefronts, and keep your eyes open for trouble."

"We can't just leave him here," said Kira. "I knew this man."

"He's frozen to the street," said Green, "and we don't have time."

Kira struggled to move him again, but he was as solid as ice. When she finally managed to budge his arm, it was only by leaving a patch of torn skin frozen to the pavement below him. She winced and let go.

"I'm sorry," she whispered, touching his frozen hair. "I'll come back." She looked up, feeling a dark foreboding. "I'll try to come back."

They ran down the street, leapfrogging from one secure position to the next, and several blocks later found the rubble of a recent explosion, now soothed by a blanket of snow. "Somebody hit a Partial emplacement," said Falin, examining the debris around the site. He picked up the barrel of a Partial-issued rifle, torn and twisted by the blast. "Maybe your friend back there."

"Probably," Kira admitted. She looked down the road, past a storefront with a faded yellow duck, and another that looked like a castle. "There're tire tracks in the snow," she said, pointing. "Not fresh, but they were made since the snow began. Whoever made those tracks might have stayed to clean up and not left until after the storm started."

"Then it's time for us to make a decision," said Green. "If Kira's right, we're only a few hours behind a platoon of Partials, which looks like it's headed east; that means they're not going home, likely because they're chasing a group of human rebels. We could follow them, or we could stay on course for East Meadow and meet up with them there."

"East Meadow will be safer," said Falin. "Humans and

Partials who are actively shooting each other at the time might be a bit less receptive to our plan of reconciliation."

"The Blood Man's probably headed to East Meadow as well," said Kira. "If he's really after a wide range of human samples, that's where he's going to find them."

"Then we go," said Green. "Move out."

CHAPTER THIRTY-ONE

It had been snowing for a week. Wet mounds of it weighed down the trees, cracking the branches, and deep drifts of it piled three feet high in the streets, with no sign of stopping. *It's like something out of a fantasy novel,* Ariel thought. The world looked unfamiliar and alien. She and her group moved from house to house even slower than before, slogging barely twenty miles through bitter cold and waist-deep snow. In each new shelter they hacked up the furniture to build as big a fire as they dared, ever wary of Partial patrols, and then peeled off their cold, wet clothes and put on new ones, desperately scavenged from whatever the house had available—a grown man's pants, shoes that didn't fit, summer dresses layered until they were warm. Ariel remembered her early days with Kira and Isolde, running giddily from house to house in the post-Break wasteland, finding cute new clothes in a hundred different styles, trying on rich women's jewelry, collecting shoes of every shape and color until their closets couldn't hold them. Now she raided old men's dressers for moldering jeans, and cut them in half to use as extra sleeves to save her arms from frostbite. The few good jackets they found they gave to Isolde, and wrapped the baby in old flannel shirts and blankets. Their one heavy coat, pulled from deep storage in the back of a rest home, was rotated between all six of them, and painstakingly dried each night by the fire.

The fires were easier to build, obviously, in homes with fireplaces, but thirteen years of neglect had left the chimneys clogged and useless, and even with the windows open, the rooms would fill with smoke. They lay on the floor, where it was easier to breathe, and hoped that no one was close enough to see the smoke and come looking—Partials were the main worry, but Ariel was just as concerned about desperate humans, starving and freezing, who would see a group of women and get all kinds of thoughts. Even with the dangers, though, it was simply too cold to forgo a fire completely. They kept their guns close and ready, and always had at least one person on watch. In spite of the fact that they disliked him—or perhaps because of it—Senator Hobb always took a double watch.

The conditions, though, did nothing to deter them from their mission to find the lab Nandita spoke of, and the first week of winter brought them as far as Middle Island, a small community that was exactly what the name implied: halfway between the west end of the island and the east.

"This is good," said Isolde. Her eyes were bloodshot, rimmed with black circles, and she stroked Khan's blistered cheek as he screamed feebly. "We're halfway there, baby. You're going to be just fine."

"Halfway from Brooklyn," said Ariel. "We started in East

Meadow, so we really haven't come that far."

"Thanks for the pep talk," said Isolde, too exhausted to manage much of a glare.

"We only made it two miles today," said Xochi. The baby was slowing them down. "The farther east we go, the worse the snow is going to be; the rain was always worse farther out on the island, at least, and I imagine the snow's going to be the same."

"We won't give up," said Hobb firmly. "This is my son we're talking about."

Ariel and Xochi gave each other a look, but said nothing.

"We're almost to Riverhead," said Kessler. "Another fifteen miles or so; a week at the most."

"We've made worse time every day," said Xochi. "Who knows how long fifteen miles could take us?"

"Riverhead is the largest community outside of East Meadow," said Kessler. "The Partials relocated everyone during the occupation, but their supplies might still be available—clean water, stored grain, smokehouses full of fish. At the very least we'll find houses with good windows, working chimneys, and clean clothes."

"We're not planning to stay there," said Xochi.

"I'm just saying we'd have the option," said Kessler. "A few days to recuperate and get our feet back under us, or a few weeks to sit out this storm."

"We don't have a few weeks," said Hobb. "There is a nuclear bomb—"

"This storm will hinder Delarosa's progress just as much as ours," said Ariel. "There's no way she's going to make it to White Plains and set that thing off."

"That only makes it more likely that she'll set it off early," said Hobb. "That she'll set it off closer."

"But if the storm ever breaks—" said Kessler, but Nandita cut her off, speaking up for the first time that evening.

"This storm isn't going to break," she said. "You heard the giant as clearly as I did—this isn't a freak storm, it's the return of winter; the first great backswing of Earth's pendulum, struggling to rebalance itself. And as far as that pendulum swung in one direction, it's going to have to swing just as far in the other. This winter could last a year or more, and this storm? I shudder to think of it."

"All the more reason to push through to Riverhead," said Xochi. "Kessler's right about their supplies, and we'll need all the help we can get if we're going to make it to Plum Island."

"You could at least call me 'Erin,'" said Kessler, "since apparently 'Mother' is too much to ask for."

"If Riverhead's such a strong community, the Partials will be holding it," said Ariel. "It's the best place to set up an outpost on the eastern half of the island, especially since we did all the work for them. Our best course is to avoid it altogether."

"We'll starve," said Kessler. "We can barely feed ourselves as it is. This house didn't have a damn thing we could eat, and unless you're volunteering to go fishing—"

"We can scrounge in stores along the way," said Ariel. "We can send out pairs to forage while the others build the fire. Anything to avoid walking into a base full of Partial soldiers."

"It would be easy enough to deal with them," said Kessler. Her voice was different, and she stole a glance at Khan.

"No," said Isolde, "I do not want to have this conversation again."

"He wouldn't be at any more risk than he already is," said

Kessler. "What, you think they're going to take him somewhere in this weather? We'll show up, they'll 'take us prisoner,' which will essentially just mean they feed us and lock us somewhere warm, and then a few days later they've died of whatever Partial plague they catch from him, and we have the place to ourselves."

"And killing an entire group of people, just like that, doesn't bother you?" asked Ariel.

"They're Partials," said Kessler, "and no, you're not the same thing, so don't look at me like you're offended. No matter where you came from, you grew up human, with human morals, and you didn't lay siege to an entire species. They attacked us in the old world and they attacked us again in this one, and now they're sitting in houses we rescued, eating food we grew and caught and stored, and I'm supposed to feel sorry for them? The hell I am."

"I don't care how good your reasons are," said Isolde, "my baby is not a bomb."

"Then we use you instead," said Kessler, "or Ariel, if she's so keen to get up close and personal with them."

Ariel spread her arms wide, waving her fingertips to beckon Kessler closer. "You wanna go, bitch? Let's do this."

"Whoa, whoa, whoa," said Hobb, positioning himself between them. "How are we supposed to use Ariel or Isolde in the same way? They're Partials—you keep saying that—but they're not sick. Are they carriers?" He scooted away from Ariel almost imperceptibly.

"They're the source of the disease," said Kessler, "which is how Isolde's baby got it. It's latent inside their bodies, but Nandita has a chemical that can trigger it."

Nandita's hand went to her chest, clutching the small bag that she wore on a chain around her neck. When she saw that all eyes were on her, she looked calmly at Senator Hobb.

"The reason I gathered the three Partial girls was because I knew they might have something inside them, waiting to be unlocked. I thought it was the cure for RM, and I spent their entire childhood trying to find a way to trigger its release. That's where I went last year—I found the facilities on Plum Island and used the equipment there to finish my research." She held up the bag, staring at the small outline of a vial faintly visible in the folds of the fabric. "But the cure was never part of the genetic code for the new models, as Kira proved, and the trigger I found is for the disease." She looked up. "If we give this to Isolde, she'll start producing the pathogen in her lungs, and spread it to kill every Partial she comes in contact with."

"Does she just drink it?" asked Kessler. "Does it have to be injected?"

"Injection only," said Nandita. "The formula's too fragile to survive the digestive system."

"Why Isolde?" asked Ariel. She remembered all the lies and deceit and experimentation, an entire childhood as a secret lab rat in this woman's hands. "Why didn't you say me?"

"I thought you didn't want to do it," said Xochi.

Ariel roared at her without looking away from Nandita's face. "Of course I don't want to do it! But I want to know why she thinks I can't." She pointed at Nandita. "That wasn't an accidental omission—you know something about me."

"Your child died," said Nandita. "Khan isn't the first Partial-human hybrid, he's the first one who lived; the plague processors in Isolde's DNA made him immune to one disease, but cursed him with another. Your baby . . . simply died."

"So you don't think I have the Partial disease in my genes."

"I don't," said Nandita. "I don't know about Kira. Isolde, as far as I know, might be the only one."

"So all the experiments," said Ariel, "all the horrible things you did to us as kids, the herbs and the physical tests and the 'alternative medicines' you gave me to try to figure this all out, that was all for nothing? You treated me like a test subject when I lived with you, and a liar and a pariah when I tried to run away, and it was all for this? So I could just turn out to be completely normal, and everything you were looking for wasn't even there?"

"Negative results are still results," said Nandita. "You have more knowledge than you did before. More truth."

"Yeah," said Ariel. "The only true thing you've ever told me."

The group mostly fell quiet after that, discussing Riverhead only briefly and deciding to follow Ariel's plan of cutting north around it. There was no more mention of diseases, or of using Khan as a living weapon, and lots of murmured worry about the worsening storm. It was becoming increasingly likely that they might never make it to Plum Island at all, though no one dared to say it out loud, and Ariel wondered what would happen then. Khan would die, at the very least. Isolde would fall apart. Hobb might very well abandon them.

And I can shoot Nandita, Ariel thought. *Helping Khan is the one decent thing she's tried to do with her life, and if she can't do that? The world will be better off without her.*

Xochi took the first watch, and Ariel slept fitfully by the fire, one side too hot and the other still freezing. She dreamed of flowers, and the garden she used to keep as a child in Nandita's house. She'd been so proud of them, and when she'd moved away she'd started a new garden: daylilies and salvia and geraniums; joe-pye weeds and black-eyed Susans. All dead now under three feet of snow.

She woke in the middle of the night to find the fire burning low; Nandita was awake, taking her watch. Ariel kept her eyes slitted, faking sleep while the old woman added more scraps of the old kitchen table to the fire. Nandita stood there a moment, warming her hands, and Ariel felt a crazy, almost overwhelming compulsion to shoot her now, right here; to rid the world of her manipulations, and save the group from their useless trek to Plum Island. They'd never make it. Killing Nandita would only hasten the inevitable and give them time to escape from the island before dying of cold or the nuclear explosion. It made so much sense. Ariel reached for her pistol, mere inches from her head, so slow and so quiet the old woman would never even notice.

Nandita pulled out the bag from around her neck, staring at it in the firelight. Ariel froze. Nandita didn't move, simply looking at the bag, until at last she reached up with her other hand and opened it, tugging apart the strings that held it closed and pulling out the small glass vial. Inside was the plague trigger, dark brown and glistening in the firelight. Nandita unscrewed the rubber cap, dumped the liquid in the fire, and watched it disappear in a hiss of bubbles and steam. Ariel watched with her. Nandita re-stoppered the vial and tucked it back in the bag, and Ariel closed her eyes again before the old woman turned around and walked back to her window to keep watch.

Ariel watched the fire for the rest of the night.

CHAPTER THIRTY-TWO

Green heard it first, stopping in midstep and raising his head to listen. The other Partials stopped an instant later, warned by the link that something was happening. Kira tried to listen as well, but when the Partial soldiers all dropped to the ground in unison, taking cover and pulling up their rifles, she realized that her ears weren't nearly as finely tuned. She pulled up her own rifle, crawling to the snow toward Green.

"What happened?"

"Gunshot," said Green, and pointed down the road to a wide-open parking lot. "Two so far. Long gun, medium caliber by the sound of it. Sniper, but he missed what he was shooting at."

"How can you tell all that?"

"If it was a real gunfight, they wouldn't have been single shots, and we would have heard more than one gun." He looked at her. "And if the sniper had hit what he was aiming for, he wouldn't have had to shoot a second time."

They crept down the road toward the sound, until the

residential street gave way to a four-lane road with a massive shopping center on the other side. The closest building was a restaurant with a silhouette of a lobster on its sign; the parking lot was mostly empty. *Looks like everyone in Hicksville decided to die at home,* thought Kira. Beyond the restaurant was a strip mall, with a few of the storefronts blackened from a decades-old fire. *Well,* thought Kira, *everyone but the looters.*

"It came from over there," said Falin, pointing past the strip mall to a multistory shopping mall two parking lots away.

"That's good open ground," said Kira, "easy to defend. Someone in a top window could shoot anyone who gets too close."

"The shot came from inside," said Green. "Which means I don't know what this means."

"It means it's easier to avoid," said Falin. "Back up a block, and we go south with cover and forget it ever happened."

"I'd like to know what it is," said Green, watching the mall with sharp eyes. "But I don't need to. On the very small chance whatever it is comes after us, we're better off out there than approaching a sniper's nest."

"What if it's someone who needs our help?" asked Kira.

"If I die before expiration," said Green, "it's going to be because you said somebody needed our help."

"I know," said Kira. She scanned the parking lot, looking for anything out of the ordinary. "If you both say it's safer to turn back, we turn—" She stopped suddenly. "Wait."

"I see it too," said Green. "A body, in the snow by that stand of trees."

"We have to check it out," said Kira.

Green sat silently, deep in thought. "It should be safe," he said at last. "We can advance under cover of that restaurant without anyone in the mall seeing a thing. Jansson can cover us from here in case of an ambush." They conveyed their plan quickly and efficiently between them, the link doing most of the work, and then Green and Kira ran forward, feet kicking up thick tufts of snow. The trees and the body beside them were just beyond the cover of the restaurant—a small strip of dirt and grass that had once separated the parking lot into traffic lanes now served as home to a full line of young trees. They glanced back, got the okay from Falin, and ran forward again to sink down in the shadows of the miniature grove.

The body lay on its stomach, barely covered with snow; he had fallen recently. Kira reached for his neck to feel for a pulse and recoiled with a disgusted curse when her hand touched a cold, wet hole.

"What is it?" asked Green.

"Gills," said Kira, recovering from the shock. She rubbed her fingers compulsively, as if she was trying to physically wipe away the memory of accidentally sticking her fingers inside them.

"Interesting," said Green. "Apparently the Blood Man brought some of his toadies with him and one of them got snagged by that sniper."

"So the sniper might be inside that mall," said Kira. "Now we have to go in."

"I know," said Green, though the slight pause before he spoke showed how reluctant he was. "I told you you were going to get me killed."

"I have three more weeks," said Kira. "Give me a chance."

Green signaled to the others, and they regrouped by the

back wall of the restaurant, well out of sight of the mall. Green explained the situation and mapped out a plan to approach the mall safely. They ran slightly to the right, around a bank and through the strip mall to another residential street beyond; this gave them cars and fences and houses to hide behind, and when they reached the larger mall they were already behind it, running across a narrow loading zone to a windowless blue wall. One of the loading bays was open, and they climbed through to the darkened warehouse.

At this point their communication became entirely nonverbal, and even with her adrenaline pumping Kira had to concentrate as hard as she could not only to detect all the link data but to interpret it. Emotional cues as simple as SEE and SUPPORT seemed to have much deeper meanings, sending one Partial ahead and another to a flanking position. The team moved seamlessly through the aisles and shelves, and eventually to the mall and the storefronts beyond, and Kira simply followed Green, stopping when he stopped, hiding when he hid. The link data sounded an alarm in her nervous system, and Kira found herself raising her rifle before she even understood why, firing down a hallway as a figure she hadn't even seen dove smoothly into cover. Falin took up a firing position by the base of an escalator, and Jansson did the same in some kind of café across the hall. Green and Kira and the final soldier, a man named Colin, raced down the hall toward the fleeing shape, only to dive to the floor and scramble for cover when the entire mall seemed to explode into gunfire, bullets flying in all directions at once. Kira crawled into a clothing store, past the racks of snarky T-shirts to the sturdier wood of the counter, and covered her head with her hands. The soldiers started firing back, and Kira was deafened by the noise, until suddenly the shooting stopped and she heard a voice echoing through the halls.

"Whoa! Whoa! Everybody stop shooting . . . everybody else. This was a carefully calibrated ambush that was not intended to catch what looks like . . . an entire squad of Partial soldiers? What? What are you even doing here?"

Kira raised her head. She recognized the voice.

"Look, fellas," said the voice, "we are trying to engage in a deadly game of cat and mouse with a psychotic murderess right now, so if you'd all just keep your noses out of other people's business, we could get back to the nightmarish hellscape that our lives have become. Or you could just help us find her. Unless you're working with her, in which case I really ought to stop talking, and we can all get back to shooting each other—"

"Marcus?" Kira shouted, standing up and edging carefully into the hallway. Green and Colin were both there, in cover positions of their own, linking their confusion. "Marcus Valencio! Is that you?"

There was a long moment of silence, and then she heard him again, his voice shocked and uncertain.

"Kira?"

CHAPTER THIRTY-THREE

Kira looked up and saw Marcus on an upper balcony, leaning over with wide eyes and his jaw hanging open in abject surprise. He looked like he'd been living in the wilderness for weeks, his bronze skin flushed with sweat and adrenaline.

"Kira!"

"Marcus!"

He ran back toward the escalators, and she did the same, racing to meet him, and he clattered down them and dropped his rifle and flung his arms around her, kissing her joyously and lifting her in the air. She clung to him, laughing and weeping and kissing him back.

"I thought you were dead," he said, over and over in her ear. "When the messages stopped and the Partials stopped looking, I thought they had you." She felt his tears on her cheek. "What has it been, a year? A year and a half? How are you even alive?"

"What are you doing here?" she demanded, too happy to let

go of him. Marcus, her best friend for years, her boyfriend for some of them. Last time she'd seen him he'd been skinny and pale, a medical intern so focused on his studies he barely left the hospital, and now he was toned and lean, quick and alert, as at home in his weathered combat fatigues as he'd ever been in his scrubs. She kissed him again. "What are you doing here?"

"Quiet down," said Falin. "Didn't you say something about an ambush and a murderer?"

"Crap, yes," said Marcus, and pulled Kira down behind the escalator. "Also: murderess. Don't be sexist, women can murder people too."

Falin looked at Kira. "You want to tell us what's going on here?"

"Marcus is one of my best friends in the entire world," said Kira. "And he's here apparently . . ." She looked at him and trailed off, waiting for him to fill in the rest.

"We were trying to find Senator Delarosa," said Marcus. "I'll get to that later. While passing through here, we got jumped by two Partials: They got three of us, we got one of them, and then we managed to set up what we thought was a pretty solid trap. A better one than we'd planned, it turns out, since we only hoped to catch one Partial, not . . ." He looked at Kira. "Six."

Her heart tightened, twisting into a nervous ball. The count of six only worked if Marcus knew her secret: the murderess he'd been hunting, the four Partials Kira was traveling with, and Kira herself. She swallowed nervously. "So you know."

"Yeah." He closed his mouth tightly, looking at the floor. "I didn't know for certain until just this moment, but we had kind of put all the pieces together last year."

Kira let out a long breath and gave a dry, humorless chuckle. "I guess that saves me the trouble of finding a good way to tell you."

"Actually I would love for you to find a good way to tell me," said Marcus. "Knowing that it's true and actually understanding anything about it are two completely different things, and this . . ."

"I wish I knew what to tell you."

"How long have you known?"

"Since Morgan captured me," said Kira. "The first time, when we broke Samm out of prison and crossed over to the mainland. When you rescued me from her, I . . . didn't know how to tell you. You hated Partials—everyone did."

"He seems fine enough working with Partials now," said Falin.

"Meeting one you can work with makes all the difference," said Marcus. "He's a buddy of mine, and he's chasing Delarosa right now, which is something else we need to talk about—"

"Movement!" shouted a gruff, older voice.

Marcus looked up sharply. "Is it the other Partial?"

"Don't know who else it would be."

"That's Commander Woolf," said Marcus. He grabbed his rifle from where he'd dropped it and shouted a question to the vast, empty mall. "Are we all pretty clear on the issue of friends and enemies? I don't want anyone getting all excited and shooting the wrong person."

"A friend of Kira's is a friend of mine," called Green.

"And a friend of Marcus has my sympathies," called Woolf. "But no, I won't shoot them."

"She just went off the link," said Green. "She probably put on a gas mask."

"Damn," said Kira. "That's going to make this a lot harder." She brought up her rifle and checked the barrel, making sure it was loaded and ready and safe. "You said you had an ambush planned?"

"We have snipers on the upper floor," said Marcus softly, "bait down there and there." He pointed along the main hallway, terminating in a clothing-filled department store, and then along a perpendicular hall that led toward a food court. "She took the main hall, probably going after Woolf, since he was the bait in that one, but he's still talking, so he's obviously okay. She must have got past him when you showed up and we all started shooting each other."

"We'll help you catch her," said Kira. "We've got some questions of our own." She stood up and jogged down the hall toward the department store, keeping close to the wall with her rifle pointed down. Falin followed close behind her, and she felt the combat coordination flare back to life on the link. Marcus followed behind, running to catch up. "Are there any other exits?" she asked him.

"Two ground-floor doors, but we have people outside both of them."

"So we won't go outside," said Kira. "Let's keep this among people who've already learned not to shoot at us."

A gunshot rang out from the department store, and Falin muttered, "Tell that to her."

"Woolf's in trouble," said Marcus, and surged forward, but Kira held him back.

"This is the third exit," she said, pointing to the mouth of the department store. "If we go in there and she gets around us, she's coming straight back here. Don't let her past you."

Marcus nodded. "I'm glad we could have our tearful reunion before I crapped my pants from fear."

She grinned and slapped him on the back, and he ran to find a good watch position while Kira and the soldiers swarmed into the department store. They walked carefully, watching one another's backs, clearing each new section and display and rack of clothes before moving on to the next one. The clothes in the store were old, but relatively well preserved; some animals had been in here, and spiders had covered the shelves and corners with gauzy white webbing, but the mannequins still stood, posing proudly, ancient sunglasses perched jauntily on their featureless, yellowed heads.

"Commander Woolf?" Kira called out. "Are you still here?"

There was no answer, and Kira proceeded grimly; the man was either dead or a prisoner. The center of the department store was a tall, open area, three stories of balconies connected by a crisscrossing series of escalators. She caught a flash of movement on the third floor, somebody jostling a rack of suits, and pointed it out to Green. He relayed it silently through the link, and soon the entire group was moving—not toward the escalators, but to the staircase in the back wall.

"The escalators are a death trap," Green whispered. "They're long and straight with no cover; she could pick us all off on the first one." He turned to Jansson. "You stay here and point out any movement you see on the link—our target's got a gas mask on, so she can't listen in." He and Falin and Colin opened the door and moved quickly up the stairs, checking each corner carefully, and Kira followed, still trying to keep up with the rapid link commands. She expected them to bypass the second floor, since the movement had been on the third, but they stopped and did a sweep of that floor as well, leaving Colin to watch the stairs and make sure the shooter didn't sneak past them on the way down. They were hemming her in, slowly but surely, clearing every possible hiding place and backing her into a final, inescapable corner. They stayed away from the edges of the balconies, but they could still feel Jansson on the link, watching out for them from below.

MOVEMENT ON THE THIRD FLOOR, came the message. She was still up there.

They moved quickly back to the stairs and went up. Kira felt her trepidation grow and was grateful that she wasn't broadcasting her fear across the link. She needed to be strong. She followed Green out onto the third floor with her rifle up, crouching low to reduce her profile, watching each corner and shadow with her heart in her throat. The gilled Partial assassin could be anywhere, lying in wait for them, cornered and desperate and deadly.

Kira glanced toward the balcony railing and the wide center shaft beyond, looking for the rack of suits she'd seen earlier. *There,* she said, locating herself mentally. *That means I'm facing left of where I was before, and Jansson is over there—*

The suits moved again. She froze in surprise, just for a split second, before dropping to the floor. She wanted to call out to the others that she'd found her, but she didn't risk it; if the assassin didn't know she'd been spotted, Kira could sneak up on her. A moment ago she was glad to not be on the link, and now cursed the fact that she was unable to silently communicate what she'd seen. She waved at Green, getting his attention, and pointed at the suits. He nodded, acknowledging that they were the same suits she'd pointed out below, and she shook her head, pointing at them more firmly. He stared back, uncomprehending, and she gritted her teeth in frustration. *Right now!* she mouthed. *She's there right now!*

He stared at her a second longer, then suddenly the link flooded with understanding, and the group of soldiers began maneuvering toward the suit display, converging on the single point with brutal efficiency. Kira followed, but a new doubt was creeping into her mind: Why hadn't the shooter moved? Why stay in one place for so long? The most obvious answer was that she'd taken up a sniping position, but she didn't seem to have a good view of anything; the railing was solid, more of a low wall, so she couldn't shoot or even see through it. That led Kira to the next most obvious answer, and she shouted a warning as soon as she realized what was really going on.

"It's a trap! She's trying to draw our attention; it's a trap."

The Partials responded immediately, fanning back out, combing over the third floor even more cautiously than before, not taking a single step forward until every step behind them had been checked and secured and cleared. When they finally turned the corner to the far side of the railing, Kira looked at the rack of suits and saw an old man, his arms and legs bound tightly with plastic ties, his mouth gagged, his body lashed to the rack. Each time he moved, the suits shook.

"It's not a trap," she growled, "it's a decoy." She ran forward and pulled the gag from the man's mouth. "Where is she?"

"Escalators," the man gasped. "She crawled down the escalators."

Kira swore, out loud this time, and stood up to peer over the edge. The escalators were such an obvious death trap that they hadn't even considered them, and their only pair of eyes watching the center of the room was Jansson, far below, where a body slithering down them would be completely hidden. A sniper up here, in her position by the suit rack, would kill everyone who tried to climb them, but their sniper at the bottom hadn't seen a thing.

And then the link data wafted up: DEATH.

"Jansson's down," said Green. "She's gotten behind us."

Kira ran, screaming as she went. "Marcus! Marcus, look out!" A gun fired, and then another, bullets roaring back and forth by the entrance to the mall, and Kira clattered down the escalators as fast as she could, desperate to reach him in time. *I just found him,* she thought. *I can't lose him again, not now, not like this, I have to help him—*

The gunfire stopped, and Kira dropped to the jagged metal steps, rifle at the ready, listening. Was she too late? Was he already dead?

"Somebody better get over here," said Marcus, and Kira closed her eyes, so relieved she could barely hold her head up. "I think it's still alive."

Kira ran down the last few stairs, creeping carefully through the bullet shells strewn on the ground floor until she saw the Partial assassin lying prone on the tiles, her rifle several feet from her hand. There was blood everywhere. Her head was turned to the side, a gas mask obscuring her face, but her pale gills flapped feebly in her neck, opening and closing in a slow, silent gasp for air. Kira approached the downed monster carefully, still terrified of what she could do, half expecting her to leap up and stab her, or bite her, consuming every last bit of life she could before death dragged her screaming down to hell.

Instead the Partial reached up and pulled off her gas mask, panting for air. She was just a girl, Kira's age, but smaller. Her eyes, dull from blood loss, focused loosely on Kira, and she moved her mouth, trying to speak.

"Who are you?" asked Kira. She kept her rifle trained on the girl, stepping slowly toward her. "Who do you work for?"

"My . . ." The girl's voice was a ragged whisper, every word a struggle. "My name is Kerri."

"Who do you work for?" asked Kira again. Her rage was slowly deflating into pity, but she fought to keep it burning hot. "Why are you killing us?"

"You need . . . to be preserved." The girl moved her finger feebly, her body still flat on the ground, her head resting on the cold, bloody floor. "We don't want to . . . lose you. When the world ends."

"The world already ended," said Kira.

"It's ending again," said Kerri, and her finger stopped moving. The life disappeared from her eyes.

Blood seeped out in a widening pool, hot and red and lost forever.

CHAPTER THIRTY-FOUR

"There's definitely someone there," said Ariel, dropping back down behind a tree-lined snowbank. The snow was worse now than it had ever been, a blizzard so thick and windblown they could barely see one another at more than fifty feet. They were north of Riverhead, slogging through wide, flat farmland, and hadn't heard the noise until it was practically on top of them. "I don't know who it is, or if they've heard us as well." Ariel shook her head, checking her rifle; it was covered with snow, but it seemed like everything still worked. She wouldn't know until she tried to fire it. "We need to find better cover if this turns into a fight."

Xochi scanned the area, though there was little to see. "We passed a farmhouse a ways back, or a church or something. Looked small, wood construction."

"Not the best defense," said Isolde. Khan was strapped to her chest, and she covered him protectively with her arms. "We're on the main road—maybe they're just passing through. If we get off it, they might not notice us at all."

"And if they follow us, who knows where we'll end up?" said Kessler. "You can smell the seawater, even through the storm—too far north and we have our backs against the ocean."

"I think they're coming toward us," said Hobb, running back from his position at the front of the line. "I can take a few shots now, try and get lucky, but that's only likely to make them mad."

"We don't even know if they're aware of us," said Nandita. "I can't feel anything on the link, but who knows how the blizzard's disrupting that?" She grimaced. "North, then, away from the road. We'll take shelter in the first suitable structure we find."

They trudged across the snowy field, Ariel shielding her face with her hands just to be able to see. The world was a white void, unshaped and unmade. Slashing pellets of ice bit into her skin. Slowly the world in front of her grew darker, a patch of gray slowly coalescing to black, and then a building appeared, wraith-like in the snow. It was stone, at least three stories high, with a heavy wooden door flanked by thick stone pillars. It felt unnatural to Ariel, like a castle made real in a realm of dreams, but she ran to the door and heaved against it. It didn't open. A plaque on the door identified it as the Bluff Hollow Country Club.

"Over here," said Xochi, "through the window." They ran to the side, where a row of tattered red curtains blew fitfully through the empty windowpanes, and crawled through to the faded opulence of the clubhouse. The curtains had done little to keep the wind and weather outside; the floor was scattered with leaves and dirt, and the front edge was mounded with snow. The wooden floor was warped and discolored from long years of water damage, and the once-elegant rugs were molding and frozen.

"I think I saw them following us," said Kessler, helping Isolde through the window before tumbling in after her. "I'm not sure."

Ariel looked around the room: overstuffed chairs, embroidered couches, central fireplace, stonework bar. "Through that door," she said. "There'll be a restroom or something back there—no windows, no snow, and as soundproof a shelter as we're likely to get. We don't want Khan to give us away."

"What's our plan?" asked Isolde. Khan was fussing, but feebly. He was too sickly now even to scream, pale and skeletal, and Isolde's eyes looked equally drained.

"Don't get shot," said Xochi. "Or captured, or separated, or anything bad."

"Does besieged count as bad?" asked Hobb. "If they know we're in here, the restroom will be the worst place we can hide—we need an exit."

"The kitchen, then," said Ariel. She jogged across the room, feeling her muscles protest, and looked through the door behind the bar. "It's small, but there's a back door, and a large central counter we can duck behind if anyone starts shooting."

"If anyone starts shooting, we're dead," said Kessler. "A kitchen counter won't protect us from an armed squad of Partials." Even so, they all hurried to the back room, crowding in among the old steel bowls and copper pans. Ariel closed the door behind them and checked the door to the back; the view was as ghostly as the one they'd just walked through, and she couldn't see anything at all past forty feet.

"We can talk to them," said Nandita. "They might not be gathering refugees for East Meadow anymore—the storm could have changed that. Certainly they won't want to take us there themselves, not in this weather. We'll be reasonable, and maybe they'll leave us alone."

"Maybe," said Kessler. "I don't like any plan that relies on 'Partial mercy.'"

"They're not evil," said Xochi, "they're just the enemy."

"That's a meaningless distinction," said Kessler.

"Quiet," said Ariel. "I think they're here."

She heard voices, dim and distant over the howling wind, and listened closely. She thought maybe she could detect something on the link, but it was too weak to tell for sure—or she was simply too unpracticed. She closed her eyes instead and tried to rely on her ears.

They're coming in the window, thought Ariel, listening to the sound of scuffling feet, thumping boots, and low, muttering voices. *I could open this door right now and take them by surprise, kill two or maybe three before they know I'm here. Except . . .* Except she didn't want to. Every Partial she'd ever met had been an enemy, like Xochi had said, but for all she knew, they *were* evil. They'd never done anything to show her otherwise. They'd invaded her home, killed her friends, and hunted them like animals; they'd harried Ariel and the rest of them at every turn, and for no reason she could possibly guess. *What do they gain from attacking us? What do they want, and how does rounding us up like prisoners possibly help them to get it? They used to want Kira, but they found her, and they haven't left, they've just . . . stayed. Like robots, or trained dogs, mindlessly following their last known orders.*

I'm one of you, she thought. *I'm a Partial, but I don't want to be a robot. I don't want to be evil. Show me you can be good.*

I don't want to be alone.

"This is the worst storm yet," said one of the Partials. His voice was muffled by the door and bore the same odd passivity that marked the other Partials she'd listened to. Without the link to convey their emotions, they really did sound like robots.

"We're due to report back in an hour," said another. "With the radio down, the sergeant's going to think something's happened."

"Something has happened," said a third voice. "At least we get to wait it out in style. Who knew this place was here?"

They weren't searching for us, thought Ariel. *They were just getting out of the storm. In the middle of that blizzard, they might not even have seen our footprints.* She looked at the others, noting from their expressions that they'd heard the same thing and come to the same conclusions. *All we have to do is wait it out,* thought Ariel. *Eventually they'll leave, and if we're quiet, they'll never even know we were here.*

"Do you have anything to eat besides this crap?" asked one. "I've had enough smoked fish to last me till expiration. It's like the only thing the humans ever ate in that town."

So they're based out of Riverhead, thought Ariel. *Just like we thought. Once we get farther east, we might be—*

"Check the kitchen," said another. Ariel froze, her fingers clutching her rifle in terror. "There might be some canned . . . I don't know, what did rich humans eat out of cans? Caviar?"

She heard footsteps and took a silent step backward, training her rifle on the door. Xochi and Hobb stood beside her. *How many are there?* she thought frantically, trying to sort out how many voices she'd heard. *Three? Four? Could there have been more that hadn't spoken?*

"Caviar sounds worse than fish," said another. "Artichokes, though. I think those come in cans."

The door pushed forward half an inch. Ariel poised her finger over the trigger, ready to fire, but the door stopped moving.

"Wait a minute," said a voice. "You're going to love this."

"Nothing in the bar will still be good," said another voice. "It'll all be separated, like the gasoline."

"Not all of it," said the first voice. The door closed again. "Stashed behind the bar they've got two unopened bottles of wine, completely sealed."

"Don't taunt me."

"I'm not."

Ariel heard a clink of glass, followed by a cheer. *Definitely more than three voices,* she thought, but she couldn't tell how many.

Xochi lowered her rifle. After a long pause, Hobb did the same. Ariel stepped quietly backward to Isolde and pressed her cheek to the other girl's ear, whispering as softly as she could. "Can you keep walking?"

"If I have to."

"They won't be occupied for long," said Ariel. "We need to get out this back door before they come looking for food." She turned to the others and motioned toward the door. They crept toward it slowly, one foot at time, barely even daring to breathe.

All of them but Kessler.

The older woman stayed rooted in place, staring at the kitchen door. *Come on!* thought Ariel. She waved her over, trying to get her attention. Nandita was already by the back door, her hand poised to open it. Kessler turned toward them, finding

Isolde. Her eyes were sad, but her jaw was set and determined.

I'm sorry, she mouthed.

Ariel screamed in her head, *Don't do it!*

"Help us," said Kessler loudly. "We have a sick child, and we need medicine. Can you help us?"

"No!" screamed Isolde.

The room beyond exploded in sound, four or five or ten Partial soldiers all standing up at once, glasses falling with a crash. "Who's there? Identify yourselves!"

"We need your help," said Kessler again. "The child is dying."

"I won't let you hurt him!" howled Isolde, clutching Khan to her chest. Kessler strode toward her, whispering softly, trying to speak as Hobb held her back.

"No one will hurt him," she whispered. "They'll just see him and get sick and take it back to their outpost to infect everyone else. We may lose a few days, but we'll be safer, we won't have any more patrols to worry about, we'll be free—"

"We're coming in," shouted a Partial, right on the other side of the door. "We want to see hands in the air and weapons on the floor."

"Leave us alone!" shouted Hobb.

The door opened a few inches, though no Partials were visible. "Weapons on the floor or we come in shooting." Isolde threw her rifle down, looking at Kessler like she wanted to tear her apart with her teeth. "That's right," said the voice, "keep going. Every gun in the room goes down." Kessler dropped her rifle, then Hobb and Xochi. "Keep going, come on." Ariel was the last to surrender her rifle, and as soon as her hands were raised, Partials swarmed into the room, four that she could see with at least one more waiting in the other room. "Hands in the air," the lead Partial repeated. "Where did you come from? We've had this area cleared for weeks."

"We need help," said Kessler. "We've been trying to make it back to East Meadow to save the child." She pointed to Isolde, but the nearest Partial shoved his gun closer to her face, and she quickly raised her arm again. "It's the storm," she said. "We weren't ready, and he's gotten sick. Can you help him?"

The Partials said nothing, but Ariel could feel a faint buzz on the edge of her perception. *The link?* she wondered. *Is that what it feels like?* After a moment the lead Partial stepped forward, his rifle down, his arm outstretched toward Isolde.

"Let me see him."

"Don't you touch him," Isolde hissed.

"We're not here to hurt you. We don't have a medic, but we do have a supply of medicine. If there's something we can do for him, we will."

"Just let him see the child," said Hobb. "We don't want any trouble."

Stay back, thought Ariel, *you might not be infected yet. Just run now and—*

He stepped forward again, keeping his eyes locked on Isolde's. "I'm just going to look. Move your hands to the side, please—hands away from the child, please." Ariel realized that they might suspect a bomb, as there was really no way of knowing that the tiny bundle on Isolde's chest was really a child. She moved her hands away, her face a mass of devastated tears. The Partial reached out, touched the edge of the blanket around Khan's head, and pulled it back.

"Bioweapon!" he screamed. "Fall back, fall back!" He practically tripped over himself trying to get away from the sick, blistered baby. Isolde wrapped her arms around the child and turned away; the soldiers scrambled for the door they came through; Kessler surged forward, shouting for them to stay, that it was all right, and a terrified Partial shot her in the chest. The shot was like a signal for the world to go mad, and in a heartbeat the entire room was filled with gunfire, Partials roaring the retreat, Ariel's group diving for cover and scrambling for their weapons. Bullets and shrapnel flew through the air, bouncing off pots and pans and showering the room in dust and plaster. Ariel drew her pistol and dropped to the cover of the central counter, firing into the wall of Partials without even pausing to aim. Xochi went down, and Nandita beside her, but Ariel couldn't see if they'd been hit or were simply hiding. Isolde ran for the back door, Hobb roaring a warning and shielding her with his body. Two tufts of red flew up from his back, and he shoved the mother and child out into the storm.

CHAPTER THIRTY-FIVE

Green and the other soldiers wanted to move quickly, hoping to travel another mile before nightfall, but Kira insisted that they bury the two Ivies. She had killed several of them by now, but this one had shaken her. They took the bodies to the nearest residential street, found a pair of shovels in the shed of a small, blocky home, and spent an hour digging a hole: first through the snow, nearly three feet high and frozen into hard-packed ice, and then through the stiff, unyielding soil below. Commander Woolf said a few words, and then Green and Falin performed a Partial ritual Kira had never seen before: They fanned at the body, spreading the link data of DEATH out into the air. If there were other Partials in the area it would give away their position, but Kira didn't bring that up. It was obviously important to them.

Marcus and Woolf were traveling with a group of forty-seven refugees, including a soldier named Galen. They traveled as far as they could that night, exchanging stories along the way: Marcus and Woolf told of their excursion up to Trimble's stronghold; Kira told of her journey out west, and of her eventual revelation about the dual cure for RM and expiration. That night they camped in a high school auditorium, tearing down the tall, moth-eaten curtains to build a series of smaller tents among the old rows of chairs. The auditorium had no exterior windows or walls, which helped keep the brutal cold at bay, and the tents helped trap their body heat where it could do the most good. Kira crawled into a small tent with Marcus and Woolf to discuss their plans.

"We're only a mile outside East Meadow," said Marcus. "We just follow this same road, but . . . I can't say how long it's going to take us to get there. The snow's been slowing us down too much."

"I remember this area from some of our salvage runs," said Kira. "We're closer here to the hospital than the hospital is to the coliseum. Do we know where the Partial army is stationed?"

"All over the island," said Marcus. "That's what I was trying to tell you earlier—the army's been scattered, hunting down Tovar and Mkele and everyone else. They've been distracting the Partials, leading them away from East Meadow so the rest of us could escape."

"Escape to where?" asked Kira. "The airport? Long Beach? You can't just hide thirty-five thousand people, they'll find us again."

"We're leaving the island," said Woolf. "And we're running out of time to do it."

"We can't leave," said Kira quickly, shaking her head. "We have to stay—we have to work together, like I told you. We have to forget all our hatred and the wars and everything else—"

"Delarosa has a nuke," said Marcus.

Kira felt like she'd been kicked in the stomach. "What?"

"She's planning to set it off in White Plains," Marcus continued. "The odds are against her, and she probably won't even make it that far, but we have to plan for the worst. We've been making our way to East Meadow ever since we escaped, gathering refugees in the wilderness as we go. We have to warn them, and we have to get out."

"Even if the nuke doesn't go off," said Woolf, "it's still best to leave. Partials and humans are never going to come to a truce—minor exceptions notwithstanding. We can't live in their shadow anymore."

"We have to stay together," said Kira, feeling her whole world slipping away. "We need them—they need us—"

"But who's going to agree to it?" asked Woolf. "A few stragglers here and there, sure, but that's not enough."

"No, it's not," said Kira hotly. "We need to convince them, on both sides, that this is the only way any of us can survive. If we run away, we're just going to put ourselves right back in the same old position again, losing every new child to RM, with no future and no hope for anything."

"Kira—" said Marcus, but she spoke right over him.

"We need to stop Delarosa," said Kira. "Warn East Meadow and evacuate and whatever you need to do, but if what you say about her is true, I don't have a choice. I'm turning around and going after that nuke. We can't let anyone else die." She started to rise, but Marcus put a hand on her arm.

"Somebody's already gone after her."

She paused in midcrouch, listening tentatively.

"He's a friend of ours," Marcus continued. "A Partial soldier named Vinci. Delarosa's got a two-week lead on you, but only a few days on him. For all we know he's already stopped her, but we can't take the chance of not warning everyone, just in case."

Kira shook her head, fighting back tears. "But what if he doesn't make it?"

"You wouldn't even know where to start looking," said Marcus. "You want to work together with the Partials? Then trust Vinci. Help us warn East Meadow—humans and Partials."

"We can't help the humans escape the occupation by telling the occupiers where we're going," said Woolf.

"This is a really terrible time to even bring that up," said Marcus, shooting him a hard glance. He looked back at Kira, who was trying her best not to scream. She breathed carefully, forcing herself to be calm. *This is just another obstacle,* she told herself. *I've overcome others, I can overcome this one.*

"This is always the hardest part," she said.

Marcus raised his eyebrow. "Evacuating the entire human population of Earth from a nuclear fallout zone?"

Kira gave a sad smile. "Accepting that I can't fix everything."

She curled up in her bedroll apart from the others and tried to sleep. They needed to rise early in the morning and get to East Meadow quickly. The Partials had to listen to reason. She'd seen too many groups like Green's and Falin's, lost and directionless as Morgan withdrew ever deeper into her obsession. They were occupying the island because they didn't know what else to do—surely she could convince them of her plan?

I need to save everyone, she thought. *I can't live with anything less. I won't leave anyone behind.*

Anyone else.

She fell asleep and dreamed of Samm.

In the morning Kira rose early, roused Green and Marcus, and set out for East Meadow. Newbridge Road was wide and straight, lined with trees and stores and crumbling houses. The center strip, which had once been grass, was now bursting up with bushes and saplings, lumpy and white with mounds of snow. The storm had stopped in the night, letting them see farther than they had in days, and the sun was blinding as it reflected off the fierce white sheet. A small breeze blew whorls of loose powder across the surface of the drifts, white ghosts on a white field. The crust was brittle, and they sank to their thighs with each freezing step.

One mile took them nearly an hour.

The closer they came to East Meadow, the more Kira felt her nerves wearing thinner, her teeth more on edge. The city was familiar—the only home she could remember—but it was intensely unfamiliar at the same time, eerily empty and buried in a death shroud of snow. When they reached the turnpike and turned west, they could see the hospital rising high above the rest of the city, the tallest building for miles, but where it was once the hub of a bustling community, it stood now pale and lifeless, the street leading up to it as silent as a tomb. Kira had lived her life among the abandoned detritus of a lost civilization—homes and buildings and cars full of skeletons; wearing dead girls' clothes and living in dead men's houses; watched by a thousand lifeless eyes from the family photos of the ones who hadn't made it. It had never bothered her because it couldn't—because it was the only world she'd ever known. The old world was gone, and they were building a new one in its ashes. Now she saw her world as theirs, her own life become a lifeless ruin. It made her feel numb, even more so than the cold and the snow and the tiny trickles of ice sliding down her frost-hardened face.

A nurse sat in the hospital lobby, alone in the cavernous silence. She looked up with a stunned expression, as shocked to see them as they were to see her, and after a moment Kira recognized her from her old days as an intern.

"Sandy?"

The woman smiled, polite but confused. Kira pulled off the long strip of blanket she'd been using as a scarf, and Sandy's eyes went wide. "Kira Walker?"

Kira smiled back, feeling suddenly self-conscious. "Hi." This city had gone through hell for her, daily executions trying to draw her out. For all she knew Sandy may have lost a loved one because of her. Kira watched her stand up and step toward her, hesitantly at first, but after a moment she was running, wrapping Kira in a tearful hug without regard for the wet slush that coated her chest and legs.

Kira hugged her back. "Where is everybody?"

"Running," said Sandy, "or getting ready to. Haru sent word that the Partials are planning a final attack, to get rid of us for good." Her face was pale with fear. "They're going to wipe us out."

"It's not the Partials," said Green darkly.

Kira furrowed her brow, thinking. "Where's Haru?"

"We haven't seen him," said Sandy, "but we've seen refugees who have. The message reached us a few weeks before the snow, and we've been sneaking people out when we can. Now there are barely any Partials left in East Meadow, just for show more than anything, and we can leave more freely."

"They've gone to fight rebels?" asked Kira.

Sandy shook her head. "They're leaving, so they can bomb the whole city and wipe us out."

"They wouldn't do that," said Kira, and got ready to explain about Delarosa and the bomb, but then decided against it. *As long as everyone is scared enough to leave,* Kira thought. "But Haru's right, we are all in danger. What about you? Why haven't you left?"

"There are still injured people in the city," said Sandy. "Someone has to stay behind to take care of them. Nurse Hardy is here, too."

"And Skousen?" asked Marcus.

Sandy shook her head. "The Partials took him weeks ago, when the bioweapon first surfaced." She noticed the confusion on their faces and frowned. "You haven't heard? There's a plague that kills Partials—their own version of RM. I guess someone's finally giving them a taste of their own . . . nonmedicine. That's the other reason their army left town; nobody wanted to stay here after Partials started falling ill."

Kira wondered how Skousen or anyone else could have engineered a Partial plague so quickly, but that was the least of her worries. Wherever the plague came from, it was one more obstacle that would convince the Partials and humans they could never dare to trust one another. She clenched her fist, as if she was trying to hold on to her hope like a tangible object. "You need to get out now," said Kira. "It was very brave of you to stay behind, but it's time to leave; the Partials will be leaving too, so there won't be any new patients to deal with. Get everyone dressed, gather all the food and medicine you can, and get out."

Sandy shook her head. "Two of our patients can't even walk."

"Then we'll pull them in rickshaws," said Kira. "I'll pull one myself. The threat is real, and we don't have long—just go."

Sandy hesitated a moment, then nodded and ran down the hall. She only got a few steps before a deep rumbling sound rippled through the air; Kira felt it first in her gut, shaking her ribs, then throbbing in her ears like a low, steady beat. She looked at Sandy, who looked back and shook her head; she didn't know what it was either.

"It's a rotor," said Marcus. "A flying vehicle, like an airplane with vertical takeoff. We saw them in White Plains." He looked at Sandy. "You didn't recognize the noise?"

"We've never seen anything fly before," said Sandy. "This is new."

The door to the stairwell flew open and Nurse Hardy burst out in a frenzy, wheezing for breath and gripping the door frame for support. "They're on the roof," she gasped. "They've come for the patients. Is that . . . Kira Walker?"

Kira took a step toward her, raising her rifle in preparation. "Partials?" Hardy snapped out of her shock and nodded, still out of breath, and Kira stepped forward again. "Where are they taking them?"

"They're not taking them anywhere," said Hardy. She staggered out into the lobby, and Kira could see now that she was bleeding from her arm. "They're going room to room, killing them." She clutched her arm and tried to breathe. "They're taking their blood."

Kira looked at Green and snarled. "The Blood Man."

"It's about damn time," said Green, raising his rifle and stalking toward the staircase. "I've been anxious for a little chat with him."

Kira followed him up the stairs, with Marcus close behind, not stopping on each floor like they had in the mall, but climbing relentlessly. They heard a scream high above them, silenced almost instantly by a gunshot and a slamming door. "Sounded like the eighth floor," said Kira.

"Morgan's army confiscated most of the solar panels when they first arrived," said Marcus. "They moved the patients up here because it made the few panels left just a little more efficient; all the power in the lower levels is cut off completely."

"Can you link them yet?" Kira asked Green.

"No. As soon as I do, though, they'll know we're here."

"They won't know who, though," said Kira. "You could be any Partial; they won't know you're an enemy."

"They'll know I'm not an Ivie," said Green, "which seems to be the only distinction that matters to them." He clenched his teeth and snarled, then stopped suddenly on the landing between floors five and six. "You go first."

"Whoa," said Marcus. "Who sends the lady into combat first?"

"A smart combatant," said Kira, not even slowing as she brushed past Green. "I can read the Ivies on the link a bit, and they can't read me. It'll give us maybe an extra ten seconds before they know we're there, but that's better than nothing."

As they neared the seventh floor she started to sense them—just a few, maybe three or four at the most. She remembered the victims she'd found so far, the Partial on the dock and the ice-cold Tovar, and she felt her blood rising. She remembered the dying girl Kerri, crying as her life slipped away. *We're trying to save you,* she'd said, and Kira still couldn't get it out of her mind. *Save us from what? From who?* She shook her head, clearing her doubts like cobwebs. The Ivies, and the Blood Man they served, were evil. She would put them down.

Eighth floor. She could feel the Ivies clearly on the link; her practice was paying off, and she fell into her combat mode like slipping on an old glove. Green was waiting below, holding his breath, giving her time to make her ambush. Marcus crouched beside her at the top of the stairs, his rifle ready in his hands. Kira closed her eyes and concentrated, trying to feel the presence of the Ivies, to pinpoint their locations as accurately as she could.

THIS ONE SAVED MOVING ON

HURRY NOT MUCH TIME

Behind their data was something else, larger and more powerful, like the vague outline of a whale swimming just beyond her perception in the deep of the sea. *The Blood Man,* she thought. It was the same kind of intense link data she'd sensed from members of the Trust, which only confused her more. *What are you?* she thought.

The hallway beyond was clear, the Ivies all working in different rooms, and she pushed open the door without a sound. She kept her rifle tight to her cheek and shoulder, the sights lined up to kill whoever appeared first. She sidestepped to a corner, taking what little cover she could, and when the first Ivie walked into her kill zone she fired a burst straight into its chest, dropping it in a heartbeat. A jar of blood fell from its lifeless hand and shattered on the floor. The alarm shot across the link: DEATH ATTACK

PREPARE CAUTION. Another head appeared just out of her view, but Marcus was already firing as she tracked her rifle toward it, and the shape ducked back behind a doorway. Green raced up the stairs to join them, and she felt a ripple of recognition on the link as the Ivies sensed him, followed by confusion as they realized they were being attacked by both humans and Partials.

The deeper presence moved, a dark shape in the back of her mind, and she tracked her rifle back again to find it. *Just step into view*, she thought, daring him to come forward. *Just give me one chance and I'll end this horror show once and for all.*

"You must understand that this is not a personal attack," said a voice, and Kira felt her heart plummet, the ground dropping away beneath it, her entire world becoming a bottomless black pit. "We are trying to save this world, so that it can be a part of the next one. Think of it as an honor, that your body and blood will provide the seeds for a new Eden." He walked into view at the end of the hall and Kira's rifle dropped from her cheek, fell from her hands, clattered to the ground as she stared at the Blood Man, walking toward her through the bright fluorescent lights.

"Kira?" said Marcus. Green raised his rifle to fire, but all Kira could do was put up her hand and shake her head.

Kira felt her legs trembling, her stomach wrenching, her arms longing to reach out and touch him even as her mind howled at her to run, to stop him, to kill him, to scream. She gripped the wall for support and stared at the face that haunted her dreams, and spoke the word she hadn't said since she was five years old.

"Daddy?"

CHAPTER THIRTY-SIX

Armin Dhurvasula stared back at Kira, his dark eyes flickering, considering her. She could feel his emotions on the link, wonder and uncertainty and a fierce determination, so strong it left her gasping. Her father took a step forward, as if trying to see her better, and a broad, almost childlike smile spread across his face.

"Kira!" he shouted. He ran toward her, wiping his hands on a towel. "Kira, you're alive!"

Green raised his rifle to fire, but Armin froze him in place with a surge of link data so powerful Kira felt her own knees buckle. Marcus grabbed her arm, holding her up, and when Armin drew close she gripped Marcus tightly.

"Don't touch me," she hissed at her father.

"Kira," said Armin. "You can't know how happy I am to see you. I thought for sure you'd died in the Break—obviously you were immune to RM, but when I finally made it home again, you were gone."

"I was . . . alone for weeks."

"It was a chaotic time," said Armin. "But you're here now, and we can do so much together—"

"What are you doing?" she demanded. "You're the Blood Man? You're the one leaving dismembered bodies all over the . . . everywhere? How could you do this?"

"I'm saving them," he said simply. "The world's ending—you thought it ended in the Break, but that was just the gunshot; the last thirteen years have been a long, slow bleeding, twitching in an illusion of life, preparing for this moment—this true death. The Partials will die in a few months, and the humans not long after. Jerry's impossible winter will only hasten the inevitable. How long do you really think we have?"

"So just because we're dying means it's all right to murder everyone?" asked Kira. "Like we're some kind of . . . sociopathic playground now? What's wrong with you?"

"I do not enjoy what I'm doing," said Armin. "Don't think me heartless for accepting the inevitable—no more than an oncologist is being cruel when he tells a cancer patient that he only has a month to live. That doctor isn't a monster, he's simply doing his job. The difference here is that I can do something no oncologist has ever been able to do; no doctor, no politician, no holy man. I can save them, Kira."

"By killing them?"

"By harvesting the best of them—their strength, their will, their creativity. All of it encoded in their DNA." He held up a jar of blood and tissue, then peered into her eyes. "Kira, what do you think is going to happen when the world ends?"

"We survived it once," she said. "We can survive again."

"We can't." He shook his head. "We had a plan for the world, you know. I still believe it would have worked. I designed that biology myself, and it was flawless. But it's all gone now. It was human nature that made it impossible, human and Partial."

"So I was right," said Kira. She looked at Green and Marcus, then back at her father. "I solved the puzzle; I discovered the process you engineered: the secrets buried in RM and expiration and the Partial DNA. I knew there was a plan, and that the plan was for peace, because I knew you." Her eyes darkened, and she stared at the jar in his hands in horror. "At least I thought I did."

"That dream is gone now."

"How can you say that?" she asked. "You were determined to care for the life you'd created; you fought for Partial rights before the Partials even existed. You knew they were destined to be a second-class species, not even accepted as people, and you devised the entire plan to ensure that Partials and humans had to see each other as equals if they wanted to survive. You tried to eliminate racism on a biological level, for all time." She gestured to the jar of tissue, to his gloved hands red with drying blood, to the Ivies behind him standing silent in the doorways of murdered patients. "How did you go from that to this? How could you ever convince yourself that this was the only way?"

Armin's face grew more serious, and he repeated his question in a somber tone. "Do you know what's going to happen when the world ends? We call it the end of the world, but it's only the end of us. The world will go on, the planet and the life that lives on it. Rivers will keep flowing, the sun and the moon will keep turning, vines will creep up across the cars and the concrete. There will come soft rain. The world will forget that we were ever here. Human thought—the glorious zenith of five billion years of evolution—will go out like a candle, gone forever. Not because it was time, not because the world moved past us, but because we, as a people, were fools. Too selfish to live in peace, and too proud to stop our wars long after they ceased to have any real meaning. Your precious human souls, your Partial brothers and sisters, all of whom you seem to think can live together in peace, are out there right now tearing this island to shreds, fighting and killing and dying not because they see a way out, not because they have a cure or a clue or a solution to any of their problems, but because that's what they do. The only thing left of any value on this entire planet is their lives, but that's not worth anything while the other guy still has his, so they kill each other. They are in a desperate race toward the final death. The winner will be the last one standing, and his prize is the final and most terrible solitude this world has ever known."

Kira wanted to protest, but her eyes fell to the body of the Ivie she'd shot, barely thirty feet away, its blood spreading thickly across the floor. She thought of the people she'd killed to get here, the bodies in her wake. A collapsed apartment building in New York City. The Manhattan Bridge. Afa Demoux. Delarosa and her nuke. Kira's own bloody hands, as red as her father's, stabbing a dagger into the skull of a dead Partial soldier.

"These people are already dead," said Armin. "Leaving them alive is no mercy, for they'll only be killed by someone else, and yet I can't abandon them. I've played my part in their destruction, don't think I've forgotten that. Don't think I've forgiven myself. But Jerry has set the stage for a new beginning. And when the snows melt and the sun returns and the world erupts in young green leaves, I will make sure that someone's there to see it. I will make sure there are eyes to behold it, and minds to understand it, and voices to carry on our story. You are breaking yourself in pieces to give a dying man a few more seconds of life. I'm going to take that man's blood and build a child and a future and a legacy that will last for another five billion years. To cover the Earth and reach out into the stars and fill the universe with poetry and laughter and art. To write new books and sing new songs."

Kira felt unable to look away from the Ivie's body and everything it represented. Too much blood. Too much loss. "You're going to build a new species."

"Human and Partial will be no more," said Armin. "There will only be one species, one perfect species. I've done it before. I've unlocked the human genome and arranged it in perfect order, like notes in a symphony. I've honed the genetic template for the human form through dozens of generations of Partial technology, and you know that better than anyone. Because you're the final result."

Kira looked up, meeting his eyes, and he smiled.

"You," he said, "my daughter, built on the model of my own DNA, polished and refined through countless drafts until I had eliminated all trace of flaw or imperfection. I had hoped some of the late-model Partials had survived, for they would be the ideal starting point for this new world, the first brushstroke on our new, blank canvas."

"Okay," said Marcus, stepping forward to place himself between Armin and Kira. "This whole conversation has been freaking me out, but that last sentence took it down a whole other path."

"You want my DNA too," said Kira. "My blood in a jar to take back to your lab."

"I want you," said Armin. "Your body and your mind."

"I won't go with you."

"You don't have a choice."

"There's always a choice," said Kira. "I learned that from someone who was more of a parent to me than you could ever be." She drew herself up as tall as she could. "If you want my blood, you're going to have to take it."

Armin sighed, and the energy in his face fell away like dead skin, leaving nothing behind but a dull, emotionless stare. "You've heard what I'm planning," he said softly. "You understand that there is no other way."

He pulled a small metal tube from a sheath on his belt, like a rounded trowel, sharpened on one end. The precise size and shape to puncture a human body and sluice out all the blood and tissue within. "None of us is more important than this. Not even my own daughter."

CHAPTER THIRTY-SEVEN

Dr. Cronus Vale used the link to clear a path through the crowded White Plains street, ignoring the stunned glances of the Partials he passed. His age alone marked him as an anomaly, for there were no Partials left who looked older than eighteen. The doctor and officer models were all part of early batches, long since expired, and his link data marked him as a god, a powerful being their biology had no choice but to obey. There were no guards at the door of his hotel, just as there were no housekeepers inside. The soldiers took turns cleaning it, infantrymen alternating with the women of the piloting corps, giving the building an austere, military feel. Everything in White Plains felt that way. Vale missed the country paradise of the Preserve, but there was no way to get back there now. He could commandeer a rotor, he supposed, but what then? Fly there in the deepening cold and worsening storm? Bring another group of Partials along and hope they would understand what he was trying to do? Rely on Morgan to not come out looking for him again? Vale wanted to see the Preserve once more, the friends that he'd made there, but more than that he wanted to keep the Preserve safe. If the only way to do that was to stay away, he'd stay away.

Especially now that there was a nuke on the loose. The stakes had been raised, and the few Partials who knew about it were clamoring to take the fight to the humans. They were already terrified by the thought of the bioweapon—Vale had left Dr. Morgan's lab partly just to keep the army under control, halting every new plan for retaliation. If he told them the humans were on the way with a nuclear device in tow, he didn't know if he'd be able to hold them back.

A Partial soldier named Vinci was waiting in the lobby; he was the one who'd warned Vale about the nuke. He'd been chasing Delarosa all the way from Long Island, but when he'd lost the canny human terrorist in Manhattan, he'd come straight to White Plains to recruit more people to the search. He watched Vale with somber eyes. "Any news?"

Vale shook his head. "Not here. We'll talk in my room." He led him up the elevator to a suite on the top floor, which Vale had converted to a command post. When the door was closed and locked, he turned to Vinci with a solemn look. "We've canvassed the Bronx with regular patrols, and put as many spotters as we can on the coast in case she tries to cross by water, but they haven't turned up anything yet. It was smart of you to come straight to us, but we have to consider the possibility that Delarosa already crossed to the mainland before we established our patrols."

"I put the men you gave me on regular routes in and around the city," said Vinci, acknowledging the possibility that Delarosa was already on their doorstep. "I just don't know if it will be enough."

"What else can we do?" asked Vale. "Everyone left in White Plains is assigned to energy, maintenance, or food production; we can spare them, but do we really want word of this to spread? It's a nuclear attack, for crying out loud—the last time someone tried to nuke the Partial army, they struck back with the biggest display of overkill in the entire Partial War. I don't want to cause a panic or a pogrom."

"All they need to know is that they're looking for a human matching her description," said Vinci. "We don't have to tell them what she's doing."

"They'll figure it out soon enough," said Vale. "They're not idiots."

"Their first assumption will be the East Meadow bioweapon," said Vinci. "The patrols I organized this morning already think that's what they're looking for, though obviously I didn't confirm or deny it."

"Congratulations," said Vale, "your cunning ruse has struck me speechless. Did you also tell them not to share their suspicions with anybody else? Do you have any faith that they'll actually follow that order? All it takes is one drunk soldier in a bar tonight, telling his mates about the paranoid snipe hunt he's been assigned to by the former AWOL traitor now serving under a member of the Trust, and the suspicions will fly and the rumors will grow and who knows what we'll have in the morning? Not three months ago this city tore itself apart in an involuntary change of leadership, because Trimble was too paralyzed by indecision to confront any of the problems her people were facing. Now Morgan's doing the same thing, too obsessed with expiration to bother with anything else, and the city's getting restless. A panic like this—nuke or bioweapon or anything similar—and we'll have a riot on our hands."

"A few Partials dead in a riot is still better than an entire city disintegrated in a mushroom cloud," said Vinci. "If it takes a public announcement and a citywide search, then that's what we do."

"Another batch dies in two weeks, give or take," said Vale. "Another fifty thousand people gone, not in the blink of an eye but in a debilitating, agonizing process. Fifty thousand death signatures saturating the air in this city until you can barely breathe without losing your mind to depression or madness. Do you know what that's going to do to the army here? Do you know who they're going to blame?"

"You?" asked Vinci.

Vale frowned. "They should, but they won't—even if the Trust's role in their expiration was common knowledge, killing me wouldn't be enough. Their problems have always had their root in humanity: the war, the poverty, the oppression, the Last Fleet. Even expiration—Morgan and I pushed the buttons, but it was the human species as a whole who asked for it, who planned it, who paid for it. Now the humans have a bioweapon? They have a nuke? Tell me you believe for one minute that the Partials won't retaliate with lethal force, falling on that island with everything they have and more. Even with two-thirds of your species dead, you outnumber them ten to one. You have rotors, you have ATVs, you even have a few tanks left—enough for an armored brigade, at least. The humans have survived this long only at your mercy, and that mercy will be gone if word of the nuke gets out. I want to find that nuke as much as you do, but we need to keep it secret."

Vale closed his eyes, exhausted and frustrated. There was a squawk from the radio.

"Arrow Team to General Vale," said the voice. "Code White, repeat, Code White."

"Code White," said Vale, his eyes snapping open. "They've found her."

"And Arrow's one of mine," said Vinci, a slow wave of fear spreading out across the link. "That means she's in the city."

"Damn." Vale climbed to his feet and crossed to the radio. "This is General Vale. This line is not secure, repeat, this line is not secure. We will come to you. State your location. Over."

"Unsecure line acknowledged," said Arrow Team. "Checkpoint Seven. Over."

Vinci spread a map across the table and scanned it quickly. "Here," he said, pointing to the western edge of the city. "It's an old college."

"Barely a mile from downtown," said Vale. "If she sets it off there, it'll kill every Partial in White Plains."

"Then we'd better make sure she doesn't."

Vinci frowned, then pressed the radio button to speak. "Checkpoint Seven: We'll see you in a few minutes. Over and out."

Vale had a small Jeep, fully electrical. The Partials maintained a nuclear power plant that supplied more than enough power—enough that Morgan had siphoned it for years while in exile, powering her secret laboratory. The drive to the old college was short, and when they arrived they found the place swarming with soldiers, far more than a single recon team could account for. Vale swore and climbed out of the Jeep.

"Report," he said firmly, and the link carried the full weight of his authority. The sergeant in charge was talking almost before she turned to face him.

"Sergeant Audra, sir." She saluted. "We found the human insurgent approximately twenty minutes ago. She attempted to activate her cargo when she saw us, and we were forced to incapacitate her."

"You shot her?" asked Vinci.

"She's wounded but alive," said Audra. "Our medic expired last year, but we've done our best to stabilize her."

Vale nodded; the medics had been among the first to be produced, due to their more advanced training requirements, and thus had been some of the first to die. He looked pointedly at the swarm of soldiers, feeling their nervous energy crackle across the link; they were scared. "Why the crowd?"

"Don't worry, sir, they all have clearance. We're all teams Commander Vinci organized." She hesitated, and Vale felt another burst of nervous fear. "When we realized what her cargo was, sir, we thought it was wise to bring in extra security."

Vale ground his teeth in frustration; the other recon teams did, technically, have clearance, but he'd have preferred if the team that found her were the only team to know what she'd been carrying. "Take me to see it."

The sergeant led Vale and Vinci into the main college building, where several soldiers in tech uniforms were milling around just as nervously as the scouts outside. "We've been using this facility for weeks," said Audra, "trying to get the satellite feeds up and working again. That's how we found her—she was farther north, trying to sneak in through a residential neighborhood, but her movement showed up on a scan from the satellites, and we brought her here, like I said, for security. We think she probably came up the river and managed to bypass our patrols."

"I used to lead a security checkpoint in Tarrytown," said Vinci. "Was nobody there?"

"I understand that checkpoint's been vacant since you abandoned it and joined the humans," said the sergeant, adding a strictly formal "Sir."

Vinci's irritation steamed across the link, but Vale steered the conversation in another direction before it could escalate. "What do you mean that you found her by satellite?" he asked. "We haven't had satellite uplinks working since the Break."

"Not until a few weeks ago," said the sergeant, and Vale could sense her pride. "General Trimble had several feeds she used to monitor the faction wars, but her control room was . . . irreversibly damaged in the civil war. This college had a new computer science department, upgraded right before the Break. Our techs have been working on it for a while, and last week we were finally able to tap into Trimble's old feeds."

"You didn't think that was something you ought to report?" asked Vinci.

"We've reported it to Morgan three times," said the sergeant. "She never got back to us. We're lucky we had the satellites, though, since Delarosa was easy to spot against the snow. Here they are."

She led them into a heavily guarded room. Marisol Delarosa, whom Vale recognized from the files he had found on her, lay on one side of it, bleeding heavily from her shoulder, with two soldiers leaning over her trying to clean and bandage the wound. In the center of the room sat a small nylon bike trailer, the kind people would use to pull their children behind their bicycles before the Break. Barely two feet across, painted a dull white, it carried a fat metal canister that had gotten an identical paint job. From some scratches on the side Vale could tell it had once been painted green, to better hide it in the forest, and he imagined she must have hurriedly repainted it when Ryssdal's insane winter storms started up. It was smaller than he'd expected, and while he marveled that she'd gotten so far, he couldn't deny that such a disguise would have made them phenomenally hard to spot. With as much trouble as the human resistance was making right now, a lone woman with a small package like this could hide in the wilderness almost indefinitely.

Until she came here, thought Vale, *and tried to kill eighty percent of the people on the planet.*

He felt himself sweating. *She'd been trying to activate it when they found her. Another minute and we'd have all been dead.*

"Is it really what we think it is?" asked Audra. "A nuclear warhead?"

Vale could hide his feelings from the link and lie if he wanted, but Vinci's data would give it away. *And they already know anyway. They've examined it, identified it, and neutralized the threat. They've done their jobs, and I can't lie to them now.* "It is."

"Damn bloody humans," said the sergeant. "Nothing's ever enough for them, is it? First the bioweapon, and now this." She gestured violently at Delarosa. "If this witch got this far without us seeing her, how do we know there's not more of them out there? What are we supposed to do?"

One of the newly appointed medics piped up from the side of the room; his name tag said Ether, and Vale couldn't help but be amused by the juxtaposition. "I'll tell you what we do," said Ether. "We take that nuke straight back and turn East Meadow into a parking lot."

Vale's amusement vanished.

Delarosa, bound and bandaged and muzzled by an oxygen tube, made a move to attack Ether, but the other medic held her down.

"No one's going to blow up anything," said Vinci, and Audra's fury burned across the link.

"We don't need a human-lover in here telling us what to do," she snapped. "After everything they've done to us, you're taking *their* side in this?"

"I'm taking any side that's not genocidal," said Vinci. "Everything that has gone wrong since the moment we came back from China has been because of one species trying to get the upper hand on the other. We're not going down that road again."

"It's going to give us some breathing room," said Audra. "It's going to give Dr. Morgan time to finish her work, maybe save some of us from expiration."

"And what if the cure was coexistence?" asked Vale. He looked around the room, holding each Partial's gaze before moving to the next one—the sergeant, the medics, the guards. "What if I told you that we could cure expiration right now, just by breathing the same air as that human in the corner." Delarosa looked at him in disbelief, and the link told him that the Partials were just as incredulous.

"That's impossible," said Vinci.

"Humor me," said Vale, but there was no humor in his voice. He looked at Vinci intently, pleading with him, and his sincerity was palpable on the link. "Pretend, for a moment, that she, and every human carrying the RM virus, is the cure for expiration. That they produce a chemical agent in their breath, the same as you do for them."

Ether answered first, hesitantly. "We'd . . . have to find a way to synthesize it and . . . make a pill or something."

Just like the humans tried to do, thought Vale. *Just what I did.* He shook his head. "You can't synthesize it. It's a two-part biological reaction: You breathe out a particle that renders RM inert in the humans, and then their body alters it and breathes it back out, curing you of expiration. You have to have both species in close proximity, and you have to have living bodies in which the reactions can take place."

"They'd kill us first," said Audra.

"Not all of them," said Vinci.

"It only takes one," said Audra. "This one smuggled a nuclear bomb right under our noses—one lone woman—and we stopped her with seconds to spare. How is the existence of one or two or even a thousand friendly humans supposed balance that out?"

"We might be able to harvest it," said Ether. "We could keep them in a controlled environment—a prison camp, or a smaller island where we can watch them more closely—and then send a few people in every morning to collect the healing particles. Then we could distribute it through the army like an inoculation."

339

Delarosa's face was livid.

Now they're re-creating my own failed plans, thought Vale. "Suppose that doesn't work," he said. "Suppose it takes"—he reversed the numbers from the Preserve—"ten humans for every two thousand Partials. One human for two hundred. If we implement this now, today, before losing any more soldiers to expiration, we'd need what, one thousand of them? Fifteen hundred? How do you support that many humans?"

"They could support themselves," said Audra. "We'd make it a . . . like a labor camp."

"And the Partials that live with them?" asked Vale. "As I said, they need to be in close proximity to Partials in order to produce the particle. Would those Partials live in the labor camp too?"

"They'd need guards anyway," said Audra. "We could take shifts."

"And what about the other thirty thousand humans?" asked Vale, feeling increasingly repelled by the entire conversation. "What do we do with the ones we don't need? Do we put them in labor camps as well, or just kill them outright?"

"Fifteen hundred is already large for a sustainable prison population," said Ether. "If we want to keep them from attacking us, or escaping and making the whole thing moot, we have to limit the population as much as we—"

"Listen to yourselves!" shouted Vale. His felt his heart pounding, his blood pressure rising even with a host of gene mods to keep it in check. "They're not animals! They created you!"

"And they tried to destroy us," said Audra. "This prison camp idea isn't all that different from what we've done all along, keeping them isolated to Long Island. But keeping them alive was a mistake. Do you know what else we've seen on the satellite? They're massing in the south—a giant human army, armed to the teeth, gathering for a final push."

"Gathering in the south?" asked Vale. "As far away from us as possible?"

"They're getting out of the blast radius," said Audra. "What else could it be? They retreat to the South Shore, send her to trigger the bomb, and then come around Manhattan and up the river to clean up any survivors."

"That's a military plan," said Vale. "They're not an army! That's what you'd do, but not—" But even as he said it, he realized he was caught in a loop of flawed logic generated by racist suspicion, one he could never hope to talk his way out of. "Just . . . get out, all of you."

"But—" Vinci protested, but Vale sent a surge of linked authority, and the Partials started filing obediently through the door.

"I'm going to talk to the prisoner," said Vale. "Keep the door closed and locked, and resume your patrols, all of you. You are not to mention any of this to anyone."

The door closed, and Vale locked it, then wearily walked to the corner where Delarosa lay red-faced and helpless. He pulled an office chair toward her and flopped down in it heavily, making no attempt at ceremony or formality. *I'm too tired,* he thought, then he said it out loud. "I'm too tired."

The woman remained still, watching him with dark, serious eyes.

"You must just be burning up right now," he said. "Aren't you? Caught in a trap by the very people you were looking to kill. And I suppose that includes me. I'm not a Partial, but I'm just as guilty as any of them for what has happened to this god-forsaken planet. No, guiltier." She saw the surprise in her eyes, and nodded. "I'm a member of the Trust, though I don't suppose you know what that is?"

She paused a moment, then shook her head. Vale let out a long breath.

"Not many humans do." He looked at the nuke, mud-spattered and scratched by a hundred thousand rocks and roots and whatever else it had passed through to get there. It was a simple metal cylinder, battered and dingy and absolutely terrifying. "The finger of God," he said softly. He leaned over to grab the wheeled cart and pulled it closer. The end screwed off, and he found the inner electronics jury-rigged with a series of yellowed plastic light switches, probably scavenged from an old abandoned home. "You're old," he said idly, then shot her a quick glance. "Not old, of course, I'd never be so rude to a lady like yourself. But you're old enough to remember the old world. The things we left behind. You remember how in all the movies and the holovids, everyone always had big red timers on their nuclear bombs? It looked like someone had stuck a digital alarm clock on there, though I suppose that's still more high-tech than these things." He gestured to the switches, their wires exposed, but he didn't dare touch them. "The bad guy sets the bomb, or the good guy sets it accidentally, and then everybody watches as it counts down: fifty-nine, fifty-eight, fifty-seven. Tick, tick, tick. None of that for you, though." He looked at her again. "No timer, no 'run like hell' period where you try to get to safety. You were just going to flip these switches and blow up right along with us." He screwed the lid back on, then looked at Delarosa, lying bleeding on the floor. He leaned forward and pulled off her oxygen mask. "I figure it's not much of an interrogation if you can't even talk."

Delarosa watched him, saying nothing. Vale said nothing back. After a moment she spoke, and Vale heard the pain in her voice.

"This is still not much of an interrogation."

"The things I want to know you don't have any answers for."

She adjusted her shoulder slightly, wincing. "Such as?"

"Such as why everybody in this entire world hates everybody else. Why I can't get four people to agree to a peaceful resolution even when I lead them by the hand ninety-five percent of the way."

"I don't hate you," said Delarosa. "You or them. Not personally."

"But you still want to blow us all to hell."

"This is going to end in war," said Delarosa. "Everyone in the world is dying, and there's no hope left, and the nerves are too raw. Look back at what's happened and tell me which part we could have avoided."

"You could have not brought a nuke into the middle of an army," said Vale. "You think your island got invaded? Just wait until word of this gets out."

"You heard them talking just now," said Delarosa. "This warhead is an excuse. You said it yourself—they're an army, bred for battle; the humans are just as desperate. War is inevitable."

"So you wanted to end it before it could start."

"It seems like the only moral option."

"'Moral,'" said Vale. "That's an interesting adjective to apply to 'genocide.'"

"Destroy White Plains and the Partial population drops to whatever's on Long Island," said Delarosa. "We'll be back on even footing again, give or take. The Partial leadership will be dead, and the ones left will stop waiting for orders that are never going to come. Maybe they'll make a treaty with the humans, I don't know, but even if they attack, the humans will be able to fight back. They'll have the courage to fight back. They'll have a chance."

Vale nodded, thinking, staring at the bomb. "The situation I spoke of earlier wasn't just smoke," he said softly. "It's real. Kira Walker discovered the biological mechanisms, and since then I've had the chance to study it out, to dig down into the science of it, and it's real. It could save everyone."

"Do you think anyone will go along with it?"

"I thought so," Vale said, closing his eyes. "A long time ago. But then the Break happened and . . . No, I don't. I told Kira that if Dr. Morgan found out about the cure for expiration, she'd enslave the entire human population. It took four soldiers less than three minutes to propose two different versions of that worst-case scenario." He tapped the bomb, listening to the metallic clang. "I had to choose once before, you know. Humans or Partials. I chose to save a group of humans, and enslaved ten Partials to do it. It was the only way." He sighed. "What else can I do?"

Delarosa furrowed her brow. "What are you saying?"

Vale took the cap off the warhead and looked at the jury-rigged switches. "I'm saying that I still think the end of all this is a choice between the species."

"Are you serious?"

Vale flipped a switch. "There's a combination, I assume?"

Delarosa took a deep breath, her voice almost reverent. "Yes." She hesitated. "Okay. On, off, on, off. Right to left."

Vale raised his eyebrow. "That's the secret password?"

"It kept it from going off accidentally," said Delarosa. "Beyond that, the simpler the better. I figured if I made it easy enough, even if you caught me someone might trigger it accidentally."

Vale looked at the switches, flipping the first three in turn. "On, off, on." He looked up. "Any last words?"

"My shoulder hurts," said Delarosa. There was steel in her voice. "Get it over with."

Vale closed his eyes, speaking not to her but to the entire world. "I'm sorry."

Off.

PART 3

CHAPTER THIRTY-EIGHT

The hospital shook, and Kira stumbled. "What was that?"

The noise continued, a distant rumble, deep in the bones of the earth.

Green raised his rifle at Armin, and one of the Ivies saw the move, perhaps even anticipated it, raising his own rifle at Green. Armin leapt through a side door and out of sight. The entire exchange was so fast Kira barely even registered it.

"Holy—" Marcus spluttered, but that was all Kira heard before Green fired a long, loud burst into the hallway, scattering the Ivies, and pulled him and Kira back into the stairwell. The Ivies took cover and returned fire, but the three companions were already diving down the first flight of stairs, throwing themselves to the floor. Bullets riddled the door above them, tearing through the wood in a furious hail of splinters and shredding the drywall on either side, only to ping and ricochet off the thick concrete steps. At the first break in the shooting Green fired back, and urged the other two farther down the stairs. The rumble they had felt hadn't gone away; instead it was gathering in intensity.

"We can't leave," Kira shouted. "That's my father!"

"Your father wants to kill you," said Green.

"I have to talk to him," Kira insisted, trying to get back up. "I have to stop him."

Green threw her back down, shouting to get through to her. "We've lost the advantage up there—they have the numbers, they have the high ground, and they have cover. Put your head above those stairs and they will shoot it off."

"But they have a rotor on the roof," Kira snarled, trying to wrench free of him. "They're not trying to occupy the floor, they're trying to get away!"

Another storm of bullets ripped through the air, and the three crouched down, covering their heads. Marcus crawled to Kira's side and shouted in her ear, barely audible above the gunfire.

"There're stairs at the other end of the hall!"

Kira nodded, and they crawled down out of the line of fire. "Each floor is a long T shape," Kira explained to Green. "We're on one branch of the T, but there's another staircase on the end of the other branch, where we can get up behind them."

"You don't think they're watching it?"

"I think they'll take their blood and run," said Kira. "I intend to stop them before that happens." They reached the seventh floor and burst out into the hallway, running at full speed. Green dropped to the floor, holding the door open behind him and raising his rifle like a sniper—but instead of looking behind him, he was looking forward to the far end of the hall. Kira didn't stop to question; if the Ivies linked him at that staircase they might not think to look for anyone at the other. She pulled out her handgun as she sprinted, cursing herself for dropping her rifle, praying she could get to the stairs and behind the Ivies before Armin had a chance to escape. Marcus puffed behind her, struggling to keep up. She poured on the speed, ready to slam into the door and race up the stairs, when suddenly it opened on its own and an Ivie peeked out into the hall, assault rifle up and ready. Kira panicked, ready to throw herself to the side, when a loud crack split the air and the Ivie went down, a red hole blossoming between his eyes.

"Go!" Green shouted, and Kira didn't even slow down, thanking him silently as she pelted up the stairs. She heard boots above her, and then the roar of a vicious windstorm; Armin and his soldiers were already fleeing to the roof.

"We don't know where they all are," said Marcus, holding her arm to stop her. "If there are still some on the eighth floor, and we go up past them to the roof, we'll be surrounded."

Kira concentrated on the link. "You're right," she said, pointing. "A big group up top, and a smaller group still down here."

"That's so weird," said Marcus. "You can . . . feel them?" The look on his face wasn't shocked or horrified, but it broke Kira's heart just the same: For the first time in his life, he was looking at her as a stranger, someone he could only barely understand. She tried to ignore her sudden emotional vertigo and whispered her strategy.

"I can't feel much detail," she said. "Not like they can. I can't tell how many there are, or pinpoint their locations. I figure there are one or two left on this floor, and a few more than that on the roof." The wind was howling wildly outside, as if a storm had risen up out of nowhere, and it had dragged their phero-monal data away and left her blind. "You stay here and watch that door like your life depends on it, because it does. Shoot at it the instant it moves—don't wait for a clear shot, just fire."

"You're not going up there alone."

"I'm not letting him get away," said Kira. She racked her gun and ran up the next flight of stairs, steeling herself for . . . she didn't know what. *Four or five Ivies with assault rifles,* she thought, and clenched her teeth as she thought of Green's words. *They have numbers and high ground, and who knows what kind of armaments on that rotor. I have a stupid handgun and . . . well, better cover than they do, probably. But what am I going to do? Kill the soldiers? Shoot my father?* She remembered her father's fevered rant about a world tearing itself apart with violence; the Ivie she'd shot was still bleeding on the hospital floor.

What else can I do?

She reached the roof access door and put her hands on it gin-gerly, just barely pushing it so she could peek out, but something was holding it closed. She shoved harder and it gave, only to slam closed again. *The wind,* she thought. *What's going on out there? And what was that rumble we felt?* Marcus screamed below her, opening fire; she prayed he would be safe, and shoved against the door with everything she had. It flew open with a bang and she stumbled out, whipped by a raging windstorm that slammed the door shut behind her, and through her flying hair she saw the rotor lift off, a dull-gray jet with a belly like a cargo bus, and two massive fans in the place of wings. Her father stood in the open door, watching her wordlessly, and then the rotors tilted and slammed her back into the door. She ran forward as soon as the pressure released, shouting into the gale-force wind for him to stop, to come back. The rotor flew south, and she watched it shrink to a dot in the slate-gray sky. With its engines gone the fierce wind grew bone-chillingly cold, and she shivered as she watched him disappear.

"You okay?" asked Marcus. She hadn't even heard him come up behind her. She nodded. His voice was a mixture of awe and terror. "What happened?"

"I didn't make it in time," she said softly. "They were already in the rotor when I—"

"Not that," said Marcus, and took her by the shoulder. "That." He turned her around, facing north toward the mainland, and she gasped. Out across the fields and forests, beyond the low hills of the island's northern face, the sky was red and roiling, burning like a low flame. A massive mushroom cloud dominated the horizon, miles wide and towering into the atmosphere.

Green joined them on the roof, his link data so black with despair that even Kira could feel it. It made her sick. His voice was soft and ghostly. "White Plains is gone."

CHAPTER THIRTY-NINE

Mohammad Khan died at 8:34 p.m., in a small house on the North Shore. The disease had brought him to the brink of death; add the pressure the winter conditions had put on his body, and it was simply too much for a weeks-old baby to handle. Isolde was in the basement, holding him and crying, completely inconsolable. Ariel stood by the back windows, overlooking a steep, rocky bluff above the sound, and looked west to the mainland. To the mushroom cloud.

The Partials were gone.

They were her enemy, but they were also her people. The only real, biological link she had in the world, behind all the lies and deceptions, and she'd never even known them. There were still Partials on the island, of course, though she figured the group that had killed Senator Kessler was gone now. *Dead of the same plague that killed Khan,* she thought, but the thought gave her no joy, no vindictive triumph at the parity of their deaths. *Nobody needed to die in that building, and yet six people did, and three more were wounded, and now Khan's gone and White Plains is gone and . . . everything's gone.* Xochi had taken a bullet in the hip, and another in her hand; Hobb had taken two in his back, which Nandita said had pierced his lung and liver. As poorly as Hobb was doing, Ariel wondered if Isolde might be the next to die. She was physically unharmed, but her soul was destroyed.

Nandita herself had been clipped in the shoulder, the lightest of the wounds, but her gene mods had accelerated her healing so dramatically that the hole was already starting to close.

Ariel played with the gun in her hands, flicking the safety on and off. On and off.

Even if we could travel, we don't have anywhere to go. That child was the entire purpose of our journey—protecting him, getting him to safety, curing his disease. He gave us a direction and a reason to hope. A reason to stay together. Now that he's gone, what do we do next?

On and off. On and off.

Ariel knew exactly what to do next; she'd been planning it since the day Khan was born. *Help Nandita save him, and then . . .*

She turned and walked downstairs.

It was warmer down there, the windows blocked with old clothes and couch cushions, and a broken nightstand burning slowly on the bare cement floor of the laundry room. The house was barely half a mile from the country club, but still farther than Xochi or Hobb could have traveled on their own. Ariel had dragged them here, sliding them over the snow on a makeshift sled while the Partials, terrified of the infant bioweapon, had fled just as quickly in the other direction. For all Ariel knew, they'd gotten back to Riverhead before they died, and given the disease to everyone else. She looked at Hobb, bandaged like a ragged mummy and sedated on the floor, still completely unaware that his son was dead. He'd risked his life to save the child, which Ariel had never expected. She crept past him, past Xochi, past the wailing form of Isolde, to the last room in the narrow hallway. Nandita was sitting in the dark.

"The mushroom cloud is gone," said Ariel. "No sign of anyone chasing us."

"I imagine they're somewhat preoccupied," said Nandita. "Under the circumstances."

Ariel sat across from her. Nandita had to see the gun in her hand, in silhouette at the very least, but she said nothing about it.

On. Off.

"You think Hobb's going to last the night?"

"I don't know," said Nandita.

"I can't help but think it'll be easier for him if he dies," said Ariel. "He sacrificed himself to save his son, and now he has to wake up and hear that his sacrifice didn't mean anything."

"His child did not survive," said Nandita. "That doesn't mean his sacrifice didn't mean anything."

The fire spit and crackled behind them.

On. Off.

Ariel wanted to shoot her now, to raise her hand and fire, but she didn't. She wanted to rage and scream and yell and make this woman pay for the hell she'd put her through—for the hand she'd had in this entire, world-ending calamity. She didn't do that either. She watched the orange lights from the fire dancing weakly on the wall, just out of reach of the room's dark shadow. "I saw what you did with the chemical trigger," said Ariel at last.

"The night you dumped it in the fire, after Erin Kessler said she wanted to use it."

"I didn't want her to try anything stupid," said Nandita.

"Looks like we didn't do enough to stop her," said Ariel.

"Looks like."

On. Off.

"Why did you do it?" asked Ariel.

"Create the Partials?" asked Nandita. "End the world? Destroy your childhood? My list of crimes is long, child. I'm afraid you'll have to be more specific."

"Why did you let them shoot us?" asked Ariel. She gripped her gun more tightly, though she still hadn't pointed it anywhere but the floor. "You can control Partial soldiers with a thought—you could have stopped that gunfight before a single shot was fired. And yet you didn't."

"I . . ." Nandita stopped, a motionless form in the darkness. "I guess I decided that if I couldn't stop Erin, I shouldn't be able to stop the Partials."

"You didn't *want* to control them?"

"I did not."

Ariel felt her voice rising. "You'd rather let them kill us all?"

"It was an inconvenient time for a moral revelation," said Nandita. "You don't have to tell me. But these things happen; I was ready to do it, and then I wasn't. The moment happened, and then it was past."

"So you think you made the right choice, then? That letting people get shot in the name of your moral revelation was worth it?"

"We didn't get killed."

"You had no way of knowing we wouldn't."

"I believe," said Nandita, "that that is precisely the point."

On. Off.

"I came down here to kill you," said Ariel.

"I know."

"I was always going to do it," said Ariel. "That was the whole reason I came. You were the only one who could save Khan, and so I was going to wait until you had done that, and as soon as you did, blam." She gestured with the gun. "No more lying, no more schemes, no more control. I figured the world would be better off."

"I can hardly disagree with you."

"Now here I am, and all I want to do is kill you, and . . ." She paused, waiting for Nandita to speak, but the woman said nothing. "You're not the person I thought you were."

"I can say the same about you," said Nandita.

"Who did you think I was?"

"I thought you were a child," said Nandita. She shook her head. "I was mistaken."

Ariel stood up, pointed the gun at Nandita's head . . .

. . . and stood there.

"Khan deserved to live," said Ariel. "Maybe Hobb does, too. Or maybe he, and you, and all those Partials in that explosion, all deserved to die. I don't know. Now here we are, and I'm the one with the control, with the power, with the ability to let you live or die with a thought. If I'm going to have any inconvenient moral revelations, now would be the time."

She lowered the gun and turned away. "I'm going to go look for water."

CHAPTER FORTY

Shon seethed, staring at the map until his vision turned red, and he slammed his fist into the table. It cracked under the force of the blow, and he collapsed to the floor of the middle-school gym he had made his base camp. Human rebels still swarmed through the forest, hiding and sniping and slipping away, killing his soldiers and attacking their supplies and leading them ever farther to the east: always north and east. Away from the mainland and away from East Meadow, and now White Plains was gone and East Meadow was emptying like a sieve. In hindsight it was obvious—the humans' actions were a powerful deception precisely *because* they weren't successful. Victory after victory, prisoner after prisoner, they had swept across the island and mopped up the guerrillas and played straight into their hands like fools. The ruse had worked, and the human civilians were getting away.

The sheer coldheartedness of it enraged him. War was war, but he had tried to conduct it honorably. He had stopped

Morgan's executions as soon as Morgan's orders stopped coming. He had gathered the humans but he hadn't hurt them; he'd tried to quell their uprisings peacefully when he could, and he'd worked to bring East Meadow food and water. They had repaid him with a vicious bioweapon, a campaign of terrorism, and now a nuclear explosion that had undoubtedly wiped most of the Partial species off the planet. His friends, his leaders . . . he had felt abandoned before, with no new orders for weeks, but now he was completely cut off. He would never receive new orders; he would never receive another message on the radio; he would never rejoin the rest of his army because it did not exist. He had twenty thousand Partials under his command, and there would never be reinforcements because they were the last living Partials in the world.

In ten more days the next batch would expire, and they would be down to seventeen thousand. A month later they'd lose six thousand more.

He was done being honorable.

A messenger walked toward him but kept his distance, probably because of the shattered table and the angry link data still boiling through the air around his head. He took a breath to calm himself before speaking.

"Report."

"One of the prisoners is talking," said the messenger. "Apparently the rebels have been spreading word of the nuke, telling people to flee south before it went off."

"And we never discovered this?"

"You had given explicit orders not to torture anyone," said the messenger. "Now that we are, they're . . . We're learning a lot."

"Who was behind it?"

"A resistance group called the White Rhinos," said the messenger. "They've been in operation since just after the occupation of East Meadow began."

"I know who they are," said Shon. "They've been notoriously hard to catch—do we have any in custody?"

"Just one, sir."

"Lead the way." He left his aides to pick up the broken table, pausing only to grab his sidearm from the rack by the door. The prisoners were kept in a pair of basement restrooms, chained to the pipes of molding sinks and dank, broken toilets. Shon nodded to the guards standing alert in the hall outside and marveled at the fierce, almost desperate anger that seemed to permeate the entire camp. As soon as they had a target for their vengeance, they would fall like a thunderbolt.

They opened the door, and Shon reeled back slightly at the smell. The messenger led him to a short, skinny girl in the back corner, who showed signs of having been interrogated.

"This is the White Rhino?"

The messenger nodded. Shon crouched down in front of the battered girl, showing her the gun. "What's your name?"

"Yoon-Ji Bak."

"And you worked with the rebel Marisol Delarosa?"

The girl's face was hard, steely and determined even through the blood and grime. "Proudly."

"Where are the rest of the humans you have been attempting to evacuate?"

The girl said nothing.

"Tell me where they're gathering, and I'll make your death quick."

The girl said nothing.

Shon raised his voice, trying to emulate as much of the sound of human anger as he could. "Where are they?"

"Shoot me," said Yoon.

Shon looked at her a moment, then handed the gun to the messenger behind him. He clamped Yoon's left wrist tightly in one hand and grabbed her little finger with his other. "You are a terrorist, a murderer, and a war criminal," he said. "That broken nose is the nicest treatment you'll get here, unless you start telling me what I want to know. I'm going to find all of you bastards, and I'm going to do what I should have done months ago—years ago. What is the rendezvous point for the human evacuation?"

"I don't know."

Shon snapped her finger backward, breaking it with an audible crack. The girl screamed, and he grabbed the next finger in line. "Let's try again. Where are the humans going?"

She screamed again, gritting her teeth against the pain. "We're getting everyone off the island."

"Be more specific, please. Where and how?"

"You'll have to kill me," she gasped.

He snapped another finger, and moved his hand to the third. "Eight more chances before I start to get creative. Where exactly can I find them?"

She was grunting now, tears streaming down her face, clenching her other fist into a tight white ball against the pain. "I don't know!"

Snap.

"Seven," said Shon. "Where?"

CHAPTER FORTY-ONE

The snow started again soon after the explosion, and Kira could only hope that the weather would diminish the spread of the fallout. Green said the windstorm was a side effect of the bomb, brought on as the fires in White Plains sucked in air like the eye of a tornado. They waited in the hospital for Falin and the others, and Kira led them all to Nandita's house, hoping to find some trace of her sisters. The wind slashed the falling snow into their faces, stinging their cheeks and eyes as they hiked through the city. When they arrived at the home it was empty.

"Sandy said that Haru was here in East Meadow," said Marcus. "If he knew about the nuke, he would have gone straight to Madison, and she wouldn't have left without Ariel and Isolde. They're probably . . . south, I guess. That's where everyone's going. They wouldn't dare try to evacuate through Manhattan, with all the bridges all booby-trapped, so I'm guessing boats."

"Do you have that many boats?" asked Green. "Thirty-five thousand people is a lot to move over water."

"We have fishing villages all along the southern beaches," said Kira. She closed her eyes as she spoke, collapsing on the old living room couch, battered and broken. She tried to remember the last time she hadn't been running, either from or to something. Even the effort of searching through her memory made her tired.

"The fishermen have some boats, but not many," said Marcus. "Still, they're better than nothing. I think Nandita has an old atlas in here somewhere. . . ." He searched the bookshelves and pulled out a thick hardback, thumping it down on the coffee table and flipping through it to find a map of Long Island. "Most of the island's protein comes from fish, caught either here, by Riverhead, or here, in the Great South Bay. There are a few smaller communities out here as well, on Jones Beach. The Riverhead boats are out of reach, but there's a pretty sizable fleet of sailboats in the bay, and while it would probably take several trips, they could start ferrying people to the mainland . . . here, I guess." He pointed to the Jersey shore. "If they follow the coast past Long Beach and Rockaway, they can cut across to New Jersey pretty easily, without ever getting out into the high seas and deep water."

"So if we want to meet up," asked Falin, "do we go to Jones Beach or look for the boats in the bay?"

"If I was trying to coordinate this I'd send everybody due south," said Marcus, looking at the map, "to get as far from the blast as possible, then west as far as they can go. If the boats are just shuttling back and forth here, between Breezy Point and Sandy Hook, they can evacuate the island a lot more quickly." He looked at Green. "Which is a long way of saying that we have a better chance of finding them if we stick to the beaches."

"Unless the fishermen haven't been able to get their boats out of the bay," said Falin. "What if the Partials are holding them? They might need our help."

Marcus leaned back on the couch, shaking his head. "Obviously you have never had the pleasure of meeting a post-Break fisherman. Where do you go if you're so traumatized by the end of the world that you can never trust civilization again? Some of them live in the woods, hunting deer and wild cats and whatever else, but most of them became fishermen: They're independent, they're mobile, and if they don't want to trade with our farms, they can ignore the rest of the world completely. That's where Kira's sister Ariel went when she left this place—straight out to Islip on the fringe of a fishing commune. I'd bet you no more than a handful of those fishing communities were ever rounded up by the Partials during the occupation at all. They could sail out to Fire Island or hide in Oyster Bay, and pretty much avoid the invasion the same way they avoided our society for the last decade."

"Then who's to say they're going to help at all?" asked Green. "Even if the other humans found the fishing communities, how do we know they agreed to let those humans use the fishing boats?"

"Oh, they definitely found each other," said Marcus. "Some of these causeways are miles long—we used to travel on them a lot when we did salvage runs—and when a fisherman sees a few thousand people crossing over he's going to get curious, and when he finds out what's going on, word will spread fast. I suppose it's possible some of them won't help, but I'd bet you dollars to doughnuts most of them will. They won't want to stay on an irradiated island any more than the rest of us, and when they leave, they're more likely to take us with them than not. They're not evil, just . . . antisocial."

Green nodded. "So what do we do?"

"We follow the other refugees," said Marcus. "South on the causeways, then west on the beaches. We take as many of the final refugees as we can—we empty East Meadow completely— and then we follow the route the others took until we manage to catch up to them."

Green asked another question, but Kira wasn't listening anymore. Marcus's analysis of the island was solid, and his plans were sound, but . . . how much of it really mattered anymore? Even if they could flee, what were they fleeing to? What hope did humans alone have for survival? They had Green and Falin and a few others, but four Partials, or even forty, couldn't save thirty thousand humans. Who even knew how many Partials were left? And surely any chance at reconciliation was consumed in the nuclear blast.

Kira stood up and walked into the kitchen, smelling the herbs that reminded her so much of home. Nandita had gone missing two years ago, and after all that had happened Kira knew she'd never see the old woman again, but this kitchen, and these herbs, brought back a flood of fond memories. Xochi had kept up the garden after Nandita left, and the ceiling was hung with sprigs of dried rosemary, sheaves of brittle brown basil and bay leaves, fragrant bunches of chamomile. Kira stared at the mess—they had obviously left in a hurry when they fled the city—and after a long moment she opened a cupboard, pulled down the blackened metal teapot, and went to the sink to fill it up. The faucet dribbled for a second and went dry; apparently the cold had been too much for their aging water system, and the pipes had finally frozen and burst. She thought about using the pump in the backyard, but eventually just opened the side door and scooped a hefty chunk of snow into the teapot. Xochi had left a pile of split logs stacked neatly by the wood-burning stove, and Kira built her fire carefully inside the cast-iron monster. Her hands moved almost by themselves, remembering the years past, night after night, doing the same thing under Nandita's watchful eye. Sometimes Madison's. The specks of snow that had landed on the outside of the teapot melted quickly as the stove warmed up, and then hissed into steam as it grew even hotter.

"Thirsty?" asked Marcus. He was standing in the doorway from the living room, watching her with tired eyes.

"No," said Kira blankly. "I just needed something to do."

Marcus nodded and walked to the counter, staring at the array of herbs. "Let's see. Mint, chamomile, lemongrass, rose hips, ginger—what sounds good?"

"Whatever." Kira put another stick in the fire, keeping the heat even. It didn't really matter, since she was only boiling water, but it was something she was good at. The fire was something she could control. She felt the heat with her hand and watched the pot.

Marcus fiddled with the herbs a bit, pulling out three of the chipped porcelain mugs and a metal mesh ball for each. He sniffed them, making sure they were clean, and dropped a few leaves into each ball as he spoke. "So that was your father."

"Yep." Kira didn't know how to feel about Armin, and so

refused to feel anything. She tested the heat again, trying to gauge the perfect temperature for the tea.

"I saw a picture of him once," said Marcus. "Heron showed it to me."

Kira looked up at this. "Heron?"

"You remember that Partial assassin who captured you when we went north with Samm? She showed up here one night last year, out of the blue. Showed me a picture of you as a little girl, standing between Nandita and that guy from the hospital. Armin . . . Walker, I guess?"

"Dhurvasula," said Kira, looking back at the stove. "I couldn't remember my last name when the soldiers found me after the Break, so they gave me one. I might be Kira Dhurvasula, I don't know. I don't know if he legally adopted me or what."

"If you were an experiment, you might not legally ex—" He stopped. "Never mind." Marcus finished with the last mesh ball and dropped one into each mug. "Is the water close?"

"Yeah," said Kira. The teapot had already started to give short, feeble whistles, gearing up for a full boil. They watched in silence, and when it piped loudly she took it off the stove and poured a steaming stream into each thin mug. The aroma of the tea rose up in a cloud, calming her, and she breathed deep. Chamomile.

"Is he going to come after you?" asked Marcus.

It was a question Kira hadn't allowed herself to think about yet, but now that it was out in the air there was no avoiding it. "Probably."

"He said you were a new model," said Marcus. "Some kind of ultimate refinement of the Partial design. If he's collecting . . .

artisanal DNA, or whatever, he's going to want yours."

"I used to wonder what I was for," said Kira. She looked up at him, meeting his eyes for the first time that evening. His face was a warm bronze, almost glowing in the firelight, and his eyes were as black as the clouded, starless sky. "When I found out I was a Partial, I thought that they must have built me for some grand purpose. Something evil, maybe, like I was a bomb carrying a new strain of RM, or a spy just waiting to be activated. I hoped, though, that just maybe I was the key to saving us all, the cure for everything or a hybrid model, or something that could bring the two species together." She smiled, but it felt sour and forced, the kind of smile that led almost instantly to tears. "Turns out I'm useless, at least as far as saving the world goes." She wiped her eye. "I don't carry the cure for RM, and while I don't think I expire, I can't do much to keep other Partials from doing so. Now Armin wants me for my DNA, and I can't help but wonder if that's all I'm good for. I used to wonder if I was really going to live through this, but now I can't help but think that maybe . . . I shouldn't."

"Don't say that."

"I thought I was made for something terrible," said Kira, "and then I thought I was made for something great, and now it turns out I wasn't made for anything. I'm just . . . here."

"You mean like everybody else?" asked Marcus. His eyes were kind, almost smiling, but Kira looked away.

"It's not like that," she said.

"It's exactly like that," said Marcus. "Nobody has a . . . destiny. I mean, nobody has some kind of inescapable path for their life. This mug was made from clay, and that clay could have

369

been anything at all until somebody made it into a mug. People aren't mugs, we're clay. Living, breathing, thinking, feeling clay, and we can shape ourselves into anything we want, and we keep shaping ourselves all our lives, getting better and better at whatever we want to be, and when we want to be something else we just smooth out the clay and start over. Your lack of 'purpose' is the single best thing about you, because it means you can be whatever you want."

She closed her eyes, her chest swelling with hope, her heart crying out to believe him, but she couldn't. Not yet. "What about the Partial soldiers?" she asked. "They were built for one thing, and one thing only—are they locked in one place? They can't even disobey orders without working against their own biology. What are they supposed to do now?"

"Believing that they had no choices is the attitude that ended the world," said Marcus. He paused, staring at the floor, and then spoke again. "I had a friend named Vinci—I suppose after the nuke you might never get the chance to meet him, but he was a good man. He was Partial infantry, a sentry in Trimble's army, but he was also funny, and clever, and smart enough to see that his world wasn't working, and brave enough to try to change it. He remade himself as much as any human ever has. Look at Green, or Falin." He shrugged, and his voice grew distant. "Look at Samm."

"Samm changed," said Kira, nodding. "So did Heron."

"You saw Heron again?"

"We were almost friends," said Kira, and stared at the swirls of her tea. "Not quite, but almost."

"She helped you get to Denver?"

Kira nodded. "I came back with Morgan, but Samm and Heron stayed behind to help the survivors. I thought one day I might see them again, but then the snow made travel almost impossible, and now with the bomb, I just . . ." She thought about Samm, and their final moments. Their one and only kiss. She searched for the right words to express feelings she wasn't even sure of. "I miss them, but I'm glad they're not here. I'm glad they're safe. I hope they stay safe, and stay in Denver, and if I'm right about the cures, they can live long, happy lives way after the rest of us all die of cancer or hypothermia or . . . bullets. Or crazy madmen who want to kill us and steal our blood."

Marcus took a sip of his tea. "You make it sound so dangerous here."

Kira laughed—not a loud laugh or a strong one, barely a chuckle, but more genuine than anything she'd felt in a long time.

"Dangerous and hopeless," said Marcus. "But I don't believe it is. You weren't 'designed' to cure RM, but you did it anyway. You weren't designed to cross the toxic wasteland, but you did that too, and then you escaped from I don't know how many bad guys, and crossed through the middle of a war zone, and while every other group of weary, bloodied refugees is getting smaller and smaller, yours is getting bigger. You're teaching people, and you're recruiting people, and it's not because you were built that way, or because you had some kind of glorious destiny to fulfill, but because you're you. You're Kira Walker. You're not going to save the world because you're the chosen one, you're going to save it because you want to save it, and nobody in this world works harder for what they want than you do."

Kira put down her mug. "I've really missed you, Marcus."

He grinned. "I'll bet you say that to all the guys."

She had loved him once, but then she'd changed and he hadn't. Now that she'd found him again . . . "You're not the man I left."

"It's been kind of a busy year."

"Put down your mug."

He blinked, surprised, then set his mug on the table just before she stepped into him, wrapping her arms around him and kissing him fiercely. He kissed her back and she pressed him against the counter, holding him tightly, needing him more in this moment than she'd ever needed anything. Outside the storm raged, the mainland burned, and the island cowered in fear. Kira forgot it all and kissed Marcus.

CHAPTER FORTY-TWO

"They're coming," said Falin.

Kira looked up from her pack, fitting in the last bottles of frozen water. "Who?"

"The whole damn Partial army," said Falin, racing to catch up. He'd been halfway up an office building, scouting behind them while Kira and Marcus and the rest of the refugees foraged for food. "They're in East Meadow now, but they're not stopping. They probably already got word that the humans had fled."

"The entire army?" asked Marcus.

"What's left of it," said Falin. He looked at Green. "Can he walk?"

"Not very well," said Kira. They'd spent five more days in East Meadow, rounding up as many people as they could and all the supplies to sustain them, and now there were only five days left before Green's expiration. Kira had never seen it happen, so she didn't know what to expect, but the Partials didn't seem surprised by Green's early signs of weakness, growing slow and weak as his body turned its energy against itself.

Kira had hoped that Green's interaction with the humans of East Meadow would save him, but it wasn't working; either it needed more time to function, or it didn't work at all. Watching him grow more frail and damaged caused the entire group's spirits to sink. They had begun to see her as a savior, but now they were terrified that Kira's shining promise was just one more false hope. They had gathered nearly four hundred human refugees, and ten more Partial soldiers had joined the group, but without any hope of salvation, Kira didn't know how long the group could stick together. She prayed that Green would pull out in time, recovering miraculously, but the prospects were bleak. A part of her still feared that this would be her end as well—not expiration, but simply death. Four hundred and twenty people, running through a snowbound hell, chased by nuclear fallout and a vast army of super-soldiers. What chance did they really have?

Kira looked at Tomas, the Partials' demolitions expert. "You're ready with the explosives?"

Tomas nodded. "All we have to do is make it across the first bridge."

Kira looked at the slow train of refugees trudging through the snow, packs of food and ammunition heavy on their shoulders. No one had brought extra clothes; there was enough of that to be found as salvage in the homes they sheltered in, and an entire continent of salvage waiting beyond the water. *If we can get there,* she reminded herself.

"Tomas, Marcus, Levi, come with me; we'll push ahead and

start setting the explosives, so they'll be ready to go when the rest of the group reaches the bridge. Falin, keep them moving, and don't let them panic. Green." She knelt down in front of the ailing soldier and grasped his hands. "You're going to be okay."

"I'm not an invalid," he said, but his voice was raspier than she'd heard it before, and his eyes looked more sunken.

"I couldn't have made it this far without you, Green. We're going to get through this."

"Then stop yakking and do your job."

Kira smiled. "That's the Green I know." She patted his arm and stood up, looking at her advance team. "Let's go."

The brief gaps of sunshine over the last few days had made the snow harder than ever to walk through, softening vast swathes of lightweight powder only to see them refreeze into crusts and chunks of ice when the weather turned dark again. Instead of hip-deep snow they forced their way across the precarious upper layers of an impossible snowbank—sometimes slipping on the ice, sometimes breaking through the brittle crust, sometimes cutting themselves on the razor-sharp edges. The fact that thousands of refugees had already passed this way, leaving jagged footprints and dropped objects frozen into the ice, only made it more treacherous.

There were two long causeways crossing from the main island to the outer beaches, and Kira's group was on the road toward the western one, Meadowbrook, which leapfrogged across four swampy islands on its way to Long Beach. Their plan was to blow each bridge as they crossed it, leaving the Partial army stranded behind them—it wouldn't stop their pursuit completely, but it would force them to find a different route. Even the Ivies, they hoped, would be reticent to follow them, deterred by the wide channels of frigid ocean water and ice floes.

Except that my father has a rotor, thought Kira. *When he comes, he could come from anywhere.*

"Do you think Armin's still searching for me?" she asked Marcus. "The explosion probably spooked him, just like it spooked all of us, but he's had days to regroup and he hasn't come back."

"He's probably raiding the rest of the refugees," said Marcus, nodding toward the road ahead. "Everyone who went before us. With that rotor and his band of Ivies, he'll have the pick of anyone's DNA he wants."

"But he still wants mine," said Kira. "He's going to make another play for it eventually, and we won't have a nuclear bomb to distract him."

"Have you considered just giving him your blood?" asked Marcus. "Peacefully, I mean—a pint or two, safely drawn, and then he can go on his way and leave us alone."

"And create another species that will smash the planet to pieces trying to justify its existence?" Kira shook her head. "No more playing God, even for people with godlike powers. When he comes for me, we have to stop him."

"That makes you sound like bait," said Marcus warily.

"It makes me feel like bait," said Kira, and nodded back to the refugees struggling behind them. "I just hope none of the others get caught when the trap goes off."

They traveled nearly a mile, and Kira felt her toes and face go numb, when Levi called out a warning. "Bridge out!"

"What?" Kira scrambled ahead to join him, and stared open-mouthed at the giant gap in the road. "Did it collapse?"

"It looks like someone ahead of us already blew it," said

Tomas, and pointed at the rubble. "That's a blast pattern, and you can see the blackened marks under the edges of the snow."

Kira walked farther forward, looking at the rocky shores of the island. "We'll have to swim across."

"In this weather?" asked Marcus. "That channel is deep and ice cold—if it weren't seawater, it'd be frozen solid. Not to mention, we were planning to blow every bridge we crossed—if whoever's ahead of us did the same, we'll never make it across every gap. We'd just be stranding ourselves out there."

Kira cursed, grinding her teeth. "They've probably blown the eastern causeway, too."

"It's not worth going three miles out of our way to find out," said Tomas. "We'll have to go back north, and then west on the mainland."

Kira shook her head. "The army's behind us."

"And now it'll be closer behind us," said Levi. "Do we really have a choice?"

"No," said Kira. She made a fist, growling in frustration, then took a breath and forced herself to think critically. "If we assume they've blown all the other bridges, our only access to the land-ing zone—or what we assume is the landing zone—is overland through Inwood and Rockaway."

"That's right," said Marcus.

She turned and started trudging back up the road. "Come on. We have to get back to the others and turn them around." She rubbed her hands together, looking at the sky as the clouds slowly closed overhead, heralding another storm. *Maybe Marcus is wrong, and I do have a destiny. Maybe we all do.*

Maybe it's our destiny to die.

CHAPTER FORTY-THREE

Kira led her refugees north, around a narrow inlet of the bay that cut deep into the ruined city, and then west along a broad thoroughfare called Merrick Road. It made them easy to find, but with the army so close behind them, they had no hope of hiding. Their only hope was to outpace the army, and Kira drove the group as hard as she could, shouting at them to run long after they had no breath to keep going.

A straggler in the back stumbled and fell, blood welling up from a gunshot wound; seconds later the sound of it reached them, echoing dully through the empty streets.

"Long-range sniper," said Green. He winced with each step, struggling to keep up even with the slowest humans. Kira opened her mouth to yell, ready to tell the group to scatter into cover, but Green stopped her. "The snowfall's getting thicker by the second; they won't get more than a few more shots that good. They're just trying to slow us down."

"I don't want to let anyone die," said Kira. But she didn't

want to leave the main road, either, and taking cover would only give the army time to catch up. *I'd hoped we might be able to talk to them,* she thought, *but if they're shooting us on sight, that's probably not an option.* She studied the road and saw an apartment building two blocks ahead that protruded farther out than its neighboring buildings; the upper windows had a commanding view of the entire road behind them. She scrambled across the ice to Levi, half a block ahead of her, and pointed it out. "With a sniper up there, we can bring their pursuit to a halt. They'll be walking straight into our fire."

He turned toward the building, ready to carry out the plan, but she stopped him. "No, not you."

"What?"

"Whoever goes up there might not come down," she said. "You're not a hired gun here, you're one of us."

"It's a solid plan," said Levi. "And I'm a—"

Kira cut him off before he could say it. "Partial, human, it doesn't matter. We're all in this together now. I'm not going to send you into that building just because you're designed for it. We're working together now, and—"

"Kira." Levi held up a hand. "I wasn't going to say 'I'm a Partial,' I was going to say 'I'm a crack shot.' But I appreciate the sentiment."

"Oh." Kira blinked. "Well, I need you with the group. You're a natural leader. And you're not the only one who can shoot." She turned to face the line of human refugees. "How many of you can shoot a rifle?"

A few people tentatively raised their hands, and Kira nodded. "Now: How many of you are trained?"

Two hands stayed up. Kira swallowed her sudden guilt and self-loathing, forcing herself to think of the group, and pointed to the heavier of the two. "What's your name?"

"Jordan." The rest of the column shuffled past them, trudging onward through the snow.

"Let me do it," said Levi. "I'm a better shot."

"You've never seen me shoot," said Jordan. Levi merely raised his eyebrow.

Kira handed Jordan a rifle and pointed to the window above them. "I want you to go up there, watch behind us, and shoot any pursuers you see."

Jordan looked back and forth between Kira and Levi, processing the request.

"Accuracy isn't as important as just keeping them busy," said Kira. "If you're as good as you said you were, you'll be fine."

"Until they shoot me or capture me," said Jordan.

Kira clenched her jaw. "Look, I know it's a lot to ask, but you would be—"

Jordan grabbed the rifle from Kira's hand. "Hells yeah, I'll do it." He checked the sights. "The world's ending anyway, and if I get to go down taking out a bunch of Partial bastards—" He glanced nervously at Levi. "I mean, enemies. Enemy soldiers. Sorry about that, friend. Old habits."

Another shot rang out, and a refugee in the back of the line fell down with a strangled cry. Kira shouted for the others to hurry, then looked back at Jordan. "You can save a lot of people."

Jordan let out a long, nervous breath, then checked the rifle one more time. "I was getting sick of walking anyway. Bad leg."

"You're a hero," said Kira.

"Then do me a favor and keep enough of these people alive to remember me." Jordan turned and stomped through the snow. Kira ran back toward the fallen refugee, but Green and the human supporting him waved her away.

"He's dead," said Green. "Get this line moving faster."

"You're the weak link," Kira shouted back, trying to sound playful but knowing she'd failed miserably.

"I'm going to catch up to you and slap you in the mouth," said Green, teasing much more successfully than Kira had. She looked at the two sniper victims, facedown and motionless in the snow, fading into the cold gray storm as the group walked on. She pushed forward, encouraging where she could, prodding and cajoling, trying to keep the column moving. Another sharp crack split the air, closer and with a markedly different sound; Jordan had started firing.

The army was getting close.

The snow stung their eyes and clung to their lashes, and the whole city seemed to blur into a pale white limbo. They passed homes and schools and parks and trees, all blended to the same featureless nothing, their steps marked by the sounds of gunfire behind them: single shots that echoed through the storm, amplified and muffled and everywhere and nowhere. The column reached a crossroads, and Marcus led them southwest on Foxhurst Road, still miles away from their destination. The single shots behind them erupted into a cacophony of automatic gunfire, a vicious onslaught that tore through the storm and then just as abruptly fell silent. *Jordan's gone,* thought Kira. *I hope he bought us enough time.*

Night fell, and the pale-white limbo darkened to a deep, black shadow that seemed to shroud the world in danger. The falling snow was even more blinding now, and the refugees begged for rest, but Kira didn't dare stop moving. More bullets flew out of the darkness, not sniper shots but advance scouts, harassing their flanks while the main army hurried to catch up. Kira assigned a team to hold them off—Levi and three of the humans—and another to explore the city on their sides, looking for Partial forces that might be trying to flank them. Kira tried to think of how she could possibly hail them and convince them of her cause, but the chances of that seemed to fall with every new attack, every new gunshot, every new fleeing victim left bleeding and dead on the side of the nightmare road.

They turned from Foxhurst to Long Beach, and from there to Atlantic Avenue, always pressing west, always trying to stay ahead of the ravenous army behind them. The suburbs slowly melded into a city, and the buildings each held terror in their shadows. A force of Partial soldiers burst out of a side street, guns blazing and the stench of DEATH wafting off them. Refugees screamed and fell, ducking behind the snowed-in hulks of old, wrecked cars and scrambling for their weapons, or simply dying in the blood-spattered snow. Kira returned fire, Marcus and Falin and even Green joining in; Falin died, and nearly fifty of the humans, before they finally fought off the attackers. Kira assumed that one or both of her scouting teams were dead as well. She ordered the humans to drop their packs, abandoning their food and its weight so they could go even faster.

"If they catch us, we're dead," said Kira, frost burning at her face and fingers. "If we're still alive in the morning, we can look for more food then."

Night closed in tightly around them. Their world was a cave full of cold and death and horror. The smell of the sea was stronger now, but so was the link data of the Partials, and even Kira could feel it coming in from both sides.

"We're surrounded," said Kira. She was guarding the rear of the column, sending the rest of the refugees as far ahead as possible.

"What do we do?" asked Marcus. "Scatter? They can't chase all of us."

"They can," said Kira. "They're everywhere, and there's more of them, and they're better at this. They can see better in the dark, they can coordinate through the link while we can barely even find each other in the snow—"

"I'm not giving up," said Green.

Kira protested. "Neither am I—"

"Then stop talking like you are," said Green, "and let's do something."

Kira nodded, struggling to think. "Tell them to go to ground," she said. "If the Partial army's in front of us now, there's no sense moving forward—send the message for everyone to seek shelter, to stay dark, to stay quiet. We'll lead the army away."

"Whoa," said Marcus. "Who's 'we'? You have to stay safe."

"I have to protect these people," said Kira. "If that means a blaze of glory, then . . . that's what it means. I'll lead them away, I'll give the army their vengeance, and maybe the others can make it to the coast."

"I'm coming with you," said Marcus.

A burst of gunfire roared out of the snow behind them, and they dove for cover. "Get down!" shouted Kira. "Everyone get down!"

She heard a muted echo of unintelligible shouts, and checked her rifle with fingers she could barely feel. She was down to her last magazine. Feet crunched behind her in the snow, and she tried to burrow deeper. Link data drifted in, closer and closer, a chemical confusion she couldn't sort through. Rifles and handguns fired in the darkness. A row of soldiers loomed over their snowbank, and Kira and Marcus and Green fired up at them, killing them or scaring them back into cover; she couldn't tell which.

"I'm out," said Marcus. "That was my last magazine."

"Mine too," said Green.

"I have maybe five shots left," said Kira. She looked at the others, dim shapes in the darkness. "I'm sorry."

"For having more bullets than us?" asked Marcus. "How dare you?"

"I mean for bringing you here," said Kira. "I thought we could make it. I wouldn't let us leave East Meadow without the rest of the refugees, and even before that I'm the one who dragged you both into this—"

"We came because we believed," said Green. "If we die for something we believe in, that's . . . more than the rest of my squad could say for themselves."

A harsh voice drifted through the storm. "This is General Shon, acting leader of the entire Partial species. Those of you who have betrayed your race and joined the human terrorists are complicit in the bombing of White Plains and the death of hundreds of thousands of Partials. Surrender now and you will be forgiven; stay with the humans and we will exterminate you with the rest of the vermin."

"We have to work together!" shouted Kira, but the only answer was another hail of bullets.

"Give me your rifle," said Marcus. "You can run for it, and I'll cover you—"

Another Partial soldier appeared above them, and Kira screamed and fired, desperate to protect her friends even if only for a moment, but more soldiers appeared, and more beside them, and Kira's rifle was empty but she still kept pulling the trigger, screaming and crying her defiance—

—and the Partial soldiers were cut down by a wave of gunfire.

"Kira!" a voice shouted. "Fall back to our position! We have you covered, fall back!"

The voice was impossible to identify in the midst of the wind and gunfire, but they were desperate for any help they could get. Kira and Marcus scrambled to their feet, dragging Green between them and stumbling through the snow. Bullets howled through the air around them, slamming into snowbanks and ricocheting loudly off the dark hulks of cars, but the vague shapes in the storm kept beckoning them forward. She didn't know who they were, but they were on the link, and she wondered how a group of friendly Partials had appeared out of nowhere from the west.

She felt something familiar and almost stopped in shock.

"Keep coming!" said the voice. "We can hold them here—fall back behind us!"

She dragged Green and Marcus forward, and then there he was, kneeling behind the protection of a snow-covered car, holding off the enemy.

"Samm?"

"Kira," he said. "I told you I'd find you."

CHAPTER FORTY-FOUR

"Where did you come from?" Kira demanded.

"West," said Samm. He kept his eyes on the road to the east and fired another short, controlled burst from his rifle.

"But how?" asked Kira. "Why? What about the Preserve? I thought I'd . . . never see you again."

"Go ahead and kiss him," said Marcus, throwing himself down behind the same car for cover. "He saved our lives—if you don't kiss him, I'm going to."

"Questions later," said Samm. "Do you have any ammo left?"

"We're out," said Kira.

"I have a pistol in my side holster," said Samm, firing another quick burst. "Take it, and get your people to safety. I'll hold this line to give you and Heron more time."

Kira took the gun. "Heron's here too?"

"Planting explosives," said Samm. "There's a bridge two blocks behind me."

Kira looked ahead, trying to spot it, but it was impossible to see anything that far through the snowfall. She looked back at Samm. "I won't leave you here."

"I'll be right behind you," said Samm, and Kira saw now that there were other soldiers with him, dug in across the width of the road. "Get your people to safety, and wait for my signal. Now go. And Kira?"

She looked at him, her heart still twisting at the confusion of seeing him here. "Yes?"

"I'm . . . glad you're safe," he said. It was a simple sentence, but the link data that came with it was so powerful it made her hands tremble. She nodded, trying to say the same thing back, but it came out as a confused mumble. She'd thought he was gone for good, trapped on the other side of the wasteland. She'd dealt with it. She glanced from Samm to Marcus and back to Samm again.

She didn't know what to do now.

"Let's go," said Marcus, and Samm gave them another burst of covering fire as they helped Green to his feet and ran forward through the howling storm. Cars and buildings and lampposts loomed like ghosts on the edge of their vision. Bodies lay in the snow, already half-buried by the relentless storm. The close buildings gave way to a wide, empty parking lot, and then they reached the bridge—the ocean inlet it crossed was narrow, barely thirty feet wide at the most, and it wouldn't hold the army for long. In this weather, though, removing it would buy Kira's people a few precious hours.

Someone waved them forward to the bridge. "They came out of nowhere," said the man; he was one of the humans Kira had sent ahead, though she couldn't remember his name. He gestured to Heron, climbing up from under the bridge with Tomas, the demolitions tech. "She says they know you."

"They do," said Kira, looking at Heron's eyes as she approached. "I'm starting to think I don't know them, though."

"Hey, girlfriend," said Heron, though her tone was hardly playful. "You miss me?"

"You're lucky I haven't already shot you for selling me out to Morgan," said Kira.

"I don't think it counts as selling if I didn't accept any payment," said Heron.

"How am I supposed to trust you? Nothing you do makes sense."

"Pay better attention," said Heron, and looked at Tomas. "You ready?"

"Samm said to wait for his signal," said Marcus. "He covered our retreat."

"Then let's shut up and cover his," said Heron, and pointed back down the road to Samm and his men, dashing from car to car for cover as the Partial army surged forward behind them. Kira fell into position next to Heron, their differences temporarily forgotten as Heron handed her a new magazine and they began firing. Samm turned and raced toward them, his arm around a wounded companion.

"Get clear!" he shouted. "Are the other two set?"

"Ready to go," said Heron calmly, and then their whole group fell back, racing away from the oncoming swarm of soldiers. Tomas unspooled a long roll of wire as he ran, and they threw themselves to the ground behind a snowbank. Kira felt the final commands race across the link:

CLEAR

READY

NOW

Tomas pressed the detonator, and the bridge exploded in a bright orange ball barely ten feet in front of the leading enemy runners. Kira turned her head away, covering her eyes against the blinding orange fireball, and felt the percussive thump of two more explosions, one and two blocks north on the same ocean inlet.

"That's it," said Samm. "Let's get as much distance between us and here as we can before they cross that canal."

CHAPTER FORTY-FIVE

Heron walked in silence, listening to the others speak.

"How did you get here?" Kira demanded, looking completely bewildered. "How did you cross the wasteland?"

"We were better prepared this time," said Samm. "We knew what to expect, and Phan and Calix have lived in Denver long enough to be experts at finding clean food and water in the poison."

As if on cue, Phan and Calix emerged from the storm, Calix barely even limping anymore. Heron had to admit she was impressed with the girl—she'd faced the journey without ever complaining; riding the horse, yes, but pulling her weight in other ways, leading them to water sources Heron would never have found on her own. Calix could read the weather in the wasteland's pastel clouds as easily as if she were reading a book, and she had kept them free from the acid rain. She was a valuable asset.

Heron watched, and listened.

"A child was born healthy," said Samm. "The pheromone you discovered, the one that cures RM, was already in her system. That's all it takes, Kira—we lived in the Preserve for weeks, just part of the same community, and it worked. That's all we have to do. We think it helped the Third Division, too."

"Who's that?" asked Kira.

"Vale's comatose Partials," said Samm. He gestured at the rugged man trudging through the storm beside them. "This is Ritter; he's the acting sergeant. He's twenty-two years old, Kira. He survived his expiration.

Kira peered at Ritter more closely. "Nice to meet you. You look like . . . I'm sorry, you're not a model I've met before: you're too old for infantry but too young to be an officer or medic."

"That's because I'm aging," said Ritter, and though Heron couldn't see it, she knew the man was smiling. The Third Division was stupidly proud of their new, human-like attributes. "When we first woke up we thought it was an effect of the muscle atrophy we experienced. Now we're fully recovered, and I still look almost thirty years old."

"It was Dr. Vale," said Kira, and Heron rolled her eyes at the eager thrill in the girl's voice. "Even with his gene mods he was still human, and it must have been his breath that set the reaction in motion. I thought it would stop expiration, but I didn't realize it would restart the normal aging process as well. That's amazing. I wonder if it also cured your sterility?"

"We haven't exactly tested that yet," said Ritter, "though Dwain was doing his best before we left."

"Shut up," said Dwain.

"It might be the human interaction," said Samm, "but we're still not sure."

Heron moved slightly closer, for this was the key to the whole thing. Now that White Plains was gone, and Morgan with it, Heron had no chance of surviving expiration except this one, small hope.

"It's possible," Samm continued, "and even probable, that what happened to the Third Division was a one-time thing—that Vale did something to them, either directly or through Williams, to keep them alive."

"Vale didn't do it on purpose," said Kira. "I spent weeks with him trying to cure expiration, and he was as clueless as I was."

Heron held her breath, listening to every word, breathing them in.

"I thought I was right before," said Kira, "but then I confirmed it firsthand. I talked to the man who designed the system, the leader of the Trust. This was his plan all along: If humans and Partials can coexist, they can live."

Heron breathed again, slow and controlled. She could live. Everything she'd done, every risk she'd taken, every gamble of trust, had led to this moment. She could live.

"It can't be that easy," said Samm. "After everything we've been through, all the hell and the wars and the end of the world . . ."

"It's not easy," said Kira. "It never has been, and it never will be. Look at the hell we've gone through just to get this far—just to convince even a tiny portion of each species to work together. It's always easier to die for your own side than to live for the other one. But that's what we have to do: to live, day after day, solving every new problem and overcoming every new prejudice and building on every common ground we can find. Waging war was the easy part—making peace will be the hardest thing we've ever done."

One of the East Meadow refugees spoke up; Heron thought she recognized him as the one called Marcus. "As important as it is that we, you know, stand around and breathe on each other, we should probably focus on getting the hell out of here. That little blown bridge isn't going to hold them forever."

"The rest of the humans are southwest of here," said Samm, "on a narrow slip of land called Breezy Point."

"That's where we figured they'd go," said Kira. "Have you talked to them?"

Samm shook his head. "We came in through Brooklyn, and since I didn't know how else to find you, we went to the closest human stronghold, which was the JFK airport; there were a few stragglers there, and they told us where the humans were gathering. Sounds like most of the island managed to make it there—twenty thousand at least, maybe thirty. They didn't know anything about you, though, so our plan was to go to East Meadow next, and that's when we heard the gunfight. I didn't know it was you until we found the front of your column and asked who was in charge."

"We were glad to see you," said Marcus, and Heron caught him glancing uncertainly at Kira. He didn't sound as glad as he claimed to.

Heron dropped back, ignoring them as their conversation turned to the more mundane topic of what to do next, and how to do it. They had more than three hundred human refugees in Kira's group, and seventeen miles to go before they could join the rest of the humans at Breezy Point. The Partial army would catch up to them, maybe not immediately, but inevitably. After this midnight chase had failed they were likely to wait before the next assault, gathering their forces and then coming down on the humans with overwhelming force. Kira's little band was doomed, and every other human on this island, and Heron did not intend to be here when that doom arrived. Thirty thousand humans were impossible to hide, even with a handful of Partials to protect them.

But one Partial, and one human to protect her from expiration, could disappear forever.

Heron looked at the group, wondering who would be the best target. Calix was the obvious choice: she was capable, she was brave, and she could help Heron more than hinder her. She might put up a struggle at first, but she had the same fierce survivor's instinct, and when all her other options were gone, she'd see the wisdom of their partnership. On the other hand, Samm seemed oddly attached to Calix, like she was a puppy, and if Heron chose her he might come after her, his stupid sense of loyalty overwhelming all his more logical priorities.

Marcus wasn't an option either, for the same reason, this time thanks to Kira's attachment, and Calix was attached to Phan. *It's like a web of dependent obsessions,* she thought. *They'd kill themselves, and maybe everyone else, just to save their friends. What good does it do? There are so many humans, all virtually identical. Why risk so much for one person?*

Heron quickened her pace, pressing forward into the long column of humans, looking for one that no one would miss. "Where's she going?" she heard Kira ask behind her, but Heron ignored them. She looked closely at each human as she passed them, assessing which ones might be best prepared for a journey out into the wilderness—who had food and water, who was dressed for the weather, who was armed and looked like they knew how to use their weapons. None of the beleaguered travelers inspired much confidence, but Heron supposed that was understandable. These were the last stragglers, the ones who hadn't dared to leave East Meadow until the bomb had actually gone off, and Kira had dragged them from their homes with dire warnings of the end of the world. *I might have to wait until we reach the others,* she thought. *Or simply take Calix and hope Samm's smart enough not to chase me.*

Someone was coming up behind her, and Heron put a hand on her sidearm, ready to pull if it turned out to be an enemy.

"I want to apologize," said Kira.

Heron slowly lowered her hand and turned to glance at the girl keeping pace with her. "Apologize?"

"I was rude to you," she said. "You came all this way, and risked your life to help me, and I treated you like . . . well, I'm sorry. You helped me, and I'm grateful."

"I didn't risk my life for you," said Heron, looking forward again as they walked.

"For Samm, then," said Kira. "The point is—"

"The point is that I didn't risk my life," said Heron. "I was always in control, and if I wasn't, I wouldn't have done it."

"Why can't you just accept the apology?" said Kira, and Heron could hear the tension in her voice.

"When have I ever made anything easy for you?" asked Heron.

"Why are you here?"

"I told you to pay better attention—"

"You want to kidnap a human," said Kira. Heron didn't respond, and Kira didn't falter a step. "You came back for the cure, and now that you're sure it's in humans, you want to take one and save yourself. I have been paying attention, better than you think, and that's the only thing that makes sense. All you've ever cared about is your own survival—you were helping Morgan because you thought she could save you, and then you helped me for a while because you thought I could. When I failed, you went straight back to Morgan, and now that she's failed you were completely out of options—until I confirmed the cure."

"I don't think you understand me half as well as you think you do," said Heron. She paused. "But a little better than I'd like you to, at least in this case."

"Then you know—"

"Did you ever stop to consider," said Heron, cutting her off, "that getting in my way is a bad idea?"

"I'm trying to save us *all*," said Kira. "You know that. Even you, if you'll let me, but I can't let you hurt anyone else."

"In the absolutely best-case scenario," said Heron, "I kill you, grab one of these humans, and no one ever sees me again. That's how things will play out if you keep trying to question me. Take it further—put up a fight, try to stop me, call for help—and I'll end up causing a lot more death and destruction before I, yes, still get away. It's not worth it. Go to Breezy Point, get on your little boat, and count the minutes until that army finally catches up and kills every last one of you. I will be safe, and whoever goes with me. It's not worth it to try to stop me."

Kira put a hand on Heron's arm; Heron stiffened but didn't pull away. Kira's voice was softer than she expected. "Survival is important," said Kira, "but not if you lose yourself in the process. Surviving just to survive is . . . empty. That's not a life, it's a feedback loop."

Heron expected her to say more, to go on and on, moralizing in classic Kira style, but she let go of Heron's arm and stepped back into the night, returning to Samm and Marcus and the others. Heron stopped, watching the line of refugees march past her in the snow, and then she turned and walked away into the city.

The buildings were dreamlike in the darkness—dull, black shapes, their outlines softened by snow and dim moonlight. Heron moved through them silently, haunting the world like a living ghost. Her stealth training was so ingrained, her skills so perfectly honed, that she left no footprints as she walked, no signs, no traces whatsoever of her passing.

If she didn't choose to leave a mark, no one would ever be able to tell that she'd been there at all.

Another shape appeared in the falling snow, low and lean. A wolf or a wild dog, sniffing hungrily through the dim gray void in a desperate search for sustenance. Heron raised her rifle silently, ready to kill it on instinct as a potential threat. Her finger hovered over the trigger. She watched the wolf stop, tense as a spring, and then burst into motion, racing through the street after a tiny white target—a cat or a rabbit, both hunter and hunted kicking up a frenzied spray of snow in their wake. The wolf pounced, shook its head three times, and the rabbit was dead in its jaws. Dark blood dripped down to the snow.

This is life, thought Heron. *Not a peace treaty, not an idealistic dream, but a grim dance of death and survival. The strong live on while the weak—the ones too small or too foolish to fight back—die in agony and blood. Kira wants a world of rabbits, safe in their warren, happy and communal and oblivious to reality, but the real world is out here. A hunter in the snow. Life is a lone wolf, scratching out a living with teeth and claws and a heart of stone.* The wolf shook its prey again, ensuring the kill, but didn't stop to feast right there in the street. It looked up, still oblivious to Heron's ghostly presence, and padded off between the drooping houses and the snow-covered boulders of old, sagging cars. Heron followed it, curious to see where the wolf deemed it safe enough to pause and eat its kill. It slipped through holes in fences, jumped over fallen trees and power lines, and all the while she followed it, watching, waiting. At last it came to its den, a crawl space below a dilapidated house, and crawled through the narrow tunnel it had dug through the snow. Heron crept up behind it, peering in softly.

The wolf laid the rabbit on the floor and watched in maternal silence as four small cubs yipped and snapped at it, eager for a meal. The mother turned toward the entrance, looking straight at Heron, and her dark eyes gleamed green in the dim, reflected light.

Heron watched the children eat, and she cried.

CHAPTER FORTY-SIX

Kira struggled through the snow, clinging to the stretcher they'd rigged to help carry Green. The Partial army was too close, and the night too cold; if they stopped they'd be cut down, or freeze to death, and so they kept walking, step after step, inch after inch, while their feet bled in their shoes and their hands froze in their gloves and the relentless storm howled around them. One mile. Two miles. Five miles. Soon almost everyone was pulling a stretcher, each one cobbled together from whatever they could find in the frozen houses on the side of the road: brooms and mops and shirts and dresses. They draped the stretchers with blankets, trying to keep the injured from freezing, and relied on their own exertion to save themselves.

On the sixth mile after the last blown bridge they were hailed by the first line of defense along the Rockaway peninsula. The land here was barely a thousand feet across from ocean to bay, and the tattered remnants of the Defense Grid were dug into homes and makeshift bunkers, headquartered in an old public school. They brought the refugees there and lit fires to warm them, pulling out all their stock of food and water. Another thirty people had died of hypothermia, and one man's feet were blackened and dead from frostbite. Kira let the soldiers help and crawled into a corner under a dry blanket to collapse into sleep.

When she woke the next day she was shocked to still be alive.

Despite the early morning light indicating the new day, her exhausted body told her she'd only been asleep a few hours. Kira forced herself up and over to the meager fire, where she held her freezing hands up to the scant heat, wondering if she would ever feel truly warm again, then sought out the leader of the outpost. He was an older man, grizzled and weary, who introduced himself as David.

"Kira Walker," said Kira, shaking his hand. She saw the shadow of recognition in his eyes and nodded. "Yeah, that one. Has the Partial army caught up to us?"

David shook his head. "We've been watching all night for them, and we have snipers and IEDs—improvised explosive devices—along the peninsula, but there's no sign."

"They're probably massing for a major assault," said Kira.

"Or defending their rear flank," said David. "Tovar and Mkele are still out there, with whatever's left of the resistance, and they might still be buying us the time to escape."

"Tovar's dead," said Kira. "I don't know about Mkele." She rubbed her eyes, feeling no more rested than when she'd fallen asleep. "Tovar was killed by a man named . . . well, they call him the Blood Man." She felt a sudden, irrational need to hide his identity, even though nobody knew who he was or that he had any connection to her. "He has a rotor and leads a group of genetically modified Partials, killing people to steal their DNA. You haven't heard of him?"

"Nothing like that," said David, shaking his head. "Some of the refugees have talked about a rotor out over Long Beach and Brosewere Bay, but none of the messengers from Breezy Point have said anything. If he's out there, he's still east of us."

"And picking off loners so they can't spread the tale," said Kira. "Keep an eye on the skies; if he does decide to come here, it's going to be trouble." She rubbed her temples, leaning wearily against a wall for support. "How about the rest of the humans? Do you know how the evacuation's going?"

"Slow but steady. Another week at least before everyone's across. This outpost was scheduled to fall back today, but I don't know if your group can make the journey."

"You have more outposts like this?"

David nodded. "Two more choke points along the peninsula, one at each bridge into Brooklyn. We've kept the bridges open in case more refugees make it across. Our plan for today was to arm our traps, rig our explosives, and fall back seven miles to the Marine Parkway—let the Cross Bay Bridge folks be the front line for a while."

"Do it," said Kira, and put up her hands to stop his protest. "We're pretty beat up, but we can make it at least as far as the next outpost. If we stop moving, we're as good as dead."

"Then we'd better get going while there's still some daylight left," said David. "Gather your people; I'll send word to mine. We can be ready in two hours, but you're welcome to get a head start."

Kira walked back to the gym full of refugees, wincing with

each step. *That doesn't bode well for the day.* She picked up a bottle of water to bring to Green, but saw that someone was already talking to him.

It was Heron.

"You're still here," said Kira, unscrewing the bottle to take a swig herself.

Heron nodded. "So are you," she said, "though I suppose that's not as surprising."

"I think she was talking about me," wheezed Green, his voice almost too weak to hear. "She thinks I'm going to die."

Kira grabbed his hand but didn't correct him, looking at Heron with tired eyes. "He's too stubborn to die."

"I know the feeling," said Heron.

Kira nodded. "We're moving out again. They have another outpost, sounds like it's about three miles away. With a break in the snow and some daylight to walk in, we should be able to make it in just a few hours."

"Two more frostbite cases this morning," said Heron, and pointed to Green, "including him. It's the people on stretchers; we have to make them walk and keep their circulation high, or they're going to lose more limbs."

"Think you can convince them?" asked Kira.

Heron smiled wickedly, walked to the nearest stretcher, and overturned it with a grunt, spilling the sleeping occupant out on the floor. He woke up spluttering, still trying to figure out where he was, when Heron tossed his stretcher onto the nearest fire.

"What are you doing?" he cried.

"She's saving your extremities," said Kira. "Find something to eat. We're leaving in an hour." The man worked his jaw wordlessly, too exhausted to argue, then walked unsteadily to the dwindling pile of emergency rations, rubbing his legs as he went. Kira nodded to Heron, who nodded back before assaulting another stretcher. Kira looked back at Green. "She's direct."

"And smoking hot," wheezed Green. "She attached?"

"You've already fought your way through Candlewood and the winter from hell and a nuclear explosion and your own body trying to kill you," said Kira. "Quit while you're ahead."

She patted him on the leg and walked away to spread the word to the rest of the group. Marcus was on one side of the room, discussing something with a refugee, and Samm was on the other talking to his group from the Preserve. Kira stood in the middle of the floor, not knowing who to talk to first, or what she would say, or . . . anything. She took a step toward Marcus, stopped herself, and walked straight instead, rousing the people in a line down the center of the room. She would worry about Samm and Marcus when she wasn't running for her life.

She snorted and shook her head. *If that ever happens.*

She had only spoken to a few more people when Samm walked up behind her. She had learned how to use the link through him, and she felt him coming now, his data as familiar to her as his face, and just as comforting. She closed her eyes, savoring it like an old, familiar smell, then wiped the emotion from her face and turned toward him. "Samm."

"Kira." He stood silent, not embarrassed or awkward but simply . . . uncertain. She loved these little flashes of vulnerability from him, like cracks in his armor of supreme, quiet confidence. Knowing that he'd led a team from the Preserve and conquered the wasteland and defeated an army to be here, only to see him hesitate, unsure what to say to her, made her heart flutter in her chest.

"I heard you say we're moving out," said Samm.

"Yes, I was just coming to tell you."

"Kira, when you left—"

"I know," said Kira. "I know . . . and I don't know."

"This isn't what I—" He stopped himself. "This isn't how I intended to do this. I had months to plan what I would say when I saw you again, but when I found you I wasn't ready."

"You made a plan and saved my life before I even knew what was happening," said Kira. "If that's not 'ready,' I don't know what is."

"That kind of thing is easy for me," said Samm. "This . . ." He paused, straightened his shoulders, and tried to start again, but she stopped him.

"I want to talk to you," she said, "for hours and days and forever, but we can't right now. Not here, and not while we're still in danger."

"You're right," he said, and she felt frustration and relief mingling on the link. "What can I do to help?"

Kira glanced around the room, wondering what to tell him; she saw the refugees trying to dry their clothes by the fire and came to a decision. "Take whoever you can and go to the nearest block of houses. We need all the dry clothes you can find— jackets or coats are ideal, but any shirt or pair of pants will help. We can't let them go outside all wet like this."

"Most of them need new shoes as well," said Samm. "We'll bring what we can." He hesitated again, as if unsure whether to salute her or embrace her, then turned and called to his group;

they followed him out, even Calix and Phan, and they recruited a few of the sturdier-looking refugees before they left. Kira watched them go, wondering if she'd said the right thing—if not taking him back on the spot meant she'd lost him forever, or if she even wanted him back at all.

Marcus, for his part, was already organizing the refugees into groups, taking stock of who had been lost and who was still there, and what resources they could muster for the next leg of the journey. She walked toward him, trying to think of what to say; now that she'd talked to Samm, she couldn't leave him out. As she walked she saw Heron, still dumping out stretchers and yelling at everyone to get up, to walk on their own, to get their blood flowing. Kira still didn't know why the girl had stayed, or if she was still planning to leave or betray them or what. *Great,* she thought. *One more thing to worry about.*

Marcus looked up as Kira approached, though he didn't smile. He nodded toward the door Samm had left through. "They scouting ahead?"

"Getting dry clothes," said Kira. "How's our food supply?"

"Grim," said Marcus, "edging toward 'disastrous,' but probably still shy of 'wanton cannibalism.' This outpost was on the last of their rations *before* three hundred refugees showed up; apparently they're scheduled to evacuate today."

"They are," said Kira. "The next outpost will probably be just as strapped when we get there."

"We can try to scavenge the area around it," said Marcus, "but you've got to remember that every human on the island has passed through here in the last month. Even scavenging, there's not going to be enough food for everyone."

Talking to Marcus is so much easier than talking to Samm, thought Kira. *Or maybe it only feels easy because we're talking about easy things. Weights and measures and nuts and bolts. Why can I talk about saving the world, but not about myself?*

Screw this, she thought. *If I don't do it now, I'll never do it at all.* She looked Marcus straight in the eyes. "Marcus, you know I'm in love with you, right?"

His mouth hung open a second, and then he smiled. "I didn't know if I'd ever hear you say it again."

"And you also know I'm in love with Samm?"

His mouth hung open a moment longer this time, his eyes clouded. "That's not what I wanted to hear next, but still . . . thanks, I suppose. Better to hear it straight out."

"I didn't think I'd ever see him again."

"So that's why you kissed me?"

"That's not why I *wanted* to kiss you, that's just why I *allowed* myself to kiss you."

Marcus shook his head. "Not sure that makes me feel better."

"I made a choice because I thought it was the only one I had," said Kira. "I know that's horrible, but there it is. When I kissed him, it was for the same reason—I thought I was going to die, and I kissed him, and I told him I loved him. It's like . . . I can throw away my whole life trying to help somebody else, but I can only do something for me if I know it doesn't matter."

"So you've kissed him, too," said Marcus. "This is becoming an intensely confusing and uncomfortable conversation."

"I'm so sorry, Marcus. I don't know what's wrong with me."

"There's nothing wrong with you," said Marcus, though he was obviously struggling to find the right words. "We're both pretty flawless specimens—I can barely choose between us either."

Kira laughed. "My choices were so much easier to make when I thought the apocalypse was making them for me."

"The apocalypse is still young," said Marcus dryly. "Do you honestly think we're all going to live through the next few days? Maybe you'll die and *I'll* end up with Samm."

"Better him than Heron," said Kira. "Whatever you do, stay away from her."

"Done and done," said Marcus. "I've only met her once, but . . . holy crap. If anyone does die in the next few days, I won't be surprised if she's the one pulling the trigger."

CHAPTER FORTY-SEVEN

The Partial army didn't arrive that day, and Kira's refugees made it to the second outpost at Cross Bay Bridge without trouble. They lit their fires and huddled together through the night, listening for the sound of the Grid's defensive traps and explosives, but they heard nothing.

"They're not coming," said Samm.

"Or they found the traps and disarmed them," said Heron. She grinned at the nearby humans wolfishly. "Sorry, I'm a bit of an optimist."

"Whose side are you on?" asked Marcus.

"This close to the end," said Kira, "we all have to be on everyone's side. We're running from them because they're trying to kill us, but we can't survive without them. That's how this works."

"So how do we reconcile that with the 'trying to kill us' part?" asked Calix. "That's going to make peaceful coexistence pretty impossible, by definition."

"We'll talk to them," said Kira. "But we'll get everyone to

safety first. They're angry—they think we blew up their home and murdered eighty percent of their species. We'll get everyone clear—of them and of the fallout—and then when they don't have anyone left to shoot at, we can talk to them."

"They can still shoot whoever tries to talk to them," said Marcus.

Kira nodded. "Here's hoping that they don't."

The next day they loaded up with more dry clothes and walked the four miles to the third outpost. Kira was surprised to find that she'd been there before, on her first trip into Manhattan; they'd gone the long way around to hide, from both the Senate and the Voice, and crossed this bridge into Brooklyn. She hadn't recognized the city in the snow, but the bridge was unmistakable. Beyond the outpost it was just three miles to the tip of the promontory, to Breezy Point itself, and Kira could already see the vast group of refugees—the entire human population—swarming over the land ahead. It filled her heart to see so many still alive, after living so long alone in the wilderness, but at the same time it chilled her, more profoundly than even the storm.

Every human on the island, she thought. *I've never seen them all in one place before.*

There's so few of us.

Breezy Point consisted of a short forest, about as narrow as the rest of the peninsula had been, terminating in a more bulbous point that seemed to be covered beach to beach in thousands of houses, packed together with nothing but narrow roads—and sometimes simply narrow sand pathways—between them. The air over the city was a gray pall of smoke from hundreds of chimneys, and the snow beneath was almost black from the ash and churned mud. The southern beach was thronged with people, and the ocean was dotted with a thin line of white sailboats, stretching out toward the distant line of the Jersey shore. Kira could see cook-fire smoke there, too, and she clenched her jaw, grateful. *Even if the rest of us die, some of them have already gotten away.*

Kira made sure her refugees had food and shelter, then left them in the outpost and struck out the last few miles with Marcus, Samm, and the rest of the group from the Preserve. She wanted to take Green as well, but he was in and out of consciousness, and the best she could do for him at this point was to keep him warm and surrounded by humans. If the interactive cure was going to kick in, this was its last chance. It occurred to her that with less than three days left until the next batch of expirations, that might explain the Partial army's sudden lack of pursuit. She was caring for one failing soldier with the dim hope that he would recover; they were caring for thousands, with no hope at all.

Will that calm them? she wondered. *Force them to slow down and take stock and reevaluate their attack?*

Or will it just make them more vengeful?

A pair of men met them on the outskirts of the town, wrapped in ponchos made from blankets and carrying a well-worn ledger. "We didn't think anyone else was going to make it. I'm Gage." The leader of the men shook Kira's hand. "Come on back to the border post; we'll get you warmed up and figure out where to put you while you wait for a boat."

"Who's in charge?" asked Kira. "We need to talk to . . . the

Senate, I guess? Is Kessler here? Hobb?"

"Neither have checked in," said Gage. "Haru Sato's been organizing everything."

"Perfect," said Marcus. "I was hoping we'd get to deal with someone talky and self-important, so this works out great."

"You know him?" asked Gage.

"We're old friends," said Kira. "I'm Kira Walker." She saw the same glimmer of surprise and recognition, and nodded. *Is this going to be a thing now?* "Yes," she said, "that one. Can you take us to Haru?"

"Let me get you squared away first," said Gage, scanning his ledger as they walked. "Looks like . . . ten of you?"

"With three hundred more in the outpost behind us," said Kira. "They'll be arriving tomorrow."

"Wow." Gage flipped more pages, studied one for a moment, then gestured to his companion. "Tell Kyle to get the West Twelfth open, we'll start putting them there." The man ran ahead, and Gage asked them more questions: how much food they'd brought with them; how many injured; how many who could care for the sick or crew a boat. Kira was reassured to see the evacuation being managed so efficiently, but it didn't lessen her concerns—efficient wasn't the same as safe. She walked faster, spurring Gage to hurry, and he led them through the snowy, soot-stained streets to an old construction warehouse in the center of town, which the refugees had converted to a command center. Haru was inside.

"Kira! Marcus!" He ran to them, wrapping them in a hug. "Madison will be so glad you're alive. She's already crossed with Arwen—we didn't want to risk losing our little girl, she's practically the species mascot at this point." He looked at Heron and the others, and his voice became more serious. "I don't know the rest of you, but welcome to Breezy Point. We think we have another good four days before we're all across, and there are already scouts pushing south and west, looking for the best routes to—don't move!" He barked the command abruptly, drawing his handgun so fast Kira barely even saw it. Haru was staring at Samm, pointing the gun straight at his chest. "Dammit, Kira, you brought a Partial?"

"I brought several," said Kira firmly, watching a group of surprised local guards draw their weapons. "Haru, this group has more Partials in it than not—including me."

He stepped back, giving himself a wider angle on the group as a whole, but his grim face faltered. "I . . . heard as much from Nandita."

"Nandita's alive?"

"She was traveling east, before the snow, trying to save Isolde's baby—"

"Isolde had her baby?" Kira cried. "Where are they?"

"They were headed east, to Plum Island," said Haru. "Hobb and Kessler and Xochi were with them. Nandita thought she could save the baby, but we haven't heard anything since. I . . . At this point we have to assume they didn't make it."

"Three minutes ago you didn't think I'd made it either," said Kira. "They're resourceful; they'll make it through."

"Can we have this conversation when they're no longer pointing guns at us?" asked Marcus. "I am just as fascinated as you are, but it's hard to concentrate with a gun in my face."

"How many of you are Partials?" asked Haru. Samm, Ritter,

and the three others raised their hands. Calix stepped forward, directly in the line of Haru's fire.

"My name is Calix," she said, "and I can personally vouch that these men have saved my life more times than I can count. They are not a threat; they are probably your biggest asset trying to protect these people."

"They're Partials," said Haru. "Kira grew up human, so I trust her, but these four could be spies, they could be assassins—they could be anything."

"Then consider for a moment that they could be friends," said Calix. "It was hard for me at first, too, but I've trusted my life to them, and they've never let me down."

Haru stared at the Partials, tightening his grip on the pistol. After a moment he spoke again. "Kira, you saved my daughter's life—whatever else you've done, you did that. If you tell me we can trust these men, I'll believe you."

"You can," said Kira. "And the woman behind you, too."

Haru lowered his gun. "Who?" He turned around and Heron stepped out of a shadow, lowering her own gun with a blank expression. Haru considered her carefully. "After that, why should I trust you?"

Heron smiled. "Because you're still alive."

Haru glowered, but after a moment he reholstered his pistol and waved away the guards. "The world has changed, and I'm not quite used to the new one yet. Kira and Marcus consider you friends, so you're welcome here."

"We understand," said Samm. "I'm glad to hear that your daughter is safe."

Haru glowered again, clearly conflicted about receiving good wishes from a Partial, but he didn't say anything out loud. Kira stepped forward and put a hand on his shoulder.

"Tell me about Isolde and her baby," she said. "How did— she?—survive the initial symptoms of RM?"

"It's a boy," said Haru, "named Mohammad Khan. And the baby never had RM. He's a hybrid."

Kira frowned. "What does that mean?"

Haru shook his head. "So you don't know. Well, we have a lot to talk about."

CHAPTER FORTY-EIGHT

"I still can't believe it," said Kira. Darkness was falling, and they were sitting in their assigned house: Kira tending the fire while Samm and the Third Division soldiers insulated the windows with couch cushions and mattresses. "Ariel and Isolde are Partials, like me—my sisters are my actual sisters, in some giant, cosmic sense."

"If they're still alive," said Marcus. "I'm not trying to kill the buzz, but the odds are against it."

"They're alive," said Kira. "Screw the snow, screw the nuke, screw the island full of revenge-fueled super-soldiers, they're alive."

Marcus held up his hands in a gesture of peace. "Okay, they're alive."

"Four more days of ferrying people in boats," said Calix. "You really think we can do it?"

"You mean get off the island?" asked Kira.

"I mean stay alive for four days."

Kira poked at the fire. "I hope so. Even if we do, it's not going to mean anything if we can't convince the Partial army to join us."

"There hasn't been any sign of them," said Marcus. "None of the explosive traps have gone off, none of the outposts have been attacked, nothing."

"Rotor," said Heron, sitting by the wide front window they'd left open for smoke. She was staring outside, and as Kira looked over, Heron pointed up at the sky. "It's running dark, but you can see its shape blocking out the stars in the background."

Samm walked over to look, the rest of the group close behind him. "Does the invasion force have rotors? They weren't using them when they were chasing us."

"The storm was too strong," said Ritter. "They wouldn't have been useful."

"It's not the army," said Kira, "it's the Blood Man."

Samm peered at the sky. "You mean your—"

"He's not my father," said Kira. "Get your gear. If he's here, he'll be looking for 'donors.' Phan, run to the command center and warn Haru, tell him to put everyone on alert." She pulled on her weather-beaten jacket and picked up her rifle, the others already scrambling for their own weapons. "The rest of you get outside, and get up on the rooftops where you can see. We're going to find where he lands, and we're going to stop him."

"There's no way we can do it while he's got that rotor," said Samm. "He can drop, kill, and take off again before we can catch him."

"We don't have to catch him," said Kira, slapping a magazine home in her rifle. "We're going to get his attention, and he's going to come for me."

The group raced outside; Kira was dimly aware that Heron was watching her intently, but she didn't have time to wonder why. Samm helped Calix onto the roof, and she shouted out directions, sending them running down Twelfth Avenue to Rockaway Point Boulevard, pelting through the dirty snow toward the eastern edge of the town. The night was clear, the first clear night in days, and Kira wondered if that was what had finally lured Armin out of hiding. Maybe they couldn't fly well in the snow, like Ritter had said? She tried to think of how that could help her now, some way to use that knowledge to stop him, but she couldn't control the weather. They reached Ocean Avenue, sprinting through the night, when suddenly the black shape in the sky darted south, high over the houses. It was barely visible, but Kira could hear the bass rumble echoing between the buildings. Shouts were already going up from the command center, too early for Phan to have raised the alarm; had they already seen the rotor, or was something else happening? She swerved south, following the rotor's path, and the rest of her group swerved with her.

"It's dropping!" yelled Samm, and the black shape swooped down against the field of stars, punching through the cloud of smoke that hung over the village. Kira heard shouts, and the pop of a gun, but she was too far away. A spotlight shone down, probing the ground like the proboscis of a fly, searching. She pushed herself, running faster than she thought she could, but the rotor didn't land—it simply circled a few times, then turned off its light and surged back up into the darkness.

"He's looking for me," said Kira. "We have to make sure he finds me before he gives up and starts taking civilians."

The streets here were narrow, revealing only a slim strip of stars, so Ritter vaulted to the top of a car, and from there to the top of a house, scanning the sky in a slow, wide circle. He found the rotor and shouted, sending the group west, and Kira took off again, determined to be there when Armin dropped back down for another look.

"He's going down!" Samm shouted again, too soon for Kira to have run more than a few blocks. She screamed her frustration, stumbling through the snow; Samm steadied her and they ran, breaking out of the narrow street into the wide central square in the middle of town. The command center was in front of them, swarming now with an armed militia, and Haru shouted to Kira as she bolted past.

"The army's here!" Haru pointed the other way, back east toward the Grid outposts. Kira could barely hear him as she ran away, his voice fading in the background. "The Partial army! They've reached the third outpost!"

Kira swore as she ran, tripping on the frozen, sooty drifts. She stopped a moment, listening, and there it was, buried underneath the deep, chopping rhythm of the rotor: distant gunfire. Enough to carry three miles through the wilderness.

"Our group is still there," she said. "All the refugees we brought out of East Meadow, people we almost died trying to save—all caught now."

"They won't kill them," said Samm.

"Of course they'll kill them!" said Kira. "You heard what they said—that humans are vermin, and every Partial who works with them. Green's back there, Samm—they're going to execute him as a traitor."

"Not tonight," said Samm. "We have time to talk to them, to make them see reason."

"Are you so sure?"

Samm didn't answer.

"Keep running," snarled Heron. "He's back up again."

Kira looked up, trying to follow the line of Heron's finger, and spotted the black patch of nothingness streaking slowly above the smoke. "South," said Kira. "Toward the beach." She took off again, running through the crowd. The streets south of the command center were the narrowest yet, skinny footpaths between close-packed houses, but Phan had rejoined them now and climbed to the top of the nearest house to shout directions.

"Four rows over!" he shouted. "No, the next one!"

Kira reached the next row and dove left, watching the rotor swoop down over an open lot between houses. The spinning blades in the wings threw up a flurry of ice and mud and shingles, cloaking the landing zone in a deadly maelstrom of debris. Kira covered her face with her arm and surged forward.

DOWN, Heron linked, then followed it by shouting out loud, warning the humans of the same thing. "Get down! Stay inside and get in cover, it's too dangerous!"

Kira ignored him, desperate to make sure Armin saw her. She gritted her teeth and charged into the swirling cloud of debris, deafened by the noise of the engines. A spotlight flared to life, probing the ground before quickly settling on her. Her arm shielded her face from the glare and the debris, but this was what she was here for. She needed him to see her, to come closer so the others could catch him. She closed her eyes and pulled her arms away, baring her face to the spotlight. Dust and ice swirled around her, stinging her face; her hair whipped frantically in the wind. The rotor hovered in place, the light streaming down, studying her, until suddenly a powerful burst of wind threw her to the ground, and she shielded her eyes as she watched the rotor lift up again into the sky.

He left. . . .

"It's going south now," said Heron, helping her to her feet. "Out over the beach."

"There's nobody there at night," said Kira. "They stop the boats at nightfall because they can't see to navigate—the whole Last Fleet is sunk out there; it's too treacherous."

"Maybe he saw the army coming," said Heron.

"Or he saw the fires across the bay," said Ritter, watching the sky. "He's past the beach and still going."

"He'll slaughter the survivors who've crossed already," said Kira.

Haru trudged toward them through the snow, flanked by a trio of guards. His face was grim. "The rotor was a distraction," he said tiredly. "A group of infiltrators sneaked into the eastern edge of the camp on foot and killed seven people. Maybe more—the reports are still coming in."

"Damn it!" screamed Kira. *Armin, you bastard. . . .*

Haru closed his eyes, rubbing them in exhaustion. "We've roused the camp and put everyone on alert, but there's not much we can do: Our food's almost gone, we have ten more cases of hypothermia, and now the Partial army's barely three miles away. A Blood Man stealing seven people here and there is almost a minor problem, relatively."

"I also have a hangnail," said Marcus, holding up his finger. "Just so we can keep the scale of major to minor in perspective."

Kira nodded, breathing deep, trying to think. "Someone has

to talk to the Partial army. To whoever's leading it."

"Anyone who tries will be shot on sight," said Heron.

"Or imprisoned at the very least," said Haru. "Convincing them they want peace instead of revenge will be virtually impossible."

"Virtually," said Kira, "but not completely. Tomorrow morning I'll go over there, under a flag of truce, and give myself up. It's the only way."

"You'll die," said Heron.

"Samm didn't think so," said Kira.

"Samm is a fool," said Heron. "The best we can hope for is . . ." She stopped suddenly, looking around at their group: Ritter, Haru, Marcus, Phan. "Where's Samm?"

Kira scanned the snowy shadows wildly, looking for his face, trying to feel him on the link. He was nowhere. "You don't think he . . ."

"Damn you," said Heron. Rage scorched the link, and she turned toward Kira with a terrifying snarl. "*You* did this!"

"He's gone to talk to the Partials?" asked Marcus.

"I never told him to do that," said Kira, "I would *never* ask him to do that—I was going to go myself—"

"Of course you were going to go yourself!" Heron roared. "That's all you ever do: You throw yourself right in the path of the nearest, deadliest problem you can find, and he knew you were going to do it, so now he's gone to do it himself."

"He's trying to save us," said Kira.

"He's trying to save you," said Heron. "And he's going to get himself killed in the process."

CHAPTER FORTY-NINE

"Three hundred and seventeen prisoners, General." Shon's aide saluted, and Shon acknowledged him wearily.

"And the trucks?" asked Shon. "We'll need to resupply before the next assault."

"They should be here tomorrow."

"Tomorrow," said Shon. He blew out a long, slow breath. "Five thousand of our soldiers may be dead by tomorrow, and certainly by the day after."

"The rest of us will avenge their deaths," said the aide.

Shon only grunted. He accepted the aide's written report and sent him away, closing the door behind him. The final outpost of the human army had been entrenched in an old army reserve compound called Fort Tilden, at the base of the Marine Parkway Bridge, and Shon had taken the main building for his army's temporary headquarters. The building was dilapidated and broken, like every other building on this forsaken island—the fence sagging, the windows broken, the few doors still on their hinges swollen from moisture and sticking in the frames—but it was clean, and it was dry, and, most of all, it was familiar. He had been born in a warehouse, dumped out of a vat by masked technicians, one of thousands in his batch, but he had been raised on a military base, so much like this one that he could close his eyes and almost hear the sounds of home: Jeeps in the street outside, shouts in the yard as a troop ran drills, the distant call of cadence as a sergeant marched his unit home to barracks. There was a baseball field outside, covered in snow and weeds and discernible only by the crumbling wooden bleachers that surrounded it. There was a part of him, a bigger part than he wanted to admit, that wanted nothing more than to go out there in the darkness and sit down in the middle of that field until he froze.

How can I fight when more are still dying? Fight or not, win or lose, five thousand of my soldiers will die tomorrow, and there's nothing I can do about it. I don't even have orders to follow. Just my own objective. The only thing left.

Revenge.

He sat down heavily in his chair, staring at the reports in his hand, wondering what to do next. He was shaken from his reverie almost immediately by the sound of pounding feet in the hallway, and the bitter link data of surprise and anger. He opened his door before the messenger even had time to knock on it.

"What's happened?"

The messenger saluted. "A prisoner, sir. A refugee from the camp." The guard's link was laced with hatred. "He's a Partial, sir."

Shon looked over the man's shoulder to see the two guards

behind him, walking slowly toward him with a bound, solemn soldier between them. He was dressed in worn, filthy clothes—practically rags—but his bearing was proud, and his link carried no hint of fear. He stopped in front of Shon and bowed his head, unable to salute with his arms cuffed behind him.

"My name is Samm," said the prisoner. "I need to talk to you." The man's resolution was so strong across the link Shon felt himself waking up.

Shon looked at the messenger. "You've frisked him?"

"No weapons," said the soldier. "All he had were the clothes on his back, and this." He held up a bottle of bourbon.

Shon looked at Samm. "Is that why you're here? You're drunk?"

"It's still sealed," said Samm. "Call it a peace offering."

"Are you joking?"

"It's a sign of goodwill."

"You're not really going to talk to him," said the messenger.

"No, I'm not," said Shon, staring at the prisoner. "After everything that's happened, I don't think I have anything to say to a traitor that a bullet couldn't say a whole hell of a lot more efficiently. But." He took a slow breath, sizing him up. Samm's link data carried the basics of his entire dossier—his rank, his unit, his history, his place in Partial society. He was an infantryman, like Shon; just like Shon, he'd fought in Zuoquan City in the final days of the Isolation War. He'd helped to take Atlanta, and he'd served under Dr. Morgan. This was a man who'd been through hell, who'd done his duty; this was a man who knew exactly what it meant to abandon your army, fight for the other side, and then turn yourself in. Shon shook his head. "No, but I have to admit I'm curious as to what could be important enough to make him throw away his life like this. So even if I don't talk, I do admit that I am willing to listen."

The messenger linked his surprise and couldn't help but link a tiny bit of disapproval, but Shon ignored him and stepped aside, inviting the prisoner into his office. The guards tried to follow, but Shon held up his hand. "Stay out here and put guards outside. They have at least one assassin in their group as well, and I don't want her climbing through that window halfway through this conversation with a dagger in her teeth." He plucked the bourbon from the messenger's hand and closed the door.

Samm stood in the center of the room, shivering slightly in his wet, snowy clothes. Shon held up the bottle. "You realize this is a fairly hollow gesture."

"I was only trying to be polite."

"I suppose I can't fault you for that," said Shon, and walked to his desk chair. He didn't offer one to Samm. The old wood creaked when he sat, but it held him well enough. "Is it still good?"

"I don't know," said Samm. "I don't drink. It's unopened, though, so it's probably fine."

Shon examined the bottle, then unscrewed the top. The smell was exactly what he remembered, and he took a small swig straight from the bottle. "I used to drink this all the time back at Benning. Something about the South spoke to me in a way the rest of the country didn't." He took another drink. "Did you know that when you brought the bottle?"

"No, sir," said Samm. "I only had time to raid one empty house before coming out here, and that's what they happened to have."

Shon took another small drink, savoring the burn in the back of his throat. "You know what goes well with bourbon? Fried chicken."

"Are we going to talk about bourbon all night, sir?"

"You came to me," said Shon. "Do you have something else you want to talk about?"

"I want you to stop this attack," said Samm.

Shon's surprise trickled out across the link. "As a thank-you for the drink?"

"I want you to put down your guns and free all your prisoners. And then you and I are going to go talk to the human refugees."

"About what?"

"About a peace settlement," said Samm.

Shon shook his head. "This is getting less and less plausible the more you talk. The humans killed our people. *You* killed our people, at least by association and probably, if I'm reading you right, by actually pulling triggers and killing them. That's not the kind of people I make peace with."

"I regret every bullet I've had to fire in this war."

"That doesn't make my soldiers any less dead."

"Neither will killing the humans," said Samm. He didn't move, but his link data swelled with urgency. "Eighty percent of our people were killed in that nuclear blast, and that was a tragedy we can never make up for. But if you don't make peace, you're signing the death warrant of the last twenty percent. The humans aren't your enemy here, General, expiration is, and killing those humans won't change that. Attack and everybody dies, on both sides, whether it's tomorrow or six months down the line. Make peace, and we can save the precious few we have left."

"You're saying the humans have a cure for expiration?"

"The humans are the cure for expiration," said Samm. "Come with me to talk to them and I can prove it to you—I can show it to you, live and in person. Are you familiar with the Third Division?"

Shon nodded. "The Third Division took Denver; it was one of the biggest battles in the revolution." He felt a sudden weight on his shoulders and took another drink, staring at the window. "They expired two years ago."

"Most of them."

"You're saying some survived?"

Samm pointed toward the human camp. "Three of them, right over there. And six more still in Denver."

Shon looked back at the bourbon, swirling it again, then capped it tightly and set it down on the desk. "Don't you dare joke about this."

Samm voice was firm as granite. "I am completely serious." His link data practically vibrated with sincerity.

"How did they survive expiration?" asked Shon.

"Human interaction."

"Are they prisoners?"

"They're allies," said Samm. "They're friends. Some of them are even . . ."

Shon felt the prisoner's emotion on the link and looked back sharply. "You're in love with a human."

"Close enough," said Samm.

"So is that why you want to save them?" asked Shon, and he felt the bitterness creep back into his link. "'Cause you found a piece of tail?"

"What can I do to convince you I'm sincere?" asked Samm. "I'm not a talker, I'm not a leader, I'm just a guy. Just a soldier from the trenches, trying to do the best he can, but this is not the kind of problem a soldier can solve. I can't cure expiration by shooting it, and I can't bring peace between the species just by following orders and marching in formation. If I were a diplomat or a politician or a . . . hell, if I were anything but what I am, maybe I could tell you what this means, how important this is, how much I believe in it. But all I can give you is my word as a soldier that this is the right thing to do. Put down your weapons and make peace."

Shon stared at him, feeling as if the ground were slipping away beneath his feet, disappearing into an inky black depth desperate to suck him down and drown him. He wasn't made for this either—he was an infantryman, not an officer; he wasn't ready for this kind of decision. Certainly not for the impossible task of supporting it after he made it. "Do you realize what will happen if I go out there and tell the army we're making peace with the humans? The same people who attacked us with a bioweapon? Who destroyed White Plains? You said it yourself: We're soldiers. We were bred for war; we were designed to fight and to kill. You talk about peace as if it were natural, as if all we had to do was stop fighting and our problems would be solved, but fighting is why we exist. War is our nature, and that makes peace the most . . . unnatural act we could perform. We even fought ourselves when we couldn't find anyone else. Sometimes I think no matter what I do we'll be fighting till the last Partial draws breath."

"I understand that," said Samm. "I've felt the same thing. But

I have to believe there's more to us than that."

"They built us for war," Shon repeated.

"They built us to love."

Shon sat in silence, staring at his desk. He traced the cracks in the wood, dry and brittle under his fingertip. He stopped, tapped the desk, and spoke quietly. "I want to believe you."

"Then believe me."

"It's hard to believe when they keep shooting at us."

"So be the bigger man and stop first."

Shon thought about the army waiting outside, the rage that still fueled them from the loss of their home. From the bio-weapon. From the years of hatred and slavery and war that dated back decades. Every memory he had of humans was drenched in hate and death and oppression.

He shook his head. *That's a coward's excuse,* he thought. *We didn't rebel so they'd treat us better, we rebelled so we could live our own lives. So we could make our choices.*

If this is the best choice, then it doesn't matter what the humans do.

"What will they do if we offer a truce?" asked Shon. "Will they accept it?"

"I can't speak for them any more than you can speak for your soldiers," said Samm. "Less, actually. I'm still an outsider in their camp."

Shon raised his eyebrow. "Then why should I trust you?"

"You shouldn't," said Samm. "You should trust Kira Walker."

CHAPTER FIFTY

Kira hadn't slept, and she couldn't imagine anyone else had, either, the entire refugee camp terrified about Armin, about the Partial army, about—

About Samm. No one had seen or heard from him since last night. She couldn't bear to think of what might have happened.

"Of course I'm coming with you," said Marcus, bundling up in as many jackets and blankets as he could find—though Kira noticed he had given the warmest ones to her, and pulled them on gratefully. The first light was peeking through the curtain of another nascent snowstorm, and they were preparing for the long walk to the Partial army. An old man from the boat lines had built them snowshoes to ease the journey, and Kira stooped to lace them tightly to her feet. *If Samm already proposed peace, and the Partials already ignored him, they're not going to listen to me.* She finished the knot on the first shoe and slowly started lacing up the next. *But I have to try. Even if I die, I have to—*

"Man on the road!" said Phan, breathless in the doorway of

the command center. Kira looked up sharply, her heart in her throat, but it was Heron who spoke first.

"Can you see who it is?" she asked.

"Middle-aged," said Phan, "maybe midforties. Dark-skinned. Probably a human prisoner. He's too old to be a Partial, but none of the East Meadow guards recognize him."

"Not Samm," said Marcus.

"He's not from the group I came here with," said Kira. "Maybe one of the guerrillas the Partials captured?"

"He's probably delivering a message," said Calix.

Haru nodded. "Let's go." He sent runners throughout the camp, warning everyone to be on their guard, and led the group to Rockaway Point Boulevard: a long, straight stretch of road from one town to the other. Human guards watched the road from makeshift bunkers, bundled against the snow in mismatched layers and armed with a loose collection of hunting rifles; the best weapons the refugees had left. Kira watched the distant man approach, and after a moment she recognized him.

"That's Duna Mkele," said Kira. "The Senate's old head of security."

"I thought it might be him," said Haru. "I guess his resistance force was finally captured."

"If he's a resistance leader, this is a prisoner release," said Heron. She looked at Kira. "Interesting."

The guards shouted at Mkele to stop a hundred feet from the bunker, and Phan ran out to check him for explosives or other tricks. "He's clean," shouted Phan, and threw a blanket around the man's shoulders, leading him in. Mkele shook Haru's hand and nodded solemnly at Kira.

"They want to meet," he said simply. "Their leaders and ours, at the intersection halfway up the road." He looked at Kira again. "They specifically requested you."

"That's getting to be a theme with them," said Marcus. "Any threats? Are they going to kill a prisoner every day until she shows up to talk?"

"Not that they mentioned," said Mkele. "Honestly, I don't know what to tell you: Our treatment has been brutal, and the Partials have been hell-bent on revenge for Delarosa's little trick, but . . . here I am."

Kira nodded, thinking. "Do you have any idea what they want to talk about?"

"Our terms of surrender," said Haru.

"Maybe," said Mkele. "He said he'd meet us in an hour, minus the time it took me to cross."

"About forty minutes left, then," said Phan. "Enough time to get some scouts out into that forest and make sure this isn't a trap."

"We'll send you and Heron," said Kira, turning to look for her, but the girl had already disappeared. "I guess she's already out there."

"Go carefully," said Marcus, stopping Phan with a hand on his arm. "Keep your eye open for any signs of a double-cross, but assume they're doing the same, and don't make any suspicious moves." Phan nodded and left.

"I guess this means we're going?" asked Haru.

"I am," said Kira. She looked at Mkele. "Did they say how many people we could send?"

Mkele shook his head. "They don't seem concerned about it.

Obviously I'm coming with you as well."

"What about weapons?" asked Calix.

"They didn't seem concerned about that either," said Mkele.

Haru growled. "Arrogant sons of—"

"We're not taking any weapons," said Kira. Haru started to protest, and Mkele with him, but Kira silenced them both. "No weapons. This is our first real chance for diplomacy, and it could be our last. If it turns into a fight we're as good as dead anyway, so let's try to look as peaceful as possible."

Haru grumbled but pulled out his handgun and set it on a table. The others piled their weapons in the same place, bundled themselves tightly, and set off down the road, careful of the slick ice hidden beneath the soft layer of snow. It was snowing again, gently at the moment, coating the empty forest in a fresh layer of white and gray. They saw a group of people walk into the far end of the road, coming to meet them; as the Partials neared, Kira saw one of them in chains, and tears sprang into her eyes when she recognized Samm.

We still don't know what this is about, she reminded herself. *Maybe they'll execute him right in front of us.*

The two groups stopped in a small T-intersection, where a third road ran south toward the ocean. Kira, Marcus, Calix, Ritter, Haru, and Mkele stood silently, facing off against five Partial soldiers and the manacled Samm. They stopped at opposite edges of the intersection, waiting.

"You okay, Samm?" Kira called out.

"Yes," said Samm, and Kira felt a surge of relief to hear his voice—followed almost immediately by frustration. *Why does he always have to be so taciturn?*

The Partial in the center of the line walked forward, his feet crunching in the snow, and stopped in the middle of the icy road. Kira hesitated a moment, then walked forward to meet him.

"My name is Shon," said the Partial. "Acting general of the Partial army."

Kira looked him in the eye. "Kira Walker. I suppose you could say that I'm the closest thing the human race has to a leader right now."

"I was told I could trust you."

Kira nodded. "Do you?"

"Samm told me some very interesting things about you and your . . . theories."

Kira couldn't help but notice that it wasn't an answer. She humored him and followed the new line of discussion. "If we work together, we can save both species. See that man behind me, second from the end? His name is Ritter, and he's from the Third Division."

"I've linked him, yes," said Shon.

"He's twenty-two years old," said Kira. "You can cure us, and we can cure you. Regular contact between the species will propagate a biological particle that—"

"Samm explained it all," said Shon. "On the other hand, he also introduced me to one of the AWOL Partials we'd already captured, a man named Green. It's hard to believe your theory when the man with the most human contact is lying on his deathbed."

Kira felt a pang of despair. "Is he already—?"

"He might as well be," said Shon. "Some of his batch already expired in the night. When I left Green this morning he could barely breathe, let alone speak or keep his eyes open."

"I'd like to see him again," said Kira. "Even if it's only . . . after."

"Friendships like yours with Green," said Shon, "or with Samm, or this other Partial behind you, are inspiring in their way, but that's not enough. You have to see that."

"I do."

"The seeds for the hatred between my people and yours were sown years ago," said Shon. "Before either of us were born. We tried living together once before, and it failed—my best friend was beaten to death by human supremacists in Chicago, five months before the revolution even started, for having the temerity to take a human girl to see a movie."

Kira was silent.

"You want peace," said Shon. "You want it, and I want it, but the two of us can't speak for everyone. For the tens of thousands of scared, flawed, fallible people who are going to be down there every day, living and working and arguing and being . . . people. They're going to fight, because that's our natural state of being, Partials and humans. It's how we were built."

"That doesn't mean we can't try," said Kira. "Things are different than they were before the Break."

"You don't know what it took just to get these other soldiers to agree to this meeting," said Shon, gesturing behind him. His link data was growing more and more exasperated. "The slightest sign of treachery from you could destroy this peace in seconds, and that's just us. That's the people I trust. What if we make an alliance and join together, and then one of your humans cracks a joke about Partial labor, or the old work programs that helped spark the revolution in the first place?"

"Don't assume the humans will be the ones to ruin this," Kira insisted, feeling her anger rise. "What happens when one of your Partials calls it the revolution, or says something about winning your freedom, standing next to a human who lost his wife and his children and his parents and everything else he ever loved—" She froze, listening. "Wait."

"I hear it too," said Shon, and looked up. The entire Partial line had gone tense, listening intently to the deep, rhythmic hum. Kira didn't dare to look behind her, too worried Shon would see it as a signal to her companions. The general's link data flooded out in frustrated confusion.

"That's a rotor," said Kira, turning south to scan the sky. The snow had come in more thickly, and she could barely see more than half a mile.

"It's not ours," said Shon, and then jabbed a finger toward the clouds. "There!" He backed away, shouting to his men. "Fall back!"

"It's an ambush!" shouted another Partial, and Kira surged forward, trying to warn them.

"Take cover!" she shouted. She heard Marcus shouting for everyone to get back, to find safe positions, but she knew it was too late for that. She was out in the open, weaponless and defenseless, and there was nothing she could do to stop Armin from killing her. Her only priority was to save the treaty, to keep this from destroying the already-too-fragile peace between the humans and the Partials. Shon and his men were taking cover in the trees, but Samm ran toward her, his chained ankles shuffling painfully across the iced road. Kira shouted to Shon, trying to explain what was happening, when suddenly the rotor burst out of the clouds in front of her, snow swirling through the massive blades in the wings. It banked toward her, swooping low over her head and knocking her and Samm to the ground with the force of its downdraft; it tilted back and dove toward her other friends, sending them sprawling. The craft set down in front of them, cutting off Kira's retreat, and the side door hissed open. Ivies poured out, rifles up and ready, and behind them came Armin: his carving knife in one hand, an empty jar in the other.

"Kira," said Armin.

"You can have my blood," Kira shouted, "but nobody else's." She pointed behind her at Shon and his sergeants, watching the scene with obvious shock. "We're making peace here, Armin. This is the end of the war, and I'm not going to let you ruin it."

Ritter ran out from behind the rotor, a branch in his fist, ripped from one of the snowy trees on the side of the road, but the Ivies had sensed him coming on the link and turned to fire before he'd even cleared the corner of the aircraft. Kira screamed, incensed by his empty sacrifice, but a moment later she saw the sense behind it: Marcus and the other humans had flanked them, charging around the other side of the rotor, surprising the Ivies from behind and tackling two of them to the frozen ground. The remaining Ivies spun again to meet the new threat, and Kira screamed again as her friends went down, as Marcus went down, blood erupting from their ragged coats in bright red clouds. She ran toward them, still screaming incoherently, Samm struggling to hold her back, when the Partials rose up behind her, drawing weapons of their own and charging

438

toward the fight, firing at the Ivies. The Ivies fired back, and Kira screamed as Samm stepped in front of her, taking a bullet in his arm. Armin stood in the middle of the battle, seemingly unafraid, and stopped the world with a thought.

NO

The command rolled out across the link, freezing Shon and his Partials midstep, binding Samm like a man of stone, stopping even the Ivies. Kira stumbled, overwhelmed by the order, by the word, by the entire concept of NO. It seemed to fill her link, her mind, her entire body. She gritted her teeth and put her hands to her head, as if she could somehow shut it out.

"That's better," said Armin. He looked at Kira, walking toward her slowly. "You were right about one thing," he said. "This is the end. Maybe not of your war—they look to still have some fight left in them—but of the war's importance. I have all the DNA I need now. The humans and Partials, so desperate to end each other's existence, can now do so without harming our future."

"It doesn't have to be that way," said Kira, forcing the words out. "It's your plan—the one you made all those years ago. It can still happen."

"For the moment, perhaps," said Armin. "But eventually they'll start fighting again. They'll blame each other for your death, for not saving you or killing me. They might even try to work together to leave this island before it irradiates them all beyond recovery, but it won't last. Their differences are too great, and the biological peace I tried to force with RM and the Partial DNA wasn't enough."

With a herculean effort Samm moved his foot, planting

himself in Armin's path. He stared at the man with clenched teeth, too rigid to speak, but determined to defend her.

Armin stopped in surprise. "Impressive. But it doesn't matter. Jerry has reset the planet, and I'll start over with a new species, built as one from the beginning instead of this ham-fisted attempt to make two coexist. They will inherit the Earth, and you will be their mother, and they will go on to greater and more glorious things than any of us could imagine. You don't understand this yet, and I suppose you never will, but that's the greatest goal of any parent: to be surpassed by his children."

"So let me live to surpass you," said Kira. "It can't be that hard—I'm already not a psychopath." She forced her legs backward—first one, then the other, draining every ounce of her will. She didn't know if she could take another step.

"Shortsighted comments like that are the surest sign that you're already not worthy of the new world." He stepped around Samm, holding up his knife, but with a guttural roar the Partial moved again, barring the Blood Man's way. "Don't make me kill you, too," said Armin calmly. "I don't wish to harm anyone, but I will have her DNA at any cost."

"If you want a new world, a world that can live in peace, you have to *let go*," said Kira. "From the beginning of this whole thing, the creation of the Partials and the formation of the Trust, you've been trying to control it, to manage every step of every process. That's what failed, Armin. Not the biology, but your attempt to control it. We have to be able to choose. We have fallen, and we have to rise up again."

"Humans have had their chance," said Armin. "They failed, and they nearly took the entire planet with them. That isn't going to happen again."

"Damn straight it won't," said a voice. Armin turned in surprise, and Kira forced her head sideways.

Heron was walking slowly out of the trees, playing idly with a handgun.

STOP

Kira felt Armin's new link data batter at her will, at her very sense of self, but Heron simply smiled and kept coming.

"I see," said Armin. "One of the Thetas." He set his glass jar carefully on the ground and straightened up with knife in hand. "This is just what I was talking about, Kira. The Thetas have free will—the others told me I was crazy to make a Partial model that couldn't be controlled through the link, but I was an idealist. I believed then, as you believe now, that the element of choice was too important to completely cut out of the species. Now I know better. I gave them choice, and all they used it for was disobedience." He tilted his head, looking at Heron with cold, calculating eyes. "I thought I'd hunted all of you down."

"You were the one who killed the other spy models?" asked Heron. "Every word out of your mouth is another reason to kick your ass."

Armin shook his head. "I might not be able to control you, but I have gene mods you can't imagine. Attacking me would be folly."

"More and more," said Heron, reaching a distance about ten feet away from him, and slowly circling to the side. "Kira, sweetie, I'm going to murder your dad."

Kira tried to answer, but the link still held her locked in place.

"I designed you to be an evolution of the Partial template, Theta, but now I know you're exactly why we need to start over," said Armin, and Kira could hear the impatience rising in his voice. "We need a species that dreams of the stars, not one that lurks in the shadows and kills for sport."

"You want a species without me in it?" asked Heron. "Bite me." She dashed forward in a blur, firing her pistol; Armin side-stepped the first shot easily, and she sent the next one to his right, missing on purpose, driving him to the left where her other hand was ready with a knife. He saw the feint coming, deflected the knife in a single swift movement, and spun back the other way, leaving her line of fire just as she was bringing the barrel of her gun back toward him; he stepped between the bullets so precisely it looked rehearsed.

"You can't be controlled through the link, but you still broadcast tactically," he said. "I know everything you're going to do before you do it." She looked unfazed, ignoring him and focusing on the fight. He danced lightly through her next several gunshots, moving so calmly he never looked like he was straining. Heron worked her way closer, sometimes leading him with bullets, sometimes trying for a hit, all the time working her way back into knife range. Kira tried to keep track of the number of shots, wondering when she would run out, when suddenly Heron slashed with her knife, dropping her gun hand and ejecting the ammo clip from the pistol; it slid across the ice, and when Armin stepped back to dodge the blade, his foot landed on the sliding metal clip and he lost his balance, throwing out his arm to keep from falling. Heron took the opening with a vicious grin, leaping forward to slash at the man's throat, but he turned his pinwheel into a parry, taking her blade on the bone of his arm and slashing back with his own knife. Heron backed up, reassessing the situation.

"That was a good trick," said Armin, "but you can't beat me."

"Probably not," said Heron. "Doesn't mean I can't win." She paused. "Kira?"

"Yes."

"Tell me you're sure about this," said Heron. "Tell me it'll work, and everyone will live, and I'm not just wasting my time."

Kira set her jaw. "I promise."

"Well then," said Heron, drawing another knife from her belt. "Let's end this."

She dashed forward, a blade in each hand, slashing and stabbing like a tornado of steel. Armin struck at her, a clear feint to drive her to the side, but Heron screamed and took the blade in her chest, catching the weapon with her own body and bearing him backward with the force of her charge. His eyes widened in shock as he tried to draw back his knife, but it was too late; Heron had her opening.

Six lightning-fast slashes from her knives, and she had cut him to ribbons.

Armin teetered on his feet, bleeding from a dozen deep slashes in his neck and chest, and collapsed into the snow.

Heron started to pivot but collapsed beside him, his knife still deep in her heart.

DEATH

Kira felt the tears on her face, hot and freezing at the same time. She forced her foot forward, first one inch, then two. Armin's overpowering command data faded from the air, and she took another step, then another. Heron's blood steamed in the frozen road, melting dark red holes in the snow below her.

Two more steps. Three.

Kira uncurled her fingers with a groan, stiff from the cold and the iron grip of Armin's link. She reached Heron and sank to her knees, checking the girl's throat. Heron's pulse was faint and erratic. She put her hands over the wound, but it was a bloody mess, and she knew it was too late.

Heron's hand reached up and found Kira's, feebly grasping with useless fingers. Her voice was a whisper. "If my life had no meaning, there was no reason not to end it."

Kira gripped the girl's hand tightly, her heart breaking. "So you ended it?"

"So I gave it meaning."

Heron's eyes fluttered and rolled back. Her hand went limp. Kira sobbed and held her, feeling the last of her life fade away.

DEATH

CHAPTER FIFTY-ONE

General Shon walked slowly up behind her and knelt in the snow at Kira's side.

"I promised her I'd make this work," said Kira. "I know it's not going to be perfect, or easy, and for all I know it's going to fail, but . . ." She clenched Heron's hand in her own. "We have to try."

Shon nudged Armin's body with his glove. The man was limp and lifeless. "After listening to this bastard tell me it was impossible, I'm inclined to give it a shot just to prove him wrong."

"There are worse reasons for saving the world," said Kira.

Samm joined them now, kneeling by Heron's side. He took her hand in his own, drawn short by the chains on his wrists, and watched her in silence. After a moment he looked to the east, toward the Partial camp. "Someone's coming to check on you."

"Must have heard the rotor," said Shon. "I don't . . . wait. There's a whole group."

Kira stood up, watching more shapes emerge from the snow. The man in the lead was walking stiffly, almost shuffling, as if he were sick. Kira took a few steps toward him and felt a rush of emotion as she recognized his face. "Green!" He waved, and she ran toward him, wrapping him in a hug. "You're alive!"

"It worked," he said, looking at his hands and arms as if they were new: strange, wondrous things he'd never seen before. "I . . . got better." He gripped her by the shoulders. "I'm not a hundred percent, but . . . you saved me, Kira."

Shon stopped next to him, staring in wonder. "Green?"

Green turned toward him and saluted. "I left the army, sir, but I'm ready to enlist in the new one."

"What new one?" asked Shon.

"A Partial just survived expiration, and you've got twenty thousand more looking for the same treatment." Green pointed behind him, at the massive wave of Partial soldiers, and grinned happily at Kira. "Is this where we sign up for the human/Partial alliance?"

An Ivie bullet had grazed the side of Marcus's head, scraping away the skin right down to the bone and knocking him out cold, but he was alive. Kira wrapped the wound and roused him, and he helped with the others—stopping blood wherever they could, stuffing holes with bits of ripped cloth, and then helping everyone back to the camp. Haru was in the worst shape, his gut punctured and his right hand mangled, but he was stable. Six Ivies were still alive as well, and surrendered on the spot with their leader dead. Kira led them back to the human camp, and Shon and Mkele stepped in for Haru, reorganizing the evacuation, slowing the frantic pace while still planning to get everyone clear of the fallout. With the Ivies' old rotor to help, they could tighten the schedule considerably.

Kira dressed Samm's wound herself, laying him on a sterilized table in their crowded makeshift medical center and cleaning his shoulder with alcohol before carefully stitching it closed. "This reminds me of being in the lab," she said, remembering their time in the East Meadow hospital when she'd studied him, talked to him, and ultimately decided to help him. She'd felt a connection to him she hadn't felt with anyone else, not even Marcus, and she'd worried for a time that it was just the link, traces of it drifting on the fringes of her mind. She looked at the next table in the row, where Marcus was stitching a bullet hole in Calix's leg—her other leg, now a mirror image of the one Heron had shot months ago.

I don't know what I'm supposed to do, Kira thought, and looked back at Samm. *But I know what I want to do.* "I need to talk to you," she said nervously.

"Are you done with my shoulder?" asked Samm.

"Didn't you hear me?"

"I did," said Samm, wincing as he raised himself upright and eased gently off the table. "But I need to talk to you, too."

Marcus looked up from his surgery. "You're going to do it right here? Just right in front of me?"

"You're a good man, and a good friend," Samm said to him. "I apologize for this." He took Kira's hands in his and looked into her eyes, and she looked back trembling. "Kira, I love you. I didn't tell you then, but I loved you in that lab, and I loved you when you broke me out of prison, and I loved you when I said good-bye on the dock, and when I said it again in the Preserve. It tore me apart to see you leave me, both times, like you were taking my heart with you. You're a part of me now, and I don't ever want to say good-bye to you again." He paused. "Everyone left on the planet is going to cross the ocean, and find a new home, and start a new life. I want to start that new life with you."

Kira was crying, holding his hands so tightly she worried she was hurting him. Around them, the medical center was crowded and buzzing with activity, but his words were the only thing she heard. Samm turned back to Marcus. "I'm sorry. I don't know how we make this work."

Marcus's face was impossible to read, but it finally broke, and he laughed. "You don't apologize for this, Samm. It's love, and love doesn't weigh its options and pick the best one—love just wants things, and it doesn't know why, and it doesn't matter why, because love is the only explanation love needs. Looking at Kira right now, I . . . know this is what she wants too. I—" He stopped and looked away sharply. His voice was thick with emotion. "I'm not going to stand in the way."

"Thank you, Marcus," Kira whispered, wiping a tear from her eye. She looked at Samm, seeing herself reflected in his eyes. "I love you Samm. I do." She pulled him close and kissed him.

Marcus wiped his eye, watching them kiss, then turned back to his surgery and sucked in a breath. "Well. Isn't that just a kick in the teeth."

"Tell me about it," said Calix.

Marcus glanced at her, then went back to work on her leg. "You and Samm?"

"Once upon a time . . ." She watched them a moment longer, then looked back at Marcus. "Did you mean all that stuff you said? About love knows what it wants and it doesn't matter why?"

"Yeah," said Marcus, "I do. I guess. It sounded right at the time, and I don't *not* mean it, but . . . You know how it is. Stop moving."

"So what are you doing tonight?"

Marcus faltered in surprise, almost stabbing her with his tweezers. "What?"

"I'm single, you're attractive, and we're both stuck in this hospital anyway. What do you say?"

"I just lost the love of my life," said Marcus. "Could you give me some time to . . . breathe, or recover, or something?"

"You lost her years ago."

"Ouch," said Marcus, and shook his head. "You know, you're very direct."

"To my frequent detriment," she said, glancing back at Samm.

Marcus laughed dryly. "That sounds like a story I need to hear."

"Then it's a date," said Calix. "Come on: It's the least you could do after fondling my leg for the last hour."

"It's a date," said Marcus, "but the first order of business is to teach you the difference between fondling and surgery. Mixing those two up could get you into trouble."

Kira stood on the shore, waiting for a ship to return for the last of the survivors. She'd insisted that she be in the last group off the island, sending everyone else to safety first. Samm stood behind her, his arms wrapped around her in perfect, comforting silence.

Before them the sea stretched out, wide and open and limitless. The crumbling remains of an old wooden dock disappeared into the waves, and she longed simply to follow it—straight out and gone, the first step onto a new path and a new horizon. White snow covered the ground like a blank parchment, wiping out the old world and waiting for them to write a new one on its pages.

"Boat!" called the lookout, and the gathered refugees looked toward Sandy Hook, but the boat wasn't there. "East," the lookout shouted, and Kira turned her head, peering into the distance. A white boat with a tall sail was hugging the coast, tacking toward them past Jones Beach.

"Did Mkele send for more?" asked Samm.

"We already have more of them than we can sail," said Kira. "Maybe it's another fisherman, finally joining the rest of us?"

They watched the boat closely, and soon Kira saw three women standing at the bow, hair whipping in the wind, one more woman behind them at the rudder.

Ariel, Isolde, Xochi, and Nandita.

Kira ran toward them, wading hip deep into the freezing Atlantic and waving to them with tears of joy streaming down her face. "You're here!" she shouted, over and over, too happy to think of anything else to say. "You're here! You're here!"

Ariel turned a sail and slowed the boat, aiming toward the dock. Kira ran back toward it and threw them a line as they bumped against it. Xochi smiled. "Want a lift?"

"I didn't know you guys could sail," said Kira.

"I spent a year in a fishing village," said Ariel. "I'd better be able to sail."

"You're alive," said Kira, so happy she was hugging herself, heedless of the freezing waves. "I love you so much." She looked at their faces: her sisters and her adopted mother. Armin may have been her father, but this was her family, real and close and wonderful. Samm walked out next to her, taking her hand. She squeezed it tightly before pulling him onto the boat with her, only letting go to hug her sisters. "Let's go somewhere."

"It's a big world," said Isolde. "We can go anywhere you want."

ACKNOWLEDGMENTS

This book owes so much to so many people. My editor, Jordan Brown, and my agent, Sara Crowe. The amazing crew at HarperCollins and Balzer + Bray. My assistant, Chersti Nieveen, and my brother, Robison Wells, both excellent writers in their own right and amazing sources of help and inspiration. My readers, who are many and varied: Steve Diamond, Nick Dianatkhah, Mary Robinette Kowal, Ben Olsen, Maija-Liisa Phipps, Brandon Sanderson, Howard Tayler, and the many others I undoubtedly forgot.

This book owes another huge debt to my wife, Dawn, who supports me more than I could ever hope for, and then some. She gives me time, ideas, advice, encouragement, food, and the freedom to do whatever I need, whenever I need to, to bring this and every other book to you. Without her I'd be flipping burgers somewhere. Thank you, Dawn, for being amazing.

Last of all, this book owes perhaps its biggest debt to the ultimate models for Kira and Heron and every other awesome girl in the Partials series: my two daughters. May you always have heroines to inspire you, role models to look up to, and the freedom and courage to make your own choices, no matter how simple or scary or hard or eternal they may be.